T3-BNV-418

The Hills Stand Watch

Books by August Derleth

NOVELS

Still Is the Summer Night · *Wind over Wisconsin* · *Bright Journey* · *Restless Is the River* · *Sweet Genevieve* · *Evening in Spring* · *The Shield of the Valiant* · *The House on the Mound* · *The Hills Stand Watch*

SHORT STORIES

Place of Hawks · *Any Day Now* · *Country Growth* · *Sac Prairie People* · *The House of Moonlight*

POETRY

Hawk on the Wind · *Man Track Here* · *Wind in the Elms* · *Here on a Darkling Plain* · *Rind of Earth* · *And You, Thoreau!* · *Selected Poems* · *The Edge of Night* · *Habitant of Dusk* · *Rendezvous in a Landscape* · *Psyche* · *Country Poems*

MISCELLANEOUS PROSE

Village Year · *Still Small Voice: The Biography of Zona Gale* · *Atmosphere of Houses* · *The Milwaukee Road* · *The Wisconsin: River of a Thousand Isles* · *Village Daybook* · *H.P.L.: A Memoir* · *Some Notes on H. P. Lovecraft*

JUVENILES

The Country of the Hawk · *The Captive Island* · *Empire of Fur* · *Oliver, the Wayward Owl* · *A Boy's Way* · *Land of Gray Gold* · *It's a Boy's World* . *Land of Sky-Blue Waters* · *Father Marquette and the Great Rivers* · *St. Ignatius and the Company of Jesus* · *Columbus and the New World* · *The Moon-Tenders* · *The Mill Creek Irregulars* · *Wilbur, the Trusting Whippoorwill*

AUGUST DERLETH

The Hills Stand Watch

DUELL, SLOAN AND PEARCE

NEW YORK

First edition

Library of Congress Catalogue Card Number: 60-5450

Manufactured in the United States of America

Acknowledgments

While the central story and characters of this narrative spring entirely from the author's imagination, certain of the people and incidents are historically accurate. The activity centering around Wisconsin's emergence from territorial status to statehood in the main closely follows the events of history, and the rise and decline of the historic lead-mining region of southwestern Wisconsin can be found in many chronicles.

I have drawn upon several books for the historical facts here chronicled as fiction, notably Joseph Schaefer's The Wisconsin Lead Region, *the* Wisconsin Historical Collections, *the* History of Iowa County, *the manuscript of* Bloomfield and Number Five, *by Oscar Hallam, the centennial supplement of* The Cathedral Tower, *and files of the* Mineral Point Democrat *and the* Wisconsin Tribune. *I owe thanks for generous assistance to Robert Neal, Elmer Mundy, Max Fernekes, Miss Alice Conger, the late Elizabeth Billings, B. J. Pellow, and Elizabeth Pellow.*

This book is for Myra and Mary
who were, in part at least,
responsible for it . . .

Contents

1. Tranquility, Farewell!

Autumn, 1844

THE AFTERNOON OF THE OCTOBER DAY WAS APPROACHING THE hour of sundown and twilight, and already the distances were lost in a pale, lavender haze. Along the ridge a stage moved steadily in a generally northeasterly direction, at a pace which suggested that its goal was not far distant, though no dwelling was in sight in all that wild country of hills and valleys. Still visible along the horizon to the southwest rose the Platte and Belmont Mounds, passed more than an hour ago—twin, rounded hills standing forth like dark, grave sentinels in a land of silence and strangeness, dominating the face of the earth at that place. An illusion of level land lay between the blue peaks and the ridge road, a tranquil country of high plateau and deep valleys, but at this hour the valleys were lost in the last sunlight lying in a soft pink and copper haze along their slopes, complementing the colors of ivy, sumach, birch trees, and hazel brush which grew at the edge of every copse and thicket. In the ravines nearby, sunlight lay pooled and warm; a kind of shimmering, colorful and mystic, filled the air, but beyond, in the deep, wooded valleys between the ridges, the first dusk already flowered where sunlight and day were withdrawn.

The two passengers who rode through the Territory of Wisconsin on this autumn day of 1844 were beset by conflicting emotions. David Pengellen was quietly happy to be so close to home once more, and proud in his young wife, Candace, whom he was bringing to her new home from Providence. He had observed her excitement, but did not know whether it rose from the unfamiliar wildness of her surroundings, from uncertainty, or from perturbation. She was pretty—dark with hazel eyes, a small, thin-lipped mouth, a pert, slightly foreshortened nose. Her long-fingered hands lay laxly in her lap, ready instantly to seize hold of him or some part of the coach each time the stage tipped and leaned or jolted and swayed on the rough roads over which they traveled.

Pride in possession of her shone in his honest, clean-shaven face; he had the look of a scrubbed schoolboy just passed in his examinations, though he was twenty-five to her twenty. He had short, dark hair, almost black, cut close to his head, but betraying a tendency to curl; his eyes were a strong blue, his mouth was wide, his lips were dominant and sensitive. He was powerfully built, broad-shouldered, and his hands were wide and strong, with spatulate fingers. In profile, his chin had a prognathous appearance because of the fullness of his mouth. His skin was dark, in contrast to her fairness, and he stood a half head taller than she, though, because of the amplitude of her clothing, in concession both to fashion and the chill of the weather, she seemed in some respects as large of frame.

The stage was now moving toward a broad thicket. She turned from the window and looked anxiously at him. "David, you said we'd be home today. It's almost dark. I hope we won't have to spend another night at an inn."

"We're almost there," he said tranquilly. "Mineral Point lies down under that ridge up ahead. Our house is the nearest one to the stage route half way up the slope—but we don't stop there."

He leaned forward, with one arm about her shoulders, turning her to the window of the stage once more. "See there—it's down past these trees. If you watch, you'll see a little of the house when we turn down High Street."

She peered intently into the glow of sunlight. Out of the corners of her eyes, she was uncomfortably aware of the sunlit mounds they had left behind, reared up like sentinels out of the plateau, like watchers on the threshold of her new world. The stage, which had traveled into the northeast ever since leaving Galena, was now describing a curve into the west, turning slowly along the ridge through a stand of thin timber toward the slope to which David had pointed. As attentively as she could, for the uncertain jolting progress of the stage, and the surrounding trees, she examined the landscape.

A wild place, certainly. A place of high hills, woods, deep valleys. Indians, too. She remembered one spot on the road not far along into the territory northeast of Galena where a colorful party of Indians had stood on horseback off to one side of the road, watching the stage roll past. Impassive, dark-skinned men, wearing little clothing. She had been briefly terrified at sight of them, recalling instantly all the horrors of massacre of which she had read. But they had made no hostile move; one of them had even offered a gesture which might have been a reply to a hail from the driver.

The country through which the stage passed was spread over with the haze of sunset glow, so that it appeared to exist on two planes—the unreality presented to the eye, the reality below. Its wildness was apparent on both; here was untamed country, a far cry from that pleasant farming land around Providence, out of which she had come as a child. She looked upon it with a troubling foreboding. It had seemed romantic from the perspective of the east; the thought of being alone in the west with her husband, in the lead mining country of the Wisconsin Territory, seemed attractive; but the realities of the frontier had grown steadily less romantic with every mile west of Vincennes. The roughness of Galena had repelled her, though it was a considerable settlement by any standard, it had attractive houses and churches, it teemed with life; but the brawling frontiersmen at the inn and in the streets of the village had filled her with apprehension. Nor had the country north of Galena offered anything to assuage her disappointment. All the inns and stopping-places along the way seemed hastily put up to accommodate the travelers in the Territory at the least expense to the innkeepers; all of them, from the Four Mile House just out of Galena to the Olmstead Inn near Belmont, were rough, barren places. So were the settlements—Hazel Green, Platteville, Belmont—crude hamlets, with none of the graciousness of similar villages in the east. The frontier was not as she had imagined it, but her confusion was such that she no longer remembered how it was she had conceived it.

In topography, the Territory here was not unlike the land around Providence, except that on occasion it was higher. But the marks of civilization were absent—there were no stone or rail fences, no old houses, no good roads, none of the signs of human habitation save only this rough, jolting road over which they had traveled since early in the day. There had been a moment of sharp familiarity at sight of Galena, for that settlement, like Providence, lay along a stream, and was built up on the slopes on both sides; but this moment had passed, for the Galena River was not the Seekonk, and the frontier houses bore little relation to the gracious homes of Providence.

This Wisconsin country was dominated primarily by three tall domes of earth, blue against the sky now—the Platte and Belmont Mounds rising out of the high plateau to the southwest, the even higher Blue Mound rising out of the northeast, on the way to the territorial capital of Madison; secondarily by the ridge along which they rode. Almost from its beginning at Galena, forty miles south, the road had followed the ridge as steadily as possible, clearly because it would have prolonged the journey and increased the difficulties to go more directly up and down hill. It was no level route; in some places the ridge was broad, in some narrow: once it was a succession of sloping knolls, again stretches of long, flat terrain, prairie-like, but not true prairie, for it was a high succession of level areas broken by low, rolling regions, grass-covered except for little thickets, which flowed from around the Platte and Belmont Mounds and constituted a true plateau, which was lost, after some miles, in the customary declivities and deep valleys. Along the ridge at this hour the sun still shone with a soft, ever-reddening glow.

Sloping away from the ridge was a succession of shallow valleys, where centuries ago erosion had taken place and been healed over; beyond these, the slopes descended less gradually but farther still to the deeper valleys. These were often very long, though never wide; they lay among the hills, with their slopes rising and flung away toward higher slopes and the ridge on all sides, for that along which the stage made its way was not the only such ridge in this portion of Wisconsin Territory. It was into one of these deeper valleys that the stage was now beginning its descent through a growth of trees.

She thought she caught a glimpse of a house among the trees, but it was a phantom; she could not recapture it, and the stage was now proceeding along an undulating road, from slope to slope, past rows of ancient oaks and flaming maples, leaving the ridge behind. The sky which only a moment ago held the setting sun, shone now only with the afterglow; the sun had vanished behind the hills rising higher and darker as they went down.

The stage lurched out of the grove, and there before her lay Mineral Point, spectral in twilight—a long, winding street of small, compact houses, stone buildings of two and sometimes three storeys, crowding almost upon the street toward which the stage moved. There were a surprising number of buildings, some of frame construction; they stood immediately before them and grouped along both sides of the street toward the north. Some of the houses had the appearance of having grown out of the slopes, though along that part of the street which led south the houses stood only on one side, along the east; across the road was a swale, with massed willows here and there, a brook, and rising land, with earthworks and crude buildings adjacent. These, then, must be the lead mines, she reasoned, and the street they were now almost upon must be Shake-Rag Street, where most of the miners lived in little homes to which they were summoned at mealtime by wives who waved white rags to signify the hour.

The stage traveled more slowly now. From the window, Candace saw enough of the near houses to be unimpressed with them; she did not like their smallness, the few windows, the cold stone exteriors, the way in which they were grouped, some of them almost eave to eave, all set into the slope behind, like outcroppings from the dark hill. A few pale yellow lights burned in scattered windows, and just ahead, a lantern hung out on a hook before a building, casting a wan light into the dusk. It was this building which was the object of the stage's journey to Mineral Point, a three-storey, clapboard building, painted or whitewashed, with porches running across the full face of every storey. The stage reached the bottom of the slope and came to a stop. A simply lettered board above the porch announced it to be the Mansion House.

"We're home, Candace," said David.

She made no answer.

The driver was dropping to the ground amidst a flurry of sudden activity. A short, hunched-over man came running toward the horses with fodder and water. A fat man wearing a white apron and carrying another lantern came out of the building. He was followed by three others, two of them dressed for travel, the third the innkeeper himself; he stood in the doorway bidding the travelers godspeed. One addressed him briefly as "Mr. Nichols," after which Nichols retired into the building once more, and the travelers, coming forward, stood aloof while the aproned man exchanged words with the driver, who had by this time come around to the door of the stage and flung it open.

"Watch en step, Ma'am," cautioned the driver.

David leaped out and stood waiting for her. She felt a pang of hesitation, as if by stepping forth now she would commit herself irrevocably. Then she gave him her hand and stepped from the stage. Behind her, the driver climbed to the top after their baggage, while the aproned man moved around him with the lantern held ineffectually low, complaining, "Why doan't 'ee come on time, Lanyon? T' Governor's bin waitin'."

At the same moment a lusty, resonant voice rang out. "Well, Pengellen—I've not seen you in almost a year. Been away?"

"Only two months, sir." David caught hold of her hand and drew her forward. "I have the honor to present my wife, Candace—General Henry Dodge, late Governor of the Territory, now Delegate to Congress."

"Madam, I'm charmed and delighted to find one so fair come to our Territory. I commend your husband's good taste."

She smiled and gave him her hand. Even in the half-light of dusk and the reflected glow of the lanterns, she was aware of his wide-set, keen eyes, which dwelt upon her without faltering, of his firm, prominent nose, of his high brow and moulded mouth, about which a faint smile seemed to linger with an air of singular permanence. A man of character and strength, she thought. A man of determination, of purpose and power. He was rugged in appearance, and yet well dressed; his paradox was briefly inexplicable to her, until she divined that he was a frontiersman risen to leadership in his domain, and the marks of his earlier years were still apparent.

But he was turning. "Allow me. My companion, Lieutenant Nathaniel Parr. Mr. and Mrs. David Pengellen."

The other traveler stepped casually forward and bowed. He shook the hand David offered him; Candace did not extend her hand, but she could not help taking notice of Parr, who was a much younger man than the Governor—near David's own age, tall, dark, thin, with brooding eyes and a sullen mouth. His cheeks were a little hollow, and his eyebrows dark and arched, so that he had a faintly sardonic expression.

"I'm in haste for Dodgeville," said Dodge. "And then I must get back to Washington."

"I tell General Dodge we'd much rather have him back in Madison as Governor," said Lieutenant Parr.

"Iss, we'd all as lev see 'im back," muttered the aproned man, passing.

The Delegate chuckled. "Tallmadge has half the legislature against him now, has he not? An honest man, but stubborn. Who can tell? I may be back. Washington often seems to me cold and alien."

"But not half so cold as here, certainly," ventured Candace.

Dodge eyed her speculatively, and at his side, Parr looked at her with some frank interest which he made no effort to conceal, his dark eyes fixed on her, hovering about her, cradling her.

"I marvel at your husband's courage in bringing you here, Madam," observed Dodge. "There are cold months coming soon, too." He turned to David. "Where did you find her, Pengellen?"

"In Providence, General."

The driver came around his six horses, touching his hat to General Dodge. "Wessen 'ee git in, Governor?"

"Are you ready to be off, Lanyon?"

"Iss, tidden far to go. I mean t' git there 'fore dark."

General Dodge bowed again to Candace. "By your leave, Madam." He walked past her and got into the stage, followed by Lieutenant Parr. The lieutenant leaned from the stage, smiling, and said politely, "I look to see you again."

The stage rolled off in a swirl of dust and fallen leaves, revealing the aproned man still standing there, his lantern held laxly.

"Arr'y hastis for hoam, Pengellen, or can 'ee step ento t' Mansion House for a spur?"

"Thank you no, not tonight, Kit. We're tired and for home."

"Do as thee wool," answered Kit, moving toward the porch. "Aunt Marget's leve a braave fire. She knaw'd ye war comin'."

There was a brief surge of voices from the Mansion House as the door closed on Kit; then David and Candace were left alone in the wan glow of the hanging lantern, against which the deepening dusk on all sides seemed suddenly profoundly dark. The impression was fleeting, for the village began to give voice almost at once in the sounds of dogs barking, the neighing of horses, distant talk and laughter, and the lights in windows shone through the twilight up and down the long street, where it turned further and seemed to dip even deeper into the valley past the Mansion House. Here and there a few lights shone on the slope which rose on the east side of the street.

"We've got a way to walk, Candy," said David. "I'll carry the portmanteau and one of the bags, if you can manage the two small ones."

"Oh, yes," she said, eager now, anxious to see the home to which her husband had brought her. "Which way is it?"

He gestured. "Over there—on a hilltop past the edge of town. We won't be alone there for long," he added, as if to reassure her. "In a few years there'll be houses all around us. Why, there are over a thousand people and more than two hundred buildings in the Point now!"

Shouldering the portmanteau and picking up the bag, he started away. She followed. The bags she carried were light; they held mostly her own things, and she wondered whether she would ever have opportunity to wear them in so rough a setting. She smiled at the thought of the stage depot's being called the Mansion House; but in a moment she sobered—if so unpretentious a building had so pretentious a name, what could she expect of her own home in this settlement? And the man, Kit, with his strange language . . .

"David?"

"Yes?"

"David, why did that man call her 'Aunt Marget'? I thought she was *your* aunt."

He laughed. "I should have explained. She's neither. It's just one of those Cornish customs you'll have to get used to, Candy. Older folks are often referred to as 'Aunt' or 'Uncle.' Marget Hoskins is just the widow of an old fellow who mined here ten years ago. She works around for a living."

She turned this over in her mind. "Does she have a key to our house, then? He said she'd left us a fire."

"Why, yes. You'll meet her in the morning. She's to come and help you till you get settled. And I want her to teach you something about making the Cornish dishes I like. Do you mind?"

"Oh, no," she cried quickly. "I didn't want to be alone every day—at least not at first."

They left the street and began to mount the hill. He cautioned her to watch her step, for the way was rough—only a wagon trail. She went so carefully that twice David paused to wait for her. And once he turned her around, so that she might look down into the valley from which they had come and see among the trees the pale eyes of the houses, yellow with candle-light and lamps. From this perspective, under the boundless stars overhead and the pale glow of the orange sickle of new moon low in the west, the valley had a kind of wild, warm beauty.

"There aren't any street-lights," she said.

"They'll come," he answered confidently.

"Oh, David!" she cried suddenly, "I feel so far away from home."

"But you aren't—you're only a few steps from the house. Come on."

It was at her lips to say that she meant Providence, but she did not speak; David was right; Providence was no longer home; this was home, Mineral Point in Wisconsin Territory—a strange place in alien country where she might never again see Benefit Street or College Hill or Prospect, or her mother or ailing father . . .

The house loomed up before her, dark against heaven. It stood among trees, neither numerous nor dense enough to obscure it: a square building. The windowpanes shone in the moonlight; there were enough of them, and from one pair came the flickering glow which could mean only a hearth fire. The house was of two storeys, a boxlike building; from one of its chimneys came a steady column of smoke, spectral on the starlit sky.

The front door opened into a small vestibule, into which he carried her, gravely. The vestibule in turn gave into a long hall which divided the lower storey and gave access to a broad stairway to the second floor. The fire was in the living-room, which was to the right of the hall in the northwest corner of the ground floor. Beyond, on the southwest, was a bedroom. Across the hall was a spacious dining-room, and behind this a kitchen and pantry. Another door led out of the house from the kitchen. As soon as David had lit a lamp, she took it and went through the house, examining each room in turn, with David following, saying nothing, watching her intently, to detect if possible any mark of displeasure, any sign of dissatisfaction. The uncertain light of the lamp told him nothing.

She could not complain for lack of space. The rooms were amply large, even to the two bedrooms and the upstairs storeroom; but, by the very absence of all the furniture it might have held, the house seemed empty. The barrenness of these rooms affected her disagreeably; she felt cold, lost, ill-at-ease; she was relieved to be back in the living-room once more, where the fire dancing on the hearth created an air of coziness.

"Do you like it, Candy?" he asked finally.

"Yes, David—it's very nice—much nicer than I thought it would be, truthfully." She smiled as he took her into his arms and kissed her. "I was afraid we might have a log cabin with two rooms instead of one. Of course"—he kissed her again—"it needs things."

"Sure it does. But what it needed most it has now you're here."

She hugged him with a brief, shuddering fierceness.

"Tired? Aunt Marget has the bed turned down . . ."

"Can't we just sit here by the fire a while? It seems such a long time since I saw a fire."

"Last night, in Galena . . ."

"Oh, last night's so far away," she cried, sinking to the floor on the rag rug before the fireplace. "And the night before that—and the one before that—and before that—does that take us no farther than Ohio, David? How far are we, then, from Providence?"

He came down beside her and held her close, putting his cheek against her hair. "Homesick—already?" he murmured. "And but come here! A thousand miles, perhaps. But it doesn't matter, for the railroads will soon be here, and once they've come, why, a thousand miles will be as nothing."

She did not answer. She looked into the flames, seeing there all she had left behind—the familiar streets of Providence, old decades before this town of Mineral Point had come into being, before even the first white man had walked here; the old buildings, the steeples and towers of that city of her birth; the long-known faces. The log on the hearth fell apart, sending a shower of sparks up the chimney; a few of them leaped past the stones to the wooden floor and faded there.

"It's comfortable just this way, David," she whispered. "I wish we didn't have to stir—ever. I'm so tired now."

"Then, come—we'll go to bed. Mr. Trelawny will expect me as early as possible tomorrow, and Aunt Marget'll be here soon after sun-up."

She lay for a long while in bed, looking toward the windows, where the outline of the panes was set forth by the contrasting lightness of the sky, and broken by the windy branches of a tree. She thought of all that had taken place since she had bidden her parents farewell, spirited and excited as she was that day, anticipating the wildness of the west, the challenge of living there at her husband's side. Somehow it seemed no different to be in this house than it did to be at an inn along the way; she felt that in the morning they would once again have to be roused in haste and hurry through breakfast in order to be on time for the stage; it seemed that they were destined to hasten on and on, blindly, pushing ever farther away from the haven of Providence, of childhood and youth, toward some destination which was unknown in an alien place beyond maps, where they would be forever lost to the world to which they had grown accustomed.

She felt indeed like one lost in a wilderness; all the events of the journey to Wisconsin Territory pushed up in her thoughts, and in this darkness all the hardships were magnified, all the difficulties promised on the horizon of tomorrow seemed insurmountable; she dreaded the adjustment which would be necessary; she dreaded the thought of meeting people; she viewed with uncertainty her own ability to meet the challenge of living in a frontier town like Mineral Point, the roughness of which David had not tried to hide.

But I will try, she told herself earnestly, with a kind of desperation that spurred her sincerity. Though everything in this dark hour was covered over and colored by her homesickness, by the nostalgic longing to wash away the memory of the past days, to be back again in the home of her childhood and youth, she told herself sensibly that the past was done, there was no returning to it, she must fit herself and conform to this new way of life she had chosen when she had told David she would become his wife. She was confident that she could overcome her doubt.

She sank at last into a troubled sleep to the keening of the October wind at the eaves and the melancholy song of a screech owl not far away.

It was dawn when she awoke.

It took her a few moments to realize where she was. She looked to David, but he still slept, turned on his side, his dark head deep in his pillow. She slipped quietly out of bed, but the room was cold. She unfolded a blanket which lay at the foot of the bed and wrapped it around her; thus clad, she walked to the window and looked into the southwest.

Beyond the house rose the grove through which the stage had made its way the previous night; great old oak trees, together with maples fired with red autumn, covered the ascending slope. The sky was visible here and there, and on top of the slope the stage road ran; beyond loomed the Platte and Belmont Mounds —thrusting out of the morning sun as they had reared up against the stars during the night. But from here, no fence-post, no sign of an axe—nothing was there to say that any other human being lived in all this wilderness.

She walked into the living-room and crossed to the windows in the northeast. Down the slope lay the village. She studied the roofs crowded along the long winding road that was Shake-Rag Street. A few small houses stood on the rise flung up from the street—of stone, of logs, of clapboards and brick. Across, on the eastern slope, were the lead diggings, some of them but pits, wide at the mouth, narrowing toward the bottom, others shaft mines with windlasses and little sheds at their openings.

Under the morning sun, the village seemed twice as large as she had thought it on their arrival. Despite its roughness, there was a tidiness about it, a compactness which belied the appearance of being strung out along one long street. Two hundred buildings, David had said. Surely, among all these people, she ought not to be lonely.

Beyond the village rose the high ridge, along which lay the road to the outside. She recalled the names of the neighboring towns—on the southwest, Belmont, which had been the territorial capital until a short time ago—a small, scattered settlement, through which they had passed yesterday; to the northeast, Dodgeville, and past that on the one side Helena and the Wisconsin River, on the other, Madison, the new capital. The ridge towered over the settlement, flung up proudly upon the sky—and the Blue Mound above, like a great sentient beast reclining there in an attitude of watchful waiting, as beneficent under the sun as it could be malign under cloud and storm. For an instant she saw the house and the town as a kind of prison, and the three great dome-like hills as guards—with an effort she thrust this thought from her.

David came silently up behind her, saying, "You'll take cold, Candy." He put his arms around her, kissed her, held her close, blanket and all. "What are you doing? Looking over the Point?"

She nodded. "I'm glad I don't have to live in any of those little houses."

"They're not all houses. There are eight dry-goods stores, four groceries, two churches, a brewery, four public houses—the Mansion House is the biggest. There are tailor shops—there's even a cabinet-maker. And, of course, there are more smelting furnaces than just Trelawny's."

"And are all these people employed in the mines?"

He laughed heartily. "Lord, no, Candy! Those are just a few of the mines. There are lead mines all over around the village. Two miles northeast of here are the copper mines—though they're not doing so well since Mr. Ansley's plan to sell stock in London fell through. I'd say there are between four and five hundred miners. And many of them also have farms of some sort, with livestock."

"You didn't say . . . is there a school?"

"Trust an ex-school teacher to think of that! Certainly—a fine brick building. It was enlarged only this year."

She turned to say something further when the sound of a key fitting into the lock of the back door arrested her.

"Here comes Aunt Marget," said David. "Go and get dressed."

Aunt Marget Hoskins was plump and apple-cheeked, with soft, warm eyes and a pleasant smile. Though she lived in reduced circumstances, she never failed to dress neatly; this morning she had come over from her home on the slope above Shake-Rag Street, behind High, dressed in a tight bodice and so many skirts beneath her apron as to create the illusion that she still had a waist line. Her brown hair, parted in the middle and worn straight to a pug behind, was covered with an ample brown shawl, which more than half swathed her.

"Mister Pengellen!" she cried at sight of David. " 'Tis good to see 'ee. I knaw'd ye'd be hoam last night. An' t' bride?"

"She's dressing, Aunt. She'll be out in a few moments."

"I'll get a crum o' fire goin'."

As she worked, she made a detailed recital of everything that had happened to her since David had gone east, and ended with the hint of a pressing problem with which she hoped he could help her. Would he?

"Of course," said David, curious to know what it might be.

She told him. Her youngest sister—"that were Bess Bishop, her that was livin' in Tintagel"—had died, leaving her child an orphan. Hard upon the letter anouncing her sister's death, her orphaned niece herself came, having obtained passage to America through the kindness of a distant relative in London, who had occasion to be traveling to St. Louis, and had come as far as Galena with her. Now the girl was to live with her, but it was certain that she would have to find some kind of work to keep herself. She was too fine a girl to go into ordinary service for long, but her speech was so Cornish that she would find adjustment difficult. She should be taught to speak as Americans spoke, so that she might improve her prospects. "Oh, 'tes suant she talks, but the cheel caa'nt go on to speak in the ould way!" she cried.

"She could go to school here, Aunt."

"Aye, but she wedn't. P'raps she's toytish, but I do thenk she's too old."

"How old is she, then?"

"Seventeen."

"Yes, she'd be uncomfortable in school. How can I help, then?"

She explained volubly. She hoped that David, who had had an education in America, might help her niece to free herself from the Cornish pattern of speech. "She's cruel smart some ways," she finished, looking at him hopefully.

"I'll see, Aunt. I'll be quite busy at the store for the next few days. Meantime, she can study in Mr. McGuffey's newly revised speller. I'll set it out. You can take it to her when you go home. You've not told me her name."

"Tamson—Tamson Bishop, Mister Pengellen."

"A pretty name."

"Iss, 'tes that."

Candace came across the hall into the kitchen, dressed plainly in brown broadcloth, which became her. She walked already with an air of possession, thought David; this pleased him. He introduced her to Aunt Marget.

"I'm fixin' a dish o' tay, Missus," said Aunt Marget respectfully.

"You'll have to be patient with Mrs. Pengellen, Aunt," said David. "I'm afraid she'll take a while to understand you. But you'll do what you can to help her?"

"I'facks, I wool."

"I'm sure we'll get along, David," said Candace.

"Once 'ee're settled, we'll make a paasty," promised Aunt Marget enthusiastically. "I fetched some 'taties, steak, and onion to fill et ento the paasty. Ye'll soon be setten' en afore him, es good es any paasty en t' Point."

The two women took each other's measure unobtrusively. Candace offered to help prepare breakfast, but Aunt Marget would not permit it—"not this first day," as if somehow her first day in her new home ought to be set apart. As Aunt Marget chattered of news in Mineral Point, she flashed hurried glances at Candace, trying to take her measure, while Candace attempted earnestly to understand the older woman's burring dialect, the rolled 'r,' the over-emphasized vowels which confused her. Candace's eyes baffled Aunt Marget; they told her less than she thought they should, no matter how much she tried to see behind them. Aunt Marget saw nothing but their blandness, like a wall shutting away her sight. Of what Candace thought, she knew nothing. She felt in Candace a burning desire to please, to like and be liked, but decided that Candace was withholding judgment on her, on the house, on Mineral Point.

Immediately after breakfast, David set out for the store. He had gone into partnership with Jonathan Trelawny four years before; between them, they owned a general store and a smelter. In that short time the store had grown from a small shop on Shake-Rag to a larger, newer building on High Street, which was expanding up the slope behind the Mansion House. In a straight line, the new store was not far from David's home, but a steep valley separated them.

The morning air was crisp and aromatic; it teased David's nostrils. A light frost had touched the leaves; here and there showers of them came down to lie in pools of scarlet or pale green or yellow, giving off the pungence which filled the air—the sweetness that was the smell of maple leaves, the musk of oak foliage, the medicinal odor of willows. The white rime, evaporating under the sun, invigorated briefly the perfumes that lay in the still, windless morning, and mingled with the acrid smell of smoke from the smelters. Though the hour was early, the village was already bustling with activity; miners were on their way to the mines, two of the five smelters were smoking fulsomely, and several women were about in the streets, baskets on arm.

The store, too, was the scene of activity—but of a different kind. Just as David stepped over the threshold, a bolt of cloth came flying at him and caught him in the chest; he prevented it from falling to the floor, and Trelawny rose up from behind his desk nearby and caught another, saying, "Good morning, David. I'd been hoping for your return. I trust your wife's well." He coughed dryly, on his way to replace the bolt of cloth, and added, "As you see, mine's in good spirits."

"I'm sorry, David. I meant that for Jonathan," Mrs. Trelawny called from the rear of the store.

Trelawny had married a high-spirited woman—tall and angular, with pronounced and coarse features, several years his junior. Seen together, they made a noticeable contrast, for Trelawny was short and rotund, with pink cheeks, a full face, full sideburns, a Quaker beard, and a cherubic eye, whereas his wife was tall, with wiry, dark hair of all lengths so that it looked forever unkempt, a fierce glance, and a sensual mouth. They had frequent arguments, of which all the village knew, for Mrs. Trelawny, being a violent woman, was not content to confine them to their home; she often followed her husband from the house, heaping abuse on him in a loud, carrying voice, and, since he paid no attention to her, she was always so much more infuriated that by the time they reached the store, she was sufficiently provoked to begin throwing things at him. He was so accustomed to these occasional outbursts that he spent his time ducking whatever she threw, and picking things up to replace them the while, saying nothing, waiting for her temper to cool, which it always did.

"What's wrong this morning?" asked David.

"Turnip pasty," answered Trelawny shortly.

"I don't cook good enough for him," cried Mrs. Trelawny.

"The turnip pasty—especially three times a day—is an invention of the devil," said Trelawny. "And my wife's partial to her relative's inventions."

Mrs. Trelawny came forward, her angry wild eyes turned now on David. "And did you bring your wife into this hole, David?" she demanded, coming up to him.

"Indeed, I did. I think she'll like it."

Mrs. Trelawny clearly did not agree. "I'll call on her this afternoon," she announced, and made her way to the door.

"You might ask her if she's got any recipes," taunted Trelawny.

She whirled around, snatched up a ball of twine, and flung it at him. He caught it. The entire building seemed to shudder at her slamming of the door. David smiled; he had witnessed such scenes before. Despite these violent quarrels, which never excited Trelawny, it was quite evident that there was a bond of affection between the Trelawnys which no violence would banish.

"If I were a preacher," mused Trelawny, sitting down, "I'd preach a sermon a year on woman as man's natural cross." He permitted himself a weary smile. "Well, now, David, since you're back, you might as well know how things are going."

"Of course."

"We'll do better this year than last—prospects have never looked brighter for the lead. We're getting two dollars, eighty-two and a half cents the hundred weight; I figure it'll be up to three dollars next year. But there's talk among more shippers about sending the lead overland to Milwaukee and by way of the lake. Ever since Doty got the New Yorkers to reduce the toll on the Erie Canal boats, it's been getting cheaper to ship by way of Milwaukee than by Galena."

David smiled at his enthusiasm. "I've been watching the market in the east," he put in.

"Likely you have. And have you been watching the political pot boil in the Territory, too?"

David laughed. "Wisconsin Territory hardly exists in eastern papers, Jonathan, except insofar as a senator from New York is now our Governor. How's Tallmadge? I heard talk last night at the Mansion House."

"Tyler's man. He and the legislature are at sixes and sevens all the time." Trelawny snorted in disgust. He went on volubly; he was confident that if Polk were elected, Tallmadge would not be reappointed. He was not sure it would be Dodge again, but Dodge's turn was bound to come up sooner or later. He leaped from talk of the Governor to the Pecatonica & Mississippi Railroad, which was to have reached Mineral Point long before.

"I can't help a smile at the thought of Moses Strong going about the country buying up pieces of property in the hope that the rails will cross there and he'll grow rich—like Doty. Poor Strong has never yet had good judgment, for all that he's smart as a whip when it comes to law. He did have a hand in some changes here—that ordinance against pigs on the streets, and the appointment of Jock Dwight as stove-pipe inspector." But suddenly he brushed all this aside. "You'll want to know about the business—it's good—nothing short of a disaster like the discovery of more lead in some other part of the country would stop us. Come, we'll go over the books if you like. Sit down here."

But before David could do so, a customer came in—the wife of one of the miners come to buy provisions and bringing in a pail of lead ore in payment, as was the prevailing custom. She engaged Trelawny in conversation while David weighed the ore and computed the credit it gave her; then he followed her about and helped her to assemble the things she wanted from the shelves and counters, for the store had just got in a large shipment of goods, and Trelawny had not yet begun to put them into order.

The woman's Cornish talk fell softly to his ears. She was a shy woman, save for talkativeness, and David answered her in Cornish. As he went about the store with her, he took note of the well-stocked shelves. Trelawny had not been idle; he had prepared well for the winter. It would take several days to put the stock away, if the time could be taken from the furnaces. Each of them spent part of every day at the smelter, though the overseer there was able and conscientious enough; it was a proprietary obligation to make an appearance at the smelter daily; if the miners who brought in lead for smelting at the customary terms of thirty-five percent for Trelawny & Pengellen had any reason for complaint, one of the proprietors was ready to listen.

Another customer came in, and another after. The accounts had to wait.

When at last he reached home for dinner, David was aware of an air of diffident tension between the two women—an intangible impression, betrayed not so much by word or glance as by their absence, the way in which Candace avoided Aunt Marget's eyes, the way the older woman kept her glance on stove or table. Candace acted as if he had been gone several days.

"We've fixed a real Cornish dinner," she cried. "Or, rather, Aunt Marget's done it . . ."

"Och, she stick'd a comfortable thoomb en et, too."

"A pasty," he said, looking at the table. "Seedy bread, apple and spice pie."

"And there's a saffron cake in the oven," added Candace.

"I thoft best we keep'd at en, there's a pure core a-doen'," said Aunt Marget. "But t' Missus es fity. Doan't 'ee let dennar cool."

They sat down. Aunt Marget waited to be specially invited, though a place had been set for her. This was an unusual act of deference to Candace, thought David. He said nothing, however, helping himself to the pasty, the savory aroma of which filled the kitchen where they sat eating, while Candace explained that she wanted to set the table in the dining-room, but Aunt Marget had thought, there being just the three of them, and the two women so busy, it would be best to set in the kitchen.

Candace chattered happily. Her animation increased the color in her cheeks, her eyes shone. She had enjoyed working on the dinner, knowing it was meant to please David, and what she had learned about Cornish food surprised her, for a pasty was not, after all, much different—except that it did not have everything in it—from a meat pie, and seedy bread was very much like the caraway bread one could buy from any baker in Providence, though it was better in flavor and texture, while the pie suggested spiced-apple pie, though it included currants and lemon peel in addition.

David was pleased at Candace's aptitude, at her response to the dishes of which he was so fond. He was reassured and confident that this beginning augured well for her complete adjustment to Mineral Point. He set forth for the store once again with an added spring to his step. He forgot the initial air of diffident tension he had caught between the women, perhaps because he was meant to forget it.

He was hardly aware, when he walked into the store, of Trelawny's angry speech against Jim Casthew, one of the miners who brought lead to be smelted, who had come in during David's absence to accuse Trelawny & Pengellen of shorting him in his percentage, trumpeting about and threatening suit.

"That assinego!" cried Trelawny wrathfully. "That twattling Glassenbury Dog! Does he take us for hoddymandoddies, eh? I sent him about his business. I say, let him sue and be damned! What do you say, David?"

"Let him," answered David tranquilly.

"Aye, 'tis agreed," said Trelawny with a pat nod, well satisfied with himself, as if he had talked David into intransigence, though David had hardly been listening.

He was tired when he started home that evening just before sundown. The day had been unseasonably warm; he had had to spend two hours at the smelter, which was off some distance from the store; and he had come back to plunge into the work of putting the store to rights so that they might move around more knowingly and not keep customers waiting while they hunted for articles.

As he walked along, he drank deeply of the evening air. Somehow the stillness of late afternoon had brought much of the smoke from the furnaces into the valley, to lie like mist along

Shake-Rag Street; but here, up the slope beyond High Street, the air was pleasant with the pungence of the frost-touched leaves, and there was also a different kind of smoke smell drifting in from the southwest, where doubtless the grass-grown plateau near the twin mounds burned, as it often did in October after the carelessness of some traveler or at the wish of the Indians, some of whom still roamed the Territory.

The place where he crossed the slope of the ridge toward that promentory on which his house stood was almost at the top. As he walked there in the haze of last sunlight, he was suddenly aware of a woman's voice raised in song, low and sweet. It came from a little way above him, from the edge of the timber there. He listened, recognized the melody, and heard the words. *Westryn wind, when wilt thou blow? The small rain down doth rain. Christ, that my love were in my arms and I in my bed again!* A pause of but a few moments; then it came a second time, the same song.

Curious, he made his way quietly forward, lest he disturb the singer.

She sat with her back to him so that he saw first her long chestnut hair, coming down softly straight to her shoulders, and there turning outward and up, a little wild. She wore a dress of some dark blue stuff resembling brocade; it was cut unlike the dresses worn by the ladies of the Territory; it was not in the fashion, for it was tight about the upper part of her body, and long and flowing about her legs where she sat with arms crossed on her knees, which were drawn up under her chin. A slim girl, with long, almost bony fingers. He did not know her.

She had not heard him and continued to sing. It was a long time, he thought, since last he had heard this ballad. Her voice was low, moving, somewhat husky; she sang the words as if they were filled with far more meaning than they had ever had before, with a kind of urgent longing he could feel. Listening to her made him go back in memory to his childhood in Cornwall, and a nostalgia began to grow in him, a longing for the place of his birth with its wild crags and deep, lonely combes. This Wisconsin Territory was like it, true, and yet it could never be the same as Cornwall, so far was it from the sea, and without the marks of generations upon it.

"Arr'y homesick, lass?" he asked during the pause that followed her song.

She sprang lithely to her feet and turned, all in one movement, her eyes flashing. "An' what buchaboo es et askin'?" she demanded spiritedly.

He did not answer, only looked at her. She was not yet twenty, that was certain. The eyes that challenged his were greenish-blue, with a sharply defined rim of clear blue; her mouth was small but competent, with an upper lip that was thin in contrast to the full lower lip now defiantly thrust out; a flush of color stood angrily in her cheeks, which were slightly hollowed beneath her high cheek bones. The tightness of her bodice praised the rounded fullness of her breasts. When he did not answer, she spoke again.

"Art' en sayen'? What do 'ee thenk? Who wud na be homesick en this land?" She paused abruptly, in the attitude of catching her words. "Och, I knaw thee! Ye're Mr. David Pengellen."

"And you must be Tamson Bishop," he said, "that I'm to teach the American speech to, and for whom I've already set out a spelling book."

She began to laugh. "Aunt Marget's made thee wise," she cried. "But 'tes true. I'm that growed up, I cud na set wi' 'ee cheel'n."

"What are you doing here, Tamson?" he asked then.

"Waiten' for Aunt Marget to set out."

"Come, then. We'll go to the house and you can set out together."

They walked down the slope through the wood, beyond which the house stood in the early shadow of the hill, the sunlight having already been thinned, though it still lay on the plateau of the Mounds toward which Tamson had been faced when he had come upon her. She talked freely as they walked; clearly Aunt Marget had disposed her to look upon him as a friend. She was anxious to see the spelling book, and promised to study it faithfully; however much she was satisfied with her own speech—and she was that, she insisted—it was disconcerting to be so often misunderstood, for by no means all Mineral Point was Cornish, and, it seemed, practically nowhere else in all this vast country harbored any of her countrymen, so that, homesick as she was for Cornwall, there were times when, in contrast to the long trip from across the sea through the eastern half of the United States, she felt herself closer to home in the Point than in any other place she had been since leaving her native country.

Aunt Marget was just leaving when they came to the house.

"Aw, ye've mit Tamson, Mr. Pengellen."

"Yes, she was up on the ridge waiting for you to start home."

Aunt Marget turned and introduced her niece to Candace, who had come to the door: she explained that Tamson was the girl for whom she had taken along the speller David had laid out.

"Perhaps I can help you later, too," offered Candace. "I used to teach school."

"P'raps," agreed Tamson, smiling gratefully.

"Come along wi' 'ee, Tammy," said Aunt Marget, walking away. She called back to Candace, "I'll come o'er t'morrow."

"I'll be waiting, Aunt Marget," answered Candace.

Once they were inside the house, Candace flung her arms around David and held him tight. No word crossed her lips, but a little smile held there. It's going to be all right, he told himself happily.

When Tamson Bishop woke up, she was alone in the house. It was her second awakening; she had responded briefly to her Aunt Marget's call earlier in the morning, but had fallen asleep again. Now the older woman was gone, and her little house was bright with the morning sunlight streaming into its small rooms through the narrow, deep-set windows which admitted it.

She lay for a long moment, stretching, cat-like, until she remembered that she should have been up long since; then she sprang from bed, conscience-stricken, knowing she must be about the little work her aunt had left for her. She pulled her nightgown over her head, and stood for a moment, naked, passing her hands through her hair.

Catching sight of herself in the sliver of mirror which hung from the wall, she went over to it and examined herself. She had no eyes for the beauty of her well-rounded breasts, nor for the fine, firm, gently mounded lines of her belly, nor for the contours of her thighs, but only for the thinness of her shoulders and back. In every other respect, she seemed to herself to have the body of a young woman, no longer just a girl; but the thinness of her back where her bones showed, troubled her; it seemed unchanged from the way it had looked when she was twelve and ten and even younger; and she looked at it now, her head turned to the glass, wondering again what she might do to round out her flesh there.

"Ye've a head filled wi' condudles, ye vain witch," she said to her reflection and turned away.

When she finished dressing, she went out into the kitchen, which was somewhat less small than the room in which she had slept. Breakfast waited for her. She looked at the clock. Just a few minutes past eight. Aunt Marget could not have been gone long. She felt less guilty and sat down to the table, after fetching the teapot from the stove. Floury milk and barley bread. Plum jam, too. Before she began to eat, she remembered David's book, and got up to get it. She put it down beside her plate. She poured her tea and opened the book at random. Holding the pages apart, she began to read.

"Brown owls live all day in the woods, but at night they come near the house, and make a great noise. Owls that live near barns eat rats and mice, and so save the wheat, oats, and corn. They take them in the night." She dropped her eyes to the next lesson. "Lesson 56. Words promiscuously arranged. De*b*t a fresh' es *say*' me*a*nt serv il*e* . . ." She wrinkled her nose in distaste and turned back to the beginning of the book. "In remodeling this work, it has been attempted, first, to introduce among others as many *primitive* words as the space would allow, and then, in subsequent lessons, to illustrate by examples and rules the formation of the more important derivatives. . . . In *pronunciation*, the authority of Dr. Webster has been followed, as presented in the late revised editions of his works; and this, without doubt, is now well established as the settled usage."

She closed the book, somewhat rebellious. "Do 'ee thenk me a cheel?" she asked the teapot indignantly. She took a swallow of tea and washed her rebellion down with it. She must learn the American way of speaking, it was true; Aunt Marget and Mr. Pengellen were right, for else she could go nowhere, save among her own people, lest she be laughed at, or worse, pitied.

She did not touch the book again until after she had done the chores left by her aunt. Then she picked it up from the table and went outside. It was now mid-morning, and Mineral Point lay flooded in the warm October sun. The house which was now her home was set part way up the slope which ended in Shake-Rag Street, at the far end of that street, though there were other houses on both sides of it. All had a marked similarity to one another; they belonged to the little group of stone dwellings erected by the early Cornish miners which had so repelled Candace Pengellen at her first sight of them; all were small, compact, seemingly too compressed to afford room to turn around in. Tamson had never known any other; indeed, except for the absence of a commodious sitting-room, it was no different from her former home in Tintagel.

She sat down in the grass beneath an oak tree at a place from which she could command a view of Shake-Rag and its junction with the High Street, down which the stage-coach must come, as well as of the slope across Shake-Rag, where the miners were at work in the pits and mines, and wagons moved to and fro, coming for loads of ore and moving to the smelters with it. How different it all was from Tintagel! There was a street in Polperro of which she was reminded at sight of the street before her; but it was possible that her memory tricked her into thinking there was a resemblance, for she had been but a little girl the last time she had visited Polperro. Yet the houses were in many respects alike. Perhaps those who had come here knew of no other kind of house to build. The valley, too, suggested Cornwall. She felt this similarity, but at the same time she was ever conscious of the wilderness.

It was not the same kind of wildness she had known along the rugged Atlantic coast. If she walked forth from the village here she would never find the ancient stones of a Kelliwic or Damelioc fortress, she would never see in this country a moor with its strange cromlechs and its brooding age, but only forests and open places dense with tall grass, rutted roads and woodland paths, where, like as not, Indians might appear. But worst of all, the sea was far away; how far she had no way of knowing. She thought she had traveled for an eternity over land; with each day that passed, the distance from the sea was increased. As long as she had sailed the Atlantic, she had the comfort of knowing that the same waters touched upon the coast near Tintagel; but now the ocean was hundreds and hundreds of miles away. It was beyond her understanding that this place, so very far from the Atlantic, should be not yet half way across America. How vast a country America must be!

"If 'twere a man, 'ee cud put all Cornwall ento 'es pocket!" she murmured. "Iss—an' still 've room for 'ee pipe!"

If she closed her eyes, she could see her beloved Tintagel again. Thinking so, she lowered her lids, but, absurdly, she did not see her native streets and byways, nor even the sea flinging itself upon the coast nearby, nor the brooding moors with their timeless cromlech, nor anything of Cornwall at all, but only David Pengellen's face as he had looked at her when he said, "And you must be Tamson Bishop that I'm to teach the American speech to . . . !"

She opened her eyes hastily and turned to the book, feeling as guilty as if she had been caught in a misdemeanor by her teacher and could expect wrath to fall upon her within the instant. She read with diligence, sometimes puzzled, sometimes annoyed at the simplicity of the task to which she had been assigned, but her mind's eye saw on every page, beyond the crowded print, past the analyses, the syllabification, the pictorial alphabet and Mr. McGuffey's lessons, the lineaments of David Pengellen.

Candace was ready to welcome Aunt Marget when the older woman came. She had already put away the breakfast dishes by that time; this did not escape Aunt Marget's notice.

" 'Tis sheamed I am to be late," said the older woman. "Ye should've leav'd dishes till I coomed."

"Oh, it wasn't for that David asked you to help me, Aunt Marget," protested Candace. "It was to help me learn to make his kind of food. What shall we start with today?"

"Scalded cream," answered Aunt Marget promptly. "An p'raps fuggan or currany 'obbin wi' figgies."

Aunt Marget bustled about with such vigor that Candace soon began to feel she sat in the older woman's kitchen, not her own;

the thought displeased her, but she pushed her displeasure resolutely from her mind. If David wished to be served these things, it was her duty to learn how to prepare them, and she should be grateful for Aunt Marget's help.

As the morning wore on, their talk moved from food, for it was only necessary that Candace see each recipe come into being, and they could talk of other things. Each of them gave free rein to her natural curiosity about the other.

Aunt Marget had lived in Mineral Point—she habitually called it simply "t' Point"—for over a decade. She and her husband had come in 1834—"a pure spur ago, Missus"—he had put up the house in which she still lived, and he had worked the mines until his death by accident. Before that, she had come out of Penzance, and met her man in Truro. They had not had children; it had not been God's will; they had wanted them, but what could they do against the will of heaven?

She spoke of Mineral Point with an almost proprietary air. She had watched it grow from a mean collection of little more than hovels to its present estate. In her eyes, Mineral Point was a settlement of considerable eminence, which Candace thought pathetic, though she made no comment; indeed, to hear Aunt Marget, Mineral Point was no less than the center of all Wisconsin, and it was plain that the rest of the world revolved about this valley of her adopted home. She spoke not with emotional enthusiasm, but with such a settled air that it did not occur to Candace that anyone could ever take issue with Aunt Marget and convince her of error.

Indeed, demanded Aunt Marget, was there another settlement in all the Territory which had in it such a Miners' Guard as Captain Rodolf was organizing? Where, outside of perhaps Milwaukee, was there another such band of fire-fighters? Were there elsewhere such a gathering of miners and such an industry in mining? To all this Candace listened patiently. Perhaps the older woman's point-of-view grew out of never really having known a better life. Candace had no knowledge of Cornwall, but, like many people satisfied with their native place, she thought of it only as a vague, foreign country, which of necessity could not offer to anyone as much as that corner of America which was hers.

"But what do 'ee thenk, Missus Pengellen?" Aunt Marget asked suddenly. "What do 'ee thenk on t' Point?"

"Oh," answered Candace, taken by surprise, "I hardly know what to think. It's all so strange to me."

It was not like Providence, then? pursued the older woman.

The very thought was laughable. She did not trust herself to speak, but only shook her head. Like Providence, indeed! In her heart she was appalled at the rawness of this settlement in the wilderness. Though there were times of the day and night, under the sun and the moon, when the stone buildings were given an aspect of mellow age and a kind of undeniable beauty, much of the village was made up of buildings which were the merest makeshift; she could not help making the comparison, so favorable to Providence, where age and gentility were one. An only child, Candace had been reared as a genteel young woman in a milieu far removed from the rigors of frontier living; though well trained in all the genteel virtues, she lacked that practical knowledge without which the ability to adjust to change is severely inhibited. The graces which served her well in the company of the Andovers, the Perkinses, the Phillipses, and those others of her relatives who had lived in and around Providence for several generations were of no avail in Mineral Point, where the principal concern of men and women alike was in a primitive kind of struggle for survival against elements with which life in Providence seldom had to cope so directly.

What then was Providence like? pressed Aunt Marget, and listened incredulously as Candace tried to re-create the sights and occasions of her home city, for it was still as home that she thought of Providence, as if she had not quite convinced herself that it was in Mineral Point that she was to live for the remainder of her days, as if she could not believe that the very exuberance and freshness which had seemed so attractively different in David during his stay in Providence were an integral part of this wild country from which he had come east, and that here all was exuberantly fresh, every moment of every day was filled with the promise of a glowing future. But how long away? None could say—tomorrow, next year, a decade hence—always around some corner yet to be reached.

Could it be that she did not like Mineral Point? Aunt Marget asked.

"It's so new to me," answered Candace. "I don't know it yet. I feel like a stranger still—even here in my own house."

"Ye sad cheel'! Ye've not ben about," said Aunt Marget, confident that a close scrutiny of the settlement would prejudice any observer in its favor. " 'Ee cud na see haalf town from here." She looked up suddenly, moved by the thought which had occurred to her. "I'll tell 'ee, Missus. Wessen 'ee walk about weth me to see a fitty part o' they housen? Thee mays't see enough to meake year vardict terrectly."

"We might walk out after lunch," agreed Candace.

But Aunt Marget would not wait. As if inflamed by a missionary zeal, she wanted to go as quickly as the work permitted; so Candace acquiesced, knowing it would not take long. In midmorning they set out, walking over to High Street, which at this hour was a mêlée of activity, for it was along this street that most new construction was being carried on, and down this road into the village came horsemen, wagons, prairie schooners, and the day's first stage.

There was no need for Candace to speak as they walked along, for Aunt Marget talked incessantly, pointing out the Court

House, a beautiful pillared building, imposing and solitary in its splendor, a building which might indeed, however incredible, have come out of her own beloved Providence. Aunt Marget pointed out the Franklin House and the Central, the other two of the town's hotels, and extolled the virtues of the business establishments—especially of Trelawny & Pengellen—in such a rush of incoherent enthusiasm, complicated by her dialect, that Candace could not be certain that she described two stores or six. Moreover, the women of the town were abroad at this hour, come shopping, and Aunt Marget knew them all, and stopped before each one she met to introduce "Mr. David Pengellen's new bride, fresh from the braave city o' Providence."

From every side rose the smell of lumber being sawed, of dust, of the smoke from the smelters riding the wind, so that it was only now and then that the wild pungence of leaves invaded the places where they walked. Aunt Marget moved about with such determination that she would have taken Candace to the pits themselves, had Candace not at last protested and warned that if they did not return soon, there would be no dinner ready for David when he came from the store. Aunt Marget turned back at once.

"An' ded 'ee see how they all gawked at 'ee?" she cried. "Doan't 'ee mind; en a few days' vallee they'll knaw ye."

In mid-afternoon two horsemen appeared on the ridge north of the village and began the descent of the slope broken in both directions by the lead mines. The forward horse was ridden by Lieutenant Nathaniel Parr; the horse coming last by an Indian, a scout and an old friend of Parr's, known as Soaring Hawk. Both carried Enfield rifles. The Indian was scantily clad, and wore three feathers in a band around his head. The feathers came up slantwise over the crown of his head from the back; his straight black hair, partly bound down by the feather-band, was lustrous. His eyes, too, were jet; his reddish-brown face was thinner than that of the average member of his Winnebago tribe, but his high cheek bones were pronounced, and his mouth more full than the lineaments of his face would have permitted, had all been perfectly balanced. His nose was long, aquiline, almost sharp; his dark body, unclad to the waist, and from there in buckskin, was lithe and powerful. He rode his roan stallion with an easy laxness. He had ridden in silence for most of the way from Dodgeville, but now, as they began the descent into the valley where Mineral Point lay, he broke forth into complaint of a kind permissible only between friends of years' standing.

Why had he, Parr, chosen to ride forth at this hour to this place? He wanted to know. The sun was hot, not a creature was in sight to invite chase and capture, they had better have gone over to the valley of the Wisconsin and hunted the bottoms along that river.

"I've told you," said Parr shortly. "Judge Dunn thought these people should know he was coming in tomorrow to hold court."

The ways of palefaces were strange indeed, Soaring Hawk went on. Since when had Judge Dunn taken to such concern for those who were to appear before him? Or had it been perhaps the idea of Parr's?

"It's no affair of mine," answered Parr. "You talk too much, Hawk." He wanted to add petulantly that the Indian's broken speech, half patois, was hard to understand; but actually he understood it very well, and he knew that the Indian would interpret his speaking so as evidence that he did not want to listen.

He, Soaring Hawk, did not understand what the white man did in his "hold court," he went on. If a man did a wrong, he should be punished. His wrong was there for all to see. It needed no other man to point to it and say, see, here it is, he did it. Still more, it needed no other man to say the contrary. Did not the white men see with eyes even as their red brothers did?

"In the white man's law, every condemned man has a right to have counsel. Counsel for the defense puts his client's case," said Parr.

"Counsel for defense?" repeated Soaring Hawk haltingly.

"He gives the devil's side, the evil spirit's side," explained Parr.

This Soaring Hawk readily understood; he nodded complacently.

By this time they had reached Shake-Rag Street north of the junction with High Street. An east wind brought a cloud of smoke from the smelters and drove it about them.

Soaring Hawk raised his voice and lamented. The white men brought evil smells into the country, they poisoned the land, they dug holes and burned out the earth, and these rascals in the Point were the worst of them all; they were too lazy even to set out crops or to keep animals; after the holes were all dug, what was to become of them? They had stolen the mines from the Winnebago in the first place, but the Winnebago had only picked up the lead that lay on the ground; they did not have such greed as to dig down into the earth for it, no. But the white men, aha!—knaves, thieves, scoundrels! He shrugged his shoulders with befitting eloquence and was still.

Parr had not been listening. He had heard all this many times before. Soaring Hawk hated everything about the mines, which had, in truth, once belonged to his people, less than twenty years before, the same Winnebago who had been ruthlessly pushed back by the rapacious easterners who came into southern Michigan Territory and seized the mines, the Indians whose dominion here had ended with the Winnebago War almost two decades ago. Parr had fixed his eye on his destination, the store of Trelawny & Pengellen not far beyond the Mansion House on the slope of High Street.

When he entered the store, followed by Soaring Hawk, Parr found David alone.

"Mr. Pengellen," said Parr, advancing with outstretched hand. "We met the other evening at the Mansion House."

"Lieutenant Parr," answered David, recognizing him at once.

Soaring Hawk sat crosslegged on the floor and watched with absorbed interest. He was constantly being perplexed by the ways of the palefaces, who, he had repeatedly observed, had an incurable habit of always circling a wood instead of going straight through it. He was convinced that Lieutenant Parr had some concealed reason for making this journey from Dodgeville, other than that he professed; he was baffled by it.

"Mr. Trelawny isn't here?"

"No, Lieutenant, he's gone to the smelter. You can find him there if need be. Just take Shake-Rag up that way . . ."

Parr shook his head. "I have no need of seeing him, Mr. Pengellen. You and he are partners; my business is with either of you. I've just come over from Dodgeville on a mission from Judge Dunn. It appears that one of your Cornish compatriots has laid an information against Trelawny & Pengellen before Judge Dunn."

David was astonished, but in a moment he recalled Trelawny's anger of the previous day against Jim Casthew. It must be he, though such haste was unusual. Yet it was like Casthew, what with his temper, to take the trouble to ride over to Dodgeville. He asked bluntly, "Was it Casthew?"

"I believe that was his name."

"Is Dunn sending a summons by your hand, Lieutenant?"

"No, sir. You anticipate me. The Judge will come over in the morning and hear the case. He'll issue a summons at that time, no doubt. I thought, since I was in any case bound in this direction, I might stop by and pass the information along to you. The summons might otherwise find you unprepared to meet the charges."

"I'm in your debt, Lieutenant."

"No, sir, not at all. I'm sure you'd do as much for me, were our positions reversed. I'll be on my way. Pray give my regards to Trelawny, and, if she hasn't forgotten me, to Mrs. Pengellen."

They rode west, up Shake-Rag Street to the top of the ridge, and then turned north once more toward Dodgeville. A south wind vyed with the wind from the east; neither was strong. On the ridge the smell of autumn lay in air with the somnolent warmth of the sunlight, and here and there little clouds of midges and gnats hung, singing thinly. In a few minutes no sign of the village was left save only, to the discerning eye, a spectre of smoke from the smelters, mounting the slope on the wind out of the coulée. They rode for a long time in silence, but at last Soaring Hawk grunted and spoke.

He was put in mind of a bewitched hunter, he said.

"Is that so?" asked Parr, wondering what was coming.

Soaring Hawk nodded gravely. The bird, he went on, was up there—he made a gesture toward the west. The hunter, starting from here, went that way—he motioned toward the southeast. True, he might in the end get the bird; it was quite possible; no one knew the wishes of Manitou, who was all-wise. But why did he not go the way of the bird and take him at once?

Parr said nothing. He was trying to follow the meaning his companion was attempting to convey.

Soaring Hawk had not expected an answer. He grunted, shrugged, grunted again. Why? he repeated. That was plain: the hunter was a white man. And the bird—aha! perhaps Manitou had only made the bird to be the victim of such an addled hunter!

Parr glanced at his companion. But the Indian rode now with

his eyes closed, and his mouth was twisted as if in derision or pain. For all Parr knew about the ways of the Winnebago, Soaring Hawk might be shaking with laughter behind his face. The moment called for an answer in kind; he grunted.

When Trelawny returned from the smelter, David told him of Parr's visit.

"Well, let Casthew do his damndest, the timdoodle!" cried Trelawny. "We're ready for him. I'll answer to him—and if I can't, you can. The figures are all in the book, as you'll see."

David had already examined the books and was satisfied that Casthew had no case against them. Why had it come to this? Why had not Trelawny tried to reason with Casthew and made him look at the figures for himself?

"You ask that, knowing his hot head, David? Faugh! even his wife, poor thing, can do nought with him."

"Who is this fellow, Parr?" asked David, after a pause.

Trelawny shrugged. "Och, I cannot say. An orphan, I'm told. He was raised by his uncle and aunt in Galena, I think. An older cousin fought with Dodge in the Black Hawk War, and Parr has conceived a great worship of the Governor. I believe he was his aide in Madison when Dodge was in the capitol."

"Well, he's hardly alone in admiring Dodge," said David dryly.

"Until the legislature in a pet took the militia away from Doty, he was a member of the militia. He still serves Dodge in some ways. Each time the Governor returns to the Territory, Parr is at his side. And as he feels toward the Governor, his Indian, Soaring Hawk, feels toward him."

"Does he employ the Indian?"

Trelawny shook his head. "No. We do."

David looked at him in amazement. "We do?" he echoed.

"Aye," answered Trelawny without looking up from the

paper he was writing. "Not just Trelawny & Pengellen, David, but the lead shippers of the country round—here and Dodgeville and Galena and the New Diggins—why, yes, to keep us informed of what goes on among the Indians. There's always this talk of uprisings—marches against the lead wagons and the boats—it would be foolish to be without information."

David chuckled. "Indian uprisings! There's about as much danger of that as there is of the collapse of the business."

Trelawny favored him with a long, humorless stare. "I don't know what any Indian will do. Do you? I don't know what my next-door neighbor will do. Do you? Why, there are times when I don't know what I myself will do. And if I don't, I guess it's a safe bet to say there's no harm keeping in touch with what the Winnebago and the Fox and the Sauk are talking about among themselves."

"Since when?"

"Since you went east, David."

"And to whom does he report?"

"To whomever it's handy for him to. If there's any news, we'll all know it soon enough by stage."

"I'd guess the stage hasn't had much business carrying word of the Indians around," said David, grinning.

"True," agreed Trelawny imperturbably. He looked up, putting down his pen. "There," he continued, handing the paper to his partner, "there are all the figures you'll need for court in the morning. You'd better take it. If Casthew becomes abusive, as he's likely to do, I'll lose my own temper."

When David went to the Court House at eleven next morning, in response to the summons against Trelawny & Pengellen, he found a considerable audience already gathered. He looked around for Candace and found her with Aunt Marget; with them sat Tamson Bishop. Judge Charles Dunn, Chief Justice of the Territorial Court, sat at a table up in front—a tall, gangling man in his middle years, with a lantern jaw upon which several days' growth of greying whiskers could be seen. His wide mouth was set; his dark eyes warm but wary. He was roughly clad, his shirt was open at the neck, and he had unbuttoned his frock coat. A shoestring tie straggled down one side of his shirt. His saddlebags stood next to one shoe, and into this the Judge reached from time to time, while he surveyed the court. Lieutenant Parr, too, was present; so was the Indian, Soaring Hawk, squatting in his customary position over against one wall. As he hesitated in the aisle, David saw someone get up from one of the seats in front and come toward him. It was young Montgomery Cothren, a man of his own age who had been admitted to the bar only a year ago; his friendly, wide-set grey eyes showed concern.

"David," he whispered, coming up. "What is this that brings you to court? Do you need representation?"

"Oh, I think not. It's just an open-and-shut matter. Jim Casthew laid a charge, and we have to answer it. But thank you just the same, Montgomery. If we'd had need of you, you know you'd have heard from us."

"Order, order," cried the Judge suddenly.

Cothren turned at once. "Nonsense, sir. Court has not yet convened."

"I'll convene it then," retorted Judge Dunn. "Is everybody here? Two cases are coming up—Casthew versus Trelawny & Pengellen, no representation, to be followed by Kilvert versus Avenell, Kilvert represented by John Cummins, Avenell represented by Montgomery Cothren. If all are present, we can go ahead." He waited a moment for any protest; there was none. He slapped the table with the palm of his hand, ignoring his gavel, and said, "This Court is in order. Nathaniel Parr, please serve as clerk of court." He leaned over, pursed his lips, and squinted into the audience. "The Court will hear Jim Casthew."

Casthew, a short, rotund man with a fringe of reddish beard and a touseled head of hair of similar color, got up immediately and recited his grievance, with many gestures and grimaces of his florid countenance. He looked accusingly at David and from David to Judge Dunn, who sat listening with remote interest, occasionally raising his head from the back of his hand where it rested, Casthew spoke volubly, in every third sentence charging Trelawny & Pengellen with having cheated him, until finally Judge Dunn interrupted him.

"The Court has heard the charge. We've heard it at least twelve times, and our patience is fraying. Plaintiff will please get on with proving the charge. In other words—you're talking too much and not saying anything, Casthew, is that clear?"

"Iss, yer honor," said Casthew, bobbing his head. He shot a vengeful glance at David, as if this reproof were his fault, and went on. What he had to say was simply that he had an arrangement with Trelawny & Pengellen, as smelters, whereby they would smelt his ore at a fee of thirty-five percent. He had brought in about five hundred dollars worth of ore and . . .

"You say 'about,'" interrupted Judge Dunn irascibly. "Was it or was it not that much?"

"I dedn' take 'en weight—they ded!" He pointed to David.

"Mr. Pengellen?"

"We called it five hundred, Judge," answered David. "Actually, it came to a little under."

"Go on, Casthew."

The miner continued. According to the agreement, therefore, he ought to have received three hundred twenty-five dollars, and Trelawny & Pengellen were to get a hundred seventy-five. But had he received that sum? he demanded, raising his voice in mounting excitement. He had not. He had received two hundred eighty-four dollars and forty-five cents. There was the proof of it; he had been cheated. And how long, shouted Casthew to the audience in his indignation, would the miners stand for being cheated and robbed by the merchants and smelters who were getting rich on their sweat and bloody toil . . . ?

The gavel banged. "Shut up and sit down, Casthew."

Casthew made haste to obey.

The Judge leaned back and looked over at Lieutenant Parr. "Have you got all that?"

"All the essential facts, yes, sir."

The Judge glanced toward David. "The Court will ask the defendant whether this is a true statement of the case."

David went forward. "The charge is false, Your Honor. But the figures, insofar as they were given, are correct."

" 'E owns up to it!" cried Casthew enthusiastically.

"I told you to shut up, Casthew," shouted Judge Dunn. "Stay shut up."

"The trouble with Jim Casthew's figures are that there's one missing," David went on. "It comes to forty dollars and fifty-five cents. The Court will take notice that that is the exact amount of the difference between the figure the plaintiff says he should have received and the figure he admits to receiving. The omitted figure represents the amount of purchases made at Trelawny & Pengellen's store by Mrs. Jim Casthew over a period of three months, two weeks, and three days."

"Is it customary to run such accounts and make such deductions?"

"It is."

"How does it come that the plaintiff was not informed of the matter?"

"I understand that the plaintiff lost his temper when he was paid by Mr. Trelawny, and immediately became so abusive that he could not be prevailed upon to listen to Mr. Trelawny's explanation. He apparently laid a charge immediately after."

Judge Dunn squinted into the audience once more. "Is Mrs. Jim Casthew here?"

A tired-looking woman got up. "Iss, please," she said quietly.

"Madam, did you buy groceries and other goods to the amount stated—that is, forty dollars and fifty-five cents worth—in the time set forth?"

"Iss, Uncle, I ded."

"Didn't you tell your husband about it?"

" 'Ee doan't lissen."

The Judge covered his mouth with his hand. He looked over at Casthew, who sat frowning and fuming silently, stirring about in his seat and waiting for the chance to speak once more. He glanced at his wife as if she had betrayed him, but she avoided his eyes and sat down, sighing, with the air of a woman who has gone through many crises, each as needless as the last.

"Come here, Casthew," commanded Judge Dunn.

Casthew got up with alacrity and came to the table.

"I want to tell you something, Casthew. You never had a case you could bring into Court, did you know that? I'm dismissing it—throwing it out of Court. But you've got to learn that you can't go to law every time you get a notion. I'm going to charge you fifteen dollars to pay the Court's expenses in this case."

Casthew flushed angrily and opened his mouth to protest.

"And if you interrupt me when I'm talking, it'll cost you five dollars more—every time," the Judge went on. He pointed to Lieutenant Parr. "Pay Mr. Parr right now. Fifteen dollars. Get your receipt and come back here."

Casthew went sullenly over to Lieutenant Parr and paid him. With his receipt in hand, he came back to stand before the Judge, who sat with his elbow resting on the table, his hand supporting his head.

"Now I want to give you a little free advice, Casthew. When the Lord made you, he gave you ears as well as mouth. You wag that jawbone too much. The sooner you start using your ears and what's between 'em, the better off you'll be. Now sit down and don't let me hear another word out of you until this Court's adjourned."

As Casthew returned to his seat, Judge Dunn spoke to David. "Is there any wish on the part of the defendant that this Court abrogate the contract between plaintiff and defendant?"

"None, sir," responded David. "Jim Casthew's a good miner. Sometimes his temper gets the best of him, but he's still a good miner."

At this unexpected praise from the object of his ire, Casthew looked up in pleased surprise, and a sheepish smile replaced his sullen scowl. Forgetting the Judge's warning, he said loudly, "I doan't want 'en contrac' broke, Judge, yer Honor, sir!" whereupon the audience burst into laughter, and the Judge replied, "That's the first sensible thing you've said this morning, Casthew! You'd better get back to the mines."

Thus adjured, Casthew lost no time escaping.

"If the Court will excuse me," said David, "I'd better return to the store."

"By all means, Mr. Pengellen. Court will now take up the case of Kilvert versus Avenell."

David smiled at his wife, as he went by. From the corner of his eye, he caught Tamson Bishop's eager smile in answer. He bethought himself of Parr's visit the previous day; had it not been for his courtesy, the convenient figures might not have been so ready to hand. He retraced a few steps and bent to Candace.

"Do you think we might ask Lieutenant Parr and his companion to dinner?"

"Oh, do!" whispered Candace.

She got up at once, beckoning Aunt Marget, and followed David from the room.

"I'll leave word for him," said David, outside.

"I hope he likes Cornish food."

"I'm sure any food is better than the fare he could pick up at the public houses," said David.

"Which one was his companion?"

"The Indian."

"The Indian!" she exclaimed, her voice raised, and immediately clapped her hand to her lips, for fear that she had disturbed some one in the room they had just quitted. She looked at David in wide-eyed surprise.

"He'll probably not sit at table with us," David went on. "But on the floor. I'm sorry, Candy. Soaring Hawk's all right, I'm sure. Mr. Trelawny vouches for him. He's a close companion of Parr's and was with him when Parr told us of the hearing. Besides, he may not come."

"An Indian in the house," said Candace faintly, shaking her head.

Aunt Marget gazed at David with a baffled smile; she said nothing to him, but to Candace said, "We best be en jeffy t' git 'en dennar on."

"And I must get to the store; so Trelawny can go to dinner," said David. "I'll probably be a little later than usual, Candy. We'll have to wait on Parr until the next case is over, unless Dunn adjourns. I'll have Parr come to the store when he's finished."

Soaring Hawk came with David and Lieutenant Parr, but even the Indian's presence in the house did not diminish the excitement Candace felt at having guests. There was in this fact itself something of the days of her life in Providence, and however different it was—David's bringing them in through the back door instead of at the front, where they would have been received in Providence—the act called forth her obligations as a hostess. She wondered fleetingly how one would receive an Indian like Soaring Hawk in Providence. She had been taken aback at his entrance; somehow, she had expected an attitude that was more servile, but no such attitude graced Soaring Hawk's entrance. He came in like a nobleman, greeted her with an unceremoniously grunted "How!" and, once in the dining-room, took a position on the floor from which he could command a clear view of everyone at the table. She had also expected someone more rugged, but Soaring Hawk was young, fine-featured, and, despite the unkempt black hair, had an air of alertness about him.

"I'm delighted to join you at dinner," said Parr, after he had introduced Candace to Soaring Hawk. "I'm afraid the food at the taverns and inns isn't very good."

As she sat down, she was keenly conscious of Parr's eyes on her. The lieutenant had a direct, unwavering gaze from under his dark, arched eyebrows. The sardonic expression she had noticed on the night of her arrival had given way to one that was rather pensive and sad; his mouth that had seemed sullen was now provocative; the eyes she had thought brooding were challenging and lively with interest. He looked at her with such intent directness as to bring a faint flush to her cheeks and, hastily, lest her pleasure be too manifest, she began to talk, her words rushing forth while Aunt Marget brought their food in from the kitchen.

"Was there ever such a court?" she asked. "Can it be that what was said and done in Judge Dunn's court this morning is legal? I could hardly credit my senses. It was all so different from the proceedings I sometimes witnessed in the east."

"Perhaps you've never heard, Mrs. Pengellen, that it's the Judge who makes the law? Well, it is. No doubt Judge Dunn must seem to you very crude; yet his decisions are as irrevocable as those of the Supreme Court of Rhode Island. And, I think, as wise."

"He seems such a rough man."

"But no fool, Mrs. Pengellen. Would you say so, sir?" Parr turned to David.

"By no means." He smiled at the memory of the Judge's instructions to Casthew. "I'm afraid my wife's accustomed to more conformity between heart and skin."

She shrugged. "To tell the truth, I know very little about it. In the east we're used to more formality."

Parr laughed. "And I don't doubt that in the east this morning's hearing would have taken half a day or longer, to fit in all the prescribed formalities."

"I suppose it would," agreed Candace amiably. "I hope you enjoy Cornish food, Lieutenant Parr."

"I'm sure that any food prepared by your good self is above reproach," said Parr.

She felt herself coloring and dropped her gaze to her plate.

David asked about the second trial; had Avenell and Kilvert managed to compose their difficulties?

"In spite of Judge Dunn's fondness for Cummins, the case was Cothren's," answered Parr. "Cothren is a very able man."

"Are you in the habit of serving as clerk of court?" asked Candace.

He shook his head. "Judge Dunn appoints anyone he's a notion to. Usually it's Cummins or Mr. Henry—but this time Cummins was appearing before him, and he could hardly serve in both capacities. I fell under his eye—that was all. I don't relish the task. But then, I've never been overly fond of work."

"Does your Indian understand English?" asked Candace innocently.

Lieutenant Parr could not help chuckling.

Before Parr could speak, Soaring Hawk grunted explosively and announced in his guttural, broken English that he was nobody's Indian, he was Soaring Hawk's Indian, his father had been a Winnebago, his mother had been a Winnebago, his forebears had all been Winnebago, his blood was pure. Having thus taken part in the conversation, he went on. "Soaring Hawk know English," he said proudly. "He not know white men." He pointed to the trial he had just witnessed. What manner of performance was that? he wanted to know. Could not the injured parties speak for themselves? What purpose had lawyers? Were they not men like other men? They were not injured, yet they spoke for the other men. But the other men were neither deaf nor dumb, neither halt nor blind. The ways of white men were beyond him. Then he grunted and was still.

Candace was astounded and embarrassed. "I meant no harm," she managed to say.

Soaring Hawk paid no attention to her. He had turned again to his food, which he ate with great gusto with his fingers, disdaining all the utensils Aunt Marget had given him.

"I'm used to him," said Parr.

David was amused, which piqued Candace. But she said nothing, for David had begun to speak of matters pertaining to the political life of Wisconsin Territory. She listened to the conversation, making mental reservations to ask David about references he made. From time to time Lieutenant Parr directed a remark at her, always with a kind of deference which pleased her. On occasion also she caught the Indian staring fixedly at her, his face a mask; she could not tell what he was thinking, but she was acutely aware of Soaring Hawk as something more than her conventionally conceived picture of an Indian. Soaring Hawk's single long contribution to the conversation had served to emphasize the profound difference in his point-of-view, and at the same time it roused some doubt in her about the validity of her own perspective. Already shaken by the contrast between Mineral Point and Providence, the Winnebago's radically altered view, which was a contrast of an even different kind, had a disturbing effect. She could not meet his gaze; she was aware that even as there existed in herself, as in other white people, a comforting sense of superiority to the savages, so there existed in these same savages a similar sense of their own superiority to the invaders who had taken their land.

When at last the meal was finished, and David had to start back for the store, he turned enthusiastically to Parr and cried, "I hope you'll feel yourself welcome to stop in any time, Lieutenant. I'm sure my wife joins me in this."

"Certainly, Lieutenant. Please feel free to call any time you're in Mineral Point."

"I'll be only too happy to do so."

Candace turned uncertainly toward Soaring Hawk. "And, of course, you, too, Soaring Hawk."

"Me," he said impassively, and grunted, rubbing his stomach in a circular motion to express appreciation for the dinner he had just had.

After they had gone, Candace dwelt for a long time on the wit and gentility so evident in Parr; happily, she thought, there were people of breeding and refinement even in this wilderness outpost. It was a comforting thought; even more comforting was the anticipation of having Lieutenant Parr again as a guest, and perhaps others like him.

When she came home at twilight, Aunt Marget heard Tamson's voice raised in song. She knew without pausing to listen that the girl sang *Westryn Wind*. It had the sound and feel of Cornwall in it; the words and melody evoked her native land, and the older woman knew that Tamson sang it because she was lonesome and homesick. It was a pity she had had to come to

America; but there was no other place she might have gone. Perhaps she might have found some kind of work in Tintagel or Boscastle, but it would have been irregular work, and she would have had to go from one place to another with nothing to look forward to but, ultimately, marriage. She could look to that here, where at least she had someone her own, less distant than those relatives still living in Polperro and Truro.

The inflections of Tamson's voice made the words she sang now soft and lulling, now intense and passionate, sometimes a cry of pain, sometimes a note of triumph. How sad a song it was! Tamson sang few others.

Aunt Marget entered her home quietly. Tamson stood at the window in the unlighted kitchen.

"Arr'y bedoled for hoam, lass?" she asked.

Tamson turned. " 'Tis this time, Aunt Marget, the last spur o' day, weth a scoy o' it fouched down west an' the colors t' make the sky all prinkt up—I thenk on the sun gone down on the sea at Tintagel. Bedoled for hoam? Mayhap."

Aunt Marget lit the lamp, saying nothing. The book she had brought home for Tamson lay on the table; it was closed. She put her shawl away and came back to the table, touching the book with her fingertips.

"An' t' book?" she asked.

"I peek'ed en et."

"Mr. Pengellen tell'd me 'ee were coomin' by, p'raps."

Tamson received this news in silence. Her eyes fell to the book. As Aunt Marget moved from the table, Tamson sat down to it, drew the book toward her once more, and opened it. She had read through twenty-four pages, to the twelfth lesson. She did not know that it had done her any good. She could understand the instructions, but the pronunciation mystified her. It did not seem to her that there was any difference between her words and those in the speller. It needed someone to say them out loud to her; yet she was not anxious that it be David, for she felt a sense of inadequacy at being unable to speak in a way that would please him.

She read patiently, while Aunt Marget moved about the small house, looking to the tasks she had set for Tamson. But all were done. She had known they would be. Tamson made no complaint, nor ever would.

In less than an hour Candace and David came.

"I wouldn't leave Candace alone," he explained. "She'll have enough of being alone later."

Aunt Marget was pleased that Candace had come along, and asked somewhat diffidently whether she might not show her little house, so that Mr. Pengellen could get on with Tamson.

"I'd like to see it," said Candace eagerly.

The two women left the kitchen as David sat down beside Tamson.

"Have you studied, Tamson?"

She answered him in a rush of words, explaining that she did not know how to pronounce the words other than she was in the habit of saying them. They seemed the same to her, just as she had learned them in Tintagel, the very same. It took someone to pronounce them for her.

He laughed. "I know. That's what I came for. You can read, but it's the way of speaking you must learn, Tamson. Now let me have the book." He took it from her and opened it at random. "Will you read this paragraph for me?"

She gazed at him for a moment in dismay; then she lowered her eyes hesitantly to the page, looking half fearfully at the lines she must read. She began, shyly.

"This boy 'as a priddy boat, weth a mas' 'n' weth sells. Ships 'r' med t' move on t' watter. They are moved by t' wind bloowin' on t' sells. Soomtimes they are verry large, 'n' 'll carr' moore 'n a thousan' men, an' food enough for 'em t' eat, a loong w'ile."

She glanced at him, to mark the degree of his displeasure. But there was neither pleasure nor displeasure in his face. He took the book and, adjuring her to listen, read the lines slowly and carefully. "Now try it again, Tamson."

She read it once more aloud, trying hard to pronounce the words as he had done, sometimes succeeding, sometimes not.

"Was 't better, David?" she asked anxiously.

"Yes, much better. Once more now."

She redoubled her efforts, though he listened with but half an ear, wondering where Candace and Aunt Marget were all this time, reflecting that this was the first time that Tamson had called him by his Christian name, being aware of some satisfaction that she had foregone the more formal address. She finished and looked shyly at him.

"Yes, that's it, Tamson. Now let's turn to one of the word lists. I'll pronounce them first, and you say them after me. Come, move closer."

Obediently, she moved her chair next to his, and their heads bent together over the spelling book. She was sharply conscious of his proximity; her pulse quickened absurdly, but she kept her eyes to the page, repeating words and saying them again, whenever David asked her to, until at last David pushed back from the table.

"That's enough for one night, Tamson. Try to say them aloud for yourself now and then. This study is tiresome now, but it will soon be over."

"I doan't find et tiresome, David."

"Well, then it will be all the easier for you." He looked toward the adjoining rooms. "Candace!" he called. "Aunt Marget?"

"Arr'y done?" asked Aunt Marget, coming in, followed by Candace.

"Yes, and tired. We'll be going." To Tamson he said, almost

brusquely, "I'll come again as soon as I can. You study now, Tamson."

"I weel, Mr. Pengellen."

Outside, the moon shone. David took Candace's hand in his, and they walked slowly homeward through the cool night, going up around the village on the slopes of the hill away from houses and buildings. The air was crisp with frost, and stars glittered from every part of heaven save that occupied by the waxing moon. A ruminant wind moved exploratively along the slope, bearing the tantalizing pungences of the deep, wooded valleys to the west.

"Where were you all that time?" he asked presently.

"Sitting on Aunt Marget's bed, talking—or rather, listening. Oh, David, how can they live in such a small house? Why, you could put almost the whole of it into our living-room."

"Oh, not quite, surely!"

"I'm glad our house isn't like that."

She tightened her hand in his. They walked in silence, Candace pitying Aunt Marget and Tamson, and pitying herself a little, too, for all that she had a big house, since it was out here so far away from Providence and home, lost in this alien wilderness. Then, looming over the ridge, she caught sight of the Platte and Belmont Mounds, like presentiments of evil, the keepers of the gate, guarding against her escape, dark on heaven and as unreal as distant clouds sure to vanish under the sun. She gazed for a moment in fascination; then she shuddered unaccountably and turned away.

At the end of that month, in answer to a direct question from her mother by letter, Candace wrote about Mineral Point.

Since you ask me how I like living here in the Wisconsin Territory, I will tell you, as honestly as I can. I have tried not to write anything before, because I wanted to wait until I could form an opinion out of a greater knowledge of this place, and because I did not want to cause you any concern, knowing how hard it is with father's health declining so. But I do not think I like this place. I have tried, truly I have. I have learned to cook and bake almost as well as the Cornish women; I can even now understand their dialect, but I discovered that I do not have to speak it, because these good people are happily unaware that it is *they* who speak with strange accents, and think it is *my* language which is different!

I have been to walk all about the village several times. It is really a village now, for it was incorporated as such only last February, and the elected officers have been wishing ever since that they were free of office, for the people are constantly sending in petitions about every matter which occurs to them—someone's pig is running loose or somebody's awning projects over the sidewalks they have put in along the stores. The people are always very kind and interested—and *curious,* about David and me. I must surely have met all of them by this time! They are not all Cornish; many are New Englanders, and some are most genteel and very cultured. Curtis and Sophia Beech, for instance—he has a store here—Montgomery Cothren, who is said to be the most promising lawyer in this part of the Territory—William Henry (he was born in St. Louis), another lawyer—and ever so many others.

In spite of this, though, the village—and indeed, the region, I am told—has a leaning toward the South; it seems more related to the South than it does to New England and the East, perhaps because many of the original miners came up from Kentucky and other points South, and because the greater part of the lead goes to market by way of New Orleans. Most of the papers published here actually carry weekly notices of steamship sailings from Galena to St. Louis, Natchez, and New Orleans!

Some of the people came from other parts of England, and even a few from Germany. But English or Cornish, it is all the same. They are a people who impress me as wishing to be enterprising without the means of being so, and they have become so dependent on the galena (which is what they call the lead) and the little amount of copper mined here, that it is only in the past few years that they have thought of raising their own food, though some of the hardier settlers in the country around took to farming at the same time as they did to mining, and they are now fairly well-to-do. (There isn't really much copper here, though. One of the men here, a Mr. Ansley, went all the way to London to interest promoters; he had some good samples with him, but someone in London had previously asked a traveler named Fetherstonhaw or something like that to look around here; somehow he took offense at someone here and made a very unfavorable report; so Mr. Ansley came home without the support he expected, and the copper mining has not been developed.) The Cornish are a lusty people, good-hearted, and they surely mean to be friendly.

Above everything else, the people here are very clannish, and they make all their judgments according to their clan-like inclinations. Not so very long ago the representative from this district, a Mr. Vinyard, shot and killed the representative from a Northern district in the council chambers in Madison, apparently with but little provocation. His trial dragged on for almost two years, during all of which time he was out on bail, and then he went free on the plea of "self-defense" because the matter had ceased to be a case of murder, but a political cause in their eyes, the merits of the charge having been lost in the fog of political prejudices. Mr. Vinyard comes from the lead-mining country; therefore, he can do no wrong. Mr. Arndt did not; therefore, he was a villain. All this in the face of the facts. By the same token, they are united in their support of Mr. Dodge, the former Governor, and poor Governor Tallmadge does not even win consideration because, in the first place, he is a New Yorker, and in the second, he followed in Governor Doty's tracks, and is a Whig, too, like Mr. Doty, who is not liked because he succeeded in having the capital site moved from Dodge's choice, nearby Belmont, to Madison, which pleased Doty because he had investments in land in Madison, and by parcelling some of it out to the legislators, he had his way in the matter.

But I am not complaining. I had no idea of what this country would be like, but it is David's country, and it looks as if it is to be my home for the rest of my life. And I am not always lonely, for people come to call, and, while Mrs. Hoskins is no longer here so often, her niece, Tamson Bishop, does come, so that I can help her study, now that David has gone through the speller with her . . .

But her letter contained nothing of the restless dissatisfaction which had taken such root in her, nothing of the longing for a place in life similar to that she held in her home in Providence, which had been her world with herself at the center of it, nor anything of her tenacity at trying to meet the challenge of the western land.

2. Something Within . . .

Spring-Summer, 1845

Despite the pelting rain and the mud, David reached the store at last. He was an hour late. He stamped the mud from his boots before he opened the door. The moment he stepped in, Trelawny took a cigar from his mouth and spoke.

"Thought you'd got stick'd in the mud somewhere, David. It's clodgy weather. Not a customer so far."

"It wasn't the mud," David said shortly. "It was Candace—she's not been feeling well. I stayed there a while longer. Now Tamson will be coming over."

"Sorry to hear that." Trelawny put his cigar back into his mouth and puffed at it while David took off his wet coat. When David was ready for work, he spoke again. "Have you heard the news, David?"

David had noticed his partner's attitude of suppressed eagerness. "What is it now? Has lead gone up?"

"No, it's the Governor. He's come home from Washington. He won't be goin' back. I had it from Parr. I predicted it. Tallmadge has been removed, and within a month President Polk will announce Dodge's reappointment as Governor of the Territory. Now Parr's been in and suggested a public dinner for Dodge. I'm for it. It will advance the interests of Mineral Point."

"Yes," agreed David with restraint, "it would be good."

Trelawny looked at him shrewdly. He rolled his cigar meditatively. "You don't sound enthusiastic, David. I know you don't prefer Tallmadge, for all that he was a good enough governor according to his lights. Come, now, tell me—is it trouble at home? I've my share of that."

"I don't know that I'd call it trouble. It seems Candace just can't like the Point."

"Och, fiddle-faddle! Women are all alike; if you mollycoddle 'em, they'll take advantage of it. For one thing, Mrs. Pengellen doesn't get out enough."

"She has no wish to." He hesitated a moment, then added, "Besides, I may as well tell you—I believe she's pregnant."

Trelawny grinned. "Well, congratulations, David! That will probably do her more good than anything else."

"I hope so."

"A child in the house—yes, that's the best medicine of all. Had we had one or two, I'd have been spared half the misery I've had." He shook his head. "But I guess we weren't meant to have children, and we've made the worst of it, as you might say."

Trelawny fell silent, and David retreated into his own thoughts. It no longer mattered that his concern about Candace showed plainly enough for his partner to see that something troubled him. During the winter just past, he had grown ever more preoccupied about Candace. He had experienced both hope and despair on more than one occasion; his concern fluctuated with her moods. And Candace's moods were unpredictable. She perplexed and baffled him; one day she gave the appearance of having adjusted to life in Mineral Point; on another she was bitter and reproachful; on yet another she was like a helpless creature caught in a trap from which there was no escape except through the beneficence of her captor. Yet always there was a certain valiance in her sincere determination to like her new home and make the best of the circumstances against which she rebelled.

It had struck David often during her first month in Mineral Point that Candace liked her new home, but with the advent of the first snow, a heavy fall in November, and the occasional isolation of the village for days at a time thereafter, she had shown a marked tendency to turn to her memories of the halcyon days of her childhood. Sometimes her unhappiness was plain, but customarily she was too spirited to permit her mood to show. She did not fail for lack of trying; indeed, at times she was so fixed in her determination that she amused and delighted him. Nevertheless, he could not help thinking that the challenge had become a kind of obsession with her; she seemed to see it as something she must defeat, or it would defeat her. She was not often irritable or angry, but she was occasionally quietly passive, which troubled him more than anger would have done. Most of the time she was animated and demonstrative, betraying nothing of her nostalgia for the occasions of the past before Tamson or others among the women who called on her, excepting Aunt Marget, who had adopted toward her a motherly attitude which came naturally to the older woman.

But beneath his occasional worry about Candace, David's spirits were buoyant with the hope that the coming of their child would divorce Candace forever from her nostalgic yearning for Providence and the scenes of her girlhood.

In mid-morning the rain ceased to fall, the clouds parted, and the sun shone. A south wind blew, bearing the perfume of wild plum and cherry and apple blossoms, growing thickly along the hill slopes, a fragrance now made stronger and more pronounced by the moisture in the air. The birds, which had been silent during the rain, began to sing again. Out of the woods rose a great mass of passenger pigeons, leaving behind them limbs broken down with the weight of the birds which had taken shelter there in the night; they made a brilliant sheen of color, flying up and making a brief shadow on the town, which they passed over into the north.

Tempted by the damp, fragrant air, Candace slipped out of the house and mounted the slope to the Galena road. She remained away from the road, however, and stood at the edge of the thicket which rose between the house and the ridge, looking into the southwest, where rose the Platte and Belmont Mounds, the magnet which drew her eyes. Unknown to David, she had taken to coming to this place; the vista drew her, in part because it represented the way back to Providence, since it was from this direction that they had come to Mineral Point, in part because the scene itself attracted her, not because of its wild beauty, but because of the Mounds, which held a singular fascination for her.

This attraction was inexplicable, because, for her, the Mounds had a sinister aspect, brooding eternally on the horizon and dominating the country all around. The natives believed that the density of the haze around the Mounds foretold the weather —if blue and not quite clear on a sunny day, rain and storm were not far away; if the trees could be distinguished on the peaks, no matter how murky the weather, the skies would surely clear soon. But it was not as prophets of the weather that Candace saw them; it was rather more as symbols of this strange, wild country, a land of almost primitive violence among men despite the growing of specious culture among some of the older families of the region. The Mounds were dark, forbidding, watchful, towering above the plateau which gave them rise and never quite out of sight or mind as long as one traveled in their vicinity; they wore the aspect of great primal beasts, doomed to sleep there as sentinels against some future waking, great beasts which might once again rise up and walk the earth in awful majesty. They brooded not only on the earth's rim, but also on the perimeter of her consciousness. Even more than as symbols of this country, Candace conceived of them as sentient barriers guarding her way of escape, and she was obsessed with the conviction that they would never permit her to go back the way she had come.

Beyond them lay her childhood and youth, and whenever now she thought of those happy days, the shadow of the Mounds lay athwart the mnemonic scenes which rose to her mind's eye. These scenes presented themselves repeatedly; the rigorous life of Mineral Point prompted them; Candace saw herself again and again as the happy, solitary child she had been, playing in the sunny room under the watchful eyes of her mother and, far back, of a grandmother who existed only spectrally in her mind; she saw herself in school, attending the sedate children's parties, walking down Benefit Street; she re-created the Providence she had known, within sight of the chasm which separated her from that city. But if she looked back with yearning and discontent, she was not the passive woman David assumed her to be; whatever her outward aspect, she was inwardly divided between rebellion against her circumstances and the honest desire to improve them by accepting her new role in this wild country. Her rebellion was selfish, she told herself often, an evidence of a too sheltered and pampered childhood and youth which had not prepared her adequately for responsibilities.

She had long ago decided that it had been a mistake to marry David and come west with him before trying to persuade him to go into business in Providence. But the mistake had been made, and there was nothing to be done about it now, for it was too much to expect David to uproot himself to suit what was only her homesickness; the most she could hope for was an alteration in the circumstances of their living of enough importance to turn events to her uses. Despite her air of passivity before David, she had no intention of waiting on events, but meant to precipitate them, if any possibility of improving her circumstances offered itself in the course of time. Sometime, surely, events would shape themselves in favor of her heart's desire.

The Mounds mocked her. She tore her fascinated gaze away and turned to hurry back to the house before Tamson might come and find her missing.

Lieutenant Parr emerged from the Mansion House, followed by Soaring Hawk. Both mounted their horses. The Winnebago, rode as he habitually did, several paces behind Parr. And where were they going now? he wanted to know.

"I'm going to see Mr. Strong," said Parr.

It meant little to Soaring Hawk to know on whom they were calling. But Lieutenant Parr planned his visits with care. The time would certainly come when his friends would be of service in advancing Parr's own ambitions, which thus far had been held strictly in rein. And Moses Strong, as a member of the Legislative Council from Mineral Point, might well be in a position to turn a hand in Parr's favor when the time came.

Lieutenant Parr was no opportunist. He had been content to drift along, basking in the favor of General Dodge, supporting himself by occasional small jobs, but primarily on the rental he received from various pieces of land he had inherited. But now, approaching thirty, he realized that he would need to look about him for some substantial position in order to insure his comfort throughout his declining years. Since statehood for Wisconsin was imminent—it could not be put off much longer—he found himself tempted by the possibilities in some public office, a sinecure which he might obtain through the good friendship of such men as Governor Dodge or the members of the Council who, like Strong, were known to him. Strong was obviously the man to inaugurate a movement for the public dinner and ovation for Dodge; his position on the Council assured him Dodge's ear, and he would have equal influence with whomever would take Dodge's place in Washington—very probably Morgan Martin, who, being from Green Bay, was beyond Parr's reach.

Parr often wondered where he would end, just as he speculated sometimes about his beginnings. An orphan, he had been told ambiguously, adopted by his Uncle Roger Parr and his Aunt Dolly—but had they been really his uncle and aunt? Had they been related to him at all? He more than half suspected he was the illegitimate or abandoned son of some personage who, traveling through the Middle West, had dallied in Galena long enough to father him. There had been a Parr daughter, too, who had died long ago. He had a vague memory of her, far far older than he, a woman, really, mothering the child he had been, a memory which was touched with an unsullied affection, existing forever in his awareness with warmth and tenderness. He thought often that she might have been his mother, for the Parrs who had brought him up had been so much older. His inclinations, his yearnings, his hopes and ambitions, such as he had had, had no relation to the background he had known. In all Galena and its environs, in all the Wisconsin Territory there was nothing which drew his interest; his ambitions sought a position superior to those commonly offered in the Territory, as complementary to a compulsion and a settled conviction that had been part of him as long as he had known. Perhaps it was the lack of parents and the affection of a closely-knit family which brought about his direction; perhaps it was something inherited from the father he had never known, a nebulous figure who could assume, unhampered, any stature in his imagination.

It was time, too, that he settled down and found himself a

wife. He smiled at the thought. Could he ever settle down to any one woman, after the women he had known? Perhaps the ease of conquest he had always experienced had been, too, however remotely, a part of his unknown heritage.

"Hawk," he said suddenly, without turning, "I'm going to find myself a wife."

Soaring Hawk grunted expressively. Were wives so easy to find then? he wanted to know. Were white women so ready to take white men at their own ideas of their worth? He did not expect his questions to be answered, and went on talking, more to himself than to Parr, but Parr listened disinterestedly. Besides, said Soaring Hawk, what would Parr do with a wife? Would she ride beside him as Soaring Hawk did? Hoh! what white woman did as the Indian women did? Would she be content to sit in one place while he, Parr, went wandering through the country? He grunted twice to express his conviction that she would not.

Parr supposed that if Soaring Hawk were in the habit of laughing, he might have laughed at the thought of Parr married. Marriage, however, might be necessary to the achievement of any position of importance in the state government which was imminent. When Soaring Hawk had finished, Parr observed only that he meant to be one of the White Fathers in Wisconsin.

This ambition the Winnebago understood. He did not sympathize with it. Were not all the White Fathers tellers of untruths? Were they not all bearers of tidings of ill omen? Were they not all desecrators of the land, destroyers of the country, thieves and poltroons? Who would be one of them when he could be a chieftain on his own horse, free to move about the country as he liked, whenever the spirit was in him to move? Parr was not meant to be one of the great White Fathers.

Parr understood Soaring Hawk's words as an expression of his fears. It was true, he could hardly have Soaring Hawk as even his occasional companion, once he found a place in the government at Madison. Soaring Hawk knew this, too; it was only natural that he would prefer to keep Parr's status unchanged.

They had now reached Moses Strong's law and agency office, and, as they approached, Strong himself came to the threshold, preparatory to going out. He was still a young man, for all his eminence in the affairs of the Territory, in his middle thirties, with a soft, wispy moustache and full, but not thick, sideburns. His chin was smooth, his nose broad, and his face, too, broad, with wide-set eyes. He was clad in a broad-brimmed hat and a black frock coat. Seeing that Lieutenant Parr was bound for his office, he stood on the threshold waiting for him.

Parr slid expertly from his horse to the edge of the wooden walk before the office.

"Mr. Strong, sir, my compliments."

"Hardly good traveling weather, eh, Parr?"

"Necessity knows no weather, sir."

Strong smiled pleasantly, but his eyes did not waver in their scrutiny of the young lieutenant, whom he knew as the emissary of information often well in advance of other sources. "Dodge is back, I hear."

"He is, sir. And no doubt you've heard he is once again to be appointed Governor of the Territory?"

"I had some intelligence of it, yes."

Thereupon Parr launched at once into his plan. Did not Strong think it an excellent idea to propose a public dinner in honor of the Governor? Mineral Point would be the logical place for it —here was the Court House for a ball, here, too, the Mansion House for the banquet.

Strong listened with interest. He avoided no occasion for adding to his own laurels, having a secret eye on the governorship himself, perhaps at some time in the future, when Wisconsin's statehood had been tested. He nodded, approving the idea of a public dinner.

"And who, sir, is the logical person to inaugurate the proposal?" pursued Parr. "Who but you?"

"Ah, indeed, you flatter me, Parr," murmured Strong. But he was pleased. Already he visualized his success in persuading the citizens of the Point, irrespective of political affiliation, to join together and sponsor a magnificent celebration to honor a man who, after all, was practically a local citizen; living as he did between the Point and Dodgeville, the Point had as much right to claim him as Dodgeville; indeed, the Governor himself had often shown his preference for the Point. "How long will he be in residence?"

"Until he assumes office, sir. The appointment should come through in ten days or so—the Governor himself has Polk's promise to make the announcement within a week. It would be my plan to call a mass meeting of the people, appoint a committee, and wait on Governor Dodge without delay, so that he can select a day for the celebration."

"Yes, of course, it must be done that way."

Parr swung himself back on his horse. "I leave it in your hands, sir."

Strong touched his hat. He scarcely noticed Parr's going or the Indian following; he was already lost in contemplation of the pomp and circumstance that must attend the banquet and ball in honor of Dodge, and even more, of the potential political consequences of a successful affair.

Parr was equally pleased with himself. Strong would lose no time in setting the celebration in motion; Trelawny would second him. Dodge might discover in good time whose idea it had been in the first place; it did not matter, since it would be even preferable to permit Strong to have the credit. Each would then be under a certain obligation to him.

Soaring Hawk grunted in appreciation. He understood the little drama quite well. When it came to a matter of white men's dealings with one another, he recognized the need for self-ingratiation.

Parr went on up High Street, Soaring Hawk coming phlegmatically after, wondering what goal Parr now sought. Parr rode past the last construction and paused. Open country lay on both sides of the high road leading to Belmont, except for the large square house in the grove two knolls removed, the Pengellen house. Abruptly, Parr turned and rode toward the house.

Candace was in the kitchen with Tamson when he came, guided by instinct this time to the front entrance. Seeing him through the windows, she cried out to Tamson who it was. "And the Indian, too!"

She threw open the door.

Parr bowed, doffing his cap. "Mrs. Pengellen, good morning. I was passing and took the liberty of stopping to bid you the time of day."

"Lieutenant! How nice to see you! Won't you step in? I'd like you to meet Tamson Bishop."

"Only a moment, I'm afraid. I'm on my way to Platteville."

"And your friend?"

"Hawk will wait for me, thank you."

He went into the house.

Soaring Hawk grunted. His immobile face betrayed nothing of what he thought. He had accompanied Parr for a time long enough to know him. It did not matter what Parr said, nor how long he stayed. Soaring Hawk suspected that it was not the house, but the woman who attracted Parr.

When David reached home that evening, Tamson was still there. Candace had asked her to stay for supper. David had not been home for dinner; he had sent word that he could not come. The village had been aroused and excited by Moses Strong's announcement, and most of the businessmen had gathered at the

Court House to discuss Strong's proposal, upsetting schedules for the group, so that they had had dinner together at the Mansion House, while debating Strong's proposition. They had decided to call a mass meeting of the citizens for the following night and elect from among them a committee to wait on Governor Dodge at his home without more than enough delay to permit of the formal announcement of Dodge's reappointment to be made in Washington.

Having explained all this, he learned that Parr had paused in going by.

"Such a handsome man!" exclaimed Tamson. "What is he, David?"

He tried to explain. Actually, he did not know more than Trelawny had told him. He knew nothing of Parr's circumstances, except that he never seemed to want for money, yet was not a spendthrift. Apart from his having been in the militia, he knew only that Parr was devoted to Dodge's interests, but no sycophant.

"And the Indian?" asked Tamson.

"Oh, Soaring Hawk's a scout, really. He keeps us all informed of the Indians' plans, what they're saying, and so on. Some of the Dodgeville shippers, and some from Platteville and the Point employ him; he moves around between the Wisconsin River near Helena, and Madison, on the one side, and down into Illinois on the other."

At supper the talk was all of Governor Dodge and the impending banquet and ball. Candace was animated and delighted at the prospect of entertainment and excitement to come, as something apart from the ordinary course of life in the village. If her cheerfulness and spirited conversation were any indication, then Trelawny had been right in suggesting that she ought to go out more, David thought. He must manage to arrange more occasions for her.

After the dishes had been washed and put away, Tamson said she must go.

"Walk with her, David," said Candace.

"Oh, I can go alone," protested Tamson.

"We could both go with you," said David.

"No, please, not me, if you don't mind. I've been on my feet all day—I'm tired," answered Candace.

David put on his hat and coat, and preceded Tamson to the door.

Twilight had fallen; it lay softly on the land, dimming the light which shone down High Street and along Shake-Rag. The evening air at this hour, with only a faint south wind blowing, was aromatic; the perfume of wild blossoms was augumented by the rich musk of newly turned soil. The waxing moon, only a day past the new, lay dark yellow, low in the west, a rind of color, beautiful in the afterglow which made the earth black against its light.

They set out along the knoll to the north, in the direction of that end of the village where Aunt Marget's house stood.

"Did you study today, Tamson?" he asked presently.

"Not much. We read in that book Mrs. Pengellen's mother sent her. *The Prose Romances of Mr. Poe.* Such dark, scarey tales, too!"

"It's good for you to read. Did Candace have you read them aloud?"

"One of them, yes. It was called *The Murders in the Rue Morgue.* It was horrible—I shall dream of it tonight, I know I shall."

At this moment she stumbled, fell against him, and caught his arm. He steadied her, holding her for a moment in his arms; when he released her, he found her hand in his. How small it is! he thought. He did not release it, but walked on holding her hand as firmly as she held his own.

"I don't think it would be necessary to study much longer, Tamson. You speak as well as you'll ever speak right now. But it won't do you any harm to read."

"I like to have the excuse to call on Mrs. Pengellen," said Tamson naïvely.

"You don't need any excuse. I'm sure she likes you to come. I know I do."

"Do you, David?"

"I mean, I like you to come see her, because otherwise she gets too lonely. I wondered, though—isn't it about time you thought of getting work somewhere?"

"Aunt Marget's talked about it." She did not sound happy.

"I don't suppose she's got much money. You'll have to do something."

"I don't know what I want to do, David."

"Perhaps I can think of something."

They crossed High Street and went on into the wanly moonlit darkness toward Tamson's home at the far end of the row of little houses before them.

"David?"

"Yes."

"What do you think of Lieutenant Parr?" She asked the question diffidently.

"He seems a very amiable young man. Handsome, too," he added, repeating her own earlier judgment. "At least—the ladies would think him so."

Was she interested in Parr? he wondered. The thought did not give him any warmth; somehow, he felt that something better awaited Tamson. In the months he had helped her with the American idiom, he had grown as fond of her as if she belonged to his own family. While he could not presume to order her life, he was loath to hold back any advice he could give her. But what could he say about Parr, except that he himself was taken by him, that he knew nothing of his background or his prospects, other than that he appeared to have affluent and influential friends throughout Wisconsin Territory.

"Yes, he is handsome," she said slowly.

Was there a note of hesitation in her voice now? He opened himself to her, trying to sense her mood. As soon as he had done so, he was aware of a kind of strangeness, almost an aloof restraint, a warmth, an attractiveness most compelling. Moonlight lay upon her face like the faint, dim glowing of a spectral light shining out of darkness far away, with the tenuousness of a planetary light; it was caught in her long chestnut hair, so that her head seemed aureoled in the moon's glow, and her hair alight with some inner burning. The dress she wore was of some smooth, shiny material; her rounded breasts caught the moonlight, so that, however wan it was, here it shone and glinted, here it was embodied, glinting not only in her hair and off her dress, but from her dark eyes, from her lips. The moment was lyrical, and for its duration he was astonished at the vitality and warmth that sheathed her, he felt an utterly irrational impulse to put his arms around her and draw her close to him and kiss the moonlight from her eyes and her mouth and her shining hair.

He almost envied Parr, if he had stirred her so; for it was clearly from her that this restrained affection moved, a tenuous, intangible thing, an emotion which caught at him, flowing forth into the May night like the perfume from a hidden blossom. And Tamson's wild beauty was certainly enough to stir any man. But—Parr? What did anyone actually know about him?

"But I would not quite trust him," she finished, with the same deliberation.

"Oh," he said, in surprise at his error.

She hastened to explain, lest she had offended him, as Parr's friend. "It was the way he looked at me. Believe me, David, a woman can tell such things by a look or a touch or a word idly spoken. If she will."

He chuckled. "A woman. And are you that, at eighteen?"

She stopped where she was and looked angrily at him, her hand taut in his. "Is it only the number of her birthdays that makes a woman?" she asked with spirit. "Is it on a certain birthday a girl becomes a woman? How is it then that some of them never become women?" She gave him no chance to reply. "I saw last autumn it was a child you thought me. Perhaps it's a child you think me still. How you must laugh at me, then!"

"I don't laugh at anyone, Tamson."

"Then you can pity me—because I'm still a child in your eyes, and I have the feelings of a woman."

He was astonished at the vehemence of her protest. That she should think herself a young woman was not surprising. He supposed all girls did. But there was an air about her, a kind of conviction that made him uneasy. He had not thought of her so much as either a girl or a woman—she was Tamson Bishop, Aunt Marget's orphaned niece. He had taken her for granted, what with his concern about Candace and business affairs. Clearly, however, Tamson was emerging from girlhood.

But where had that tenuous moment of mystical lyricism gone? He had sensed it, as well as a warmth of affection he had thought meant for Parr.

They reached the Hoskins house, where lamplight in the kitchen told them that Aunt Marget waited for Tamson.

"Good night, Tamson."

She pressed his hand. "Good night, David." she stood for a moment with her eyes fixed on his face, as if searching for something she hoped to see. Then she turned and went into the house.

He stood for a moment outside the door. This Tamson had not been like the Tamson he had known; something of her wildness had been subdued, something of the girl she had been had become a young woman. She had begun to live that secret and mysterious life which every woman lives, he thought, something men can never understand, something toward which men grope haltingly forever. He had not been wrong in feeling the affection like an aura radiating from her. But dared he now suppose that it had been meant for him? Surely not! Surely it must be Parr, despite her words. It could not mean what he feared it might mean. How could he have been so blind, if so? No, no, certainly it must be Parr, the thought of whom stirred her. In his anxiety to believe himself, he pushed back the memory of her denial of Parr.

He turned and began to run toward home, trying not to recognize the leaping of his pulse.

In less than a month the public banquet and ball in honor of Governor Henry Dodge took place. The Governor himself had set the date—the fifth of June—when the committee from Mineral Point had waited on him at his home. The day was in the nature of a holiday; though shops and stores would be opened on demand, no regular business would be transacted, and the mines were all but abandoned. In the middle of the morning Captain John O'Neill led his company of Mineral Point Dragoons, colorfully uniformed, all the way to Dodge's home five miles north of the village, to escort him back to the village.

When the procession reached Mineral Point, Candace and David were in the company of citizens who formed at the Methodist Church and joined the parade at the head of High Street. David was touched by Candace's excitement. She had been afraid, when she had learned the date set by the Governor, that her condition would not permit her appearance, with propriety, in public; but she had laced herself so tightly that no one could have guessed that she was months pregnant. She wore one of her best dresses, suitable either for the street or for inside—a violet-colored terry velvet, trimmed with black quipure, almost daringly low at her shoulders, with a waist as tight as she dared make it, and a full skirt hooped around her and descending gracefully and almost severely under an equally severe blouse to a quintet of wide ruchings, a pattern repeated in the fullness of her sleeves. Her bonnet was black, with violet-colored trimmings in the shapes of flowers and a wide ribbon. She saw with pride that she was one of the most strikingly dressed women on the streets, and she drew many eyes, including those of Lieutenant Parr, who managed to come to her side, doff his high hat, whisper, so that David could hear it very well, that certainly she was the "most stunning sight to be seen this day in Mineral Point, and I do not except—though it may be heresy—the Governor himself!"

Governor Dodge was conventionally dressed, for he wore the customary black frock coat, slender at the waist, and rather more full above and below, with tight-fitting sleeves, trousers, and waistcoat, a white shirt and black string-tie. He carried a tall beaver hat in one hand; this he waved at the cheering crowd, as he rode, bowing and smiling, through the rows of people. Candace had not thought him so distinguished in appearance when first she had seen him, but the strength of his character was always to be seen in his firm features. Now he seemed a little tired or weary. His wife, who rode at his side, was also dressed conservatively, as if she would not be seen in grand clothes lest the less fortunate among her husband's constituents take offense at what they might consider an unseemly flaunting of wealth Governor Dodge did not in fact possess.

The procession swept along Shake-Rag Street and High Street to the Court House, where the official welcoming committee waited to receive the Governor. The committee of citizens had appointed Moses Strong as the official toastmaster of the banquet which was to follow, and the Governor's old friend, William Smith, the District Attorney of Iowa County, to introduce the Governor at the Court House—which was a formality, since everyone knew Dodge.

When the carriage came to a stop and the dragoons began to dismount to form a guard of honor on either side of the passageway up the few steps to the imposing portico of the Court House, Parr appeared as if by some legerdemain at the door of the carriage and opened it. Candace saw the Governor, following his wife from the carriage, pat Parr affectionately on the shoulder. The Governor and Mrs. Dodge walked up the *allée* of the dragoons to the portico, where Moses Strong welcomed them, and sat down on the seats presented to them.

Having shaken hands with the Governor, the District Attorney—a tall, heavy-set man of grave mien, bearded and jowled—began to speak. Candace listened as he outlined Dodge's career—his birth at Vincennes in 1781, his boyhood in Missouri, his term as youthful sheriff of Ste. Genevieve County, his captaincy of the border volunteers, his appointment to the rank of Brigadier General by President Madison, his reputation as an Indian fighter and his occupation of the Winnebago lead mines, followed by his part in both the Winnebago and Black Hawk Wars. As he enumerated Dodge's offices, it seemed to Candace that no man had ever held so many. Smith held up the Governor as the champion of freedom for all men, revealing that it was not popularly known, but at the time of the Governor's coming to the Territory, he had owned three families of slaves, all of whom he had set free, bestowing upon them sufficient improved land and goods to enable them to make their own living thereafter. This was the man who was now destined to lead Wisconsin into history as the newest star in the flag of the United States.

The ovation which followed the District Attorney's address

quieted only when Governor Dodge rose and came forward to acknowledge the introduction. Candace stood so close that it seemed to her she could see the fusion of the Indian fighter and the canny politician in the stalwart figure who bowed slightly and began to speak.

"My friends and neighbors, as I understand my old compatriot, Mr. Smith, I fear he expects me to duplicate in the years to come the exciting events of my earlier years. I'm afraid I can't promise to do so—not that I'm unwilling to make the attempt—but that I'm no longer a young man, and there are now more important things to be done.

"Here in the Territory of Wisconsin, we wait upon history. I believe you know that the events of the nation are commencing to move with ever increasing speed, now that Mr. Morse's telegraph has connected Washington to the important cities of the east, and will no doubt soon also bring about a connection to cities much closer to us. The annexation of Texas, I fear, may yet lead to war, though I'm happy to say it would appear imminent that a treaty will soon be signed between our country and Great Britain to settle the issue of the Oregon boundary. Our problems here are dwarfed in comparison to those facing the nation of which we are a part. We are moving to fulfil a manifest destiny, for statehood is not far away.

"In the meantime, there are countless small tasks which attend our rapid growth; but a short two years ago, there were within our Territorial boundaries only fifty thousand people, exclusive of the native Indian population; today there are close to three times as many. By mid-century, I'm confident that we have every right to expect a population of three hundred thousand. We are no longer a frontier Territory, and the transition to statehood is a task which has been entrusted to my care.

"I am conscious of the honor you do me in this gathering, but I can do no more than assure you I shall do all in my power to fulfil the obligations entrusted to me, and I should take it as a favor if you good people here today would consider that I speak to you not only as your Governor, but as a man who has mined at your side, who has fought at your side, who has tilled the same soil, as neighbor and friend."

The bedlam of cheers, whistles, shouts, stamping, and handclapping was diminished only by the Governor's leading the way from the portico of the Court House into the *allée* of dragoons, his wife on his arm. The dragoons filed off smartly at the far end, as the Governor and Mrs. Dodge passed, and double-timed to the front, thus forming a continual line arched over by their swords all the way to the Mansion House, where the banquet had been laid.

Candace and David were joined by the Trelawnys, who were also bound for the banquet. Mrs. Trelawny was as voluble in praise of the Governor's address as she was likely to be in her criticism of it tomorrow. The crowd was thinning. Trelawny caught David's eye, raised his eyebrows, and nodded in Candace's direction, as if to emphasize the wisdom of his advice to David. But David needed no prompting; he had already seen that Candace was radiant as she had not been since she left Providence.

It was after midnight when they reached home. They had walked up from the Court House, first taking Tamson home—for Candace had remembered Tamson and sent David to bring her to the ball. Both were tired, but Candace chattered incessantly of the events of the day, and particularly of the ball, saying several times, "Why it was almost like Providence!" which represented the height of an expression of favor and brought a smile to David's lips each time she said it. "And those toasts!"

"I liked the one he made to the Protective Tariff," said David —" 'A cruel and cunning invention by which the great body of the working men of our country are made to pay all the taxes for the support of the Government.' "

"Don't forget the one to 'the Fair of Wisconsin.' It seemed as if Mr. Strong looked directly at me when he proposed it."

"He did."

"It was a good thing," she went on, as they were getting ready for bed, "that Lieutenant Parr was there! I don't know what I'd have done, the way you had to go here and there. I know you couldn't help it, but I'd have felt terrible just sitting there. I hope I didn't make a spectacle of myself by dancing with him too often."

"Of course not, Candy."

"But I did dance with him often—three times, I think. I did one of the waltzes, a quadrille, and I was with him in the cotillion. He dances well."

"Better than I do, I marked that."

"Oh, I wouldn't say that."

He laughed good-naturedly. "I suppose you wouldn't, but I may. It doesn't matter. The only thing that matters is that you had a good time. I know it hasn't been easy to fit in here, Candy. I never expected it to be. But it did seem to me tonight you were happy."

"Oh, I was! Everyone was so nice to me. Even the Governor came up and spoke to me—he introduced me to Mrs. Dodge."

"Piloted by Parr, I have no doubt."

"Well, yes, Lieutenant Parr was with them at the time. But the Governor recalled meeting me the evening we came."

"Did Parr dance more than once with Tamson? I didn't see."

"I don't know, David."

"I couldn't dance more than twice with her myself. I had the feeling at the outset she didn't want to come. She felt out of place, for lack of the fine clothing the women had, though I thought she was well enough dressed."

"Oh, there are a great many things men never seem to notice," said Candace lightly. "Come to bed, David. I'm tired."

But neither of them slept. Each lay cradled in his own thoughts. David's were a confusion of impressions which remained from the day's political activity, of which there had been a great deal carried on in the most casual fashion at both banquet and ball, a confusion of images and scenes through which moved the figure of Lieutenant Parr, like a man sure of his position—though he had none of which David was aware; Candace's were an ordered kaleidoscope of the day's events, begun with the arrival of Governor Dodge, events through which moved constantly Lieutenant Nathaniel Parr, with an ease and a facility which she envied him because David did not have them. If only David had such connections as Lieutenant Parr! But there was little future in David's position, while surely there must be a great future ahead for a man like Lieutenant Parr. She basked still in the envy she had aroused in many of the women—she had been sharply aware of it, and took a passive satisfaction in it.

Over David's thoughts on the edge of sleep lay a feeling of contentment in Candace's happiness and the knowledge that the day had helped her make progress toward liking the Point. But it was not happiness that colored Candace's thoughts—it was a growing restlessness, seeded there by the assiduous attentions of Lieutenant Parr, and the admiration and respect that gentleman seemed to excite wherever he went.

They were not the only ones who lay sleepless.

In her small, narrow bed, Tamson Bishop lay awake and dry-eyed, though there were unshed tears in her. She was too stubborn to shed them. She should not have gone to the ball, she knew. The severe plainness of her dress made so great a contrast against the fine clothes of so many of the ladies as to have made her conspicuous. Moreover, the fullness of the ladies' skirts only served to emphasize her own unfashionable clothing. She had no other clothes. She had had no lack of dances, for all that—once with Mr. Trelawny, then with Lieutenant Parr, once with a strange young man who told her his name, too, was Bishop, and that he came from Dodgeville, once with a Mr. Gundry, one of the newest citizens of the Point, and twice with David. Those had been the best of her dances, the two with David, who though he lacked Lieutenant Parr's polished elegance and smoothness, nevertheless had a sureness and stability she missed in Parr.

Too, Parr's conversation had been odd. "I could wish to see more of the ladies of the Point," he said, lightly. She had replied that no doubt there were many who could echo his wish. She had said then, that he had not been to call on the Pengellens for some time. "It's not for the lack of wanting to do so," he had answered, and given her such a queer look, his eyes looking to probe behind hers.

But David, who had spoken almost less, had nevertheless said more—in the way he held her in his arms, in his smile, his eyes. But I'm just a girl to him, she said to herself, closing her eyes against the darkness of her little room, so that she might see again the brilliance of the ballroom and feel herself once more in the haven of David's arms, in a place of light and music from which all other people washed away, swept out of her mind's eye, and she and David were alone in all the world.

On a knoll not far from Governor Dodge's farm, Lieutenant Parr sat astride his horse under the stars of autumn pulling up into the late spring heavens at this hour. Soaring Hawk sat on his own horse not far away. They were watching the safe homecoming of Governor Dodge and his wife, escorted now by no full company of dragoons, but only by Captain O'Neill and two others. The lights of the carriage marked their passage. The little company swept off the highway and into the farmyard, where Toby, the Governor's aged Negro servant, was on hand with a lantern. There, after a brief pause, the three dragoons from Mineral Point left them, the sound of their horses' hooves loud in darkness broken otherwise only by the yawping of a fox or the screaming of a lynx. Parr had followed the riders at a modest distance, but, on the approach to the Governor's home, he had taken a short cut through the woods to come forth upon the knoll where he now sat. His day was done with the Governor's safe arrival at his home.

Soaring Hawk muttered in complaint. Was it not like the white men to begin a thing and not finish it? he wanted to know. What a grand company they had made, prancing up to the Governor's carriage the previous morning! What a great spectacle they had made all that morning, indeed! And now? More than half of them had fallen victim to firewater, most of the remainder had been too tired to remember the obligation they had undertaken. Three of all that company remained to return the Governor to his home. And these were the men he had to govern! Pity the white chief!

"The Governor knows how to deal with men, Hawk," observed Parr.

He was not thinking particularly of the Indian's words. Here under heaven, he was, as always, at peace with himself. The restlessness, the ambition, the desire for preference and power, the compulsion to seek forgetfulness in women, the conflict within him between his manifold duties to himself and his far-reaching ambitions, the gnawing doubt about his heritage—all these were stilled, subdued, not forgotten, but diminished in stature and pushed to the perimeter of his consciousness. Here he was aware only of the vastness of the earth, the beauty of the land, the wild, surging power of the rugged hills and the high plateaus, of the deep, dark valleys, and the swift, cool streams. There was a singular harmony between him and the stars overhead, as well as the earth underfoot, and he could think with tranquility of the days and months to come, looking forward to the time when the Governor would assume his office and convene the Territorial Legislature, to the steps leading to statehood, looking backward to the success of the Point's public homage to Dodge, congratulating himself not only on his perspicacity in suggesting it, but also on his canny foresight in rising in response to a toast and coupling Dodge's name with Morgan Martin's, who was sure to take Dodge's place in Washington. Martin would not forget if indeed he won the Democratic nomination in Madison later in the month.

The Indian grunted and said, "Rain come." He gestured toward the west, where an almost invisible bank of cloud was beginning to push up into the heavens. "Hawk know." He raised his head and sniffed the wind. "Wind say rain come."

"We're not far from home," answered Parr. "We'll be there long before rain comes."

Soaring Hawk muttered that it was time to be starting for home, by which he meant for the time being, Dodgeville, where Parr had his quarters.

Without a word, Parr urged his horse forward, descending the slope through the wood there to the road that led to the north. He was in no haste. The night was temperate and still, save for the susurrus of wind in the trees, and the voice of Soaring Hawk, who was delivering his verdict on the celebration at Mineral Point, expressing in various ways his restless irritation at the increasing evidence of the flourishing of the white race, which in his eyes was peculiarly unfitted to survive, despite its occasional honest leaders. Because he was familiar with this kind of reflection from Soaring Hawk, Parr paid no attention. His thoughts were elsewhere, now, back once more at the ball, and he saw before him once more the face and form of Candace Pengellen, her hazel eyes, merry as he had seldom seen them, her thin mouth smiling, her small nose provocative and challenging.

He was drawn to her. Perhaps it was because he recognized in her a restrained ambition which had its complement in him. He had responded to something in her at his first sight of her, but his conviction then had settled into one of her desirability, he thought of her as he had thought of other women who had been his conquests and from whose arms he had disentangled himself at will. But his second sight of her had revealed something more of her restlessness, though no complaint had crossed her lips, and no one could have been more decorous than she. He had left her on that occasion uneasy within himself because he recognized a response in himself that was something more than the customary reaction he knew for attractive women. There was no question of her attractiveness; he had seen the frank and covert attention of other men of whom she appeared to be wholly unaware; but her attraction for him did not rest alone in such physical beauty as she possessed. He had known other beautiful women—both with the quiet, smouldering beauty of Candace and with the wild and untouched beauty that was the Bishop girl's.

He contemplated Candace now with more honesty than he had permitted himself before. He had tried at first to dismiss his attraction to her as but another evidence of a tendency of which he did not always approve, but to which he was soft enough to yield time and again. But, being sensitive, he was aware of her growing approval of him; she was far from a state of mind which would entertain even the thought of disloyalty, far less faithlessness, to her husband, but Parr recognized that the first step had been taken. If he never saw her again, that step was irrevocable, but she would never go beyond it. Perhaps it would be better if he did not see her again; there were women far more beautiful than Candace. But he would not promise himself that, despite a feeling that it was the most sensible course he could take. He was convinced that a kind of destiny would see him safely through any peril which lay in wait for him on any course he chose to follow.

Behind him, Soaring Hawk was silent. If he had been given to pondering human relationships, he might have thought this friendship between Parr and himself a curious one. But he was not. There were many things about Parr which puzzled him; he believed there were as many things about him that baffled Parr. Soaring Hawk did not trouble himself about them. He accepted their relationship without question. Looking westward, he saw the clouds moving rapidly toward the zenith, black out the stars; Parr had not yet seen them; they would barely reach Dodgeville before rain would be upon them. His usually immobile features crinkled into the ghost of a smile.

Yes, thought Parr, I'll see her again. He felt himself committed to every course he undertook, this one no less than that which must inevitably lead to political preferment. But far back in his mind he was troubled by the recurring premonition of danger, which rose perhaps from a latent morality. He had had similar premonitions before; all had come to nothing, among them the association of danger with Soaring Hawk, who had soon after saved his life at a fording of the Wisconsin during a time of high water when thawing snow came down from the north and drove the river up. He was passively irritated with himself for entertaining vague fears and uncertainties upon any act, however trivial, to which a man might commit himself.

From the top of the rise where they now rode, they could see Dodgeville, the rows of houses and other buildings straggling down a long winding street and clustered about the diggings. They began the descent of the slope into the settlement just as the first rain-drops fell.

"Rain come," said Soaring Hawk in triumph. "Wind never say wrong."

Candace's delight in the celebration for the Governor lasted less than a fortnight; by the end of that time restless dissatisfaction had replaced her pleasure in the events and memories of that day. David saw the return of her mood with resignation, for it manifested itself in irritability and a kind of complaint which was difficult to bear, because it was in essence so unanswerable. When Candace cried out that the crudeness of the village could not be concealed by any number of celebrations, there was no effective contradiction, only the patient answer David had made before, that Mineral Point was growing fast, and time would erase those cruder aspects of the settlement. When she complained that the Pointers did not speak her language, his reply, that many of the ladies now coming to Mineral Point hailed from New England and were as well educated as she, elicited from her only the admission that she knew none of them. Yet she had met them all; if she failed to seek their company, they could not be held responsible for not calling on her. It was true that there were not many younger women without families in the Point, but soon she, too, would bear the same responsibilities as most of the women in the village.

The excitement of the ball had had the effect not of increasing her satisfaction with Mineral Point, but of subtly eating away at her determination to meet the challenge of western life. The ball had brought to the surface once more, sharpened by desire repressed for so long a time, her longing for a life of more excitement in some city like Providence. It divided her against herself, for at the same time that she tried earnestly to be the wife David wanted her to be, she fought against rebellion. Of this, David saw no sign, for she was careful that he should not. The very formlessness of her plans, as well as her indecision and indirection, made it necessary for her to be cautious; but even this racked her with a feeling of guilt, as if she were being disloyal. If he sensed anything of her conflict, he put it down to her pregnancy and dismissed it from his thoughts. He did not dream that there were days when she was bent upon escaping Mineral Point, when she looked back toward Providence as her goal, or some city like Providence, in the east, out of savage country; he had no suspicion that her mind vyed between sincere resolutions to overcome her dislike of Mineral Point and plans—most of them unworkable—for escape.

Her mood increased the uncertainty of David's daily routine, and this was a source of irritation. He never knew when he set out for the store each morning, how he would find Candace at noon or at evening; he was grateful for every visit Tamson or Aunt Marget made, for the older woman, understanding Candace's troubled mind, had resumed her visits whenever it was possible, and gradually Candace came to welcome her company. In a short time she was once more helping Candace to manage the household. It seemed almost as if Candace now took a perverse comfort in the older woman's dialect, which rose and fell in a kind of pleasant rune throughout the hours she was in the house; but, in fact, Candace had come to accept and like Aunt Marget as she had not yet learned to like the Point.

Aunt Marget had succeeded in enlisting Candace's interest in Tamson to the extent that Candace reminded David one morning of his promise to see about finding work for Tamson.

"I forgot," admitted David. "We've been so busy at the store, I hardly know which way to turn. And one of us had to go to the smelter today."

"The store!" exclaimed Candace. "Wouldn't that be just the thing? She could work there, David."

He had not thought of that. "I suppose she could. But the trade's pretty rough sometimes."

"Tamson can take care of herself."

"No doubt. Well, I'll mention it to Trelawny."

He was chagrined that he had not thought of it himself, and spoke to Trelawny at once on his arrival at the store. Much to his surprise, Trelawny accepted the suggestion without reservations.

"Just what we need!" he cried. "Here I've been wondering how we'd make out, what with all the things we've got to do. You've got to go to Helena today, David— Curwen seems to question the amount of lead we sent over. You'll probably find him at the tower; he's got it into his head to make shot again—it's been over three years since last he made any—instead of shipping all the lead down to St. Louis. I have our bill of lading here; you might ask at the smelter what he loaded—I think Lewis took the lead over that day—a week today, I think. Have you asked the girl whether she'd work?"

"No. But I'm sure she will."

"Well, why not walk up and get her now, then? You'll not have to hurry about Helena if I'm not alone here."

David found Tamson working with her aunt in the kitchen. A book lay face down on the edge of the table; Tamson had evidently been reading it. He glanced at the title—*Charlotte Temple, a Tale of Truth*—and wondered where she had found it; perhaps a traveler had left it at the Mansion House, for the traffic through the Point was increasing by the month, since the village was on the route to Madison from the south, and on the Galena-Milwaukee run of the stages, too.

He explained the purpose of his call. Would Tamson come to work?

She was delighted. "Surely, that I will, David. Aunt Marget's been wanting me to turn my hand to something useful."

"An' she's na ben wantin' et," supplemented the older woman.

"Mr. Trelawny says you're to come now, if you can."

"I doan't need 'ee for bakin'," put in Aunt Marget.

He waited a little impatiently for Tamson to make herself ready, knowing that the ride to Helena would take at least three hours, even on a horse of better than average speed. He would hardly have time to go home and tell Candace he had to go. But he need not. Aunt Marget could tell her not to expect him for dinner—perhaps not for supper; it might well be after dark before he reached Mineral Point again.

At the store, he picked up the bill of lading. Despite his work, Trelawny had got a horse ready for David, a black stallion that was one of Abner Nichols'; David had ridden him before. Trelawny saw him off with many warnings to stand firm, not to be taken in by any complaint of Curwen's.

He rode down to where Oliver Jeffries was in charge of the blast furnace where most of the ore brought to Trelawny & Pengellen was smelted for shipment either down the Wisconsin or overland to Milwaukee, and from there by the lake route through the Erie Canal to New York.

Jeffries, a short, scrawny man, hailed him on his arrival. "It's a long time since you were here, Mr. Pengellen. What brings you?"

"This shipment to Curwen. He claims he's short almost two hundred pounds of the thousand we sent him."

"We sent him a thousand," said Jeffries confidently. "At least, a thousand pounds left here. Let me get Lewis; you can talk to him; he hauled it over. Feed the furnace, will you, Mr. Pengellen?"

Jeffries went off, leaving David no alternative but to feed the galena into the shaft furnace, where it mixed with fluxing materials and coke to be reduced to metallic lead, slag and by-products, taken out at the bottom of the shaft. Perhaps Lewis was at work below, though there were two other men employed by Jeffries, in addition to Lewis, whose principal task was to haul away the smelted lead. But it was not Lewis below, for he came in but a few moments—a tall, burly man, very rough in appearance, dressed in buckskin in spite of the warm June weather.

"Ye werr afterr seein' me, Mr. Pengellen?"

"Yes, we've had some questions about the amount of lead you took to Curwen. I'm just on the way to see him. He claims he got only eight hundred pounds. We've billed him for a thousand."

"Aye, an' he got a thousand."

"All right, Lewis. Go back to your work. I'll take care of this."

He rode out of the village into the north, crossing back of the smelters and the mines toward the Dodgeville road, for Helena lay almost twenty miles beyond that town, and he had no time to lose, since the hour was already almost nine. The day was warm, the sky occasionally crossed by cumulus clouds, which shut out the sun from time to time, and diminished its head. Between Mineral Point and Dodgeville a great many travelers were on the road; he met and passed the stage from Milwaukee on its way to Galena; he overtook and passed a small train of seven ox-drawn lead wagons and several horsemen traveling more leisurely. The stages and the lead wagons were responsible for the comparative smoothness of the road, which followed a winding course up and down hill, around the slopes, with the woods cut wide away on both sides in the vicinity of the villages. These same lead wagons and stages, however, cut deep ruts into the muddy roads in spring, and at every prolonged wet period, arousing anguished demands from the lead miners for a railroad connecting them to shipping points.

Beyond Dodgeville, David met fewer travelers, for the road to Madison branched off there, and the route to Helena had fallen off in popularity ever since the shot tower at that place had ceased to manufacture and ship shot in any quantity, and many of its inhabitants had moved away. He wondered what would happen if the galena at Mineral Point gave out, and the smelting ended. It seemed unlikely, for no other place in the entire nation yielded so much lead as the area from the Wisconsin River on the north down into Illinois—the veins seemed endless; wherever lead was sought, it was likely to be found. Helena had been ruined not only by the failure of the shot tower, but by the disastrous regime of old Knapp, who had collapsed in defeat when his bank in Mineral Point had closed its doors.

But David's thoughts turned from speculation to Candace. She was never absent from his mind; she held to the perimeter of his awareness and rode with him all the way, hour after hour. It seemed to him, now that he had had time to see Candace against the background of Mineral Point and in another perspective, that the ties which bound her to childhood and youth were not only sentiment and nostalgia, but also in part the overweening attention her mother had always bestowed on her in a home where her father was less the master than he should have been. This bondage was still in her, and it imposed a kind of pattern of its own; since she was no more the center of the world in which she lived, as she had been in the house in Providence, it was only natural that she should be discontented and plaintive until she managed to reach the maturity which must eventually come. He was moved whenever he thought of how sturdily and valiantly she tried to meet the Point on its own terms.

Though he rode rapidly, it was after noon when he reached the site of the shot tower. The tower was a deep shaft bored into a bluff which faced upon the Wisconsin, flowing beautifully there among wooded islands and past a high escarpment, along the water's edge of which lay an exposed rock face on which the Indians of perhaps centuries ago had drawn crude emblems and figures—men at hunting, pictures of tribal war, tribal symbols—cut into rock and painted over with the red of their war paint, though the rising and falling waters of the river had begun to dim the outlines of their drawings.

Curwen had gone to dinner in what remained of the settlement which lay back a little way from the bluff of the tower, but one of his employees was at work there, and opined that Curwen would be back within a short time. When he did come, he would go directly to the top of the bluff, where lead was being melted and poured down to the chamber where the employee was at work. He was at the moment taking the lead which had fallen down the perpendicular tower—two hundred feet or more—out of the tub of water into which it had fallen, and putting the pellets out to dry, preparatory to being poured over the inclined planes, divided by troughs, where the round shot would be separated from the imperfect shot.

It did not seem to David a favorable occupation. The shot tower had been abandoned for good reason; the manufacture of shot could no longer compete with more skilled workmanship along the Mississippi and elsewhere. Besides, while there was no evidence that Curwen had resumed his trade for any length of time, the water-bath leaked, and the grading machine was badly rusted. Plainly Curwen would not be at shot-making for very long; the height of the tower's usefulness had passed.

David made his way out of the cavern-like chamber at the foot of the tower, so painstakingly hewn out of the rock almost two decades before, and climbed up the steep ascent of the bluff some distance past the tower itself, for the face of the bluff out of which the shaft had been cut was impossible to climb. As he climbed, the vista of the Wisconsin River valley at that place unfolded before him. The river here curved down out of the north, around the bluff on the west, and then leisurely into the southwest—a broad, blue stream, flowing its way among many islands, with a wide sweep of lowland and prairie to the north and northwest, and high rolling hills beyond, all but one or two covered with trees. Tall hills and craggy bluffs rose in the southwest, too, broken by the mouths of deep valleys, and here and there among the trees wound the clear, turbulent streams that emptied into the river.

Curwen had already returned to his crude smelter at the mouth of the shaft. He was a rough-looking man who had not shaved for some days, and with the look of not having changed his clothes for as long a time; out of his stubbled face his thick mouth shone redly, and his pale blue eyes seemed almost bright. As David came up, Curwen was just beginning to drop the melted lead into the shaft through the perforated ladle.

"By God! It's Pengellen!" he cried. "I'll bet that word I sent by Lassiter fetched you."

"Well, yes, we thought we'd find out where the difference lay."

"I'm sorry, Pengellen. There ain't any, and that's a fact. I'm sorry you had the trip for nothing, but I did think you cut me out two hundred pounds. It was all the fault of that jackass down below; he separated the shipment and set off two hundred pounds somewhere else. When I started to work on it, it didn't look like a thousand; so I weighed it, and it came out to eight hundred. 'Twas only after I sent you word that he owned up to putting out some of the lead. I could've kicked him—and I did."

"I'm glad our figures jibe," said David with relief. He sat down on a crude bench not far from the shaft. "Lewis remembered delivering it."

"Just a little matter of a temporary separation, you might say," said Curwen. "You stayin'?"

"No, I'll be going back directly. I'll rest a little. There's too much work at the store for me to loaf anywhere." He gestured toward Curwen's work. "What are you up to, Curwen?"

Curwen threw down his ladle and came over to sit beside him. "Well, I'll tell you, Pengellen," he said earnestly, "I thought to go back into the business of makin' shot. I figured what with trouble stirring in Mexico—I got a strong notion we'll be in it —we could use all the shot we had. But that damned knave, Knapp, just about ruined everything here, and I guess I won't be at it as long as I thought. It'd cost too much to fix everything up; I can't afford it. I'll finish what I started and then I'll stick to the shipping. Lead's going up, too."

"Yes, I thought Knapp didn't leave much behind when he hightailed it out of the country," said David.

Curwen got up again, restlessly, and picked up his ladle once more—a man of little judgment, thought David, with hindsight instead of foresight. But certainly he was not alone in these shortcomings.

He got up himself, stood for a little while watching Curwen at work, then bade him good-bye. He went back to where he had left his horse cropping the long grass that grew along the edge of the inlet from the river which came up almost to the mouth of the chamber at the bottom of the shot-tower shaft. The employee there hardly noticed him. He thought he ought to stop for something to eat, but he had little appetite; now that the difficulty about the lead shipment had been so easily resolved, his thoughts returned again to Candace.

The hour was not late. He should reach home in time for supper.

Aunt Marget left the house in late afternoon. She dallied a little, not wanting to leave Candace alone; but Candace could not have been more alone without the older woman than with her, for she had heard nothing all day but a recital of small talk, of incidents which had taken place during the past weeks, which David had never mentioned—of drunken brawls, near duels, vicious fights which had occurred within the Point and in neighboring towns—all of which only emphasized the roughness of the region. It seemed to her that no matter how much she tried to find compensation for her relative isolation in this wild country, it was certain that each time disillusionment would come, wearing away at her determination to best the challenge of this frontier life. Moreover, Aunt Marget's dreary recital of the number of deaths in the wake of a cholera epidemic which had scourged the Point only a few months before her own coming to it last October filled Candace with dismay, not so much for her own life, as for that she carried within her.

She was fully aware that the transition from the life she had known in Providence to that of this Wisconsin village had been too abrupt, and had been made to seem all the more so by the violence of the contrast between her sheltered early years and the raw practicality of life in Mineral Point. She had tried repeatedly to forget her earlier years, but she could not. She had made many attempts to see Mineral Point as her permanent home, to accept it, to belong to it. Her mother had urged her in letters to "make the best of things, and you will soon find that a change will come about, for the better, for it is never what is outside and around one that is so important as what is on the inside." Though Candace believed this, her belief could not entirely overcome her consuming ambition which was somehow bound up with the conviction that there was no future for her or her family in the Point.

As a girl, she had early determined that she would make something of herself—like Anne Bradstreet, whom she admired. Though this adolescent ambition to justify herself in the eyes of her companions and her family had been swallowed up in time, a faint aspect of it still lingered and sprang to life in the restless dissatisfaction which so often moved her. And because of this unrest, she was too often torn between the wish to compromise for David's sake, and the desire to escape for her own. But she did not suspect that the wish to escape was not for freedom from

Mineral Point so much as flight from maturity and the responsibilities she was afraid to assume.

Alone, she did not know what to do with herself. She had long ago grown to dislike reading. Her mother had sent her the popular books of the day as well as those acclaimed by critics. She had for a while enjoyed such dramatic romances as *Kate Walsingham, Humility Before Honor,* and *The Drooping Lily;* then slowly, insidiously, her interest lagged, the setting distracted her; she had scarcely been able to finish the first chapter of *Typee,* and at last she did not even look into the books her mother sent. She was unhappy alone; she fell back upon herself, seeking in vain for something to which to cling for comfort; but in all the genteel instruction in the manners and customs of the day which she had been given, there was nothing to help her plan a course through the rough realities of frontier existence.

The sun drew westward, the shadows lengthened; outside, in the drowsy summer afternoon, the birds made a scattering of songs—no longer the carols of spring, but the more settled melodies of summer, the robins' singing having given way to the nostalgia of pewees, the mourning doves' keening being replaced by the liquid notes of wood thrushes, the larks' threnodies lost among the songs of field sparrows and vireos. All these rose from the woods south of the house, all sounded sweetly through the open windows, and the exploratory south wind pervaded the house with the perfume of wild honeysuckles, late to flower in the depth of the grove. But she was unaware of their enchantment in her preoccupation with herself; it seemed to her at one moment that she must and would find somewhere the strength to overcome her unhappiness, and at the next that there must be some way of escape, some egress from the four walls pressing in upon her, from the crude, boisterous, brawling village lying in wait beyond. If only she could discover one solution or another!

She walked restlessly from window to window, but she avoided any view of the Mounds. Looking northeast, she was struck with the physical fact of the village's expansion, for whole blocks of building had been erected since October, and other streets were springing up, parallel to both High and Shake-Rag Streets. Raw, unpainted houses were encroaching even toward this house, which she had at first thought so isolated from the rest of Mineral Point, but she no longer looked upon this promise of an end to her solitude as pleasurable. The one vista which always gave her pleasure was in danger of being shut away; that was the view of High Street which permitted her sight of the Doric columns and entablature of the Court House, which, during evening hours when the late sunlight glowed redly about it, brought back vividly certain scenes in Providence, and, looking at it, she experienced that strange, psychic feeling of being transported thither; it was not just an experience of her mind, but one which carried with it a physical involvement, so that she believed for those moments that everything about her situation now was but a dream, and that this vista of Providence alone was real, that she need but walk toward those columns and that twilight to the familiar streets and lanes, and, beyond, into the gracious vestibules and drawing-rooms of her childhood's city.

She stood at the window looking toward the Court House, waiting for that hour when the light of the setting sun would create the magic illusion. Beyond, along Shake-Rag, the Cornish women were coming out of their little white and yellow stone houses to wave their white cloths to their husbands on the opposite slope, signifying that the evening meal was now ready. The warm friendliness of the women as they stood talking to one another along the street was lost to her; it did not occur to her that their street and its confined life offered precisely as much in human joy and travail as any street in Providence, for they remained fundamentally foreign to her. As she watched, the women, one by one, went back into their houses, and on the opposite slope men began to come down from the pits.

She glanced again toward the Court House. Her restlessness subsided as anticipation took its place; but before the sun had descended sufficiently far to surround the entablature of the Court House with that rose haze of evening, she caught sight of a horseman coming into the village over the pitted ridge from the north, she concluded instantly that it was David, for he rode rapidly toward High Street, and she realized in panic that she had not yet begun their supper. She abandoned her post, pushed down her concern with herself, and hurried to the kitchen, hoping that he would be delayed long enough for her to prepare the evening meal. In this, she acted by habit; she had been taught that these duties of a wife came before all else, and she fulfilled them faithfully not because it was her desire to do so, but simply because they were integral to the tradition in which she had been reared.

She was ready with supper when David came.

"I missed you, David," she said quite truthfully.

He tweaked her nose solemnly, kissed her, and said he had hastened to be back before dark. "I didn't like to think of you alone here after sundown—not that there's any danger."

"How is it like up there where you were?" she asked, as they sat down to table.

"Helena? Oh, it's a dying town; it has no future."

She smiled at this. Had Mineral Point? she wondered.

"But the Wisconsin is a beautiful river. I think you'd like it. It's broad, with many islands, and the bluffs along the river still show some of those strange drawings done by Indians."

"Is it like the Seekonk?"

"Yes, in a way. But wilder, of course. Broad and quiet, too. Yes, I think it is."

"But an Indians' waterway!"

He laughed. "And where do you think the Seekonk got its name, Candy? From the Puritans? There were Indians there, too. I sometimes think you never realize that Providence was also once a crude frontier town rising among the Indians."

She ignored this. "Some day perhaps we can ride over to see it."

On a hot July day Lieutenant Parr rode into the village on his way to Platteville. He cantered down the slope from the north, across Shake-Rag, and up the High Street, tipping his hat to various acquaintances on the way. The hour was past noon, approaching one o'clock. He cast a speculative glance toward the Pengellen house, but did not venture in its direction. Just as he fixed his gaze on the grove of trees through which he was to make his way to the high road beyond Mineral Point, he caught sight of a young woman hastening toward the street from the direction of the Pengellen house. He thought at first it might be Candace, and slowed his horse to a walk.

As she came close, however, he discovered that it was Tamson Bishop. He reined his horse to a stop and got off. He removed his hat and wiped the moisture from his forehead and temples, dabbing also at his upper lip, and waited for her to come to where he stood.

Tamson did not see him until she was almost upon him. She was hurrying so that she would not be late to work.

"Good afternoon, Miss Bishop," said Parr, making her a courtly bow.

She returned his greeting circumspectly, wondering why he had stopped to talk to her.

"Soaring Hawk tells me you've taken up employment at the store," he said. "I hope you find it congenial?"

"I do, Mr. Parr, thank you."

"I'm sure the patrons must appreciate someone other than the partners behind the counter, all due respects to those worthy gentlemen. I'm just on my way through to Platteville and Galena. You've been to visit Mrs. Pengellen, I observe; I hope they're both well."

"Both, sir."

"Pray give my best wishes to them when next you see them," he went on. But his mind was not on his words; he knew that Tamson Bishop had ready entree to the Pengellen household; she might make it more easily possible for him to be seen there, if it seemed that his interest lay in her. How to bring this about gave him little trouble. "I've wondered ever since the ball last month whether I might some day have the privilege of calling on you, Miss Bishop," he said candidly.

Tamson did not think he had any interest in her, but she was not perceptive enough to understand his purpose. She was puzzled and intrigued, just the same. She was not averse to pretense on her own. She lowered her eyes with becoming modesty and was silent.

Parr immediately launched into a suave, persuasive little speech in which he seemed to praise her modesty at the expense of his boldness. She was amused.

She looked up with a faint smile. "Perhaps, some day, Mr. Parr."

"Perhaps this day week, at seven o'clock in the evening?"

"Very well," she agreed.

He thanked her. As he went on up the road out of the village, Tamson could not help thinking that he possessed an undeniable fascination.

Toward evening, Soaring Hawk came into the store. He was alone. He left his horse standing in the road, not tied to the wooden hitching posts set in along the street there. In his usual silent manner, he walked through the store and sat down cross-legged near Trelawny's desk.

"Hello, Soaring Hawk," said Trelawny, who was at the moment busy with his wife.

Mrs. Trelawny sniffed. "Perhaps you'd better take care of your Indian friend."

"Soaring Hawk will wait," said Trelawny, undisturbed.

"I don't like being hurried," she said shortly, and went out.

Trelawny turned to the Winnebago and shrugged expressively.

"Make squaw work," said Soaring Hawk simply. "Squaw make papoose."

"All very well," agreed Trelawny. "But it doesn't always work. What goes on wherever you've been?"

Soaring Hawk explained that he had been to the north. Up past Helena, across the river, past Sac Prairie in the vicinity of Baraboo, which was the seat of the adjoining county and much newer than Mineral Point. There were still many Indians in the vicinity, though all the Winnebago had been supposedly shipped down the Wisconsin into Iowa lands five years ago. There were even more palefaces, more coming every day. But old Chief Yellow Thunder had come back with his squaw. He had become a white man. He had bought land—his own land—he had bought it and was now to be a farmer, raise crops, live as a white man. Soaring Hawk's eyes alone expressed his scorn for Yellow Thunder's chosen way. There were others among the Winnebago doing the same thing. It was not good for an Indian to live as white men lived.

Trelawny listened without interrupting him. There was no good in asking questions. The Indian would say only what he had a mind to say.

Soaring Hawk came presently back to the lead region. Did

Trelawny know a certain chieftain styling himself Kinnieshek?

"I've heard of him."

Kinnieshek had gathered about him a band of dissident Indians. Some were Fox, some Winnebago. There was even a Dakota among them. They belonged in Iowa country, but they had come over a wooded area not far from New Diggings, to the west, commanding the route of the lead wagons to Galena. Now there was sullen talk among them about the way in which the white men had stolen the lead mines from the Winnebago. There was talk about a raid upon the lead wagons traveling south. They were poorly guarded; no incidents had taken place for so long a time that the guards had been relaxed; the Indians in numbers could seize an entire train and make off with the lead, hiding it in the woods until they could sell it.

"They haven't got a chance in hell of carrying it off," said Trelawny. "Think so, Dave?"

David had come up to listen to Soaring Hawk. He shook his head. "They could try it, though. Give them a little liquor and God knows what they'll do."

Soaring Hawk agreed. There were men who would give them all the firewater they wanted. There might be a white man or two who would share in the lead, Soaring Hawk hinted impassively. The price was rising; it might never rise as high again.

"Well, what can we do about it?" asked David.

Someone might be able to scare Kinnieshek, opined Soaring Hawk. The Winnebago believed that it was quite possible to find out whether Kinnieshek had white accomplices. An Indian coming in with much lead to sell would invite questions. It would be wiser for white men to carry it in. The Indians would raid, then hide, and the whites would later bring out the lead.

David began to question Soaring Hawk. Did he have any information about the identity of Kinnieshek's accomplices?

None, said Soaring Hawk.

Had he talked with Kinnieshek himself?

He had. He felt Kinnieshek's dishonesty, his restlessness, his smouldering anger, his hatred. He would do it. But he was no less afraid, should the white men discover who had done it.

Trelawny took a cigar from his desk and lit it. He puffed thoughtfully at it while David and Soaring Hawk talked. David's questions achieved nothing. He might have expected as much. Soaring Hawk had told all he knew or wished to tell for the moment. He listened to him say that he had not yet told all the lead shippers, but that they would soon know; he was going to Platteville tonight.

"Dave," Trelawny said suddenly, his round face sober, "do you know Kester McAvity?"

"I've heard his name."

"He hangs around Galena and Dubuque. A gambler. You know him, Soaring Hawk?"

The Winnebago knew him. It was evident that he had no good opinion of him.

"I wonder if he knows you, Dave," Trelawny went on. "It seems to me it might be a good idea for someone to spend a day in Galena and scout around. There are places where an Indian couldn't go with as little suspicion as a white man." He turned to the Indian once more. "Can you be in Galena tomorrow, Hawk?"

The Winnebago nodded. He expected to be in Galena by noon or before.

"Good. You can meet the stage—but not too openly. If you find out where McAvity is, point him out to Dave."

Soaring Hawk objected at once. He did not think this a good idea. If by any chance any of Kinnieshek's Indians were about, he, Soaring Hawk, would be recognized; David would thus be associated with him; he would then accomplish nothing with McAvity. He had a far better idea. Perhaps Trelawny did not know it, but Lieutenant Parr was in Galena. He, Soaring Hawk, would find Parr, Parr would meet the stage, Parr would show McAvity to David. In that way he, Soaring Hawk, would not be seen with David.

"Excellent," agreed Trelawny. "We'll leave it at that."

After Soaring Hawk had gone, David questioned his information.

"The only fault I have to find with Soaring Hawk," said Trelawny, "is that he's more apt to understate a matter than to exaggerate it. If he sees fit to mention that Kinnieshek is thinking about raiding a lead train, you can be sure Kinnieshek more than just talked about it in his cups. And it's not an idea that a band of Indians would be likely to get without prompting. McAvity looks like the man to do it. I may be wrong. See for yourself."

"Do you expect me to go up to him and ask him?" protested David.

"I guess you'll be able to find out where he stands. He's a gambler. He's not a buyer of lead, nor a shipper. He might be interested in lead. Talk lead to him. You're a buyer and not too curious about the source."

"I see."

At supper, David explained that he would be gone all the next day. "I've got to go to Galena."

"Oh, David, take me along!" cried Candace.

"I hardly think the ride would be good for you, would it? And you oughtn't to go out."

"David—I hardly show, you know that."

"But the risk."

"It isn't any greater than leaving me here all by myself. Aunt Marget works out tomorrow at Mrs. Lanyon's in the morning and Mrs. Penberthy's in the afternoon. And you may not be back."

"I'll try to be. The stage goes faster now, and there are more stages. I could be here before midnight."

But there was no denying her. She begged and pleaded. All his protests were useless.

Early next morning they took the stage for Galena.

David had dressed in rather colorful fashion, like a gentleman of leisure and questionable occupation; he wore a high hat, a lavender waistcoat, with a watch-chain across it, and a purple cravat. Moreover, he carried a cane, and he felt certain he looked the part Trelawny expected him to play. Candace was dressed in the height of fashion; she had so little opportunity to wear her good clothes that she took this advantage to do so. Her dress was a grey tarlatan, over which she wore a pelerine of cardinal muslin, trimmed in moire and lace. David had remonstrated gently with her, suggesting that some other outer covering would be better fitted for travel than this pelerine, which was more suited to evening wear, but she paid no attention.

Fortunately, the coach was not crowded. Only two other passengers rode at this hour; one was a fat, well-dressed man who gazed at them drowsily and closed his eyes directly after, though he did not sleep; the other was a priest. He, too, seemed tired, but he looked familiar to David—a thin man with intense, dark, burning eyes, with a lean, ascetic face that bore the marks of ill health or physical exhaustion. The priest returned his gaze as if he recognized him, and finally, as the coach was moving along toward Belmont, he spoke.

"Forgive me, but aren't you the younger partner of Trelawny & Pengellen?"

"I am, sir—traveling with my wife."

The priest smiled at Candace, allowing his eyes to linger on her for a long moment. "Father Samuel Mazzuchelli," he said.

"Of course. You were in Galena for several years," said David.

"Yes. But I'm not long back from Italy. I've come to stay

now, I hope. I went there to rest for a while, and now I'm at another parish. I'm just on my way back there."

David explained to Candace that the priest with whom they rode was widely known throughout the Wisconsin Territory, as well as in Illinois and Iowa, for his indefatigable labors as an architect. He had built many churches in the neighborhood of Mineral Point, and he had been the first chaplain of the Wisconsin Territorial Legislature in Belmont. He turned again to the priest. "And now, Father?"

"Now? Who knows? It's in God's hands, surely. I've been authorized to establish a Dominican Province at Sinsinawa. I've worked there for some time. Next month Bishop Henni will bless my church there—St. Dominic's. The college will come, God willing."

"How long have you been gone?"

"Almost two years."

"Don't you find the growth of our village surprising?" pressed David, with a sidelong glance at Candace.

"Yes, indeed. But one expected it."

"Not I," put in Candace. "My husband is always trying to convince me that if we wait long enough, we may grow as big as cities in the east."

"Who knows?" asked Father Mazzuchelli.

His voice was gentle, pleasant. His eyes moved from David to Candace and rested there, seeming to see into her, through her, and beyond. She was fascinated by his eyes. She had an ingrained prejudice against Catholicism, fed by generations of Protestant antipathy; but this tired, friendly man suggested nothing of the legends upon which she had been brought up. If the traveling habit he wore—a long black coat over a priestly habit of the same color—was repugnant to her, she forgot her repugnance before the almost hypnotic warmth of his tranquil eyes and the soft persuasiveness of his words. He spoke of the changes in the Territory since last he had been here. He had come this morning from Madison, which but a few years ago had been little more than a hamlet and was now a flourishing young city. He should perhaps have gone directly back to Sinsinawa, but he wanted to pass through the villages where he had served as pastor, especially Galena and Dubuque, before he went to Prairie du Chien and his present charge.

Their fellow traveler opened his eyes from time to time and interjected vague comments, none of which was pertinent. He appeared to exist in a world of his own, into which the priest, Candace, and David happened to have been projected against his knowledge and will; he spoke like a man roused from unawareness; if the priest mentioned Platteville, he spoke of New Diggings; when the priest spoke of Dubuque, he was somehow reminded of Governor Dodge, who had little relation to that city. There was a faint air of the comic about him, but there was no harm in him, only a kind of aimlessness.

Their talk, with its distracting interruptions, was not enough to hold Candace's roving attention; besides, it was primarily between David and the priest. She turned her head from time to time and gazed from the coach, dwelling upon her last journey over this terrain. The road which had been rutted and rough on that occasion, was now dry and dusty, so that the stage rolled smoothly along with only occasional joltings, though it swayed dangerously around the many curves in the road. This was hardly preventable, for the coach was top-heavy with the baggage and the driver and his companion on top. Candace's perspective was different now; it had undergone a subtle alteration; there was a division, however slight, in the loyalty which previously had been solely behind her; instead of moving from a place long familiar and dear to an alien country, she traveled between places of some familiarity, and was thus able to compare the landscape favorably with that she had seen on that dark day up from Galena.

The day, which had begun with clouds, was now sunny; the clouds had rolled back, the hot July sun shone down, the air was windless. The landscape was lushly green, with that deep green of mid-summer; the leaves of trees pressing close upon the road at the edge of groves and more extensively wooded tracts had a hard, bright sheen of sunlight, where shade did not soften them; the depths of each wood looked cool, inviting; the waters of the Pecatonica, crossed not far beyond Mineral Point, were cobalt and clear.

Yet there was something about the plateau of grassland which flowed toward the twin Mounds of Belmont and Platte that was forbidding; here in this expanse, which was largely treeless, the sunlight seemed to brood, not pensively, but almost darkly, the grass seemed to undulate gently without wind, the two Mounds towered over far down against the horizon. It was incredible that they should be riding here along a ridge and not down on a plain, for the illusion of prairie-land was here in the long sweep of grass, tall as a sea of grain, swirling distantly to the Mounds on the one side, and to a downward slope on the other side of the road along which they moved.

There was a sentience about the grass, a watchful vitality, as were it constantly waiting to recover once more the road which had been cut through its expanse, to heal this wound and do away with this mark of civilization. At the same time, the sea of grass had an undeniable fascination; its windless undulations caught the eye, the sheer mass of it quickened the imagination. How must an area like this have impressed a traveler among the surrounding hills at first sight twenty or thirty years ago! All else was hilly terrain; the road dipped into a valley, swept up a slope to follow a ridge, descended once more into lower, sometimes swampy ground, and mounted another hill, for all the distance to Galena, save only for a few miles over the border of Illinois, where the road followed along another region of high land which was less a plateau than land on a higher level, sloping down sharply to the valleys and the knolls on which Galena was built.

Over all the terrain brooded the Mounds, rising with an illusion of intimacy that was overshadowed by that insistent aura of the ominous which seemed to emanate alike from Mounds and plateau. Indeed, behind this outwardly pleasant landscape there seemed to peer the face of terror; yet Candace could not take her eyes from it; she found herself looking constantly over the plateau to the Mounds, first at the Belmont Mound, which was the nearer, then at the Platte, for the road curved in a wide half circle partly around them, and they were visible for most of the trip. They drew her eyes, compelled her glance, rose like sentient symbols of this harsh, wild country, defying her rebellion, scorning her hatred, aloof from such concerns as hers or of any man or woman who chose to live within sight of their high rounded slopes. The very sight of them chilled her gaiety, pushed back her first tentative acceptance of this land; yet she could not keep her eyes from the Mounds, but viewed them as long as they were within the orbit of her sight, almost mesmerized by their looming on the landscape of earth and mind.

But at last they were passed. She could no longer see them except by turning to look back; she resisted the impulse to do so and looked out upon the passing country with a feeling of freedom from their menace. Man-made changes were everywhere. Thickets were being leveled, fields of grain stood in many places, and, perhaps because she had looked at them first with so jaundiced an eye, the settlements themselves seemed larger. As she rode along, she became more and more certain that she was winning her struggle against her prejudices; time and patience would wash away her yearning for the east and bring her an inner peace, come with her acceptance of this wilderness that was Wisconsin Territory, where everything, even human life, was held cheaply.

The stage came at last into Galena, slowing down the long winding slope which led to the inn where the stage customarily stopped. The priest had long since grown silent; he sat with his eyes closed; occasionally his lips moved, as if he were in prayer. Their comical fellow-traveler had come to life and was now looking appreciatively from the carriage, speaking with great animation of the advantages of living in Dubuque, whither he appeared to be going. David was wondering how Candace would occupy herself in Galena, for it might be impossible to return before the next day.

Parr waited for them. David saw him at once, and with a sense of relief. He did not completely depend upon Soaring Hawk, as Trelawny did; he had not had Trelawny's experience with Indians. Parr stood there with a certain elegance, and was quick to help Candace from the coach, saying with marked emphasis how very pleasant it was to see her. Then he caught sight of the priest, and a broad smile came to his lips, he made a slight bow, and greeted him.

"You're certainly ubiquitous, Nathaniel," observed the priest. "One never knows where you'll turn up next."

"Ah, but even I haven't wandered so far—nor a tithe so fruitfully—as you, Father," replied Parr.

The priest smiled and, taking his portmanteau from the driver, he set off up the slope in the direction of St. Michael's, the church he had built a decade before.

"Is there anyone you don't know, Lieutenant?" asked Candace, laughing.

"Indeed, yes. Many people. Ten years ago Father Mazzuchelli and I lived here in Galena; it's only natural we'd know each other." He turned from her to David. "I'm surprised to find Mrs. Pengellen with you."

David shrugged. "It was her wish, not mine. I didn't have the heart to leave her, even though I can't very well take her with me here in Galena. I thought she might wait somewhere until we could rejoin her."

"That won't be necessary. As a matter of fact, I've just left McAvity. I won't have to return with you; I can stay with Mrs. Pengellen. McAvity's not easily mistaken. He's a man of fifty or so, stocky of build, with a cleft chin and red hair. You'll find him at a tavern called the One-Mile House, on the Mississippi side of town. He'll take your measure, David. If you like, use my horse; he's tethered up ahead."

"No, I'll walk, Nate. I want to plan what to say."

"If you're not back here in two hours, I'll come for you," said Parr meaningly.

David quelled Candace's quick alarm. "I'll be here before then."

"May I show you Galena, Mrs. Pengellen?" asked Parr, offering her his arm.

David strode off in the direction of the One-Mile House. He was not sure how he should proceed, but he was not hesitant for all that. Perhaps the best approach would be simply to ask for McAvity. Yet he felt intuitively that this would be an error; it would be better to bring about McAvity's coming to him. He walked rapidly along the winding streets of Galena, crossed the Galena River, and took a footpath to his destination—a shoddy-looking inn built of logs facing a road leading from Galena toward the Mississippi. A rough sign identified it.

He went in.

Since it was now past the noon hour, the proprietor, and a woman who might have been his wife, were sitting at a meal at one of the four tables in the poorly apportioned room which served as both tavern and vestibule for his innkeeping activities. At yet another table sat a thick-headed, red-haired man, with such a cleft chin as Parr had described; he had small, black eyes. He looked calculatingly at David when he entered. Judging by the smell in the place, the proprietor and his wife were eating kidney stew. McAvity was not eating; he had a bottle of whiskey and a glass before him. He had the air of waiting for someone; perhaps he had appointed the inn a meeting-place.

The proprietor eyed David suspiciously from his one good eye. He had a crude patch over the other, made of some purple stuff, which lent him a faintly comic appearance. David sat down. As soon as the proprietor came to his feet, David called for a bottle of whiskey and a glass. McAvity looked him over boldly. David took a notebook out of his pocket and made a pretense of studying figures in it. He poured himself some whiskey, but refrained from drinking too much of it on his empty stomach.

Within ten minutes, McAvity's curiosity impelled him to push his own table out of the way and walk over to David's.

"Stranger here, ain't ye?" he asked, sitting down.

David nodded.

"In business?" pursued McAvity.

David looked at him coldly. "I'm buying lead," he said levelly.

"Ain't one a the regular buyers, are ye?"

David shook his head. It would not do to seem interested too soon.

"Thought I never seen ye 'round before. Mind if I have a drink?"

David nodded toward the bottle. McAvity crossed to get his glass. He poured himself a full measure.

"You buyin' a lot?" asked McAvity.

"Don't look like it," answered David with an irritated manner. "I guess I'm too late. The regulars got in ahead of me. They

send their men up from St. Louis, and a lone wolf won't stan
much chance."

"Where you shippin' from?"

David favored him with a long glance. "I'm not particular."

McAvity ran his tongue out over his lips. He appeared t
think this over. Then he said, "I got friends in the mines. Ho
much d'ye need?" He spoke hastily, with ill-concealed eagerness
glancing at a clock on one wall.

"I'll take what I can get," answered David, assuming a sus
picious air.

"I might be able to git ye some. But up river from Galena
though."

"That's agreeable enough."

A pair of travelers came into the tavern, but neither, judgin
by McAvity's disinterest, was the object of his tryst. Neverthe
less, McAvity lowered his voice to a more confidential tone
though he had not seemed to mind the eavesdropping of th
proprietor and his wife, who were probably old friends, he too
care that the newcomers heard nothing.

"How'll I let ye know if I can get any?" he asked cautiously

"Just send a letter to D. F. Lengro, care of the Galena post
master. I travel around. I get back here often enough to pick i
up in time."

"How're you buyin'?"

"I'm paying the market price at the time of purchase," sai
David. Then, giving him a long hard look, he added, "Look her
—I don't know your name, but I reckon I can trust you—
might be able to pay a little more than the market price. I'n
shipping lead out through New Orleans."

McAvity grinned. He seemed at once more at ease. David'
tone suggested illegality in his hint of exportation without clear
ance, as David had meant it to.

"I'm McAvity," he said, with a certain pride. "Everybod

hereabouts knows K. McAvity. You can always find me here or over in Dubuque." He glanced once again, a little apprehensively, toward the clock.

Despite an impulse to sit and talk, David felt that he should go, since McAvity might not want him to be here when the friend for whom he waited came. He got up to go.

McAvity leaned over and whispered hoarsely, "Who sent you here, Lengro?"

David smiled and shook his head.

"You *was* sent?"

"I understood I might meet somebody named McAvity who might help me out. Good day, sir. Till we meet again."

McAvity's puzzled eyes followed him to the door.

When he had walked a short distance from the inn, David slowed his pace. Directly ahead of him, a growth of scrub and brush afforded concealment for anyone who might want to watch the inn's front entrance. Dare he chance it? he wondered. He was curious to catch sight of the caller McAvity expected; yet he did not know but that his own retreat from the inn was being watched. His steps faltered. McAvity would be suspicious enough without giving him further cause. Reluctantly, he went on, looking back from time to time.

Just as he reached the crest of the descent toward the Galena River, he saw a rider on a horse reach the inn from the direction of the Mississippi. He was now too far from the inn to make out any details about the rider, except that he appeared to be an Indian. He was vexed that he had not dawdled or taken a chance, but there was nothing for it now but to go on. Just after he had crossed the bridge, a horseman galloped past from behind; in passing, he leaned toward him and spoke.

"Kinnieshek," he said.

David looked after him in surprise. But, of course, it was Soaring Hawk; he had been watching the One-Mile House from some safe vantage point, probably at Parr's suggestion. He had seen Kinnieshek come.

When he reached the stage depot, Candace and Parr had not yet returned. Soaring Hawk was there, but he paid no attention to David; he sat astride his horse in the shade of a tall poplar not far away, his eyes half-closed, yet doubtless aware of everything that went on. David ordered something to eat, and sat turning over in his mind the problem of Kinnieshek and McAvity. It was entirely likely that McAvity intended to urge the Indians to raid a lead train for him. How to deal with the proposed raid? —whether to urge the guards to stay and fight it off, and risk someone's being killed, or whether to order them to scatter, risking the loss of horses and lead. The Indians would probably not keep the horses, which could be traced too easily. But the problem would have to be submitted to all the shippers in a meeting called for that purpose.

He had just finished eating when Candace and Parr came. He had gone outside to look for Soaring Hawk, who had gone, when he saw them coming up the street; so he waited for them amid the bustle of arrivals and departures on the various stage routes that met in Galena.

"Have you been waiting long?" asked Candace anxiously.

"No. I've just had time for lunch. Have you eaten?"

"Yes, Lieutenant Parr knew a place to go."

"Good. I'm in Nate's debt."

"Escorting Mrs. Pengellen is a pleasure any time, Dave." He bowed to her and surrendered her to David. "And you—how'd you fare?"

"I think I got what I went after."

"Good. Have you seen the Hawk?"

"He was just here."

"If you'll excuse me, I'll hunt him up. My horse is just behind the depot, and he'll be waiting for me."

"Thank you, Lieutenant," said Candace. "I didn't know Galena could be so interesting."

Parr turned, a little frown on his forehead. "I don't want to be forward, but since David and myself have done away with formality, I could be more at ease if Mrs. Pengellen would do likewise. I realize that it isn't customary in the east"—was there a note of irony in his voice? David wondered—"but in this part of the country, it comes more easily."

"I'm no stickler for formality myself," said David, "and I'm sure Candy would just as soon call you 'Nate' as 'Lieutenant.' "

Candace colored faintly. "Well, then, thank you, Nate—if you like that better."

"Indeed I do. Thank you. Now I must be off. I hope to see you soon."

After Parr had gone, David asked Candace whether she had not now come to realize that Galena was made up of something more than the uncomfortable inn at which they had spent a night in the previous autumn.

"Yes, David," she said quietly. "Nate took me to see that priest's church and also a Methodist church. He showed me some beautiful old houses which are almost as nice as some of those in Providence."

"It was certainly good of Nate to see you about. I couldn't have taken you with me, and he knew it, of course. He wasn't too trying?"

"I like him very much. He's every inch a gentleman. Perhaps he's too much one for this setting."

He thought this ambiguous, but he did not ask her to explain it. It was enough that she had enjoyed herself. No one knew Galena better than Parr, who had grown up here. Galena was beautiful, and it had an air about it, discernible through all its brashness and brawling roughness; there were trees along many of its streets; its houses had charm and simple, honest beauty some of them; its public buildings commanded respect; and built as it was on the slope of the low hills rising from the river it offered many surprising perspectives.

Later, as they were riding homeward on the stage, he noticed a distant preoccupation about her. He put an arm around her and drew her close. Perhaps the visit to Galena had served only to sharpen her longing for Providence. He looked ahead with hope to the coming child. In this he paralleled her thoughts for she, too, was hoping desperately that the birth of their child would change things, she did not know how, hoping with a tenacity which was far more intense than David could know

3. . . . Which Passeth Show

Summer, 1845

When Tamson had finished cleaning the kitchen, she went to where her aunt lay resting and asked, "How do you feel now, Aunt Marget?"

"Och, but for a croom o' hurt en my cheens, I be feelin' better. I'm summat hoozy. Comin' down weth a cold, p'raps."

"If anyone comes looking for me, I'm going up the hill a way. I'll be sitting there; you can send him right up."

"Es et a man ye're expectin', Tammy?"

"Lieutenant Parr said he might call."

"All right, cheel."

She went out of the house, taking along one of the books Candace had given her. The evening was warm. The July day had been hot and windless, but now, as so often happened just before sundown, a west wind had begun to blow, an idling, capricious wind, which soon lessened the day's lingering heat. A kind of hush lay in the air out here beyond the houses, though there were sometimes sounds from the Dodgeville road, which was not far away, and from the village itself. Few birds sang—out of the nearest woods pewees called pensively, thrushes sang, a pileated woodpecker rattled; but the grassy slopes were still except for the tremulous sibilance of the wind passing among the blades.

The sun was not yet down. It lay low above the western rim, bathing the earth in a rose and saffron haze. As she mounted the ridge, the sounds of the village receded, dropping deeper into the valley behind, and the voice of the wind grew louder. It spoke to her of Cornwall, it made her to think again of the west wind's blowing in Tintagel, with the smell of the sea in it, blowing over the moors with the pungence and perfume of the flowers and herbs that grew there.

Her objective was a knoll from which she could look beyond the village and watch the moon rise. It was scarcely a day past the full, and should be up not long after sundown. Reaching the knoll, she sat down. She turned to the first page of the book and read the opening lines of *The Amber Witch;* but her thoughts were not on the book; she thought instead of Parr's coming, still puzzled as to his motives, curious to learn what they might be. And she thought of David, who had seemed so preoccupied ever since his return from Galena. He had not gone to the shippers' meeting at Belmont; Trelawny had gone instead.

Throughout that week, David had done little save the routine of work; he had been disinclined to journey anywhere, even to the smelters; so Trelawny had gone, muttering good-naturedly, but in complaint just the same. From the shippers' meeting Trelawny had returned to report that the shippers planned to permit any raid inspired by McAvity to take place and then to try to catch McAvity through the opening David had made. It could be done simply—once the raid had taken place, McAvity would try to get in touch with "Lengro," who would make an appointment. Then McAvity could be taken at the rendezvous, which would probably be above Dubuque, in the vicinity of Sinissippi. There was nothing to be done now but wait.

The rising wind made a hushing sound in the grass, where already an early twilight lay, though the red ball of the sun was just now touching the horizon. A gopher, running along through the grass, came upon her suddenly, and sat up in startled surprise with a little whistle of alarm, to look at her in wide-eyed wonder, its little front paws held before it in trembling tensity, turning its head one way and then the other; but, since she made no move, the creature resumed its course, passing so close to her that she could have touched it. She sat so that she could command both east and west horizons at once, watching the sundown while being ready for the moon. She was grateful for the wind at her temples, at her throat, cooling and soothing. As evening advanced, the air grew fragrant with the musks and perfumes of the wilderness just beyond the village, the scents of leaves, of mould, of wild clematis and woodbine beginning to flower.

When she thought of David, she thought also of Candace, for it was surely with her that David had been so preoccupied for the past days. She could understand Candace's nostalgia, and she sympathized with her; but it did seem to Tamson that Candace had not exhausted either her capacity for adjusting herself to Mineral Point or her will to do so. She knew how hard Candace had tried, but she resented a little the slow progress Candace made because this disturbed David. Tamson had an interest in David that preceded her actual meeting with him. A long time ago, when she still lived in Cornwall, Aunt Marget had written her all about the handsome young man for whom she kept house, and for whom she had cooked ever since Uncle Ben had died. David Pengellen had come to signify a tangible link to Tintagel, and the girl she had been in that ancient Cornish city had fallen in love with the picture of him her aunt had painted. She had had little difficulty recognizing him at first sight; Aunt Marget's description had fitted none but him;

and if that adolescent affection for the unknown David had been childish, the knowledge of him, of his steadiness, his patience, his kindness, was not calculated to diminish it. She could not find a like attraction in any other man or boy in Mineral Point, for all that David was ten years her senior and well married.

She thought with fleeting regret that it was so, that it was not as it had been when she was still in Tintagel, with David a lonely young man whom she might someday see as Aunt Marget saw him. In that interval of her mother's death and her own coming to America, David had married, as she had learned at her arrival in the Point, for Aunt Marget had then already had the word of it, and the knowledge of David's coming return with his wife.

The sun vanished. From the zenith, a deeper blue washed down the western slopes of heaven upon the aquamarine and lemon in the upper west, pressing irrevocably down, down upon the cerise and magenta and smoky orange closer to the darkening rim of earth. The eye of Venus shone through, cold and blue, pale still in the lemon band of afterglow, brightening slowly as the afterglow drew horizonward and the twilight came over the land from the east. She turned and gazed into the east. Already lights were up in the village, candles and lamps flickered in windows all along Shake-Rag Street, and across it, the smelters smouldered redly.

Presently a glow shone in heaven over the eastern hills, and in a little while the moon began to push up from the horizon, silhouetting the trees of that hilltop blackly upon its yellow face. She began to sing again, subdued now, lest someone hear; it must soon be time for Lieutenant Parr to come, unless he had forgotten. She sang *Westryn Wind*, but at sight of someone walking up the slope in the dusk she was still, the sound of her voice dying away into the calling of whippoorwills and the strange cries and sky-coasting of nighthawks.

Parr came to where she sat, having descried her white face in the moonlight.

"Good evening, Miss Bishop," he said.

"You're very formal, Lieutenant. Just call me Tamson. Will you sit down?"

"Thank you, I will." He sat down beside her, not failing to notice the discarded book. "A beautiful night. I couldn't have arranged one more so."

"Yes. I wanted to see the moon rise."

"I've come in time, then." He was silent for a moment. Then he said, "I couldn't help overhearing your song. Isn't that a curious song for a young lady to be singing?"

In the twilight he could not see the color that rushed to her cheeks. "It's an old Cornish ballad. I sing it often—but I don't sing it for company. It's a lonely song."

"Are you lonely, then?"

"No, Lieutenant."

"Nate, if you please."

"All right, Nate."

"If not lonely, homesick?"

"A little. It wears off, though."

"Strange," he mused. "You're not alone in that."

"I suppose not. Some of the women from the east find it hard here," she agreed. "But the Point is growing so fast they hardly have time to sit and think of what's past."

"All but Mrs. Pengellen."

She was surprised that he should have noticed Candace's devotion to the past. She said only, "Yes. I guess we've all noticed that."

"Have you seen her recently, Tamson?"

"Not since last week. But you saw her then yourself. I heard David tell Mr. Trelawny you were kind enough to squire her about Galena."

"Yes, I did show her Galena. I believe she enjoyed it. Just the same, I don't think she was meant for the frontier."

"She doesn't go out enough," said Tamson. "Of course, now it's hard for her to go out, but even so, before this . . ."

He did not appear to be listening; he was gazing at the moon, which had now risen above the tree-line and was shedding a winelike light over the dark earth.

"Perhaps we could walk over and pay them a visit," he said casually.

She sprang to her feet. "Let's do that, Nate. It will take her mind off all the troubles she thinks she has. We'll have to stop at the house to tell Aunt Marget where we're going; otherwise she'll fret."

Approaching the Pengellen house, she would have gone to the back door, but he led her around to the front, explaining the difference between calling at the back door and the front; tonight, the front door was proper. She decided silently that he entertained some conflict about the occasions for formality.

David and Candace were glad to see them, though both showed surprise that they should be together. Tamson saw it especially in David's eyes; it gave her a sense of well-being to recognize it, knowing intuitively that he was trying to reconcile her reaction to Lieutenant Parr as given him not long ago with her appearance now in Parr's company. But if David's short-lived surprise satisfied her, Parr's subdued attitude puzzled her; a kind of wariness had come over him, superimposed upon the restraint he had exercised in her own company, and if his manner toward David was frank and friendly, toward Candace he was almost deferential. Because she was puzzled, she watched Parr surreptitiously throughout the evening.

She lay for a long time sleepless that night.

Her observation of Lieutenant Parr had given her insight into his motives. Despite his cunning—and he was clever and suave, notwithstanding an affectation of casualness—he was disarming in this, in spite of his seeming attention to David, Tamson divined that Parr was principally interested in Candace. It was incredible, but it must be so, for every evidence supported her belief. It lay not only in his first noticeable deference to her and in her eager acceptance of that deference, but also in the way his eyes flickered in her direction time and again, even when she was silent and he was speaking to David, in the frequency with which he managed to bring the conversation around to Candace, in the subtle flattery he conveyed her. Indeed, there was such a singular harmony about all his words and actions in Candace's presence, that no other conclusion was possible.

But, just as her conclusion was evident, so was also the fact that the whole drama Parr played was beyond David's awareness. He was too much concerned with furthering Candace's happiness to correctly interpret Parr's interest, and any attempt to suggest to him that Parr might be entertaining more than a friendly regard for David's wife would be met with stony disbelief. She knew this intuitively, but she had no question about her conclusions concerning Parr's motives; she recognized that he hoped to have readier ingress to David's home through her, Tamson, so that he might call on Candace without exciting gossip.

The decision she faced in the darkness of that night was twofold. Her first impulse, to speak to David, she discarded; he would not believe her, not because he would think her too imaginative, but simply because he would be unable to see through her eyes and intuition; she knew that women often saw things men did not. Any attempt to make him see might only reflect on her. This decision was therefore beyond her power to alter. Her second was more difficult. Recognizing Parr's motives, should she permit him to use her? This involved her principles more directly. She had to consider her own feeling for

David, to which he was as blind as he was to Parr's interest in Candace; she must not let her affection for him direct her course. By the very token of that affection, if David loved Candace, as surely he did, then she, Tamson, must do everything in her power to assure his happiness.

But she was troubled, nevertheless, and when she slept at last, her sleep was uneasy.

In mid-August the expected raid on the lead wagons took place. It was carried off at night, near Hazel Green, but far enough away from that village so that no alarm could be sounded. By pre-arranged plan, the guards offered but token resistance and fled, returning after a suitable interval with reinforcements from Hazel Green. But the Indians had come prepared to take away the lead; they had emptied five wagons, leaving wagons and horses unharmed, and had gone to the west, toward the Mississippi. The shippers involved were Poad & Tredinnick of Linden, William Prideaux and Spensley & Penhallegon of the Point.

Soaring Hawk was in Mineral Point with word of the raid even before the guards had returned to the scene. The shippers met him at the Court House, after they had been called together, and listened to what he had to say.

Kinnieshek had conducted the raid, said Soaring Hawk. There was no question about this, since he, Soaring Hawk, had witnessed it. He had followed the shipment because he had learned that the raid would take place sometime during the present week, and very probably at night. Parr had kept an eye on shipments moving south by day. Sixteen Indians were involved, in addition to a white man who did not appear, but remained west of the road. He could not identify him. It might have been Red Hair—which was Soaring Hawk's name for McAvity. Some pursuit had taken place, but the Indians got away, as expected, for few white men could follow a trail in the dark. Soaring Hawk had followed the raiding Indians long enough to catch sight of the white man of their party. The raiders had gone in the direction of Sinsinawa, then turned north along the Mississippi.

"Why in the devil didn't you keep after them?" demanded Colonel Billings.

Soaring Hawk gazed at him impassively. What could he have accomplished by doing so? he wanted to know. Did not the shippers wish to capture the man who had urged Kinnieshek to make the raid? No one knew that he was with the party. True, the Indians carried the lead. If he, Soaring Hawk, had been discovered, he would have been slain. He did not believe this was the wish of Manitou. It was not his own wish. Besides, he added cogently, he did not know how his spirit could be of as much service to the shippers.

"You might have found out where they cached the lead," offered another shipper.

This was true, agreed the Winnebago. But the plan was for McAvity to sell it to Pengellen as "Lengro." Unless that were done, they might have only the lead, not the raiders. Kinnieshek could be found at any time; Soaring Hawk would lead them to him when the moment came. McAvity might escape. It would be better to follow the plan on which they had agreed.

The shippers agreed. Parr was instructed to look at the post office in Galena for a letter addressed to "D. F. Lengro." The postmaster should be taken into his confidence, so that Parr need not show himself indiscriminately, should someone in McAvity's pay be watching the post office.

In ten days, Parr rode into Mineral Point with the letter from McAvity. He brought it to David. Trelawny, David, and Parr studied it. Written illiterately, it offered "Lengro" five thousand pounds of lead if he would bring a flatboat and prepare to move it down river without delay from the point specified. The point McAvity named was north, not on the Mississippi, but on the Wisconsin, mid-way between the shot tower at Helena and the village of Sac Prairie on the other side. That made it over thirty miles from the Point, but the Mississippi in the vicinity of the raid would have been almost as far.

"How did they get way up there with it?" Trelawny wanted to know.

Parr explained that Soaring Hawk had reported a movement of Indians back and forth across the region from Hazel Green northeast toward Helena, none by the regular routes, but all west of the roads used by the inhabitants. But it did not matter where the lead was; the Indians, urged by McAvity and pressed by the search being carried on in the neighborhood of Hazel Green, had lost no time in moving the lead to a place of comparative safety on the north edge of the lead region. The place chosen was a low, deeply wooded area of the Wisconsin River bottomland, for several miles on both sides of which there was not so much as a squatter's cabin.

The date set for the rendezvous was four days past the night of the full moon, the twenty-first of the month, a Thursday. The hour was seven o'clock in the morning, which could not have been more suitable to the shippers if they themselves had chosen it. McAvity also had no scruples about naming his price: $200—which was a dollar over the prevailing price of three dollars a hundred pounds. He had evidently decided that "Lengro's" business was as illegitimate as his own.

The shippers had a plan ready; it required only one change in view of McAvity's demands. That one was readily settled—a flatboat could be rented from Count Brogmar at Sac Prairie; since he knew the Count, Parr could make the arrangements, though David would have to accompany him, since he would need to come down river that morning on the boat. In the night preceding the hour set for the meeting, Soaring Hawk would scout the country to determine whether or not McAvity was alone; if so, as was likely, since the presence of Indians would draw unwelcome attention to him if they were seen by residents of nearby Helena or Arena, a picked group of shippers, on horse and armed, would infiltrate the woods during the night, cutting off all avenues of escape for McAvity.

On the twentieth, David set out with Parr to ride to Sac Prairie. The way led through familiar territory to the Blue Mound, and from there across country to intersect the road leading from Madison to the adjoining county, newly set off and named Sauk only the preceding year. The character of the terrain north of the Blue Mound was different; the country was more rolling, the hills lower, except for a few, which were tall, but not as craggy or as much part of a ridge as those around the Point. Reaching a moraine east of the Wisconsin, they saw Sac Prairie spread out on a great paw of land which was the west bank of the river at that place, a kind of wide valley surrounded by low hills and a ridge of bluffs in the north. The Wisconsin flowed in from the north around the unusual prairie area and out by the southwest.

Parr gestured to the south. "It's down there about ten miles we're to meet McAvity."

The region toward which Parr pointed was one of dense woods, well away from the hills which were back from the river at that place.

"We could ford the river at Pierneau's hill," Parr went on, waving a hand in the direction of a solitary peak which pushed up from the river's edge south of the village and was crowned by a large house and several outbuildings, girt by trees, "but we might as well take the ferry—Brogmar owns that, too, and it'll fetch us out at his store."

They began to canter down the slope on the rough road.

"Who is this man Brogmar?" David felt impelled to ask. "I hear his name from time to time."

"I suppose you might say he made Sac Prairie—maybe he did. He's got his fingers in practically every pie over there. But his cousin, Pierneau, was there a long time before Brogmar came. As to who he is—well, he's one of those people who came over here because Europe was too uncomfortable for them. He calls himself 'Colonel' now, but he's really a Count—Hungarian—and they say he came here to grow grapes and to write a book about his experiences in America. But there's also a tale that Metternich's police were after him for being too outspoken about political matters over there. If so, he wouldn't be the only one."

As they approached the shore of the Wisconsin, the ferry came from the west toward the road's end and the dock screened by willows. They met at the water's edge. Both riders rode out on to the craft. Parr hailed the boatman genially, as if he were an old friend, and immediately began a conversation with him. He called him Richards. An Englishman, apparently, concluded David. According to Richards, Count Brogmar was at the store; usually his father, the old General, was there, but the old man had been indisposed, and the Count himself was there, as restless and energetic as ever, what with all the fires he had to tend.

The ferry reached the west bank of the river. Parr and David rode off and up the low slope to the main street of the village, a dusty road, where they found themselves before an unusually large store flaunting a great sign: Brogmar & Bryant—General Merchandise. Following Parr's lead, David dismounted.

They went into the store, walking past a clerk who came to meet them straight to the back of the long room, where David saw a tall, broad-shouldered man with a ledger in his hand standing at a window. He was in shirt-sleeves, worn open at the cuffs, and around his waist he wore a wide sash of scarlet, which appeared to be of some kind of silk. Becoming aware of their approach, he turned. David found himself looking into a pair of sharp dark eyes set in a broad, intelligent face, distinguished by a sense of impressive dominance.

"Lieutenant Parr! Aren't you out of your orbit?"

"We're looking for a lead thief, sir."

The Count barked a short laugh. "He's not employed by me. I keep my men too busy to permit peccadillos."

Parr introduced David.

"Pengellen," repeated Brogmar, as if he savored the name. "That has a good Cornish sound. They call you 'Cousin Jacks,' I think. But then, most of you people in the Point are Cornish—just as most of us here are either German or Yankee. Sit down, gentlemen. As usual, I'm in haste—I began to look over my ledgers six months ago, I've promised myself daily to finish the task—it wants but a day—and I'm running out of promises. But if I can do anything. . . ." He left the sentence suggestively unfinished.

"We believe you can," answered David. "We understand you might have a flatboat you could let us use."

Brogmar looked at him with frank appraisal. "I use flatboats to haul bricks from my yard, yes. Have you ever operated one, Pengellen?"

"No, I haven't."

The Count turned to Parr. "He has, I know. You'll need an extra man, then. Do you have him?"

"I'm afraid we don't," answered David.

Parr broke in. He explained their need for the boat, while Brogmar listened restlessly.

"Yes," Brogmar said when Parr finished, "I'll have the boat for you. I'll get you an extra man, too—" He turned impulsively and shouted to the clerk they had passed. "Herman, take one of the horses, ride down to Pierneau's, and find out if I can have

Clement beginning at about three o'clock tomorrow morning." He turned back to David and Parr. "It'll take you that long to get down there; it's about ten miles. You have to figure on sandbars and obstructions, you know. Clement is a good man; nobody here knows the woods or the river any better. Oh, if one of the traders were here—Lapiage or Souligne—perhaps they'd be better on the river, but neither has half the strength of Clement, and if it comes to a fight, why, he'll be just the man to have along."

"When we've finished with it, we'll arrange to have it brought back."

"Just take it to Helena, and I'll have Clement bring it back as a tow when the next steamboat comes up. Now, you'll want some place to stay over night; there's no sense going back to the Point. I'll attend to that. And you'd better turn in early—it won't be easy to take a flatboat down the Wisconsin."

Darkness still shrouded Sac Prairie when they were awakened by Brogmar himself, coming to their room clad in a long, silken robe, emblazoned with a coat of arms. He carried a lamp, and, having awakened them, left it, making his way in the dark back to the kitchen. They followed him as soon as they had dressed. Two steaming cups stood there. In the absence of his wife, the energetic Count had himself prepared a little coffee for them.

David could not help commenting on its excellence.

A deep chuckle rumbled from the big man in the dressing-gown. "It contains some of the finest brandy, Pengellen; it ought to be good. Here, have some more. There's plenty. I'll join you. Is there anything you'd like to eat? There are some cold meats, there's bread, even a few cakes, if you've a fancy to them."

But they wanted no food. They were anxious to get away now. Where was Clement?

"He'll be at the landing. Don't worry about him. The boat's

there. Let him take charge of it; he knows the river. He may say little; he's a Frenchman, but he's not like so many of his countrymen—he's been here too long for that. Besides, a man who spends most of his time in the woods knows how to be silent."

Brogmar's house was not far from the landing, only two or three blocks; in the moonlit darkness David could not be sure. Already at this hour a faint glow in the east heralded the dawn. Not far above the horizon in the east shone Jupiter, the morning star, undimmed by the gibbous moon already well past the zenith in the western heavens.

Aristide Clement waited at the flatboat. While they exchanged introductions, David took note of his bigness, which was similar to the Count's. Clement weighed over two hundred pounds and stood more than six feet in height; he had thick, sensuous lips, deep-set eyes, and a massive roman nose beneath which he wore a heavy moustache. His hair was longer than that of most men. His voice surprised David; instead of the booming voice he expected, it was quiet, self-assured, and entirely without accent of any kind. He had anticipated their coming and had already brought their horses from the stable next to the store and put them on to the flatboat, together with his own.

The boat was not one of the largest which plied the river, yet had ample room for horses and men and other cargo. As soon as David and Parr had boarded it, Clement shoved off, handling his pole with great dexterity, and shoving the boat out into the current as rapidly as possible. The current caught and turned it, carrying it with slowly increasing speed down past the settlement, past the long island which began just below the village and curved with the Wisconsin at the beginning of its bend into the southwest, past the bluff crowned by the house of Chalfonte Pierneau, Brogmar's cousin, to where dense woods crowded upon the water from both banks.

Dawn fanned up the eastern heavens. Already, going past the Pierneau house, they could see the reflection of that pale light in the windows. And now along the Wisconsin the morning song of birds began—solitary sandpipers and killdeers ran along the shores where the water was shallow, giving their wild, sweet cries, their voices blending into the purling and rushing of the water, where it swirled around the rocks at the base of Pierneau's hill and at his landing, where it poured through the branches of trees torn from island banks and drawn out into the river, where it cascaded over rocky ledges or ate away sandbars. A small flock of mergansers flew up river; now and then wood ducks, teal, and mallards started up, crying in alarm; herons, fishing at the shallows, screamed at them harshly, *krark, krark;* ospreys and eagles moved high over the surface of the water and, with the rising sun, long files of crows began to show themselves from time to time, in flight from one shore to another. The lush banks were hardily overgrown with trees, bushes, and vines, and in every open place blossoms shone—yellow coneflowers and loosestrife, sky-blue fringed gentians, lavender bergamotte, and Joe-Pye weed, white boneset and balmony, cardinal lobelias.

Save for the birds and the occasionally glimpsed animals—otters and beavers at mouths of lesser streams emptying into the Wisconsin, minks and muskrats near sloughs and backwaters—they were alone on the river. For the first few miles they spoke little; Parr needed to accustom himself anew to the use of the pole; Clement was intent on guiding the boat and keeping it away from sandbars on which it might lodge and cause them to lose precious time. David took his stand with the horses; though Clement's was quiet, his and Parr's were restive, not being used to this mode of travel. But presently the horses calmed down, the boat entered the quieter water beyond the long islands which reached past Pierneau's to where the Wisconsin widened at the beginning of a ridge of bluffs rising opposite the head of woods which held to the east shore. Here they passed a stern-wheeled steamboat, bound out of Prairie du Chien for Portage; the craft saluted them with three blasts of its whistle.

Clement observed at its passing that it was not like "the old days," when there were no steamboats, but only the canoes of the voyageurs and the traders, and occasional flatboats and rafts, the days when the Wisconsin was the only highway across the southern part of the Territory, and down past Pierneau's high house had come missionaries, soldiers, Indians, *engagés,* and all manner of traders and travelers, down from Quebec and New York, by way of Lake Michigan and the Fox River to the Portage. How much longer Clement had lived in the Territory than he, thought David. He turned to look at him just as Clement spoke to Parr.

"You handle a pole well. But you're not a river man."

"How can you tell?" asked Parr.

"Oh, it's the way you have. You're a horseman. Been in the militia?"

Parr had dressed roughly, to fit the role of an employee of David's and rouse no suspicion in McAvity. He admitted that Clement had guessed well.

"Won't take us long now," said Clement then. "I figure there's only about two miles to go." He looked at the sun, now well up the east, though a bank of cumulus, dark from the rim of earth to its white convoluted flank, presaging rain, was pushing up to overtake it. "It's after six now."

McAvity had chosen well. The Wisconsin at this point flowed between woods like walls, dense and dark. All along the west bank rose hills of varying heights, covered except for small areas of calcareous rock by thick undergrowth and tall old trees; wherever any openings occurred, they were of shallow valleys, closing not far back from the water's edge—a wild, desolate country, which had yet to know the invasion of white men. The east shore was equally wild, but flat and low, giving rise to many small streams, sheltering dark ponds and sloughs. The eastern hills were as far as two miles back from the Wisconsin's edge, and all the distance between the river and the hills was a mass of unbroken trees—the haunt of lynx and deer, of raccoon and bear.

Clouds overtaking the sun cast an even deeper darkness over the river and the woods. David had moved forward, to scan the east bank for sign or sight of McAvity. He did not expect him to be alone, but he was not likely to have more than one or two men along. The raft moved slowly down along the east bank, through more sluggish water; McAvity would be careful that no passerby would catch sight of the lead being loaded and would perhaps choose a point opposite an island, which would screen the site from anyone passing on the river in the main channel.

Clement saw him first. Without turning, he said, "He's up ahead, Mr. Pengellen. Just opposite the middle of that long island."

McAvity stood out from under the trees, flanked by one other man on his right. David raised one arm; McAvity responded. Clement eased the flatboat over toward shore.

"Ye're on time, Lengro," said McAvity as they came within hearing.

"I make it a point to be," answered David curtly. "Got what I want?"

McAvity jerked his head backward. "Ye got the money?"

"I've got it."

The flatboat scraped bottom and was grounded. David turned to Parr, saying gruffly, "Mind the horses." He beckoned to Clement and leaped off the boat, unmindful of the shallow water into which he jumped. Clement followed.

McAvity watched with cautious eyes. His right cheek was

distended by a wad of tobacco, which he rolled free and chewed briefly. He spat.

"I'll see the lead, McAvity," said David.

McAvity shrugged. "Ye're mighty pertikelar, Lengro. A man'd think ye didn't trust me."

His companion looked unblinkingly at David; when David caught his glance, he had the fleeting sense of familiarity, and, glancing back at McAvity's companion a few seconds later, he saw that he, too, was trying to remember where he had seen David before. With a sharp stab of alarm, David thought he might have been in the store at some time. But now McAvity was leading the way back into the woods.

"I hope it's not too far away to be loaded easily," grumbled David. "I'm not in the mind to haul it down by hand, two and a half ton of it."

"It's right back here," answered McAvity.

As he spoke, he rounded a fallen tree. There, skillfully concealed beneath the spreading limbs of the still leafed tree, was the smelted lead.

"I take it this lead is honestly come by?" said David. "I don't intend to buy stolen lead."

"What d'ye take me for?" snarled McAvity, turning angrily.

At that moment, McAvity's companion spoke. "Your name been Lengro long? 'Pears to me you look like one of them Mineral Point shippers."

McAvity reached for his weapon, but Clement was too fast for him. A sidearm appeared in one of his big, capable hands; it spoke louder than any words. An ugly look came into McAvity's face; a mottled color rose in his cheeks. His companion paled, as if he had some premonition of what was to come. Before McAvity could speak, the sound of a twig snapping behind him caught his ear; he turned his head in time to see the first of the surrounding shippers emerge from the woods, his rifle cocked and ready. In a few moments the woods gave up thirty determined men, the silence of whose encirclement of the little group standing beside the stolen lead was ominous.

McAvity looked his fury at David. "God damn you, Lengro! —or whatever your name is!"

"Pengellen," muttered his companion. "I knowed I'd see him before."

"I'll git you, Pengellen," muttered McAvity.

"Hold tha tongue, McAvity," said the foremost among the men. Without turning, he called, "Michael Poad, coom look a thicky lead."

A grim-faced man of forty years of age came forward. His features were almost forbiddingly dark, but he was not ill-favored in looks. He moved into the foliage of the fallen tree breaking away branches as if they were reeds. He knelt and picked up some of the bars.

"Aye," he said, after five minutes of examination, " 'tis the lead we shipped, some of et. We put a small *t* weth the look of a cross on't, made hard to see. 'Tis there."

At this, Captain John O'Neill pushed out of the group and took charge. "All right, gentlemen. We'll ask Mr. McAvity a few questions. How'd you come by this lead, McAvity?"

"I bought it."

"From whom?"

"That's my business."

"You can talk here or in court, McAvity. This is the lead taken from our wagons by a band of Indians near Hazel Green two weeks ago. You heard Poad identify it; he was one of the shippers. Now then, what have you got to say?"

"I bought it off some Indians," admitted McAvity sullenly.

"Did you put 'em up to taking it?"

"Ye got no proof of anything like that," answered McAvity angrily. "Ye'll git nowhere sayin' so."

"Got a bill of sale?"

"No."

"Or any other proof you bought it?"

"I can prove I didn't steal it."

"You'd be sure to have an alibi, I'd guess." O'Neill turned to the men. "What do you say, men? Shall we take care of him?"

"Now! Now!" cried some of the men. "String him up!" cried others.

McAvity pulled nervously at his open collar. His face grew rigid and pale. "I got rights," he shouted. "I ain't been arrested. The law . . ."

"Don't quote the law to us, McAvity," said O'Neill roughly. "What about your companion. Is he in this, too?"

"I just hired him," protested McAvity. "He don't know a thing. He's just a man to help me move the lead."

"I see your horses over there," continued O'Neill. "But two horses didn't bring five thousand pounds of lead. Where are your wagons, if you brought it? Or did your Indian friends fetch it here for you?"

An angry murmur grew in the crowd pressing around O'Neill. "What're we waitin' for? String 'em both up! Hang the thieves!" Various conflicting cries arose. Some voices appealed to reason; some recalled the laws of the Territory against lynching; some were for arresting McAvity and his man and taking both off to jail. The immediate result of this difference of opinion was confusion in the ranks of the men behind O'Neill. When O'Neill himself turned to remonstrate with them, McAvity and his companion made a frantic dash for their horses, weaving in and out among the trees. Amid a mêlée of angry cries and some scattered shots, they reached the horses, mounted, and, crouching low, rode off. A handful of men set out in pursuit, though Captain O'Neill and the majority of them did not move.

Presently O'Neill smiled. "Well, David, I'll wager that rascal will make himself scarce in the Territory for a good while. We've taken Kinnieshek; he's in jail at the Point now, and he'll stay there for a few years. Then he'll be sent out west."

"Looked as if you wanted them to get away," said Clement.

O'Neill shrugged. "We had nothing to go to court with, did we? You can't convict a man of encouraging the Indians to steal just because he offered to sell some lead. No, we've put a scare into him; we'll let him think he'll be lynched if he ever comes back. But not a one of us ever meant to lay a hand on him. The best we could have done with him was to get his testimony against Kinnieshek, and that was chancy for him. He knew it. Besides, the guards and drivers can or will identify Kinnieshek."

"Shall 'ee git 'en wagons?" asked one of the men.

"Yes, go ahead. We'll have to move fast; it looks like rain."

The men scattered immediately. They went into the woods in all directions in search of their horses, which had been left well away from the scene, lest McAvity and his henchman become suspicious at sight of them in this lonely spot, should he have come in during the morning hours before eight. But the place where he had camped for the night had been reported by Soaring Hawk and was easily found not far from the cache.

The lead had to be loaded, which was a heavy task, for the woods were so dense that extensive cutting had to be done before the wagons could be got close to the cache. Some of the lead would be returned to Mineral Point to be used as evidence against Kinnieshek, but the bulk of it could be shipped on down the Wisconsin from Helena.

It was Clement who suggested the obvious solution to the problem. The flatboat was at hand; why not use it to carry the lead to Helena? One of the owners could go with him, or better, both. The lead could be sent on from there, as the shippers wished. Perhaps Count Brogmar might make a charge for the use of his boat, but it would surely not amount to much, and time would be lost cutting a road through the woods to get at the lead brought in so diligently and secretly by the Indian renegades, a little at a time.

Poad and Penhallegon elected to accompany Clement. Parr brought the horses ashore, and the shippers' horses went on board in their place. The men—except for those who had gone for the wagons and those who were still in noisy pursuit of McAvity—fell to at once and began to load the lead on to the flatboat, to the accompaniment of much banter and jollity, released by the relaxing of their angry tension. Now that the serious business of the morning had been concluded successfully, their natural boisterousness reasserted itself, and, amid a great deal of friendly jocularity, the lead moved in a steady stream from McAvity's cache to the boat.

Parr and David presently set out for home as soon as Clement, with Poad and Penhallegon, pushed off from shore down the shallower channel around the southern tip of the island and out into the Wisconsin's current. The rest of the men scattered, some for Helena to arrange for the disposal of the lead, some for the wagons and home.

"It wasn't good that McAvity found out who you were, Dave," said Parr, thoughtfully, as they rode along.

"What can he do about it? He'll lie low for a long time. He's too well known to risk coming up to the Point to have it out with me."

Parr did not answer.

"It can't be much past nine," said David then. "If we ride fast enough, we can make the Point in time for dinner. You'll come up, of course? We'll surprise Candy."

"Come on, then," cried Parr, digging his heels into his horse. They went flying down the trail shouting at each other like carefree boys.

Just as Parr started out for Dodgeville that evening, Soaring Hawk joined him. The Winnebago had been in Galena and Dubuque that afternoon. After scouting the region of the rendezvous appointed by McAvity and reporting that the two men were encamped not far from the river, thus permitting infiltration of the woods during the night, he had ridden to the south, into Illinois and the southwestern corner of the Wisconsin Territory. He had gone there to look for others among the Indians who had been with Kinnieshek on the night of the raid. He knew most of them, and most of them were firewater-drinking, slothful renegades of no worth to their tribes, corrupted by the seductive example of men like Red Hair and his companions in leisurely troublemaking. Kinnieshek's arrest would scare most of them into other country, except perhaps Bald Turtle, a cunning Fox, and Black Wolf, the Dakota.

He rode out of Dodgeville with Parr, his usually impassive manner giving way to questions. How had the raid gone? Had Red Hair been taken?

Parr told him.

Soaring Hawk was puzzled. He grew voluble. He did not understand the ways of the palefaces, he said. His was a familiar complaint. It was well known that Red Hair had urged Kinnieshek and his band to raid the wagons. Red Hair had paid them in firewater; that was why Kinnieshek had been so easily taken—he had been drunk. Now he was sober enough, but it did him no good to be sober in the white man's jail. Why had they not held Red Hair?

Parr tried to explain, quoting laws governing evidence.

The white man's law was a thing of two heads, said Soaring

Hawk bitterly. It was one thing in word, and another in deed. White men would try Kinnieshek by the white man's law; but they would not try Red Hair. Parr spoke fine words about the need for proof. But proof would be there to convict Kinnieshek; though none of the guards had actually seen him, still they would swear to his being there at the raid on the wagons. Why could they not do the same to Red Hair? Was it because he was a white man? But the Indians would not do likewise. The offender in their ranks became an outcast.

"Unless his crime was against white men," interposed Parr.

Soaring Hawk ignored this, continuing his complaint. The palefaces were strange creatures. They claimed brotherhood for the Indians, but they acted otherwise. It had always been so; it would always be so. They put their names to treaties and broke them before the ink had dried. Many a chieftain had tried to deal with the white invaders of his land in fairness, but to what end? If they rebelled, the white men called it "war" and took them, killing many. It had happened to Red Bird of the Winnebago. It had happened to Black Hawk of the Sauk. They took Red Bird and he died. They took Black Hawk and put him on their iron horse and took him away. They brought him back, conquered, broken, and he died. That was the way of the white man—to talk brave and fine, to act in a different manner. The white man spoke lies. The truth lay only in his actions. When the white man committed a crime against the Indian, and the Indian sought justice, the white man cried out that it was the red man who had done the thing in the first place.

This was a theme which enlisted Soaring Hawk's earnestness. He seized every opportunity to declaim at length on the inequalities visited upon the Indians by the very people who had come boldly with their guns and bowie-knives to take the land from the Winnebago. His reference to bowie-knives was shrewdly calculated to needle Parr, despite his affection for him, since Soaring Hawk knew that Governor Dodge still wore a bowie-knife on occasion.

But the Winnebago noticed presently that Parr was unusually silent. Even in the darkness, fragrant with the perfumes of the summer night, heightened by the afternoon's rain, he could sense Parr's preoccupation. Could it be that Parr, too, was dissatisfied with the justice of his race?

He asked presently. What troubled him?

Parr had been thinking of Candace—of how she had looked, of how glad she had been to see them safely home, of her small talk about Tamson's staying with her the previous night, how she had worried for their safety, having no way of knowing what was taking place, once the men of the posse had ridden out of the Point last evening. Her concern had been genuine, and Parr was trying to assess it in proper perspective. It was not something he could tell the Hawk.

"I didn't like it that McAvity recognized and threatened Dave," he said instead. "McAvity's a vengeful skunk. He'll get even, if he can."

All the more reason he should have been kept, said Soaring Hawk.

Parr shrugged.

Soaring Hawk said no more. But Parr's attitude puzzled him still further. Perhaps no Indian could ever understand a white man. He knew very well that Parr was interested in Candace, even though he could not fathom her attraction—a pale, weak thing, he thought her, unworthy of a man like Parr. But since this was so, he could not comprehend why Parr should concern himself about David, if he coveted his woman. Perhaps he had not accounted sufficiently the friendship between the two men; it was not impossible that such a friendship should exist. Soaring Hawk had not thought about it before.

They rode in silence for the rest of the way home. The waning moon pushed yellowly up, shedding a wan glow over the landscape. Parr was still lost in the thought of Candace; he desired her, but at the same time he was in conflict about her. The currents of friendship for David, David's trust in him, a sense of loyalty all crossed this inexplicable desire, and he told himself repeatedly that there was some flaw, some error in his make-up which inspired such conflict. Soaring Hawk misunderstood his meditation; in his sight it was Red Hair and his threat which troubled Parr, and he considered dispassionately the ways in which Red Hair might avenge himself on David. He could shoot him, he thought tranquilly. Red Hair might do so. Soaring Hawk could not understand why Parr should worry over this possibility, since it would open his way to the woman.

They reached Dodgeville, and went to the hostelry where Parr kept a room. Soaring Hawk lay on the floor in the same room and slept. Long after the Indian had fallen asleep, Parr still sat restlessly at the window in the darkness. Soaring Hawk watched him from under his lids before he himself slept, and when he woke later. He was astonished that Parr was so deeply troubled about Red Hair's threat. It would be so simple to prevent Red Hair from carrying out his threat. He did not like to see his white friend so disturbed. If danger to the storekeeper upset Parr, then that danger must be removed. It was simple. It was so simple in solution that it was another baffling aspect of the white man's nature that he did not seek it. But since Parr would not, he would. He closed his eyes again, composed and confident.

In the morning Soaring Hawk rose before Parr woke. He went outside and took care of his horse. He was very fond of his horse. The stallion, a spirited roan, showed the Winnebago's care; his coat was glossy and thick, his mane was less wild, he was well fed. He responded without demur to Soaring Hawk's ministrations as well as to his orders; he was less respectful of attention from anyone else. At dawn, Soaring Hawk mounted him and rode leisurely south.

He came into Mineral Point in the early hours of the morning. There was already a great bustling about of people. Soaring Hawk looked upon them with dubious eyes. They did not seem to know the value of leisurely living; they did not know how to enjoy the earth itself; they knew only how to deface and despoil it. For all his liking for some members of the white race, he did not know what the race had, to justify its pride. He rode up to the jail in the Court House and asked to see Kinnieshek.

Since the jailer knew him, there was only a brief debate before he was taken in to see the captured chieftain.

Kinnieshek sat with his face to the wall. He was a short, stout Indian, with a tendency to fat; he was not very clean, his hair was matted, his clothing was not well kept. He did not turn at their entrance, but sat looking stonily at the wall. The jailer said he had brought someone to see him, but that he must remain here until they finished talking. No answer from Kinnieshek. Soaring Hawk talked with him in the Winnebago language.

He had discovered, he said, who had informed on Kinnieshek.

Kennieshek was interested, though he would not turn. Who was it?

"Red Hair," said Soaring Hawk. He went on to say that what Kinnieshek must do when he came to trial was to say that Red Hair had urged him and paid him to rob the lead wagons; this might incline the white men to mercy; instead of imprisoning him, they might be satisfied just to exile him.

There was no need to say anything further. Having delivered this message, Soaring Hawk took his departure, only grinning with purposeful inanity at the jailer's complaints that he had not understood what they had talked about, how did he know but that they were planning Kinnieshek's escape from prison? At this, Soaring Hawk said bluntly that he did not run with flea-ridden foxes, which was an allusion the jailer understood.

Soaring Hawk went on about his business.

Four days later it was reported from Galena that the body of McAvity had been discovered not far from a lonely inn west of Dubuque. His skull had been crushed in by one blow. There had been nothing to show whether an Indian or a white man had done the crime, unless a small piece of scalp which appeared to be missing indicated anything. It might have been gouged out by an animal. When he heard this news, Parr looked to Soaring Hawk with some suspicion; but since he knew nothing of the Winnebago's visit to Kinnieshek, and knew that Soaring Hawk had not been farther west than Galena throughout the four days, he at least could have had no hand in it. Soaring Hawk's impassive face betrayed nothing. He knew that Kinnieshek had managed to send out word to his friends, scattered as they were; the Dakota, Black Wolf, had killed Red Hair. Now the storekeeper was safe, and Parr should be rid of his concern.

This was the end Soaring Hawk had desired.

Early in September, the postmaster sent over to Trelawny & Pengellen's store a letter for Candace. Moses Strong brought it. He had been on his way to the Court House and it was but a few steps out of his way to deliver it. It was more bulky than usual, and was from Candace's mother. Some time had elapsed between letters from the east, and Candace had been concerned about not hearing from home; so David took the letter up to the house. Tamson had gone home to dinner, and he was in any case soon to go; so he went without waiting for Tamson to return, leaving Trelawny alone.

He was touched to see how delighted she was to receive it. He thought sometimes he did not appreciate the meaning of Providence and her family for Candace, and this made him uneasy, as if some blame attached to him for this failure, and as if this, too, contributed to Candace's occasional unhappiness. For it was sometimes evident that Candace was not happy; discontent and nostalgia shone through her words and actions now and then, though she always tried very hard to conceal them, and that very striving made it impossible for him to take notice of her state of mind, lest the struggle she made be weakened and her depression grow. Moreover, in the past fortnight, she had not been well; she had grown noticeably heavier and Dr. Stonecroft had called twice to recommend less activity, even though she was not often active around the house and seldom went out beyond the area of the yard or the little woods near the high road to Platteville.

She broke the seal on the letter and opened it. It consisted of two large sheets of paper and a newspaper clipping; in her haste to see what the letter contained, Candace did not notice that the clipping fluttered to the table at which David had seated himself. One of the sheets was less large than the other; this had been enclosed within the larger, which had been folded and sealed, then turned for the address, written in a hand which seemed spidery in contrast to the large, decorative "25" the postmaster at Providence had scrawled on the upper right corner to show that the fee had been paid.

David picked up the clipping as Candace started to read her mother's letter. He saw that it was an obituary notice; then he read the name of his father-in-law. He looked up, startled. Candace read with one hand pressed to her lips; she was agitated. He got up at once and came around to her side.

"Oh, David!" she cried. "Father's dead! Dead and buried these three weeks!"

He took the letter gently from her hand. "Let me read it. Sit down, Candy." Expecting her to burst into tears, he was surprised that no tears came. She sat down, incredulous, as if she could not accept the fact that her father was gone. He stood beside her, reading the letter rapidly. Her mother had written in the fullest detail, almost with a kind of cruelty, as if she meant to spare her daughter nothing. Yet the old man's death had not been unexpected; he had not been well for many years; it was believed that he had been in a decline which could end only in death. He had died quite suddenly one night in mid-August in his sleep, without so much as a cry. Her mother had found him dead in the morning. There was no hope of reaching Candace; there had been no warning that death was imminent. He had been buried on the third day thereafter.

He turned the page. There were some paragraphs about the funeral services—who had come, who had not. Then came a final paragraph, extending to the last page of the letter. "And now, my dear child, I feel that you should know I can no longer keep up the house alone. I am not as well, either, as I have been in the past; it is nothing to worry you, but it is just too much to keep up the house any longer. Agnes has asked me to stay with her; she has lived alone now for two years, ever since Henry died, and it seems much the wisest and most sensible thing to do. She is five years my junior, and is both strong and capable. Nor is she in any way demanding. I kept up the house, of course, as long as your father was alive; he would never have consented to my selling it; but now I have no alternative. I have already had three very good offers, one from Colonel Howard Phillips, who has more of an appreciation for such a fine old house as this than any of the others."

He looked down at Candace, trying to estimate how this further blow would affect her. She had loved the house, the neighborhood, the street. Her Aunt Agnes lived in another part of the city, closer to the western edge, almost in the country. But Candace was already holding out her hand for the letter, her face drawn but tearless.

"I'm all right, David. Please."

He gave it to her, filled with misgivings. Then he sat down once more, watching her intently. But there was no sign of tears.

She read with perfect impassivity, except for the patent strain which was not altered by the subject of the house and what was to become of it. After she had finished, she turned to the beginning and forced herself to read the letter over, word for word, as if to impress it upon her mind indelibly. Then she read the obituary notice.

"I'm sorry, Candy," he said, when she met his eyes.

"It had to happen sometime," she said quietly. "But she shouldn't sell the house without asking me. She could have let it."

"It's her house," he countered gently.

She laid the letter away and began to set the table. He sprang to help her, saying he had understood Aunt Marget was to come over today, and where was she?

"Not till this afternoon. I want to clean house."

"I hope you remember, Candy, Dr. Stonecroft said . . ."

"I know, I know. But I can't sit idle all the time. I feel all right."

He was upset by her reaction to her mother's letter; he had expected tears, perhaps even frantic grief; he had not been prepared for dry-eyed stoicism. Perhaps, he told himself, this was but evidence of how well Candace was learning to accept Mineral Point. Just the same, when he met Aunt Marget on his way back to the store, he asked her to see to it that Candace did not over-work.

When Aunt Marget stopped in at the store late that afternoon, he was apprehensive; but she had come only to shop. David went up to her to ask her how she had left Candace.

"Och, she's fair tired. Runnen en an' out, boostering all they day," she said. "She worked like a mazed woman, to clean all, even they scoanes an' they drang. She washed down they durnes, an' a body duss'en say no to she. She'll be glad of sleep."

Soon after, David went home for supper. He found Candace

sitting at the table. She had evidently been reading her mother's letter again, for it lay at her elbow. She greeted him affectionately, but her eyes were far away; no doubt her thoughts were back in Providence—it was natural that it should be so. He understood that all her fury of working this afternoon had been in an effort to push out of her consciousness the shock of the news from Providence.

She was not talkative. She had no news to tell him because, she said, Aunt Marget had been uncommunicative that afternoon—probably, thought David, because Candace had pushed the work so diligently. Nor did he have much to say, being unwilling to intrude upon her thoughts. In any event, what happened in the store always seemed to him of no interest to her; he was not given to carrying home common gossip, though there was always plenty of that, most of it utterly unfounded in fact. Nor was Candace much interested in hearing it; however much she tried, she could not become absorbed in the affairs of the other women in Mineral Point.

Soon after supper, Candace went to bed.

When he came to bed two hours later, she was not yet asleep. By the light of the shaded lamp he carried, he saw that she lay wide-eyed in bed, her gaze fixed on the ceiling. A gentle breeze blew in through the open window, swaying the curtains a little; a late whippoorwill sang outside; crickets and katydids churred beneath the window—but she was oblivious of them.

He undressed and put out the light as he got into bed with her.

"Candy," he said tentatively.

"Yes?"

"Won't you try to sleep?"

"I can't sleep."

"It doesn't matter about the house, Candy," he said. "Home is where the heart is."

"That was home," she answered. "I always hoped to go back there some day. I thought after . . . after. . . . Oh, how could Mother have done it! She knew what the house meant to me."

He put his arms around her and drew her close. "Candy, Candy—no one can ever go home again, never again to that home. Childhood has to end, youth ends, just as life itself ends."

"But as long as it was there—just as long as I knew I could go back there . . ."

So it was this that was in her heart; this knowledge had been her refuge from Mineral Point; this had helped to give her the strength to make the adjustment life in the Territory demanded of her. Now it was gone. He understood instantly how much this action of her mother's meant to her. If he could have wished the act out of existence, he would have done so instantly. The distant security of the house in Providence had bolstered her determination, had made her struggle to meet the challenge of Mineral Point a little easier. There was nothing he could say that would not remind Candace of the increasing tenuousness of the bonds that still existed to bind her to Providence.

She began to shudder; her hands reached blindly for him. He felt the tears come, and held her while she sobbed with a dreadful, hopeless despair which was a torment for him because he believed obscurely that it was he who had brought it about. If he had not gone to Providence, if he had not met her, fallen in love with her, taken her away from that milieu and the occasions to which she belonged! But this was futility itself, this was a maze of accusation and challenge from which there was no escape, and he closed his mind to it, while Candace wept against him, the first wild grief giving way to a more restrained sobbing, and at last subsiding to tearless sighs and finally to sleep.

In the deep night he was awakened by her cry.

"Candy!" he called, struggling upward.

"Oh, David! David, my back hurts so." She spoke with patent effort. "And my side, too. I'm afraid I'm going to be sick."

He was out of bed on the instant. He lit the lamp, then crossed quickly to shut the window, thinking that the cool night air might have chilled her. He dressed rapidly.

"I'm going for the doctor. Will you be all right until we get back?"

She nodded, biting her lower lip. Her face was drawn with pain.

He left the lamp burning and ran through a light, misting rain to the doctor's home, which was one of the new buildings put up within a few blocks of his own house. After he had awakened him and asked him to come, he ran back to the house, not waiting for him.

Candace still lay as he had left her. At the moment of his entrance, her face was relaxed, but even as he threw off his coat and sat down beside her, the grimace of pain crossed once more. He recognized, in alarm, that her pain was spasmodic. He put his hand on her forehead; there did not seem to be fever. He took her pulse; it seemed fast.

"Dr. Stonecroft will be here in a little while, Candy," he said, reassuringly. "I'll go light a lamp for him in the kitchen."

The doctor came while he was in the kitchen—a cheery, hearty man of early middle-age, wearing spectacles and a goatee. His professional manner inspired confidence. David led the way to the bedroom.

"Well, well, what have we here, Mrs. Pengellen?" asked the doctor. "Pain in the back, Mr. Pengellen tells me. And in the side. Eh, eh? What else?"

Candace passed her hand wordlessly over her abdomen.

"I see," he said. "Pulse fast, too. No fever—that's good. Just try to relax, Mrs. Pengellen. You've been overdoing it." He stood up and walked back to his bag, which stood beside David. "Better fetch Mrs. Hoskins, Mr. Pengellen."

The doctor avoided David's questioning glance.

When David came back with Aunt Marget, the doctor met him at the threshold of the bedroom. He admitted Aunt Marget, but not David. "Better wait out here, Mr. Pengellen."

David waited apprehensively, pacing from the dining-room through the living-room to the kitchen and back. He lost track of time in his anxiety. In the east the sky grew pale, and the first pink shone on the low-hanging clouds there. The rain ceased, and the clouds broke. The west wind began to blow, rich with the pungences of late summer, sharpened by the mist and rain of the night. He heard Candace cry out several times. Each time he went to the door of the bedroom. Each time he retreated, afraid to think of what might be taking place.

At last the doctor came out.

"All right, Mr. Pengellen. She'll be all right. You may go in now."

David brushed past his almost apologetic smile of sympathy. Aunt Marget had left the room through the hall door. He strode over to the bed where Candace lay looking for him. She was exhausted; tears still lay in her eyes; her lips trembled as on the verge of new grief. He sank to the bed at her side, clasping her hand.

"Oh, David," she whispered brokenly, "oh, David—I lost our baby."

The misery and despair in her voice found their counterpart in him. For one intuitive moment, a spectral terror stood tangibly in the room between them.

"We'll try again, Candy," he promised reassuringly.

The walls flung his hushed words back at him, and, as if in answer, the doctor appeared at the threshold and said, "I'm sorry, but the hour is late . . ."

4. The Stamp of One Defect

Winter, 1846

JONATHAN TRELAWNY HABITUALLY APPROACHED HIS BREAKfast table with interest. He could never be sure what he would find on it. Though his wife betrayed a passionate addiction to detestable turnip pasties at dinner, her breakfasts were infinitely varied; he was as likely to face a pork chop as eggs or saffron buns. Nor could he foresee the topics of conversation which his wife chose with the same penchant for variety. She seldom elected to speak of the weather. He was surprised when she did so this January morning.

"It's going to thaw," she said. "I've been outside."

It was still dark, though the sky was clear and the sun was soon to rise. He looked at her warily, though an expectant smile concealed his wariness; she seemed deep in contemplation of something beyond the weather, for her habitually fierce glance was soft and thoughtful.

"It's a good thing," he said agreeably.

"I thought so. December was bad enough. Are the roads open?"

"The stages have been going through."

She set his plate down before him. Fried kidneys. He goggled at them.

"Jonathan, we haven't been out of the Point for a long time."

"Not in winter," he answered firmly.

She paid no attention. "The Governor's going to address the Council and the representatives on the sixth, and Colonel Bird's sponsoring a ball at his Madison Hotel that evening. I think we should go."

He gaped at her. When he found his voice, he said, "I've got a pretty good idea of what Dodge is planning to say. Besides, who'd take care of the business?"

"You've got a partner, haven't you? He spent enough time away from the store two years ago. Are you going to sit in this rut all the rest of your life? I don't intend to. Two days in Madison won't do you any harm, either." She dared him with a look to deny her.

"P'r'aps not," he conceded.

"Besides," she went on, "I think we'd better take Candace along. She hasn't been herself since her miscarriage. She mopes too much. If she won't do anything for herself, somebody'd better do it for her. She'll enjoy getting to Madison. Talk to David this morning and let me know this noon. Mrs. Bird is holding rooms for us till the evening of the fifth."

His protests were of no avail. His suggestion that David take his place was brushed aside. "That poor thing," as Mrs. Trelawny referred to Candace, needed to get away even from David. Two days was not long. She saw him to the door and shouted instructions and adjurations at him for half a block.

When David came in that morning, Trelawny approached him diffidently. How was Mrs. Pengellen? he wanted to know.

"I wish I could give you a straight answer, Jonathan," said David. "She seems to just pine."

"Is she strong enough to travel?" pressed Trelawny, hoping

selfishly that she was not, for he had no wish to journey to Madison, close as the capital was.

"Oh, she's strong enough. She just has no interest in things."

"My wife thinks she should get out and around more," said Trelawny then, and went on to tell him of his wife's plan.

"It sounds like a good idea," agreed David. "I don't know what she'll say."

Trelawny shrugged. "I guess it won't make much difference what she says—my wife has made up her mind that she must go, and what can any of us do in the face of that?" He smiled ruefully. "Just the same, for once I think my wife may be right. We all know it hasn't been good for Mrs. Pengellen to brood as she does. And to think of how well she was getting along before you lost the baby! You said yourself she's hardly looked at the piano you got her Christmas."

David nodded. "Well, anything's worth trying."

"Yes, and my wife wants to know by noon. She's reserved rooms at the Madison Hotel; they're being held for us till Monday night. We'll set out on Monday by stage and come back Wednesday. So you'd better take a run back to your house and ask her now."

Candace saw him return with surprise. "Why, David, what are you doing here so soon? Is anything wrong?"

"No. Trelawny sent me back to ask whether you'd like to go in to Madison with them for the Governor's message and the ball at the Madison Hotel."

She hesitated, then shook her head.

He sat down on one of the kitchen chairs and drew her to his knees. "Candy, they want you to go. It may be what you need—a change of scene."

"In mid-winter?"

"Any time is good."

"Do you want me to go, David?"

"Yes, I think you'll enjoy it."

"But you—you're not going?"

"No. This time it's Trelawny's turn. But you'll see everything with them. And you'll meet people from all over."

She wondered, as she listened, what people she might meet—and what she could see in Madison. But it was true, she ought to go, she needed to get away even for just a little while. "I'll go, David," she said.

He kissed her. "I want you to have a good time—for our sake."

She smiled. "I will, David."

How different she was from the girl who had married him in such high, romantic anticipation that day in Providence! he thought, as he hurried back to Trelawny.

The early winter dusk had given way to darkness, illumined by the quarter moon riding high over the city, when Lieutenant Nathaniel Parr rode into Madison from the south. He had been away for over a month, almost two, as far south as Kentucky, and west into the new state of Iowa, which had taken from the Wisconsin Territory old Julien Dubuque's city, once so strong a contender for the site of Wisconsin's capitol. The brilliance of Venus still shone in the west, but redly now, for it was close to the horizon, and in the east the bright winter constellations gleamed.

The territorial capital was sprawled over a wider area than most of the settlements in Wisconsin, except Milwaukee. This was because of the way in which Madison had grown since its inception less than a decade before; settlement had followed the shores of the four lakes, close to two of which lay the heart of the town and the capitol square, with the still unfinished capitol building—a large, stone structure, much of it in use—rising on a square of land set off by a fence of aromatic cedar. From this public square, streets radiated in all directions, with little semblance of order. While in spring and after every rain, the streets were seas of mud, sheltering pigs, ducks and geese—as did one wing of the capitol, also, its cellar being open and inviting wandering swine, so that critics of the administration were wont to declare that there were times when an impartial listener could not truly distinguish between the squealing below the floors and that in the halls of the legislators—at this time of the year, the streets were equally difficult because of snow. Many of the streets were no more than narrow lanes, scarcely adequate for stage-coaches, though when Parr rode, he was not crowded.

The night was crisp, but not unseasonably cold. The day's thaw had left a pleasant musk in air, and the moisture of the thaw had not entirely congealed; here and there it held the odors of cooking food, of coffee, of liquor—for there were several taverns close to the capitol for the convenience of the legislators and all such persons, of whom there were always legion, who came crowding to Madison to seek special favors of the government. Parr rode steadily down one side of the capitol square and along a road not far from the lake, arriving presently at the Madison Hotel, where he dismounted and led his horse around to the stables. These were crowded to capacity; so he left the horse, after finding some feed for it.

He entered the hotel by the back door, leading directly into the kitchen, where a florid, middle-aged woman stood working over a stove, and a young girl, with a kind of doll-like prettyness, was putting food on a tray.

"Sakes alive!" exclaimed the cook. "It's Mr. Parr. I wonder if we've room for you tonight."

"You look overworked, Millie," he said genially. "But then, you're used to it. And you, Myra—I thought by this time you'd have trapped a councillor or at least a representative. I had no idea you liked it so well here."

Both were used to his raillery. He stopped frequently at the hotel, and was as familiar with the kitchen as he was with the private quarters of Colonel Bird and his family.

"Room?" he went on, walking through the kitchen. "As long as there's food, I can always find room. Has anyone seen Soaring Hawk?"

"No, Mr. Parr," said both simultaneously.

He went into the dining-room, which was crowded with people, among whom moved three waitresses. There were people he knew among the diners, and he returned their hails and greetings, but none whom he sought. He went on around into the lobby. This was equally crowded; from the adjoining bar-room came a bedlam of talk. Along the walls of the lobby away from the outer doors lay bedding, preparatory for shake-downs there later at night; evidently, then, the hotel was filled to capacity. He expected this, for it was usually so on opening days of the session.

No one was at the desk, but even as he looked for Colonel Augustus Bird, the proprietor himself came hurrying out of the bar-room—a big, broad-shouldered man, with long arms and solid, capable hands. He was in his shirt-sleeves, and wore a loose tie with a stick-pin in it. His heavy, jowled face was bewhiskered. His eyes, as he caught sight of Parr, flowered with friendliness.

"Parr!" he cried. "You can sleep on the roof! Where've you been? The Governor's been asking after you."

"Has he, indeed!"

Bird threw a powerful arm across his shoulders. "Have you had supper?" he inquired solicitously. "But, of course not—or perhaps you wouldn't be here. There's not a chair in the dining-room. All the better. You can go in and eat with the family. We've some friends in from Mineral Point, but you'll not mind them. Pleasant people. He's in business there."

As he talked, he drew Parr around the desk to the door of his own rooms. He threw open the door and, shoving Parr into the room, bawled, "My dear—we've another guest for supper," after which he withdrew.

Three small children ran curiously into the room, and, seeing him, ran up to him, dancing and shouting, "It's Uncle Parr! It's Uncle Parr!" A handsome, buxom woman appeared from an inner room and advanced upon him, crying out, "My dear Nathaniel! We'd almost given you up. When did you come? But, of course, just now, or you'd have been here before." She had reached his side and now lowered her voice to whisper rapidly, "We've guests. A Pointer and his wife—old friends. And the wife of his partner—a quiet mouse." The children scampered around them, following them into the dining-room, one after another, like a parade, still crying wildly, "It's Uncle Parr!"

From the threshold he saw who sat at the table.

"Mr. Trelawny!" he exclaimed. "What a pleasant surprise! Mrs. Trelawny—how are you? And Can—Mrs. Pengellen!" He added to his hostess, "But, of course, I know these people very well, Mrs. Bird."

"How nice!" said Mrs. Bird. "Augustus junior, give your place to Lieutenant Parr. Perhaps now we'll be able to do justice to that fine roast pork."

Parr sat down beside Candace. Despite her reserve, it seemed to him that she looked upon his arrival with subdued pleasure. At the moment, however, his hostess demanded his attention. She overwhelmed him with a flood of questions, giving him little time to answer any one of them, and said several times that he was a much sought-after man, Governor Dodge himself had sent about trying to find him.

"I'll see the Governor tomorrow," he assured her. "It can't be important, whatever he wants to see me about." He looked at Trelawny. "How are things at the Point?"

"We're almost snowbound," answered Trelawny. "Where've you been keeping yourself?"

Parr explained that he had been in lower Illinois and Kentucky. "And how does it come I find you here?"

"Mrs. Trelawny," answered Trelawny promptly.

"The man needed to get out," said Mrs. Trelawny in a challenging voice. "Look at him! A bewizened creature, and no need for it, either. Besides," she added, turning, "I believed Candace would like to go. Isn't it so, Candace?"

"Oh, yes," replied Candace. She would not truthfully have answered thus only half an hour ago, but now that Parr had come, she was relieved of the weariness she had felt in this city, to which she had looked forward with such interest, since she had heard so much of it, only to find it much like Mineral Point.

"We're planning to hear the Governor's message tomorrow," Mrs. Trelawny went on, emphasizing her words with several jerks of her dark head, and with a look that was meant to show that they would find a place to hear and see, or Mrs. Trelawny would know the reason why.

Parr turned to Candace. "Pray permit me to offer you my arm at the capitol tomorrow."

She lowered her eyes, momentarily confused by his directness. "I think we'd all enjoy your company," she said quietly.

"Good! We'll go over directly after breakfast, even though the Governor likely won't appear in the Hall of Representatives till eleven o'clock or so."

"I much prefer to have someone along who knows his way around," said Trelawny, with obvious relief. "I'm no hand to push my way through crowds."

"We'll meet at breakfast then," said Parr.

Mrs. Bird again demanded his attention, explaining that she would soon have to take her husband's place at the desk, while he came in to eat, and thereafter they talked animatedly about the events of that first day of the session—the election of Nelson Dewey as President of the Council and Mason Darling as Speaker of the House, but particularly of the discussion about the act of Congress authorizing the President to sell the mineral lands of Wisconsin, which profoundly affected the entire area southwest from the Wisconsin River at Helena down. In this fashion they spent the evening, while outside these private rooms, guests crowded to their small quarters, while others, less fortunate, slept wherever Colonel Bird provided space for makeshift beds.

In the morning they went to the capitol early. Even so, they were not the first. Parr had made his way to the Hall of Representatives, knowing that the Governor would address both legislative bodies there. He found seats for the Trelawnys in the gallery, and two more nearby for Candace and himself. Across these he laid a walking stick he had picked up at the hotel to use. He was not in uniform, but wore a high-collared coat, a roll-collared waistcoat, with tight-fitting trousers strapped under his feet, a cravat of black silk knotted about his stiff white collar, and a beaver hat. He attracted attention wherever he went; Candace was surprised at the number of people who knew him.

"If you don't mind," Parr said to the Trelawnys, "Mrs. Pengellen might like to see the capitol before the session begins."

"Go right ahead," said Mrs. Trelawny as if she were giving an order.

Thus bidden, Parr escorted Candace through the building, even to the unfinished portion, which was but one small part of the capitol. She was impressed, for the building was large and not without dignity, even if it lacked much of the polish and classic lines of others like it in the east, and everywhere there was still evidence of haste which resolved into crudenesses no amount of time would erase. Parr nodded to many men he identified as members of Council or representatives, and, as they were passing the main entrance on their way back to the Hall of Representatives, they met Governor Dodge coming in.

He, too, was fashionably clad. Like Parr, he had doffed his hat. It seemed to Candace that he had grown noticeably greyer since she had last seen him. He smiled broadly at sight of them. When he came up, he bowed to Candace, and clasped Parr's arms briefly in his hands.

"I looked for you yesterday, Nate. I must see you sometime today. Not now though—I'm too busy."

"Tonight, Governor?"

"Are you at Bird's?"

"Yes."

"Will you be at the ball?"

"I plan to be—" He turned to Candace. "If Mrs. Pengellen will do me the honor of permitting me to escort her there."

Taken by surprise, so that in her confusion she thought her refusal to accompany Parr would deprive the Governor of his opportunity to see him, she nodded. A wash of color appeared in her cheeks.

"Tonight, then," said Governor Dodge. He paused before Candace, touched her chin with his fingers, and murmured, "My dear Mrs. Pengellen, only a lady could blush so becomingly."

He went on.

She meant to protest to Parr, but did not. The propriety of attending a public ball in the company of a man who was not her husband troubled her, but then, the Trelawnys would be with them, and therefore, in a sense, they would be properly chaperoned. And surely David would not care—if he knew, he would urge her to go. But did she want to dance? She thought, faintly, she did not, she ought not to want to; her inclination was not strong, but she remembered how pleasant it had been to dance with Parr at the Court House in Mineral Point; at the ball she might feel different.

"Would you like to meet some of the gentlemen, Candace?" Parr whispered.

"Oh—I don't know," she answered.

But they were already moving toward two men who had evidently just arrived. One was tall, commanding, with firm, warm eyes looking out of a broad, intelligent face, half of which was concealed by a flowing black beard; though otherwise well dressed, he wore a purple sash around his waist. The other was more slight of build; he was thin-faced, with carefully trimmed moustache and beard, soft, touseled hair, handsome and, though lithe, powerful. He had fine grey eyes, long thin fingers, and was elegantly dressed. There was an air of reserve about him, in contrast to the sense of belonging that seemed to radiate from the other. But Parr had reached them, they had seen him, they smiled.

Parr bowed. "Gentlemen, may I present Mrs. David Pengellen of Mineral Point? Count Augustin Brogmar—Baron Chalfonte Pierneau."

Brogmar made a sweeping bow and kissed her hand gallantly. "Madam, a pleasure. I had the privilege of playing host to your husband one night last August before he set out down river on my flatboat."

Baron Pierneau was somewhat more formal, but no less friendly. He added to his cousin's speech the fact that his man, Clement, who had also gone down river on the expedition to catch the lead-thief, had spoken well of her husband. "And, of course, there was no need to speak to me of you, Parr," he added.

"Pray excuse us," said Brogmar, "we're on our way to Council."

They parted, but already Parr was advancing upon another man, dressed in sombre black, except for his white shirt and grey cravat, a man in middle age, of firm, impressive features—a long, large nose, dark, wide-set eyes, high brow, and long black hair worn straight down to his shoulders. His face was lean, his look provocative. He was clean-shaven, and thus in a minority among the gentlemen in the capitol. Parr presented Candace to Hercules Dousman of Prairie du Chien.

"Mr. Dousman has the reputation of being the wealthiest man in all the Northwest Territory," added Parr.

"And, like all reputations, greatly exaggerated," said Dousman gravely. "My dear lady, your escort has far greater riches than I. He has youth."

He held her hand for a moment, looked searchingly into her eyes, and, bowing, went past.

"It's almost time for the session to begin," said Parr then. "We'd better take our seats or risk losing them."

They returned to the Hall of Representatives and sat down. The gentlemen of the legislature, however, still milled about. Some stood talking animatedly in little groups; some strode from one group to another; others stood alone; and here and there men who were not members harangued isolated councillors.

"These are the men in whose hands the fate of our statehood rests," Parr said with gentle irony, almost as if talking to himself. "I should be afraid of some of them. Mr. Strong, whom you know, is talking with Byron Kilbourn of Milwaukee—see them down there!—Mr. Kilbourn has been interested in the Rock River Canal, but they say he's all for a railroad now, and means to have a charter for one as soon as he can talk the legislature into giving him one. Strong, of course, prefers that the railroad shall begin at the Point; so they're at loggerheads.

"See there—that tall, severe-looking man without a beard—that's Councillor Marshall Strong of Racine, a great conservative—no relative of Moses'. He's talking to Edward Ryan—he's a Racine lawyer, and they say he's as wild and radical as Strong is conservative. He's a great enemy of the banks. And over there, with at least one ear on their conversation—that reserved young fellow with the Quaker beard and the round, red-cheeked face—he's bound to be interested in what goes on; he's Alexander Mitchell. His Wisconsin Marine & Fire Insurance Company of Milwaukee is the only sound bank in the entire Territory and the states around—only the statutes prohibit banks; so they call it an insurance company."

She looked from one to the other of the men as he pointed them out. There was something in his eager words that spoke for the cross-currents and conflicts of the drama slowly shaping the Territory toward maturity. Kilbourn looked like a petulant man, though he had a fine appearance with haughty eyes and a small mouth. Marshall Strong seemed to be little more than a youth, with wide-set warm brown eyes and a high brow crowned by dark hair cropped shorter than the hair of most members. Ryan, also a young man, made her think of a great, shaggy, friendly dog, while Mitchell was somehow, in his very solitude, as well as in the dignity that was his, the most impressive of them all.

Even as Parr was talking, President Nelson Dewey of the Council strode to the front of the hall, mounted the rostrum, and pounded for attention. "The members will please take their seats," he cried. "Governor Dodge is ready to address this Legislative Assembly. The audience will please refrain from making any disturbance, for the Sergeants-at-Arms have been instructed to remove all offenders forthwith. Gentlemen, the Governor of the Territory."

The Governor strode up to rousing applause. He put on his spectacles unhurriedly and arranged such notes as he had scribbled for his guidance. "Members of the Council," he began, paused, and began anew: "Honorable Members of the Council" —laughter interrupted him—"Honorable Members of the House of Representatives"—he paused and looked up, peering over his spectacles. Spontaneous applause broke out once more and he smiled.

"Gentlemen, I shall presently speak of the various needs which will come before this session—of matters pertaining to school laws, the Territorial debt, the building of a penitentiary, the sale of the mineral lands, the new harbors along the lake cities, the pending railroad—but there is another matter of sovereign importance which must be placed before this body without delay.

"I refer, gentlemen, to the question of the formation of a State government to replace the present form. We've been informed by Mr. Morgan Martin, our Delegate in Congress, that an enabling act has been passed by Congress authorizing us to form a constitution and State government for the purpose of being admitted into the Union as the State of Wisconsin. I must tell you, with deep regret, that the Congress, which has already gratuitously bestowed upon Illinois part of our Territory, and a further amount to Iowa, has now taken yet more from our lands by setting forth that our northwest boundary pass through Lake Superior to the St. Louis River's mouth and then follow up the main channel of said river to the first rapids above the Indian village, according to Nicollet's map; thence due south to the main branch of the St. Croix; thence down the channel of said river to the Mississippi."

He was interrupted by cries of "Shame!" "Outrage!" "Robbery!"

He shrugged and waited for the Members' indignation to die down. Then he went on. "I'm sorry; there's nothing we can do in protest. This action was taken for the purpose of deliberately creating another non-slave-holding state out of the old Northwest Territory. The enabling act further stipulates that section sixteen in every township shall be granted to the State for the use of schools, and goes on to make further similar stipulations regarding the need for public buildings. It stipulates also that net proceeds of sales of all public lands lying within our boundaries shall be paid to us for the purpose of making public roads. I am therefore recommending that the honorable Members prepare and pass without delay a law submitting to the people the question of the formation of a State government, as the most important legislation to be undertaken at this session."

The temper of the Members was demonstrated by prolonged applause, in which the audience joined. The applause continued until the Sergeants-at-Arms came to their feet; then it rippled away and died. The Governor continued, expanding on the subjects he had mentioned at the beginning of his message.

When at last he finished, he had spoken for an hour. It had not seemed so long to Candace. She had not thought that Governor Dodge could command her interest to such an extent—even her enthusiasm—but perhaps it rose from the impressiveness of her surroundings, the proximity of Parr, the conviction of the importance of the ladies and gentlemen present as much as from the tangible machinery of government.

As the Governor stepped down and began to walk away, the President of the Council adjourned the gathering. The crowd rose and began to move toward the doors. The Trelawnys joined Candace and Parr. Mrs. Trelawny was equally voluble in praise of the Governor and in condemnation of the Congress for "robbing us of our land," while Trelawny himself spoke of the projected railroad between the lake and the river, hoping the road would run through the Point. Men stood in little groups everywhere, some expostulating earnestly, others listening impatiently. Outside the capitol, several gentlemen rode horses away from the capitol enclosure, and Candace saw the colorful Count Brogmar with his cousin and Hercules Dousman walking away together.

Candace hardly listened to what Mrs. Trelawny said. She was lost in her own thoughts as they walked back to the hotel. The movement of many people, the sense of urgence, indeed, of history, that was all around her, the aura of importance that hung over the capitol all impressed her and filled her with a new vitality which was in sharp contrast to the listless disinterest which had been her mood on the way to Madison. At the same time, she was conscious of a harmlessly vain pleasure in meeting people like those to whom Parr had introduced her. It seemed to her that Lieutenant Parr was somehow the epitome of everything the capital city was coming to represent.

She dressed with great care that evening. She had brought : ball dress she had not had a chance to wear since coming fron Providence. Her mother had often disapproved of it as too dar ing, but she herself liked it. It was of white gros de Naples, witl a low corsage, tight about her breasts, and pointed with lace an a stomacher. The sleeves were puffed and short, with a *bouillo* at the bottom, and the skirt was ornamented with small bow and tassels and two rows of pearls. She wore a high-backed coml in her hair and dressed it with a ribbon of blue and a festoon o pearls borrowed from Mrs. Bird.

"More than one man will look twice at her," opined Trelawn in a whisper to his wife, as they waited for her.

"This is just what she needed," asserted Mrs. Trelawny "Didn't I say so? To get out and enjoy herself and not sit hom moping."

Parr's eyes spoke for him when he came for them, though h said nothing until he led her out to the floor of the ballroom fo their first waltz.

"I shall be the envy of every young blood here, Candace," h whispered. "I swear it! I've never seen you look so ravishing. declare, I believe when I look at you at this moment I've neve seen you before at all. You look enchanting."

"Oh, Nate, stop. People are looking at us."

"Do you wonder that they do? And do you think they'll loo any the less if I'm silent? It isn't me they're looking at—it's yo I'll wager that not a page of *Godey's Lady Book* dare stand be side you!"

"Oh, Nate, please!"

"Must I surrender you to Trelawny for a dance? And to Colo nel Bird? I'll resent every moment apart from you."

"Nate, I'll blush. I *am* blushing," she cried.

"And what of me? I'm burning."

She was delighted, amazed, even a little alarmed. Her puls

quickened. That Nate should speak so, despite his correctness, both touched her vanity and surprised her. At the same time, he held her with unnecessary tightness, quite as if indeed he did not wish to relinquish her. And he spoke with neither banter nor ightness in his voice, but with a tense and meaningful air. She was not displeased. She felt that perhaps she ought not to listen, but listening would do her no harm. It was a long time since any man had spoken to her so extravagantly. Even David had never spoken to her in this fashion. She was keenly aware of being looked at, sometimes with frank, open stares, sometimes with discreet glances. She knew people would ask about her, who she was, and she realized that very few of the ladies were dressed any more fashionably than she. She closed her eyes and sighed.

"What is it, Candace?" asked Parr quickly.

"I do believe I'm a little giddy."

"And who could help being? Shall we leave the floor?"

"Oh, no! The dance will soon be done."

"Too soon, alas!"

She smiled. "If I weren't married, I'd certainly be taken up."

"If you weren't married you'd be taken up indeed—I wouldn't urrender you to anyone. I'd carry you off the floor," he said passionately.

She looked at him, wide-eyed. That he should speak so, without the ghost of a smile! His dark, brooding eyes met hers, and for the first time she looked behind his suavity, correctness, his cool, calculated efficience. She lowered her eyes. At that moment she was conscious of a disturbing rapport between them. Her pulse quickened anew. The sense of giddiness diminished, and a sharp awareness took its place—an awareness not only of place and of the man who held her here so formally in his arms, but of her relation to David, to Mineral Point, and the wider world that reached to Providence. The perspective trembled and righted itself.

"I'm afraid, Nate, you've flattered so many ladies you lose your sense of proportion."

"Or gain it."

The dance came to an end. She took his arm and walked across to where the Trelawnys stood. There they waited until Colonel and Mrs. Bird stepped out on the floor to lead off in a Virginia reel. Parr joined with Mrs. Trelawny on his arm. Trelawny took Candace. Several times during the reel Candace met Parr's eyes, and read in their gaze no retreat from his words. She was conscious of an excitement induced not alone by the rapidity of the dance.

Just as the reel ended, a burst of applause came from the main entrance. Governor and Mrs. Dodge had just entered. The floor cleared, and Candace rejoined Parr, both a little breathless. People moved casually back, making room for the Governor and his wife, and for the remainder of their party, Judge Dunn and Mrs. Dunn, Councillors Dewey and Catlin with Major Rountree and their wives, and several more couples Candace did not know. Colonel Bird hurried to find a place for the Governor, while the fiddlers tuned up and waited on the settling of the party to begin a cotillion.

Mrs. Dodge sat down, but the Governor remained standing, looking all around him, bowing now and then. He saw Parr at last and signalled him to come to him. Then he sat down until Parr, with Candace still on his arm, reached his side. He came to his feet once more and bowed to Candace.

"One would hardly have known you, Mrs. Pengellen," he said, "but for the familiar radiance of your features. Pray sit down beside Mrs. Dodge." To Parr he added, "We'll leave the ladies to each other."

They stepped away a little, but not far enough to keep Candace from hearing their conversation, despite her own formal talk with Mrs. Dodge.

"My dear Nathaniel, I have private information from Martin hat war with Mexico is inevitable," said the Governor. "Some novement of troops may have begun already. Slidell hasn't made ny progress on his mission to buy the territory of New Mexico, nd General Taylor's in the country of the Nueces and Rio Grande Rivers. It's regrettable, but it's so. What will you do?"

"I have no choice, sir. I'll go."

"Let's not be too hasty, Nathaniel. I'll perhaps want you for time to be in Washington. I'm sure there'll be volunteers from he Territory. Someone should be in the capital. Your commis-ion as a captain could be assured. I don't know how much fight-ng there'll be, and I need you here, too."

"I'll bear that in mind, sir."

"Good. There isn't any need to say anything about this. Only few of us are informed."

They returned to the ladies. Since a cotillion was now begin-ing, the ladies joined the gentlemen, Candace on the Governor's rm, Parr escorting Mrs. Dodge. Not until she was dancing a valtz with Parr did Candace have a chance to say what she was hinking.

"Nate, I couldn't help overhearing the Governor. If there's a var—will you have to go?"

"It would be better if I went."

"Why?"

"For several reasons. I'm needed. I should go. Finally, I ought o go away for my own peace of mind. In confidence, that was vhat I looked for in Kentucky these past weeks. I thought I'd ound it. I find now I was in error."

"I'm afraid you speak in riddles, Nate."

He smiled. His dark mood was passing. "But you're no riddle, Candace—except only as every woman is a riddle to every man. Tell me, will you dare dance the pigeon wing with me if they lay it—or the double shuffle?"

"Oh, they are such—such violent dances," she protested faintly.

"Yes, I know. I've danced them. Haven't you?"

She nodded. "It seems a long time ago."

"Shall we try?"

He was challenging her. His eyes dared her, his mouth—she saw for the first time how proud it was, with a hint of scorn in the set of his lips—provoked her.

"All right," she said.

The waltz ended, and Colonel Bird came over to lead Candace off in a rapidly-paced dance called *Hunt the Squirrel.* This was the evening's fastest dance, and she was not to have another with Parr.

By midnight, Candace was tired. The Trelawnys had already gone to their room, which immediately adjoined the Birds' private quarters, where Candace was to sleep. Both Colonel and Mrs. Bird were still on the floor, though the Dodge party had taken their leave an hour ago.

"Oh, for a breath of fresh air!" cried Candace.

"Let me get your cloak. Perhaps then we can step outside."

"Please do, Nate."

"As for me," he continued, coming back with her velvet cardinal, "I'll have plenty of fresh air. I'm off for Dodgeville within the hour."

"At this time of night!"

"Traveling isn't crowded. Besides, Soaring Hawk is anxious to head south as soon as possible. He came in this afternoon."

They left the hotel, crossed the verandah, and walked to the street. The windows of the ballroom and of the adjoining barroom were steamed up from the great crowd of people still inside, but at this hour, few people were outside. They walked slowly down the street and stood looking out to the lake, a great, spectral mass of white, frozen over and snowed upon. Across its expanse the far shore rose ghostlike upon the darkening heaven, for the moon was setting among clouds, and an overcast was moving across the stars.

"I hope you haven't had cause to regret your holiday, Candace," Parr said quietly.

"Oh, no," she cried, turning to him. "It's been wonderful! I didn't want to come—but now, I'm glad I did—it's been like a beautiful dream."

"But it wasn't a dream," he said soberly.

She looked at him wonderingly. "Nate, you've been strange tonight. Won't you tell me why?"

"I couldn't."

She drew her cardinal around her and pressed closer to him. "Don't you know how dangerous it is to rouse a woman's curiosity, Nate?"

"Is it?"

His hands rested lightly on her arms at her shoulders; he stood for a moment thus, while she looked up at him. Then his hands slipped past her shoulders, his arms went around her, he bent and kissed her, taking her mouth fiercely, out of pent-up desire, holding her so tightly she could not move. But her instinctive struggle against him diminished, died away; she gave herself up to his kiss, and he realized with bounding pulse, that she returned the pressure of his lips.

She was trembling when he released her.

"I know I ought to ask your pardon," he said, "but that would be a kind of acknowledgment of error, wouldn't it? I haven't made any. I've wanted to kiss you ever since I first saw you."

For a long, troubled moment, she said nothing. Then, "I'd better go in, Nate."

"Yes, I think you'd better," he agreed.

She took his arm. They walked back to the hotel in silence, through the crowds about the ballroom, to the proprietor's quarters. She turned at the door.

"Thank you, Nate," she said quietly.

"Thank *you*, Candace."

She slipped into the darkened room and closed the door behind her. She stood with her back to the door, her hands pressed flat against its smooth surface, her eyes tightly closed. She waited there for her pulse to subside, for it still pounded with unnatural rapidity. She touched her lips with her fingers; her mouth still felt hot from the pressure of his, and it seemed to her that her fingers, too, grew warm, pressed there where he had kissed her. Her conscience rebuked her; she had made no protest, expressed no displeasure, given him no sign that she was angry. But she was not angry; astonishingly, she was aware of a kind of wild exultation in the midst of the shame she felt.

She went to her room, cautiously, lest she stumble against something and awaken the children. She undressed in the dark, thinking of Nate, and growing warm all over, as if his sudden, moody eyes were upon her here in this unlit room; and indeed, in thus accepting his kiss, she felt a sense of shame similar to the thought of his sight of her unclothed. But her shame was not strong enough to put down the exhilaration she felt, an exhilaration that seemed to exist apart from censure in a corner of her mind which no memory, no code, no previous training could touch. In the conflict between shame and exultation, the confusion of her mind grew and kept her for a long time sleepless in this strange bed, suspended somewhere between her beloved Providence and Mineral Point, which she had come slowly to tolerate almost to liking, between irresponsible youth and the denial of maturity.

Soaring Hawk, warmly clad in buckskin, with even his traditional feathers put off in favor of a tight-fitting coonskin cap, had observed Parr's every move. He had entered the ballroom early in the evening, taken an inconspicuous place, and watched the dances of the palefaces, which afforded him considerable entertainment. He scorned them. They were nothing like the grave dances of his own people—the dances to the rain god, the dance to the west wind, the dance for war, accompanied by their runic songs—in which few of the squaws ever took part. He could not understand the meaning of a waltz; he assumed that the cotillion had some significance but was unable to fathom it; at least, it had pattern. The violence of the double shuffle amazed him insofar as it was possible for him to experience amazement at anything these incredible palefaces did.

He had seen Parr go out with Candace on his arm. He had followed. By the time Parr came back out alone, having first changed clothes and then presented his compliments to Colonel and Mrs. Bird, to bid them farewell, Soaring Hawk was waiting with the horses. It had been understood at their meeting that afternoon that they were to return to Dodgeville after the ball, though Soaring Hawk was no longer convinced they would go.

When Parr came, he said, "Snow coming."

"You rascal," said Parr heartily, "you've been listening to the wind again. That wind of yours is a teller of tall tales."

Soaring Hawk took no notice of Parr's raillery. For himself, he did not mind snow. He welcomed it. It was a sign from Manitou, like the rain and the wind, like the rolling thunder and the forked lightning. He mounted his horse and waited patiently for Parr to do likewise.

They rode out of the yard and turned south. The night was windless. Clouds covered the sky, save in one or two places where stars looked through. Low along the western rim, a band of sky still showed, and there lay the setting moon, large and deep yellow, spreading an eerie glow over the snowbound earth.

Soaring Hawk was silent until they had gone well away from

Madison. Then he began to speak. He had seen the White Chief signal to Parr in the ballroom; he had seen him speak privately to him, though the woman had listened. He had seen the expression of Parr's face at the Chief's speech. It meant a change in all Parr's plans.

"Yes," Parr answered the question the Indian disdained to ask. "The country may go to war."

"Hoh!" barked the Winnebago with savage scorn. He supplemented this indication of his sentiments presently by saying that this was surely nothing unusual, for did not white men always make war? Indeed, they did. And was it not customary to fight against other men, red or brown or even white-skinned like themselves, who were less in number and not so warlike? The palefaces were war-makers; they were born to make war, they died making war, they did so with nothing of the simple cruelty of the Indians, but with a kind of torture which filled the heart with false promises and lulled the brain with hope, all of which were lies, dishonesty, cheating. If indeed Manitou had created white men, even he must have forgotten his special reason for doing so.

Parr said that this time Soaring Hawk spoke more wisdom than he knew.

Satisfied, the Winnebago lapsed into silence.

The sky closed. Clouds lowered over the setting moon and the dim yellow glow there filtered briefly through. Overhead, the last stars vanished. The air was moist, sweet with the musk of thawing snow, a fresh, crisp smell pervading everything, even the thick clothing both of them wore. Somewhere in a wood not far from the road a pair of saw-whet owls made their bell-like notes; they rang out into the night air with a strange, ventriloquial quality. There was no other sound but that of their horses' hooves and the crunching snow.

They rode steadily. Parr pushed the thought of impending war from his mind. Candace was uppermost in his thoughts. He turned over in memory every inflection of her voice, every word she had spoken, every glance of her eyes; all remained in his memory with such clarity that he found her face superimposed on every place toward which he turned his eyes; and, riding there, he had only to lower his lids to imagine himself once more in the ballroom, with Candace in his arms, hearing her voice, seeing her smile and that look in her eyes which spoke far more than she knew of the confusion within her. He had feared for a moment that her reaction to his kiss would have been otherwise, but it was not; it had confused her, but his kiss had not been unwelcome, and he felt that she was drawn to him even as he was to her.

There was a kind of harmony between them that all their differences could not dispel. Perhaps her restlessness found its counterpart in him; the occasional dissatisfaction in Candace reflected his own reaction to his milieu, however different their grounds. Perhaps it was because of this harmony that the familiar road of conquest along which he had set out had turned into something more, so that it was no longer the conquest of Candace that he desired, but Candace herself. He had discovered this during his weeks in Kentucky on an errand for Chief Justice Dunn; there Parr had thought constantly of Candace, until it had seemed that she had an importance in his mind equally as great as his ambition for his own advancement. And, indeed, there were times when it seemed that of the two, she was the more important.

That this should be so when she had seemed unattainable he could understand; that it should still be so now, when he was satisfied that she was not unattainable, was a source of wonder. But he could not deny it. She had never been so beautiful, so desirable as she had been tonight. Parr had never been in love; in casual dalliance he had found no need for love, no compulsion to surrender himself; he was by nature solitary, though in a passive way he cherished the friendship of Soaring Hawk, Governor Dodge, and of other men and some women of the Wisconsin Territory and the country south. To them he gave generously of his time and such small abilities as he possessed; but of himself he gave little. He kept himself secure in a little cocoon of self-assurance which cradled his ambitions and desires, his hopes and all the lost longings he had known from childhood, the unanswered question of his paternity and the unresolved fate of his carefully-wrought plans. Candace touched upon this inner self, hitherto inviolate. Her prisoned helplessness, her dream of the past, her hope of the future she envisioned in terms of honor and glory, her restlessness all appealed to him out of a core which was equally solitary, equally unshared, equally unknown.

Behind him, Soaring Hawk was aware of his meditation. He sensed that a problem of some gravity troubled Parr. He was baffled. War would not bother Parr, he was certain. Even if he went, he might not see much of it. Nor could it be danger menacing the storekeeper, for Red Hair was long since dead. It could be only the woman, a conclusion which baffled him all the more, for it was inconceivable to him that any man should trouble himself about a woman. But the ways of white men were riddles; they were strange beyond comparison with anything in Soaring Hawk's experience. The Indian, who was direct in all his dealings, could not understand the need of deviousness, which was the distinguishing mark of the white man in all things.

He smelled the air several times. It was moist, almost sweet. "Snow come," he said.

"Let it come," answered Parr.

The problem that confronted Parr waited upon circumstances. But his intuition told him that, circumstances permitting, his pursuit of Candace would not abate, all considerations of friendship with David, even of ambition, notwithstanding. Yet he was not without scruples; it was only that he now found himself caught by a passion beyond his control, stronger than he himself was, the fancied need for a woman like Candace to be his. And though part of him rebelled in resentment against it, sufficiently for him to welcome escape into war with Mexico, he knew that his course was irrevocable.

They were half way back to Dodgeville when snow began to fall. Parr rode for a long time before noticing it, so brightly did the image of Candace burn before his mind's eye, so fully did she occupy his thoughts.

On Wednesday morning Tamson rose early. She got out of bed and dressed hurriedly in the chilly room. It was not yet daylight. Snow fell steadily outside, quietly, without wind; she could hear it sifting against the windows, making a gentle *hush-hush* against the glass, a sibilant whispering. Aunt Marget was herself just up; she looked upon her with astonishment.

"Es et en a maze y'arr, Tammy?" she asked, as she bustled to get breakfast. "En all my boorn days I ne'er seed 'ee so hastis."

She shook her head. "No. There's so much work at the store. And David's all alone till Mr. Trelawny comes back today."

"Stage'll be some'at late en they lashes o' snow," judged the older woman.

Tamson made no reply. She ate hastily, while a grey day dawned outside. After breakfast she put on her cap, her long coat, and her high shoes, and set out through the snow for the store. It had snowed since the early hours of the day, and three inches of it lay over everything. The smelters made a red glowing here and there in the falling snow, the flakes catching and reflecting the firelight. Light still shone in the windows of many houses, and some places the lights were going up at the entrance of the mine shafts. The air was not cold, only pleasantly crisp, and the smell of snow was fresh and good in the nostrils, thinning the pungence and acridity of the smoke from the smelters.

David was already at the store. She knew he would be. He had come down before dawn each morning; he had gone home long after dark each night, taking his meals at the Mansion House. But it was not his work she thought about; it was his silent preoccupation which had been maintained with almost painful consistence ever since the loss of the baby, and which seemed to have lightened only with Candace's visit to Madison on Monday. His worry about Candace touched everything he said or did; this brief freedom from Candace had served him well.

"Good morning, Tamson," he called out as she entered.

"Oh, David!" she cried. "Sweeping! That's my job."

She walked down the length of the store without stopping to remove her coat or fur cap, took the broom away from him, and held it with one hand while she flung off her cap and began to shrug out of her coat. He came over to help her, grinning.

"If I didn't know better, I'd think you were the proprietor," he said.

"You needn't laugh at me. You have better things to do than sweep the store. Besides, didn't I sweep it last night?"

"But I was here, working after supper. People came in." He shrugged. "It doesn't matter, only I like to see the place clean for part of the day."

"With this snow, it won't be clean long."

She swept diligently, as if the success of the entire day depended upon her finishing this trivial task in record time. He walked to the north wall to set prices down on new merchandise stacked there; but when she finished, she found him watching her.

"Now rest a bit," he said, laughing. "Come and tell me how you and Nate are getting along."

"How is it you think we should be getting along, David?" she countered, thinking: How strange he should ask that! She walked slowly toward him, marking every aspect of his face, challenging his blue eyes.

"Surely Nate doesn't call on you to talk about the weather!"

"He hasn't called on me very often, David," she answered. "Three or four times—no more. And you know that almost every time—the only exception was that week last September when Candace was ill—we've walked over to your house. Nate's always been a gentleman; I wouldn't expect him to be anything else. I told you once how I felt about him."

He remembered and smiled. "Sometimes I don't understand women."

"Perhaps that's a good thing."

They stood facing each other. He was aware of a certain air about her, as if by main force she held herself from speaking words she wanted to say. His casualness gave way to a feeling of unease. She marked the alteration in his eyes and the set of his wide mouth.

"Since you asked me that, David, I want to ask you something, too—what's the matter with you? All these months, half of you hasn't been here. Except, perhaps, these past days."

He blinked and looked past her toward the door—almost, she thought compassionately, as if he hoped the entrance of a customer might make his answer unnecessary. But the falling snow and the earliness of the hour were against him. His eyes wavered back to her. At sight of the unhappiness in them, she found it an effort to keep from running to him, throwing her arms around him, trying to comfort him.

"It's Candace, isn't it?" she said, rather than asked.

He nodded. "I can't say, though, it's exactly her fault. She did seem to grow more tolerant just before she lost the baby. I thought now and then she had grown to like the Point. She showed it. But now I wonder if she's ever really been happy here

—or whether she ever will be. I suppose it was her mother selling the house and the miscarriage that turned her again. Tamson, she tries so hard, she does. I've thought of sending her back east, but she won't go now. The house was her anchor. I have all I can do to get her to answer her mother's letters, and when she does, she never writes very much. I'd like to do something more for her—but there's nothing I can do."

"Perhaps you try too hard."

"No, I guess I shouldn't have brought her here. I didn't realize how attached she was to her home, and how hard it would be for her to change. She has changed, though—you know she has."

"Yes," she admitted reluctantly. "But I don't know, David, if it's in her heart or in her will."

"I'm sure it was both, Tamson."

"It's been plain to see," she said then, "the way you felt since Sunday. I suppose it was just the relief that you didn't have to go back to your home and find her there and be reminded."

He looked at her reproachfully.

"David, you can't go on living like that."

"Oh, it will change."

The door opened and one of the miners came in, calling for wicks. David hurried to wait on him, and Tamson took up the task he had left. She felt both sorry for him and angry with him, sorry because she understood his dilemma, angry because she believed he was too ready to assume guilt when none was his. The small talk in the front of the store died away; the door opened and closed. David came back and stood above her, where she crouched among the stacks of merchandise.

"I've often thought, Tamson, seeing you here like this, if things were otherwise, it might be Candace here, helping me," he said musingly.

She came to her feet, her eyes flashing. "And I, David Pengellen, I've often thought, too, that if you hadn't been so hasty in

Providence, it might be me, up there as well as here." She was instantly sorry that she had spoken; she had taken him by surprise, and at once, remorseful, she flung her arms around him and said, "Och, David, I'm sorry, I shouldn't have said et. But I mean et, only I shouldn't have said et." She raised her head and looked at him. "Say you forgive me!"

"It was unfair of you to say it," he said. "Perhaps you couldn't help thinking it—for I've thought it, too."

"Oh, David," she cried, and held him tighter. She closed her eyes against his and waited for his kiss. It came. His lips brushed her cheek and moved upon her mouth, at first hesitant, almost wary, then fiercely possessive. All the pent-up passion within her answered him.

But it was he who started away. "Now we've done it. I'm sorry."

"For that," she said proudly, "I am not. We've done nothing but what was wanting to be done a long time. You know it, David, unless you have no sensibilities at all, I could never look at another man."

He shook his head, as if he did not want to hear her words. "Tamson! I'm married—it couldn't be. Think of Nate . . ."

"Oh, Nate!" she cried passionately. "Do you know how I feel toward Nate? I pity him—I pity him from the bottom of my heart, for he's lost and he doesn't know it."

What she said went unheard. "We must forget this happened, Tamson."

"If it eases your mind, David, you forget it. I cannot."

"Tamson, please. You don't know what love is."

"Oh, and don't I? I'll tell you what it is—it's what I feel for you, it's what I've always felt for you, with all the pity, too, and it's what you've got deep down in your heart for me—if you weren't afraid to let it come."

"Tamson!"

"You needn't say me no, David. Your mouth was as hungry as mine. You're the first man to kiss me, David, and there'll be no other."

"Tamson, you don't know how dangerous . . ."

She interrupted him in a reproving voice. "We've no right to spend this day arguing. The time is half Mr. Trelawny's, and there's work to be done. I'll ask you to remember—you were a-setting out to forget this happened. Get on with it."

Candace rode all the way to Mineral Point in contemplative silence. She did not notice that the stage took almost twice as long to reach the Point as it had taken to go to Madison from that place two days before. The stage was crowded with people the Trelawnys knew; so there was little demand for her conversation. Such part as she took was purposeful. She asked Jonathan Trelawny who Count Brogmar was, and was told; she asked him to identify Hercules Dousman, and learned of that gentleman's eminence in Mr. John Jacob Astor's fur company; and she asked about Baron Pierneau, but of him Trelawny knew nothing.

She dwelled upon these people in her thoughts—they were rich, influential, they were personages on any stage, and Nate appeared to be on intimate terms with them. Indeed, Nate seemed to know everyone of importance in the Territory, just as he had been everywhere in a dazzling round of activity. Nate was the trusted emissary of the Governor, the Chief Justice, and others in high places; he was the friend of Indians, kitchen maids, soldiers and miners. She was naïvely impressed and could not help making the contrast between Nate and David; beside Nate, David paled and faded.

Her confusion of the past night had resolved itself. The attention Nate had paid her, against the background of the holiday, had lifted her spirits to a buoyancy they had not reached for months. David had guessed correctly that the shock of anger and grief which had been in some part responsible for the loss of the baby took rise not alone from her father's death, but from her mother's summary sale of the house which had been talisman and touchstone, refuge and retreat. Her mother had thus deprived her of past and future at once; the haven which had always existed in the back of Candace's mind as a place to which to escape if the wilderness pressed too close was gone without warning in a change as abrupt and sudden as death. For three months she had been lost—three weary, desolate months, without refuge for her spirit, without the promise of the house in Providence to return to. She had always tried to show her best face to David, to conceal her misery, but she knew he had felt it, just the same. Even alone, she had tried to turn her thoughts outward, to look at Mineral Point with acceptance and affection, but little had taken her interest for long, and only Nate's occasional visits with Tamson had freed her briefly from her mood.

As they jogged along through the thickly falling snow, Candace saw Nate in a new light—not only as the confidant of men in high places, not only as the friend of all men, not only as the polished and informed courier, not only as the soldier and the man who had flaunted convention to escort her to the Governor's Ball, had breached etiquette to kiss her and refused to ask her pardon for doing so, but as a way of escape, a new talisman and refuge. Nate's proximity alone would go far to help her learn to like Mineral Point; in the buoyancy of her spirits now she felt a new strength, a new sureness.

On the morning of the second day of February, Soaring Hawk rode into Mineral Point with disturbing news. He came into the store and stood in the middle of the floor, in contrast to his customary easy squatting posture; this was a measure of his agitation, though there was no sign of it in his face.

"Where are you bound for?" asked Trelawny. "Parr with you? Where's he been keeping himself?"

The Winnebago's attitude arrested further questions. He replied that he was going no farther. He had stopped in at Dodgeville; Parr had come in the previous night from the east. Soaring Hawk said he had come at the behest of Thomas Parish, a shipper of Muscoday, a settlement on the Wisconsin River sometimes also called English Prairie, which lay some thirty miles northwest of the Point. There had been trouble at that place the previous evening—an outbreak.

"Of Indians?" asked David, incredulous.

Soaring Hawk answered that Parish had some question as to whether the outbreak was of the Winnebago against white men or of white men against the Indians; it could as likely have been one as the other. There were no Indians to say; there were only some white settlers along the river above Muscoday who were loud to curse the Indians in the manner natural to white men.

"What the devil is this?" demanded Trelawny impatiently. "Is it another rumor? We've heard hundreds of them."

There had been a skirmish already, Soaring Hawk continued, telling his story in his own way. A band of Indians had met or been met by a party of whites. Someone had opened fire—the white men, of course, said it had been the Winnebago. Four Indians had fallen, and two white men had been injured. There had been an exchange of shots before the Indians retreated. Now the Muscoday country was aflame with tales that the Indians had sent runners to their scattered bands in preparation for war, and the white men had sent for aid by dispatching a courier to the Legislature, which was closing its session this week in Madison.

Trelawny swore heartily. "That could start trouble all through the region!"

That was why Parish had sent him, Soaring Hawk went on. They needed level heads, and preferred men who had served with the militia. He had already looked for Captain O'Neill, but he was gone. Parr had promised to interrupt the task now occupying him and join any group of men who wished to set out for Muscoday in the morning to make an attempt at peace between whites and Indians. The men of Muscoday and its vicinity were organizing; twenty of them had banded together and chosen James Estes to be their captain. They were determined to drive every Indian along the Wisconsin to the Mississippi, and, as usual in such matters, it would give none pause to kill the Indians instead.

"I'll go," offered David.

They would set out from Parr's place in Dodgeville at seven in the morning next day, said Soaring Hawk.

"We can both try to find a few other men," said David. "You go down and see Tom Prisk, Hawk. I'll hunt up a few volunteers myself."

"All hotheads, hotheads," muttered Trelawny, shaking his head in disapproval. "Too many of 'em would rather fire off a gun than sit down to reason. You reason with 'em, David, or first thing we'll have a war in the Territory."

David heeded the warning implied in his partner's words; he avoided seeing any of the younger men who would have gone for sport. There would be enough of them from Muscoday to keep under control. When they set out for Dodgeville in the morning there were only four of them—Tom Prisk, Simon Lanyon, Tubal Harris, and himself. They found Parr and Soaring Hawk with two men from Dodgeville, Charlie Bilkey and Jack Bartle, waiting for them. The eight men took the trail to Muscoday.

The morning air was crisp and still, but the sky was clear and the sun, when it rose, brought additional warmth. The snow was not deep; some days of thaw had lessened it, and traveling was not too difficult for the horses. The road led through many thickets and some interminable groves, where trees were closely pressed together and stood singularly dark against the white earth. They rode in pairs whenever the road permitted; it was not a commonly used trail, and in some places there was scarcely room for more than a single rider. David rode beside Parr most of the time. Soaring Hawk invariably rode alone at the rear.

Parr was preoccupied. David made small talk about the prospect of trouble; Parr foresaw no extensive difficulties, but agreed that the Muscoday matter was a nuisance, which, if not abated, might involve the whole lead mining country. Behind them, their companions laughed and joked and discussed business, making comparisons between the growth of Mineral Point and of Dodgeville, the men from the latter town insisting that before many more years passed they would wrest the county seat from Mineral Point, an expression of long-standing rivalry.

"I believe I'm in your debt again, Nate," said David casually. "You certainly helped Candace out of her doldrums. You must stop in again soon."

"At the moment I'm on an assignment of the Governor's," answered Parr. He did not explain, except to add that he could not be anywhere but on the Governor's business for some weeks to come.

David was mystified at Parr's restraint. Something in his manner suggested a reluctance to stop and visit them.

They reached Muscoday at noon and rode directly to Parish's smelting furnace. Parish, a brawny, ruddy-faced man, with a bluff, hearty manner, came out to meet them. He was delighted at their arrival.

"Glad you're here," he cried. Looking at Parr's uniform—for Parr was in the garb of the militia, he added, "They'll likely listen to you, Parr. You're just in time, too—there's more than thirty men just chomping at the bit to go fight Indians. That ain't what we want. Have you et?"

They had not; so Parish dispatched two of his men to make arrangements for them to eat at his own home. He sent another to call on Captain Estes and instruct him to wait for reinforcements coming from him. Then he was introduced to those men he did not know. David had met him before; he understood Parish's interest. Parish had been one of the first men to ship lead by wagon train directly across the Territory to Milwaukee; the routes Parish and his fellow smelters from this part of the lead-mining region used would be under easy, open attack by Indians in case of spreading trouble with the Winnebago.

Parish mounted his own horse and led them to his home, where he sat talking with them while they ate. As far as he could make out, he said, the whole flare-up had happened because of a conflict between two hunting parties. Then that difficulty had been followed by the Indians taking a canoe belonging to Captain Horatio Smith, who lived up river from Muscoday. One thing had led to another till the skirmish of the previous night.

"It happened about supper time," said Parish. "Some men went out to talk to the Indians—that's the story. They say the Indians fired on 'em. Now they've tasted blood—two of 'em got hurt, and four redskins went down. Killed or not, nobody knows. The Indians took 'em along back into the hills."

"Where are the Winnebago now, Parish?" asked Parr.

"Who knows?" asked Parish, shrugging.

Soaring Hawk interposed and said softly that the Winnebago were in the hills north of the Wisconsin. This was across the river from Muscoday, in a series of low, densely-wooded hills which grew into taller slopes beyond—a difficult country in which to engage them.

"Just the same," said Parish doggedly, "we've got to talk to 'em. And we've got to settle the men in town who're ready to start trouble."

"The strategy calls for a reconnoitering party," suggested Parr. "We'll take a dozen men or so, including Estes. We'll leave the hotheads trailing us. That'll keep them away from the Indians—if we can find them."

"We find," said Soaring Hawk confidently.

After they had eaten, they rode into Muscoday, where three dozen men milled around in the main street, excitedly watched by a handful of children and some apprehensive women, who called out words of warning from time to time. The men were boisterous, fully armed, and steaming with self-assurance, deceived into confidence by the apparent strength of their numbers. They set up a cheer at sight of Parr's uniform.

"Told ye we'd git some militia outa the gov'mint," shouted one of them.

Parr did not disabuse them of the mistaken notion that he had been sent from Madison.

Parish muttered. "It was a damn' fool thing to do, to vote out the militia just to make things harder for Doty. Maybe this will put some sense into them politicians' heads. I never gave a damn whether Doty spelled it 'Wiskonsan' or not, and I don't know what all that infernal fuss was about up in Madison, anyway. All I know's that now when we need it we ain't got no militia."

The mistaken impression that he represented the Territorial government won Parr an immediate hearing. Captain Estes presented himself and announced that he would be perfectly willing to follow his lead.

Parr scrutinized Estes—a young man, firm of purpose, he judged, and able. "No, Captain—you've been elected leader of this group. I'm but a lieutenant, as you see. I'm at your service. So are we all. But I do have a suggestion to make. In any group there are likely to be men with itchy fingers on a trigger. It won't take much to start serious trouble. I propose that we take a small group—pick half a dozen of your men; I'll go with this party, and Soaring Hawk, who can talk with the Winnebago in their tongue, and form an advance party to attempt a peaceful settlement. Who's the chieftain of this band?"

"I believe it's Star Walker," answered Estes.

Parr shot a glance at Soaring Hawk, who gave a barely perceptible nod.

"Very well, then. We'll try to find him. Soaring Hawk believes the band is in the hills across the river. Where's the fording place?"

"I'll show you after I talk to the men."

Estes turned and shouted an order for silence. Then he outlined Parr's strategy, selected six men to accompany him, and joined the men from Mineral Point and Dodgeville.

They set out, Estes riding ahead with Parr, who lost no time in impressing Estes again with the need for avoiding a shooting war. If one broke out, he said, what was to prevent the Sioux, cousins of the Winnebago, from filtering down into southern Wisconsin from the northwest along the Mississippi? Nothing. Captain Estes was visibly impressed. When they reached the river, he rode back to instruct the main body of the troops to follow only at a distance of more than a mile, preferably two.

The Wisconsin at this season was all but covered with ice. Only a narrow channel remained open, and this flowed for the most part over shallows. They rode over the ice, plunged through the shallow waters of the fording place, went along another tract of ice, and then moved directly up into the hills which brooded darkly above the Wisconsin's shore.

The hills were covered with oak and cedar trees, with occasional birch, elm, ironwood, and maple trees, rising among groves of wild crabapple and hawthorn. The cedars added darkness to the snow-covered slopes, but many tracks were to be seen. This was where the encounter of the previous evening had taken place, explained Estes. The Indians had fled north from here.

Soaring Hawk rode forward with Parr and Estes from the place of the outbreak.

The tracks were numerous. They appeared to trail off in at least three directions. They might unite farther in the woods, but for the time being they were confusing. The deeper the men moved into the woods, too, the less sunlight reached them. The hills were compounded of ledges, knolls, dark little valleys; in some places the snow was surprisingly deep, and the greatest care had to be exercised to keep from slipping into pockets or off ledges. The conflicting tracks were puzzling, the woods' stillness almost oppressive. A few birds fluttered up and flew away; now and then ruffed grouse whirred up from the snow; rarely, a fox or a lynx sped away from his lair at their approach. The sun vanished under clouds now and then; each shadow brought to the woods a sense of brooding expectancy, as if every silent tree waited upon the sudden meeting with the Winnebago, lurking somewhere in the security of these wooded hills.

Presently Soaring Hawk came to a stop. The men would have to spread out, he told Parr. There were four distinct trails. Though doubtless three of them might lead to the same place, one might be the correct trail to the Winnebago encampment; the other three would be but to a rendezvous away from the camp.

They divided. Parr, Estes, David, and Soaring Hawk followed along individual trails. Sometimes they were close together, sometimes farther apart, but they were never out of shouting distance. An eerie air of unreality lay over their pursuit. Sometimes each of them was briefly alone in the woods. Behind them came the others of the advance party, and farther behind still the main body of the pursuers.

David presently found himself well over to the right of the others. As he rode along among the trees, following a well-marked trail, he heard the call of a barred owl, thrice repeated. He listened for the answer which often came from another of its kind. The answer came, far ahead.

Soaring Hawk, however, had interpreted the calls differently. He beckoned vigorously to Parr and Estes.

In a few moments the three of them came riding toward David over the ridge. Hearing them, David turned to face them.

At that moment Parr caught sight of an Indian partly concealed behind an old oak tree against the trunk of which grew cedar brush. The Indian had his gun turned on David; he was just rising into position to fire. Parr had one terrible moment of indecision—Candace flashed across his mind's eye. Then he acted; he swiveled, brought his gun up, and fired at the hand holding the trigger of the weapon trained on David. Two shots rang out together, but David, having seen Parr's sudden movement, had instinctively thrown himself from his mount into the snow. The bullet intended for him whistled over his saddle and buried itself in a tree.

The shot roused shouts from the rest of the advance party. They came charging through the snow toward the scene. Parr rode forward to make sure David was not hurt. Soaring Hawk started after the wounded Indian, who had dropped his gun and was running through the woods. He barked at him in Winnebago.

After a few steps, the Indian stopped and turned.

Soaring Hawk shouted again.

The Indian answered.

Soaring Hawk, turning, ostentatiously threw his gun to Captain Estes, and rode toward the Indian. He stopped beside him, reached down, lifted him on to the horse before him, and rode away into the woods ahead.

"That was close," said Estes, riding up to David.

Parr was bent over the trail David had been following. "This is their main trail, all right. Some of the youngsters have been walking here. They wouldn't likely be on any but the main trail. They can't be far ahead." He smiled at David. "You just had the luck of coming up against their first outpost, Dave."

The rest of the advance party rode up, swirling around them, demanding excitedly to know what had happened. Captain Estes explained graphically, taking added opportunity to damn traders who sold firearms and firewater to the Indians. As to what they were waiting for, Estes answered when asked, it was the return of Soaring Hawk, who had presumably gone to talk to Star Walker.

Soaring Hawk was gone almost an hour.

By that time the main body of the troops under Estes' command had come up. Estes had told them that there was every hope for a peaceful discussion of their differences with the Winnebago. He warned again that every man was to keep his hands off his gun until he or Lieutenant Parr commanded otherwise. The men had built a bonfire at which to warm themselves and were circled around it when Soaring Hawk returned.

He came alone, but he announced that Star Walker was coming himself to talk with Captain Estes. They were to ride forward several hundred paces in advance of their men; the Winnebago chieftain would meet them at that place.

Captain Estes, followed by David, and flanked by Soaring Hawk, rode out at once. They were not out of sight of the men, among whom Parr had stayed, when they reached the place of the meeting.

Star Walker came presently in silence out of the woods, sitting astride his horse. He was followed by two other horsemen and several Winnebago on foot. Star Walker was a short, unimpressive man. He wore buckskin, but his face was unpainted. Those of the Indians who attended him were all in war paint and carried arms; it was an ominous sign, but the fact that the chieftain had come himself was encouraging.

He met Estes' upraised arm with a similar gesture. Sitting with their horses' heads almost touching each other, Soaring Hawk in impassive attendance as an interpreter, they began to talk.

The chieftain's story was an old one; white men had heard it often, when they stopped to listen. He did not want war, Star Walker said. His people did not want war. Would any chieftain make war with all his women, children, and aged on his back? It did not make sense. Why, then, did the white men fire upon him? Four Indians had been wounded. Four members of his band might die. And why? All because a number of his young warriors had gone to hunt deer, and, after tracking and shooting him, had had their deer taken from them by a party of white hunters from Muscoday. The Indians had protested. They had been fired upon. They had then tried to follow in a canoe they had taken from Captain Smith. Smith had fired on them as thieves. They had lost their deer. They had gone back for reinforcements, they had met a band of white men. They had exchanged words, but the white men did not want to listen. There had been shots. And now here they were, ready to fight. Did the white men want war over the stolen deer?

Estes knew very well which of the young men of Muscoday had brought in a deer. He raised up in his saddle and turned to look back. One of them was among the men around the bonfire. He shouted for Mark Buchanan to come forward.

Buchanan, a lanky woodsman, rode to where Captain Estes sat.

"Buchanan, did you and your party take a deer from the Indians two days ago?"

"Ye gonna take his word against mine, Cap?" asked the young man angrily.

"I'm asking you, Buchanan. I don't give a damn for the deer. I don't give a damn for your hide, either. I'm thinking about women and children who are apt to be massacred if this breaks out into a war. Answer me."

"God damn it, Cap, we was follerin' that deer."

"Give me that gun, Buchanan."

"It's mine."

"Give it to me, I say."

Buchanan muttered but handed up his weapon. Estes took it and ordered Buchanan back into the ranks. There was an excited, menacing murmur among the Winnebago behind Star Walker. It died away when Estes handed the weapon to David.

Star Walker spoke gutturally in his native tongue.

Soaring Hawk translated. Star Walker was pleased, he said. He had correctly understood Captain Estes' gesture. Buchanan was not worthy to carry a gun; he could not be trusted. Captain Estes believed the Indians and not the thieves who had stolen the deer. It was good. They would now talk, as one man to another, as one man who loved this Wisconsin River land to another who loved it as well, and there would be no differences between them.

It was late afternoon when they returned to Muscoday.

Much to their astonishment, they found a crowd of people gathered in the town's main street. But they had not gathered to welcome them home. They were attentive to someone else who was talking to them from his horse, where he rode, flanked by several other men and encircled by the crowd.

Seeing Estes and his men, the people cheered. They made way for them, clearing a path so that they could ride up to the other horsemen. Parr and Estes, riding ahead, recognized the party—Governor Dodge had ridden in from Madison.

"My good Nate!" cried the Governor. "And is it all over, then?"

The Governor's eyes shone with excitement or pleasure, or both; the hair that looked out from under his fur cap was whitening now, his sideburns were thinning, but his face seemed as young as ever, and there was a kind of boyish eagerness in it. The old Indian-fighter is living his youth over again, thought Parr affectionately.

"I'm not surprised that the Governor finds it difficult to keep away from the scene of trouble," said Parr, grinning. "How the blood quickens at the thought of fighting again!"

Dodge laughed heartily. "You rascal! You know I don't want trouble."

"Not even just a little?"

"None, Nate. Just the same, the petition from Muscoday brought action. Tom Burnett penned a bill reviving the militia, the Legislature passed it, and I signed it—all within half an hour. Now here I am to find out if we ought to memorialize the Secretary of War asking for a corps of dragoons."

"We've settled the trouble, Governor," said Captain Estes.

"Capital, gentlemen! I'm happy to hear it. Come tell me about it while we take supper."

David and Parr rode back toward Dodgeville that night together. The other members of their party rode ahead; the murmur of their conversation drifted pleasantly back through the penetrating, moist air. Soaring Hawk rode behind. The sky was clear. Venus shone low in the west, and the quarter moon shed a soft white glow over the landscape.

They rode in silence. They had spoken but briefly after leaving Muscoday. David had said, "I seem to be forever in your debt, Nate. You'll have to let me know how I can balance the score." Parr had answered, "I haven't done anything any other man wouldn't have done. Forgive me, Dave, but it troubles me to have you think otherwise."

Neither chill air nor moonlight witchery penetrated the sheaths of their private thoughts.

David's perplexity was boundless. Something had happened to Parr; what it was he did not know. He reflected, as he rode along, that he knew very little about Parr's private life; he saw him usually only as Parr meant to be seen; there were aspects of Parr's existence which were utterly unknown to him. How could he know what ate at Parr? It was not his part to pry into his life. Yet he could not avoid the intuitive feeling that the restraint between them had its origin somehow in something he himself had done or had not done. How could he tell if Parr would not speak?

Parr himself contemplated his momentary hesitation of the afternoon. David might have been killed in that instant of indecision. He shuddered within himself at the thought. How had he come to this, for desire of any woman, that he should have experienced even that brief, brief hesitation when a man's life was the forfeit? He scourged himself.

Soaring Hawk rode in his customary wonder at the ways of white men. He had marked and understood Parr's hesitation. Though he was able to appreciate Parr's act, he was unable to understand why Parr had not hesitated longer, if David were all that stood between him and the woman he wanted.

5. The Pales of Reason

Spring, 1846

NONE WAS MORE AWARE OF THE ALTERATION IN CANDACE THAN she herself. Nor did anyone suspect the reason. At her return from Madison, she had seemed a different person. To David it was almost as if somehow she had become once again the girl he had loved and married in Providence—she was as gay, as lighthearted, as amiable and complacent. She chattered incessantly about the ball, the Governor's speech, the kindness of the Birds, Parr's courtesy, and the people she had met. Her manner was a delight to David, the change in her filled him with profound relief, and he resolved that if so brief a holiday meant so much to her, she must go again, whenever she wished.

She was no longer listless as she had been for so long after the loss of the baby. Yet the mood of exuberance did not last. She grew quieter, and a speculative preoccupation replaced her garrulousness. David thought that she was returning to a mood of depression, but, though she was increasingly silent, she did not seem unhappy. She was occupied with thought of Parr, and the fact that she had seen and heard nothing of him. She did not know what to expect of him, but she hoped he would call. What had happened between them had brought about a change in her view of Parr, as well as in her outlook; Mineral Point now seemed easily endurable, her dormant ambitions and hopes had been given new life, and Mineral Point no longer seemed an anchor in an alien sea.

She thought often of Parr. He seemed so dignified, almost aloof, when he had bidden her good-night after the ball. Perhaps his feelings had been hurt at her abrupt leavetaking? But no, it could not be. It was far more likely that she had disappointed him in some other way. She could not imagine how. There was something inscrutable about Parr which she could not penetrate. In this, he was profoundly different from David, whose every thought was plain on his honest face. She knew Parr existed in a world of his own, hedged round by barriers against the outside world. She knew intuitively, too, that Parr's kiss had not been the act of an impulsive moment.

But as day followed day, and week succeeded week, she grew more silent and sometimes a little irritable. To all David's suggestions that she take another holiday, she responded with a flat negative, but he was relieved when, in response to a tentative proposal that she go to visit her mother in Providence, she replied, "I can never go back there, David," with all the intensity of which she was capable. She felt occasional remorse because David was so concerned about her; in all her contemplation of Parr, she was aware of no diminution of her love for David, and little change in her attitude toward him; she never thought of any future—even one to which Parr might lead the way—without David, projecting all three of them into a fantasy only tenuously attached to reality.

Late in the afternoon of a windy March day, Parr dismounted at the Mansion House and went in. Colonel Abner Nichols was just crossing to the tap-room.

"Can you put me up for the night, Nichols?" asked Parr.

"Reckon so. Where've you been? I haven't seen you around for a spell. Come along in and have a drink."

Parr walked into the tap-room. He had no appetite for liquor, but he was not inclined to refuse Nichols' invitation. Except for a table at which four old men sat playing at some game, they were alone in the tap-room; the players were too absorbed to notice them. Nichols went around behind the bar. What would Parr have?

"Oh, a little whiskey."

They would have one together, said Nichols. He poured the amber fluid from a large clay jug; the liquor gleamed and shone in the half-light of the tap-room. Outside, the wind lashed a tree beyond the window; it made a rattling sound. Where had he been? Nichols asked again, shoving his glass toward Parr.

Parr told him. He had been journeying here and there in the Territory, wherever the sodden roads would permit, talking to people about the impending election at which they were to vote on the question of statehood. Nichols guessed that Parr had been acting on Dodge's behalf. Parr estimated that the total vote would be at least three to one in favor of statehood.

Nichols leaned on the bar and listened. He thought but did not say that there was no need for chasing all around the Territory to discover the sentiment of the people; one had only to be the proprietor of a hostelry like the Mansion House to know what people were talking about. When Parr finished, he opined that he could pass on some news Parr very likely did not know. Parr raised his eyebrows. Nichols leaned closer and said confidentially that President Polk had ordered troops into some of the Mexican lands.

Parr smiled. "Not Mexican, Nichols. That's the area between the rivers—the Nueces and Rio Grande—that's been under dispute. What do you hear about Slidell?"

"Failed," said Nichols succinctly. Did Parr think the Mexicans would stand for that?

Parr did not think so. It would be only a matter of time before hostilities began between the two countries.

And what of the troop levy in case of war? Nichols wanted to know.

"The Governor's said no draft would be levied against any of the territories," answered Parr. "But there's nothing to prevent us from enlisting with the volunteers of neighboring states. Amasa Cobb is joining with Illinois volunteers. I heard that an entire company's forming near the Illinois line—Jim Collins is the captain."

"Will you go, Parr?" asked Nichols bluntly.

"I believe I may."

Nichols left him to wait on other customers who came into the tap-room from the street door. Parr lingered over his whiskey. He had drunk but little of it; it lay warmly inside, and its pungence rose to his nostrils from the glass he cradled in one hand. He was thinking of the impending Mexican war, trying to guess how long it might last—certainly not more than a year, he was confident—trying to make a decision about his participation. He felt under no obligation to go, and even the Governor was of two minds about his going—he wanted him both to go and to stay, the former because he, himself, if he had been younger, would have enjoyed the fighting again, the latter because Parr was of service in the countless little things too many men hesitated to undertake lest it demean them.

The thought of being too long away from the Wisconsin Territory was not pleasing to him. For one thing, with Wisconsin now moving so rapidly toward statehood, it behooved him to be on hand when major changes came into being; if he wanted to better his position, he could not do so from so great a distance as the Mexican border. For another, there was Candace.

Nichols came back.

And what was the news of the Point? asked Parr, reminding Nichols that he had not been in the village for two months.

Nichols shrugged. The town was growing as fast as ever, even though it had lost its newspaper. Though the *Miners Free Press* had suspended, the word was that a new paper, the *Mineral Point Tribune*, was soon to start up. Nichols offered him another drink with the gesture of reaching for the jug, but Parr shook his head and revealed that he still had whiskey in his glass. Nichols poured himself another.

A boy stuck his head into the room and called, "Ab Nichols is wanted."

Nichols went without comment.

Parr returned in his thoughts to Candace. He had contemplated her often during his wanderings through the Territory. With each day that separated him from the night of the ball at the Madison Hotel, he struggled to adjust his perspective. He was prey to all the attitudes from which he thought he had divorced himself—fairmindedness, loyalty to his principles, the ethics even of seeing David and Candace while he considered plans to make Candace his own. He had pursued his solitary way from one community to another, turning Candace over and over in his mind, trying to fit her into his plans and, whenever that did not seem possible, to alter his plans so that she might be included. He had tried to look at himself from every perspective. It did not matter, in the end, what David might think. But what would the Governor have to say?

No matter how he tried, he could not reconcile his ambitions with Candace in any plan which included Dodge. The Governor was a rough man, but a fair one. Whatever question there might have been about the old man's treatment of the Winnebago in seizing their lead mines two decades before, there was no question about his sincerity in anything he undertook. It was inconceivable that he would look with favor upon Parr's invasion of another man's household, or indeed any liaison which involved a reflection upon his character. Parr might more readily kill another man with impunity than rob him of his wife. However rough the Territory was, it nevertheless sustained its own code, and Parr was well aware of it. He was loath to retreat on either course, though in the back of his mind lurked an ever-present belief that ultimately he must surrender either Candace or the career toward which he had so skillfully impelled himself.

The tap-room was now filling up. Miners were coming from the shafts and stopping to have a drink or a game before going home, while others were stopping for supper and to spend the better part of the night gambling and enjoying themselves. A fiddler had come in from the street, and sat in one corner playing none too skillfully a series of sentimental strains. Miners gathered around the roulette wheel and lined the bar. Parr put down his glass and sauntered into the spacious dining-room.

The table had been set and several miners were already at it. Four passengers from the stage which had just arrived came in and took places, while the driver went on through into the tap-room, loudly cursing the muddy roads over which he was obliged to travel.

Parr sat down by himself at one end of the table.

One of the passengers from the stage detached himself from the party and came over to sit beside Parr—a tall, portly man with a domelike brow from which his dark hair was brushed back from ear to ear. His wide mouth, pursed of lip, was surmounted by an impressively large nose.

"If I'm not mistaken," he said suavely, "I have the privilege of addressing one of Henry Dodge's errand boys."

Parr looked up angrily. At sight of the face leaning toward him, his anger cooled and vanished; caution took its place. The ex-Governor of the Territory likewise had powerful friends in

Washington as well as in Madison; indeed, had he not named the capital city in honor of either Dolly Madison or the President, currying favor in Washington?

"Mr. Doty," he said. "You honor me."

"I hear reports of you everywhere, Parr," said Doty. "That is to say—you've been everywhere."

Parr smiled. "Greatly exaggerated, I have no doubt."

"As to that, I don't know."

"But you, sir—aren't you lost in this part of the Territory?"

Doty smiled. "I consider it necessary to invade the stronghold of my opposition from time to time."

"Actually, it's you who are now in opposition," interrupted Parr.

"Though, of course," continued Doty, ignoring Parr's thrust, "no area is out of my ken. I've been traveling Wisconsin for years, as you should know." His eyes flickered back to Parr, scrutinizing him frankly. "But you, my dear fellow—what brought you north and west last month? Even into Green Bay?"

Parr laughed. However irascible and impatient, however impetuous and dictatorial James Doty had been as Governor, there was no disliking him. His eyes smiled even when he looked deep, his face, despite its largeness, had a pixyish expression which was almost ludicrous on so large a body, and yet was not without dignity. "You're well informed, Mr. Doty."

"I believe it wise to be informed. I suppose you were running some errand for Henry. But, stay—let me guess. He sent you about to find out whether it would be safe for him to declare in favor of statehood? Ah, I have hit it." He chuckled.

"The Governor has always been for statehood, Mr. Doty."

"Your memory fails you, Parr. He was against it as long as I was Governor and he was in opposition. I need hardly remind you that statehood was my idea, and that, perhaps because of its origin, it was defeated by your mining gentry each time it was proposed to the electorate." He sighed. "But now that it comes as Henry's idea, no doubt the miners are all for it."

"Not quite. But statehood will win. And what are your plans, sir?"

"I have none at the moment. In good time I expect to stand for Congress from my District. I tell you this because no power on earth can prevent my election. I don't have to contend with your miners." He rose. "Pardon me, I must rejoin my party. My compliments to the Governor, next time you see him."

"Permit me to have something to drink sent you and your party, sir."

Doty showed his surprise. "Well, thank you, Parr."

"And do me the honor to bear in mind, sir, that I am no one's errand boy but Nathaniel Parr's."

Doty smiled, nodded, and was gone.

Parr was not displeased. Doty would remember him as far more than the Governor's "errand boy," an appellation he despised, though he recognized that it was not entirely unjust. It was as well to be somewhat less than openly antagonistic to men of Doty's power, lest the pendulum of fickle popular favor swing away from the Governor and back to Doty and the men around him. It represented no disloyalty to the Governor to hold a little of the sunlight around Doty.

Seeing Nichols moving toward the tap-room, he called him over and ordered whiskey sent to Doty and his party. He waited for Doty's nod of acknowledgment and bowed, smiling. Then he turned to his own meal.

An hour later he walked leisurely from the Mansion House. The Pengellen house looked phantasmal in the deeper dusk on the edge of night. Mineral Point encroached upon it from both west and north, and in time the house would be surrounded. As he walked up the slope toward it, he saw that a light burned only in the living-room. Perhaps David and Candace sat there.

As he stood before the door, he felt an impulse to go silently away, as if from danger. He scorned it and tapped smartly on the panel.

The lamplight moved from the living-room toward the hall, down the hall to the door. He saw it, distorted, through the panes beside the door, though, because of the nature of the glass in the panes, he could not make out who carried it.

The door opened. Candace stood there, holding the lamp high.

"I thought it must be you, Nate," she said. "No one else ever comes to the front door. Do come in."

He stepped into the hall, closing the door.

"You've been away a long time," she went on, as she led the way back to the living-room. "We've missed you."

"And I've missed you, Candace."

She turned and faced him. "Have you, Nate?"

His eyes fixed upon hers, held there. "You should know I have, Candace. I had to travel through the Territory. There wasn't a day I didn't think of you."

"Oh, Nate!" she cried. "And not a word!"

Her cry was deprecatingly happy.

He moved forward with mounting confidence. She had been expecting some word from him, a visit, a letter. "I wouldn't have troubled you now, Candace," he said, "but I thought perhaps I had taken an unforgivable liberty . . ."

She brushed this aside with a gesture of a clenched fist.

"But then, as days and weeks passed, and I went from one town to another, thinking of you, thinking of how beautiful you looked in that white dress, with the pearls in your hair, and of how well we danced together, and of that last wonderful moment, when I held you in my arms and knew the bitterness of realizing that you were not mine, but another's . . ."

"Oh, Nate—please." She was upset.

"I don't mean to distress you."

She shook her head, saying nothing.

He touched her hands; her fingers tightened in his.

"Where's David?" he asked.

"Gone to work a while in the store."

"He shouldn't have left you alone, Candace."

"It doesn't matter—I'm used to it now."

His hands left her fingers, followed up her arms to her shoulders. Then she was in his arms, mouth to mouth, with her hands pushing against him and her mouth straining to his. They held together for a long moment. Then she broke away and stepped back.

"David . . . David," she murmured.

He sat down and she, seeing, took a chair opposite him. She was trembling, he saw. He was aware of the wild leaping of his own pulse. It was a rash thing to have done, to have kissed her when at any moment David might walk in. But no one had seen; the house was not yet close enough to its neighbors to permit of anyone's seeing, and David was not here.

"There was no word from you, Nate," she said with some strain in her voice, "no one had seen you. We wondered what had happened to you."

"I didn't think anyone would trouble over my whereabouts. I could easily have written to you—to both of you." He shrugged. "It wasn't for the lack of thinking of you. I thought so often of that night . . ."

She wanted to say, "I, too," but she forebore, thinking of David and the loyalty she had for him.

Seen in this dim yellow lamplight, wearing clothes of great plainness and herself seeming utterly plain, there was a singular beauty about Candace, not only in her eyes fixed so intently upon him, or on the lips which invited him, but in her entire attitude. But instinct armed him against any further advance.

"Candace," he said thoughtfully, "I think we have a good many things in common." He groped blindly, haltingly. "I think there are things both of us expect from life, but neither of us has yet found them."

"Yes," she whispered, thinking that he spoke her own thoughts.

"I think neither of us is content with what we have, each of us wants more," he went on. "I suppose there are a lot of people like us in the world, but at this moment, in this place, there are only the two of us . . ."

At the store, David completed his work. Trelawny had already gone. David went around and put out the lamps, one by one. Then he put on his coat, went out, and locked the door. He stood there for a moment, deliberating about going down to the Mansion House for a while; he did not want to go home immediately, though he knew Candace was alone and expected him. He listened to the thin sawing of someone's fiddle, to singing and shouting at the games in the Mansion House; he was restless, and tonight the inns drew him. But he turned away and began to walk up High Street.

The board walk had been extended well up the slope, for buildings now rose on both sides of the street along the road to Platteville. The familiar smell of freshly sawed lumber lay in the air. Would Mineral Point ever be without it? he wondered. The expansion of the village was so steady that there was hardly a day in season when a new building of some kind was not begun. And no place of business was ever vacated but that another merchant or professional man was not ready to take possession. The expansion of Mineral Point gave him a sense of well-being, even though the shippers were now receiving slightly less for lead. But the change was infinitesimal; the price had decreased less than ten cents per hundred pounds. In the year past the

Point shippers had sent out millions of pounds; Trelawny had shown him estimates of the region's production for 1845 which went above fifty million pounds and represented only the lead shipped from Mississippi ports, and did not take into account lead sent out of lake ports. However uncertain the lead market might be at the moment, there was bound to be a rising demand for it if hostilities commenced between the United States and Mexico.

Away from the row of houses the wind caught him more easily. It blew out of the south and southwest, warming, aromatic, stirring, filled with the pungence of earth opening again, the smell of thaw and mud, of sap flowing and the sweetness of early blossoms. As he was about to turn off High Street, he heard a woman singing. He stood listening. *Westryn Wind*. Only Tamson would be singing it. He turned impulsively and walked along the ridge diagonally back toward Shake-Rag Street.

He found her high on the ridge. She was walking along the trunk of a fallen tree.

"What are you doing here at this hour, Tamson?" he asked.

"I might ask you that same question, David. I know Aunt Marget's home; so Candace must be alone, too. But I'd know what you'd say—you've been working, you were on your way home; then you heard me singing here, and you couldn't resist the song—is that it?"

He laughed. "You've not answered my question."

"And you've not answered mine," she retorted. "But since it's true as I said it, you needn't. As for me, I got tired reading, I couldn't sleep so early; so I walked out."

"I don't know that it's a good idea—walking way up here, apart from town—and some of the miners drinking the way they do."

"I can take care of myself, David." She jumped off the tree and stood leaning back against it. "Why aren't you on the way home, David?"

"I just don't feel like going home. Spring fever, maybe. For a while I thought I'd go down and mix with the men at the Mansion House. Nichols always offers good entertainment."

"And a good table—either to feed at or lose money at."

He raised himself to the bole and sat down. She reached for his hand to help her climb up beside him.

"Besides," he went on, "it's such a fine night . . ."

"Is it Candace again?" she asked bluntly.

"You seem to know." He shook his head. "But, no—I can't say it is. Ever since that Madison visit, Candace has been different somehow. Sometimes just like her old self. But just the same, there's something. I'm afraid I've failed her, somehow; I don't know how. We have money and we're making more all the time; all you have to do for money in Point is work for it; the more you work, the more you make. It can't be money—I've failed somewhere else."

She looked at him in baffled helplessness. "Why is it always *you* who have failed?" she cried passionately. "Why it is always *you* who feel guilty?"

He gazed at her in astonishment. "You know how hard Candace has tried," he said reproachfully. "But then, Tamson, perhaps you're partial."

"Perhaps." She frowned. "But you're partial, too. I wouldn't know how else a man can act if it isn't enough for him to work as hard as he can. And you haven't begrudged Candace anything."

"There are a lot of ways in which a man can fail a woman, Tamson."

Tamson protested. "But, David, if a woman loves a man, I'd think she'd try to accustom herself to the way he lives."

He chuckled. "Tamson, love isn't as simple as that. You learn about it as you grow."

"I know now."

"I wonder."

"I know enough to ask myself often—many times—whether Candace loves you—or only herself."

"You aren't being fair, Tamson."

She was silent for a long time. "I thought you might think so. But I believe I'm fair. I do know how hard Candace has tried. I know she's sincere—but it's always like she's holding something back—as if she tried only because she counted on getting away."

She ceased talking abruptly. By the quizzical, curious look on his face, she recognized that he doubted her. She was hurt; she withdrew into herself. Then she slipped off the trunk of the tree.

"I've got to get back home. Aunt Marget'll wonder what became of me."

He fell into step at her side.

"Do you walk out this way, often, Tamson?" he asked quietly.

"When I don't care to read, yes. I like it outside. I always did. When I was a little girl, I used to go off toward the moors away from Tintagel or down to the sea. I've been way up and around all the woods and hills here already."

He marveled that he knew so little of her doings. But he had been too busy at the store, and with the lead. The thought made him uneasy. If he knew so little of Tamson, perhaps he knew too little as well about Candace. Perhaps he owed it to her to study her needs with more care.

They came to the little house where Tamson lived. She bade him good-night and slipped inside. The house was dark. Aunt Marget was either sitting in darkness or already in bed. It was mid-evening, nine o'clock or later. He quickened his steps toward home.

Jim Casthew entered the store on David's heels.

"Hello, Casthew," David greeted him, wondering what the

miner had come about so early in the morning. Certainly no complaint this time; he had mended his ways and was now more prosperous than many of the miners who still worked at a salary of four dollars a day. Casthew had bought his own land years before, and he had recently begun to mine this, too.

"Time o' day t' 'ee," replied Casthew, a friendly smile on his chubby face.

"What can we do for you today, Casthew?"

"I'll tell 'ee," said the miner gravely. He sat down on a box and began to talk. He had been thinking matters over in the past few weeks and had decided to sell out his holdings and go elsewhere. West, perhaps. He had made a good deal of money now, his health was no longer what it should be, his wife was failing too. His newest shaft showed a good vein of galenite. Did Trelawny & Pengellen want to buy?

"I'll have to ask Mr. Trelawny. Just wait a minute."

He walked to the back of the store where Trelawny sat at his desk.

"Jim Casthew's up front. He's been getting nervous about the government's pending sale of the lead mines, and wants to sell out. Are we interested?"

"Have you had a look at the vein?"

"No."

"Well, it might be worth buying. Just go along with him, will you, Dave, and take a look at what he's offering us."

David walked back to where Casthew stood waiting, brushing at his fringe of red beard. He took his hat and put on his coat, seeing which, Casthew came with alacrity, realizing that David meant to look at the mine, and explained that it was on the far ridge, which meant that it was not on the near slope at Shake-Rag, but beyond, over half a mile from the store.

Casthew talked animatedly in his heavy Cornish speech while they walked, telling David how he had come to dig for lead at this place. He had no use for divining rods, but he did believe that the masonic weed was a good indicator of lead. Besides, he had discovered some float mineral near the surface in this place, and the slope had the look of good lead ground; so he had dug the new shaft, and had had to go down only fifty feet before striking a most promising vein. He had taken out some of the lead. It was a good quality. He had begun to tunnel in both directions, and his man, Pike, was down working now. But the vein was still new, and most of the ore remained to be taken out.

They arrived presently at the mine. It had the appearance, as did all the mines, of an ordinary well shaft, with an opening almost five feet in diameter. A windlass, fixed upon posts set on either side of the opening, supported the rope which raised and lowered the miners as well as the ore buckets. Two men were busy at the mouth of the mine, and a wagon stood nearby for the load of the galena to be sent to the smelters.

David knew both the men and greeted them.

"I dug et en the haard time, en winter," explained Casthew. "I'll go on down."

He took a candle from his pocket, lit it with a locofoco match, and, holding it in one hand, stepped into the sling at the end of the rope; the two men, one at each handle of the windlass, let him down slowly. David stood peering down. Some timbers were laid in against the soft soil immediately below the mouth of the shaft, but the walls were not yet fully timbered. This would be a point to count in any consideration of price, and Casthew was likely to haggle, however erratic he might be in wanting to dispose of his property at a time when the price of lead was sure to advance.

He followed Casthew down the shaft, marking the depth of soil, the stratification of the rock, and came finally to the lead-bearing fracture. He saw by the light of a candle, set in a gob of fire clay and affixed to the wall, that considerable progress had been made in the construction of a tunnel two ways from the bottom of the shaft. The man, Pike, clad in the customary clothing of the miners—heavy shoes, felt hats, hickory shirts, jackets, and bedtick overalls—was busy beside a wheelbarrow down one end of the tunnel. Casthew led the way toward him, holding his candle high and talking volubly, pointing out the virtues of the vein. Both of them got out of the way when Pike, with a full ore bucket on his wheelbarrow, went past them to the foot of the shaft.

Casthew had reached the end of the tunnel. He declared that the vein would reach to the edge of his property, and past it. Moreover, the breadth of the vein had not been reached on either side of the shaft.

They turned to walk back along the tunnel to the other end.

At this moment, there was a sudden cry from Pike. He fell back, but too late to avoid being struck by a falling piece of ore. Then, with a horrible crushing and rushing sound, the ore bucket came down upon the wheelbarrow, smashing it, followed by a cascade of earth, which poured out of the shaft and into the tunnel.

After a moment of stunned astonishment, Casthew ran forward, crying, "Cave-in, Mr. Pengellen!"

David paused long enough to snuff out the candle by which Pike had been working. A second candle, which had burned near the foot of the shaft, had been put out by the falling earth. Casthew's alone remained lit. He ran forward to where Casthew lamented, picking up Pike's shovel on the way.

"Put your candle up till we see how Pike is," said David. "If he's all right, we'd better start digging."

Casthew obediently stuck his candle to the rock wall. Both bent over Pike, who had reeled to the floor of the tunnel after receiving the blow which had felled him. But he was not grievously wounded; though unconscious, he would soon be able to lend a hand at the digging. They seized him and dragged him back along the tunnel, where they set him up against one of the rock pillars which had been left to support the roof.

There was only one shovel, but there was also a pick. Casthew took the pick, and the two of them set to work. They dug the earth out of the shaft and threw it into the tunnel behind them. There was no way of knowing how extensive the collapse of the shaft was; the rock ceiling held, the considerable portion of untimbered earth had undoubtedly given way, the shaft was probably filled, and the entrance overhead fallen in.

"I'll take en shovel," said Casthew, seizing it.

David took the pick, recognizing that Casthew could accomplish more with the shovel than he.

"They'll be gittin' us," said Casthew.

David was not so confident.

They dug furiously. Behind them, Pike came to, groaning. He got to his feet unsteadily and joined them. They worked in silent suspense.

In an hour they had cleared the bottom of the shaft and dug out part of the shaft up as far as they could reach. Farther they could not go, for the earth was packed like moulding clay into the shaft.

"We'd better put out the candle," said David. "No use taking up the oxygen with it. We can wait just as well in the dark."

"They'll be gittin' us," said Casthew stubbornly, desperately eager to believe it.

Strangely, David was not afraid. His first alarm had passed. It did not seem possible for them to die in so small a mine, but, of course, it was. There was nothing to prevent its taking place except the diligence of those who would be trying to reach them from above. The alarm would have sounded in the Point by this time. But if anything should happen, he thought, what would become of Candace? And, far back on the perimeter of his consciousness, growing every moment in magnitude, an echo of this thought asked: And Tamson?

Word of the accident at Casthew's shaft spread through Mineral Point like the wind. Candace was one of the last to hear it. Because of the isolation of the house as well as because of David's being caught in the mine, she had not learned at once. She heard it only because Mrs. Trelawny thought of telling her and ran over.

She could not credit Mrs. Trelawny's grim words. "But what would David be doing in the mine?" she cried, agitated.

"They were thinking of buying the mine," explained Mrs. Trelawny. "Are you comin' or not? They've started digging."

Candace had already put on a muslin cape. She snatched her hat and ran from the house, not stopping to lock the door. The two women went down the near slope directly to Shake-Rag Street and hurried across, joining the throng who were on the way to the scene of the accident.

A crowd of people had already gathered at the pit where once the shaft had stood. Many miners were digging frantically at the earth there, and others were widening the pit. Candace pushed through to the edge of the crowd, where she found herself among a group of the most concerned spectators—the wives of Casthew and Pike, Trelawny, and Tamson. Seeing Candace, Trelawny came over at once to reassure her.

"Don't you fret, Mrs. Pengellen. They'll have him out."

She stared at the place where David was buried.

At this moment a giant of a man strode into the digging group. Candace recognized him as a Platteville miner named Hausmann. Despite the order which prevailed at the scene, he took charge instantly, shouting questions. Was it a well tunnelled mine? If not, why were they digging so frantically? Didn't they know the air would be exhausted before they could get down?

"Find a pipe," he shouted. "Bring it here. A long one!"

A score of miners who had been standing helplessly by rushed off at once in search of a pipe. So rapidly had the miners worked, that already they had reached a depth of more than ten feet from the level of the surrounding terrain, and they were now at work in the clay of the shaft. This was painstaking work, for the clay packed almost as quickly as it was loosened; it needed only to fall back from shovel or pick to pack anew. The men persevered, to the shouts of encouragement from the crowd, which had backed away respectfully from the little group where Candace stood, leaving the six of them isolated.

Two of the miners pushed their way through the crowd with a long pipe. Hausmann immediately directed that it be pushed through the clay down the shaft so that the trapped men could get air while the digging proceeded.

The pipe was set up. Many hands sought to turn and push it down. The distance now could not be much more than twenty feet, estimated Hausmann, and for half that distance the pipe went down by the sheer weight of those who pushed it. Thereafter it required additional force. The energetic Hausmann backed a wagon up beside the pipe and climbed up, carrying a heavy sledge-hammer. But even then he could not quite reach the top of the pipe. Two of the miners then mounted the wagon, braced themselves, and permitted Hausmann to stand on their shoulders. From this height, Hausmann drove the pipe down steadily with the help of the hands that pushed at it.

It went down reluctantly. Men waited with long rods to free the pipe of any soil adhering to the inside of it. Hausmann descended to the wagon, then to the ground, pounding lustily, with a savage pleasure plain on his heavy, moustached face, as if he were personally vanquishing death. Other miners, returned with further lengths of pipe, stood waiting; around Hausmann, digging continued.

Candace tore her gaze almost guiltily from the diggers. She had been in an agony of fear for David, when the thought of Parr intruded. She bit her lip, thrusting Parr from her mind. On one side of her, the wives of Pike and Casthew were weeping into their aprons; they had evidently come running from their houses without coats, but the sun was bright and the wind warm. On the other side of her stood Trelawny, and, past him, Tamson. Her glance fell upon Tamson's clenched fists, held rigidly at her side. Her eyes flickered to her face; it was tensely expressionless. Tamson stared straight before her, her gaze never once leaving the diggers. It seemed to Candace that Tamson repressed a disturbed fear more profound than her own. She looked away.

There was a sudden shout from Hausmann. "She's through, boys!"

Instantly the men with the rods sprang into action. They plunged the rods down the pipe. But there was not much clay in the pipe; such clay as had entered the lower end of the pipe had quickly packed, blunting the drive end, but allowing most of the pipe to stay open. The rods were withdrawn, and Hausmann stepped forward, put his lips to the hammered end of the pipe, and shouted. Then he put his ear to the pipe and waited. He smiled.

"They're all right," he called out.

Then he grabbed a shovel from one of the miners and began to dig.

Trelawny touched Candace's arm. "This'll take quite a while, Mrs. Pengellen. I think it'd be better if we went back to the store."

"How long?"

"At least three hours, I'd guess. They'll have to timber it in as they go now. When they come to rock, it'll go faster, but not till then. If you want to come back, we can have one of the miners come to the store and let us know just about when they reach them."

She nodded and turned. She met Tamson's eyes. Tamson looked relieved now, with the tension drawing from her face, which was less a mask than it had been during the time of uncertainty. Candace went down the slope with Mrs. Trelawny. Tamson waited for Trelawny, who went to speak to one of the miners.

Though Mrs. Trelawny went home from the store, Candace remained. She sat down to Trelawny's desk, to which he solicitously directed her. There her tension broke; she began to weep quietly. Almost immediately Tamson was at her side, one hand on her shoulder.

"Don't cry, Candace," she murmured. "David's all right."

Candace's sobs subsided. She looked up. "And you—are you glad, too?"

"Of course. David's my best friend here," said Tamson simply.

Their eyes met, Candace's probing, Tamson's frank but inscrutable.

"Yes, yes," said Candace. And it was true—how could it be otherwise? Though she was convinced that Tamson's feeling for David was far more than just friendship, it did not occur to her that David might even have noticed it, much less reciprocated it in any way.

The moment ended. Tamson went back to help Trelawny. Candace sat quietly watching. Away from the mine, she thought more readily of Parr. She understood, ever since his visit of the other night, that Parr loved her. He had not said so in as many words, but other words and actions had spoken more plainly. The excitement of the discovery, the appeal to her vanity, had been mitigated by a sober realization that the undeniable attraction she felt for Parr was not the same as the love she bore David.

The store was filling with customers now. It was the middle of the morning, and there were not only women come down from the mine, but also the usual shoppers. Both Trelawny and Tamson were kept busy. Watching Tamson, Candace envied her ability to laugh and joke with the customers, men as well as women. Now and then one of the women, catching sight of Candace, came back to offer words of comfort, which had the unhappy effect of making her feel that she did not merit them. She rose finally and said she must go back to the house, telling Trelawny to send up any message when it came, and she would then return to the mine at once.

It was not three hours, but five, before the message came.

She returned to the mine immediately. Tamson and Trelawny were already there. Mrs. Casthew and Mrs. Pike welcomed her with glances which plainly showed their kinship with her in this accident. She met Tamson's confident smile with one of her own.

The pipe was just being removed from the shaft. A windlass had already been set up, and the last of the clay was being brought up in ore buckets. The crowd around the mouth of the shaft had swollen again. Men and women stirred restlessly on all sides, up the slope and down, standing uncovered in the sun, which, at this hour of the afternoon, was unseasonably hot. The crowd was no longer tense and watchful, but a social gathering. On all sides conversation rose and fell.

The last of the diggers came up in the bucket, and the bucket was detached.

In a little while the first of the men came up. It was Pike. He was grinning happily. A little blood showed on his temple. At his appearance, the crowd set up a tumultuous cheer and, as he stepped out of the sling to solid ground, his wife ran forward and threw herself upon him with such violence as almost to upset him. The crowd cheered anew.

Candace felt her pulse quicken as the rope went down again.

But it was Casthew who came up next, somewhat apologetically, crying out that David had made him go second, he should have come last, being the owner, protesting until he in turn was overwhelmed by his wife and drowned out by the roar of the crowd.

The rope went down for the last time.

David came up almost as unruffled as he had gone down. Though she had resolved not to make a spectacle of herself, Candace ran to David. He caught her in his arms and kissed her.

"Oh, David!" she cried. "I was so afraid. Don't you ever go down again."

He smiled. As he started to walk toward Trelawny, he made a sign to indicate that the mine was all right for their purchase. Then he saw Tamson. He turned, with Candace on his arm, and offered his other arm to Tamson. The three of them moved down the slope with the dispersing crowd. Trelawny walked over toward Casthew, resolved to lose no time in buying his mine.

High up on the slope, crowning the ridge, Parr and Soaring Hawk had witnessed the rescue. They had been riding in from Dodgeville and had been attracted by the crowd's roar at sight of Pike. Coming to the top of the ridge, they had halted, looking down the slope at the concourse of people there. It took but a few moments to ascertain what went on. Soaring Hawk saw Candace and Tamson first, since they stood apart, beside the other women, between the open shaft and the encircling crowd. He grunted. Parr followed the direction of his gaze. They were not so widely separated as to make recognition difficult.

He saw Casthew brought up, and then David, and he watched with mixed feelings how Candace ran to David. Even from this place apart, he thought of himself as an interloper. A shudder of distaste ran through him. He watched the crowd disperse. Then he rode after them, silent and thoughtful.

Soaring Hawk rose before the sun and went out to care for his roan stallion. The horse whinnied familiarly, switching his tail. A kind of communication existed between them. The horse responded to the Winnebago's touch with easy precision, and accepted Soaring Hawk's ministrations with pleasure. Nearby, Parr's horse waited expectantly.

The April morning was a choir of birdsong responding to the glow of dawn, at first a grey, then almost white, then pink and copper, as clouds broke away and the sun shone through. In Dodgeville a few roosters crowed, the dogs barked, cattle lowed, and the stirring of the day's life in the village began again.

Parr came out, his dark eyes flickering from the horses to the Indian. "It seems foolish for you to ride along, Hawk."

Soaring Hawk said he had made up his mind to ride as far as Galena. If Parr must go to war, he could go that far with him. He would go all the way, but he knew very well that Indians were not welcomed in the White Father's army, save as scouts in familiar territory. And where was Mexico? He did not even know.

"We can get breakfast at Nichols'," said Parr, mounting. "But first I want to stop at the Governor's farm."

They started away, Parr riding ahead, as usual, Soaring Hawk close behind. The morning was fragrant with spring. The smell of opened earth, of growing things, of blade and leaf, of catkins powdering the air with pollen, rode the gentle southeast wind. Crows flew in long files over the land, cawing, and small flocks of passenger pigeons flew northward, the early morning sunlight touching their breasts and making a wonderful show of colors there.

They rode the few miles to Dodge's farm in silence. The house lay in a little grove of trees not far off the road. Toby, one of the former slaves of the Governor's household, was up and about in the yard. He started over toward Parr and Soaring Hawk until he recognized Parr and heard the door of the house open and close where Governor Dodge himself came out toward Parr. The Governor was in trousers, shirt-sleeves, and slippers, with his prized bowie-knife in his belt.

Parr dismounted. "Good morning, Governor. I took the liberty of stopping to say good-bye."

"You're going then, Nathaniel? I could wish you weren't, but I'll not try to dissuade you. You've served me far better than many another—and more—you've been not only a supporter, but a friend."

He had come up to Parr while he was talking. Now he clasped his right hand in his and rested his left paternally on Parr's shoulder, his keen eyes searching the younger man's face. The wind passed gently through his white hair.

"Thank you, Governor."

"I shall hope to see you as soon as you're back, Nathaniel. Surely it won't be more than a year?"

Parr shrugged. "Who can say?"

"The troops are under General Taylor—Zachary Taylor. I knew him well when he was at Fort Crawford. I could give you a letter to him—but," he laughed, "with your penchant for getting around, perhaps you knew him."

"I knew him," said Parr.

"Good luck, Nathaniel. My best wishes go with you."

The pressure of his hand relaxed. He stepped back. Parr thanked him soberly and mounted his horse. With a wave of his hand, he rode out of the yard. The Governor seemed to him at this moment rather more of a father than his foster-father had been.

They rode along the road to Mineral Point. The sun was higher now; its warmth was beginning to be felt. The early morning birdsong had changed its character as the hosts of migrant birds added their voices. Bees hummed in the blossoming catkins of alder and willow trees.

A mile from the Governor's home, Soaring Hawk began to speak. There was a grievance in his voice. Though he did not ask the direct question, in his way, there was nevertheless in his complaint the wonder about what need impelled Parr to go to enlist from Illinois. The Wisconsin Territory did not need to send troops, only the states. There was no obligation upon Parr to go.

Parr agreed.

The Winnebago went on. Perhaps this country, Mexico, was so great that Parr feared for the defeat of the White Father in Washington?

"No," said Parr, "Mexico's a small country. Undeveloped."

Ah, replied Soaring Hawk, stung by the well-known word so often applied to his people's lands, stolen by invading settlers, then the Mexicans were like the Indians. Perhaps the White Father and his soldiers had taken their lands, too?

Parr chuckled. How readily every problem reduced itself to Soaring Hawk's terms, he thought. Yet it could not be denied that there was a hard core of truth in the Winnebago's understanding of American progress. And Soaring Hawk's curiosity was understandable, for he knew better than anyone that Parr was not in the habit of taking ill-considered action at any time.

He answered Soaring Hawk briefly, conceding that the trouble was about land. He knew this would set the Indian off in a triumphant expression of his contempt for the lust and greed of the palefaces. But Parr did not listen to it. He was lost in thought of his impending enlistment. He was not anxious to go. Indeed, every instinct impelled him to stay. All his friends and many of his acquaintances had urged him to abandon his plan to enlist, even the Governor having suggested within the past week that, in view of Washington's attitude about territorial enlistments, he ought not to be precipitate.

But now he was going, in spite of all the reasons he could adduce for staying, because it seemed to him that his reasons for going were stronger, though they were but two—the additional benefits which might accrue to him as a veteran of a war in his search for preferment in political office, either appointive or elective, in the coming state of Wisconsin, and the flight from the conflict which raged within him between his desire for Candace and his compelling ambition to achieve an eminence among his fellow men, an eminence he was convinced obscurely was his right and obligation to himself to achieve.

They began the descent into Mineral Point. Soaring Hawk lapsed into an aggrieved silence. Parr had not yet answered him. In the devious ways of white men, he had told him nothing.

They dismounted at the Mansion House, and moved among miners on their way to work, travelers waiting upon the stage, speculators and their sycophants. Breakfast was being served inside in the large dining-room, and Abner Nichols himself was passing among his guests.

"I guess the election suited you all right, Parr, eh?" said Nichols, coming over to where Parr and Soaring Hawk had seated themselves.

"Except that I under-estimated the result," said Parr.

"Three to one, you said. It was more than six to one for statehood—just as Doty guessed."

"Well, this time it's done. I guess Mr. Doty has a better eye for this kind of prophecy than I. The Governor's working on his announcement about apportionment of the delegates to the constitutional convention. Have them bring us something to eat, will you, Colonel?"

"What'll you have?"

"Oh, I'm not particular. Hawk'll have the same."

After breakfast, they stopped at the Trelawny & Pengellen store. Parr went in alone. There were several customers in the store, but Trelawny himself was not busy. Parr walked back to where he stood.

Trelawny hailed him with pleasure, as always. "Where to today, Parr?"

"I came to say good-bye for a while. I'm off to war."

"War!" exclaimed Trelawny. "Mexico?"

Parr nodded.

Trelawny called out to the front of the store. "Tamson, Dave—come and say good-bye to Lieutenant Parr. He's going to war!"

David came back at once and flung an arm about Parr's shoulders. "You'll have to stop at the house and say good-bye to Candace, Nate."

"I will," promised Parr.

Tamson came, after finishing with her customer. She gave him her hand and said coolly, "Good luck, Nate!"

He stood for a few moments, laughing and joking with them. He felt that there was something unreal about the fact of his farewell. But in a little while, he left the store to rejoin Soaring Hawk. Tamson, David, and Trelawny followed to the threshold and waved him off.

Candace, seeing him come, ran from the house, suspecting his purpose. She stood beside his horse as he dismounted, her hazel eyes fixed challengingly on him, her thin-lipped mouth stubborn. Before he could say anything, she spoke.

"So you're going, Nate?"

"Yes, Candace."

"Why?"

The question lay there between them. He did not put the answer into words. "I must."

"You needn't tell me that. I know you don't have to go. You want to go. You're running away."

His smile, his steady eyes, the gravity of his gaze, touched her. She softened.

"Oh, Nate," she cried. "Don't go away—please!"

Grunting, Soaring Hawk turned his stallion and went around the corner of the house.

Then she was in his arms. He held her as if he never wanted to let her go again, kissing her headily, passionately, again and again, until Soaring Hawk reappeared and said sibilantly, "Woman come."

They broke apart. Candace clung to his hand.

"What woman?" asked Parr.

"Aunt Marget, I expect." Then, "Nate—you'll write to me?"

"How dare I?"

"To us, then—I'll read between the lines."

"I'll try, Candace."

"Please do. I'll look for your letters."

"I'll try."

"And Nate—I hope you'll think of me now and then."

He smiled wryly. "How could I not?—when you've been in my thoughts so much."

He pressed her hand and swung himself back on to his horse. "Good-bye, Candace."

"Good-bye, Nate."

He saw that her mouth trembled, but she held back her tears. The woman in the house would see, thought Parr. He leaned down and said, "I wish we were riding away together, Candace."

At the corner of the house he turned and waved. Candace was still standing where he had left her, one hand clenched at her side, the other pressed to her lips. He went on, and she was lost to his sight.

Soaring Hawk waited for him on the high road. The Indian gave him a baffled glance, edged with scorn. He fell in behind him as they took the road to Belmont and Platteville, where he would stop to pay his respects to Major Rountree and one or two other friends. Soaring Hawk's silence did not last long, however; they were scarcely past the grove of trees which separated the ridge road from Mineral Point, when the Winnebago began to talk.

The white men, he said, did not know how to care for their women. Or how to handle them. Indeed, many times it seemed that it was the squaws of the white men who handled them instead.

Parr said shortly that white men did not make slaves and pack horses out of their women.

That was where the white men made a mistake, Soaring Hawk said with conviction, as if this could not be gainsaid. He went on in his customary direct manner to say what he thought about men who were set to running away by women. In his instinctive way, he had divined one of Parr's reasons for traveling to enlist.

Parr made no reply. It did not matter that Soaring Hawk believed that Parr was in flight. He was not in flight from Candace. He was trying to escape the conflict within himself, but there was nothing to be gained by explaining that to the Winnebago, who would not understand his failure to make an immediate choice in order to end the conflict. The desire he experienced for Candace was complicated by more than the cross purpose of the ambition which drove him forward relentlessly toward the destiny he sought. There was a bondage between Candace and David; it was not one readily dissolved. Parr saw it, felt it, and understood it. Parr's love for her was a thing impossible of consummation, impossible of fulfilment. Better to hold it in abeyance, to suppress it, let it die—if that were possible. He did not know that it was, but he would find out in the adventure to which he rode.

They reached Galena in mid-afternoon. There they parted. Soaring Hawk showed no emotion, but betrayed the affection he felt for Parr in the formal embrace he gave him. Then Parr remounted his horse and rode to the south.

He did not look back.

6. The Dram of Eale

Autumn, 1847

DAVID DROVE THE CARRIAGE AROUND TO THE FRONT OF THE house and waited there for Candace. He got out and walked up and down the new driveway, which had been put in but two weeks ago. It looked firm. Perhaps it would not be too muddy in the spring. Leaves came fluttering down out of the evening, and lay yellow and claret along the driveway and on the lawn. A few drifted to the verandah, and shone against the recently painted floor.

He walked back to the horses, checking their harnesses. It seemed absurd that they should have to drive over to the Foster house for the masked ball, but Candace insisted on it. They could have walked as easily. But perhaps, since they were in costume, it would be better to ride. Candace, as usual, was taking time, though the hour was early, an afterglow still lingered lemon and magenta in the west, the warmth of the October day lay in the drowsy, leaf-pungent air. He felt stiff and uncomfortable in his George Washington costume.

Seeing the *Mineral Point Tribune* on a chair on the verandah, he sat down to look at it. He had not had time to look at the paper for a fortnight. It had been opened and folded to the page of advertisements, and he knew that Candace had again been contemplating the advertisement of the steamer *St. Croix*—"This splendid and fast sailing steamer will run regularly and positively, during the high stage of water, leaving Galena for St. Louis and New Orleans, every Thursday . . ."—as so often she did. This was the principal sign which remained to tell him that Candace's compromise with Mineral Point was not entirely complete, though he had no complaint to make. He turned its pages casually, skipping news of the lead mines, glancing idly at the personal notes, reading the bulletin from Washington—"General Scott entered Mexico City on September 13th, we learn today. At the same time, the blockade of both coasts of Mexico by our fleet continues. It is the opinion of the government that peace with Mexico cannot long be delayed. The *El Arco Iris,* published at Vera Cruz, states that the moment Santa Anna abandoned the capital, the disorder commenced, and as soon as the populace considered themselves free from the bayonets which might have controlled them, the *Leperos* commenced to sack the city . . ."

He turned to the secondary story, and read the opening sentence: "Work has not yet been begun on the proposed railroad between Milwaukee and Waukesha, for which a charter was granted last February by the Territorial Legislature at the behest of Byron Kilbourn and a group of Milwaukeeans who are far more interested in trade between that city and Waukesha than they are in the plight of the lead miners of Mineral Point and its neighbors, who are finding it daily more difficult and expensive to ship lead across country while our roads remain in good condition only seasonally."

But the paper, as usual, told him nothing he could not hear across the counter. He dropped it, got up, and walked back down and around the carriage, where he stood looking out over

Mineral Point. How the village had grown! A good thing I bought part of that woods, he told himself. The rest had been sold now, houses had sprung up, his home was surrounded on three sides by the growing village. Across High Street, on the knolls and ridge where Tamson had once loved to walk of an evening, houses now stood. A secondary road had been cut along the ridge so that travelers between Dodgeville and Belmont need no longer thread their way through Mineral Point traffic. He looked toward the smelters. Half a dozen of them belched smoke into the quiet autumn air, each of them—except for Beech & Company's copper furnace, which was responsible for fifteen thousand pounds of that mineral per week—producing eighteen thousand pounds of lead daily. The prosperity of Mineral Point approached affluence.

Even at this hour, there was a constant hum of sound from High Street, where the public houses were thronged with miners, speculators, shippers, and travelers, among them a steady stream of land-seekers who had been drawn to the lead shipment by its prosperity. Carriages, horsemen, wagons, and the stage moved in and out of the village.

The afterglow washed down the western heavens. A few flocculent clouds drifted slowly across the southern sky; a light wind began to rise out of the west. Lights began to burn in the village, and the smelters shone redly against the darkening sky. He walked back to the verandah and sat down once more, kicking the paper aside. It felt good to relax. He wondered if Tamson would be at the party. He hoped she would be. She had said very little about it at the store, but she was usually invited to all the balls and parties because her challenging beauty ornamented any gathering. Only Candace could hold a candle to her, he conceded.

His impatience grew. Though there was ample time to reach the party before the hour set for the masked ball, he disliked the way in which Candace sent him out to get the carriage ready and then kept him waiting. Perhaps this was a part of her compromise between the way of life she had hoped for and that she lived. But she had adjusted herself so well to Mineral Point that the death of her mother in June had raised no desire in her to return to Providence to settle her mother's estate; she had left it to her Aunt Agnes, and had been too disinterested even to question any of her aunt's decisions. Candace had given over being negative and silent to become positive—and sometimes demanding. Ever since they had begun to go to parties in Mineral Point and the neighboring towns, Candace's acceptance of her world had come with more grace.

He opened the door finally and called, "Candy! What in the world are you doing? I'm waiting."

"I'll be there in just a moment."

She was almost ready, but she did not hurry. It would do David no harm to sit quietly for a while; he drove himself too much in his work. Her Martha Washington costume made her look demure, yet dignified, plain, yet interesting. She wondered who would be at Foster's, and how large a ball it would be. She wondered if the weather would hold. And she was troubled because they had not heard from Parr for such a long time. Could he have been wounded?

She had followed the course of the war with fascination in his curiously impersonal letters. She had fought the battle of Buena Vista, she had laid the siege of Vera Cruz, and she had battled Santa Anna at Cerro Gordo in his letters. She knew the personalities of his officers—he himself was a captain, though he would still be only a lieutenant in the Territorial militia when he returned. *If* he returned. That he might not return was a possibility she would not consider, with all the stubbornness so integral in her character. She wondered whether he had received the little painted miniature of herself she had dared to send him.

She looked at herself for the last time in the glass, trying on her domino. Then she put on her powdered wig. She was satisfied with what she saw. She doubted that anyone but those who recognized their carriage driving up would know who they were.

She slipped her cloak over her shoulders, took her gloves and fan, and left the bedroom. She went around to where David waited. He locked the door after her, then followed her to the carriage.

"David, put on your mask."

"It's in my pocket. I'll put it on when we get there. It's hard enough to drive this way."

They drove out into the street. The horses, with the carriage pressing after, negotiated the declivity and the adjoining rise to High Street, with caution. They crossed High Street. A passing horseman shouted jeeringly, "Honest George Washington himself! Tell us a lie, Jack!" Down another slope they went and then up the winding road that led to the Foster house, which crowned the knoll upon which it was built, set in the midst of a little parklike area of old and young trees. It was a new house, perhaps the most magnificent in Mineral Point. The first time Candace had been in it, she had grown a little envious. But the Pengellen house, for all its spaciousness, was no longer alone in its bigness. Mr. Cothren had brought property for a new stone house nearby, and Mr. Lanyon had announced his intention of building a fine house of brick.

The entranceway of the Foster house was lit by a row of Paul Revere lanterns, in which candles or torches flared fitfully in the rising wind. They made an avenue of lights from the carriage stop to the front door. Several men were at hand to remove the carriages as their occupants left them, and presently it was David's turn. Candace was helped out by one of the men while David got down from the driver's seat.

Candace straightened her dress, looked David over critically, and went into the house on his arm. They passed through the vestibule into the narrow hall and on into the three connecting rooms which were being used for the ball. She saw that a great many people were already present, and she met the curious stares turned on them with hard, direct eyes, determined not to give her identity away, though, much to her annoyance, she overheard someone nearby whisper her name at once. But in a moment her irritation turned to pleasure, for the whisperer added that there was not another woman as pretty in the house.

David moved leisurely among the maskers until he came to Moses Strong, who, clad as Robespierre, was holding forth on the dissensions of the constitutional convention, which, after battling over putting together a constitution, had had its work repudiated at the polls that spring, when the voters had overwhelmingly rejected the constitution, to the embarrassment of Congress, which had already passed an act for the admission of the State of Wisconsin. There was a strong smell of liquor about Strong; his addiction to whiskey was evident now and then, but he was at the moment at his most loquacious and betrayed none of the effects of over-indulgence.

"No, my dear people," he was saying, "there were but a few factors which were responsible for the defeat of the constitution. Certain articles were incorporated which shouldn't have been put in—they put all the people into an uproar—Whigs, Democrats, Locofocos alike. Ed Ryan's article prohibiting banks, for instance . . ."

"You voted for that one, Moses," said one of his listeners.

"I know I did. I still believe in it. But at the same time Alex Mitchell's Milwaukee Fire & Marine Insurance Company has been carrying on just like a bank—what's more embarrassing, it has several times saved the credit of the Territorial government itself—while all the banks in the adjoining states have failed and robbed the people with their worthless forms of currency. So Mitchell's friends united against the constitution on that count. Then there were the very progressive articles so opposed by Marshall Strong—granting a wife separate property rights and guaranteeing a homestead from forced sale . . ."

"Didn't you vote for those, too, Moses?"

"Well, yes, I did."

At this moment the little group of musicians hired for the occasion struck up a waltz. Moses Strong turned instantly, and, though he had shown no previous awareness of the Pengellens, stuck out his arm to Candace and said, "I believe this is our dance, Madam. Will you do me the honor?"

"If M. Robespierre will promise to leave me my head," said Candace.

"Surely not even Robespierre could have separated so beautiful a head from so bewitching a form." He chuckled and indicated David. "But if this gentleman should happen to be your husband, perhaps it might be well to introduce *him* to M. Guillotine?"

They swung out into the group of dancers, Strong guiding her skillfully, though by no means all the maskers danced. Many sat along the walls, in twos and threes, talking or watching.

"I promised myself I'd dance with every beautiful woman at the ball," said Strong. "It's surely fitting that I should begin with the most beautiful of all."

"Mr. Strong, you flatterer! I don't wonder you never have any trouble winning your elections, if you can talk as glibly to the electors."

He laughed heartily. "I should feel reprimanded, but I don't." He gazed past her. "Aha! there's that tempting Bishop girl. I'll have to dance with her, too. Dressed as Little Bo-Peep! Bo-Peep indeed! Gathering sheep when she could be gathering men. Believe me, my dear lady, some women have no enterprise."

Before their dance had finished, Strong had identified fully a dozen of the ladies. He had never once been so ungallant as to mention her name within anyone's hearing, though she reflected that he would very likely do so as soon as he found himself with another partner.

They finished in another room. David was nowhere in sight. Anxious to find Tamson Bishop, Strong excused himself and went off, leaving her alone. But she was not long alone. A masker dressed in the costume of the United States army approached her. He walked like a young man, but wore a heavy black beard; she could not determine whether it was part of his mask or real. A domino concealed his eyes. He bowed to her and extended his long-fingered hands, palms upward, expressively, without a word asking her to be his partner. She was piqued. She was certain that she knew him; tantalizingly, his identity lay on the rim of awareness, but she could not fasten upon it.

She smiled and moved into his arms. The musicians played another waltz. Because of the elaborateness of many of the costumes, the musicians had been instructed to confine themselves to the slower dances. They danced for a few moments in silence.

"You are silent, sir," murmured Candace.

"At a dance, one dances," he replied provocatively. "Besides, I'm unmoved by Madam Washington's beauty, I confess, for I wear next my heart a portrait of the most beautiful woman in existence."

"Indeed," she replied, stung.

"I believe Madam knows her very well," he went on.

"Who are you, Captain?" she demanded.

"Dare one say before the unmasking?" he teased her. "But I have the honor of Madam's acquaintance. I saw her once in a most beautiful gros de Naples gown of white at a ball in Madison; I was encouraged to present myself for a dance with her tonight."

Her curiosity was fired. She was conscious of mounting excitement. Since they were at the moment close to one of the double doors leading out to the lanternlit porch along the south wall of the house, and away from the press of dancers, she was emboldened to ask, "And may I see the portrait of your most beautiful woman?"

"Do I detect irony or envy in Madam's voice?"

She was positive he spoke in a deliberately disguised voice. Who could he be? Whom had she met that night in Madison? It seemed so very long ago now. But he had stopped; in the absence of her answer, he was drawing his watch from his breast pocket.

"Madam insists?"

"Please."

He opened his watch and flashed the picture laid opposite its face at her. She saw it for only a moment; then the watch was shut again, being put away. It was familiar, indeed—it was her own picture—the miniature she had sent to Parr. She shot a startled, wide-eyed glance at him.

"Nate!" she cried in a low voice. "Oh, Nate! You're back!"

"I'm sure no one will notice in the informality if I keep on dancing with you through the next dance."

"Of course not. Oh, Nate! I'm glad you're here." Her voice trembled with the excitement she felt. "Tell me all about yourself. Are you all right?"

"If we don't dance, someone might claim you. Come on."

They swung back on the floor. She clung to him as tightly as she dared, her pulse singing. How like him to appear in this manner! But, of course, he had just come to town, he had learned of the ball, borrowed a domino—the beard was his own. He was talking rapidly in a low voice.

He had been wounded, not severely, and invalided out. The fighting was all but over, anyway. He did not want to speak of the war; he could find it possible to sympathize with the Mexicans. Soaring Hawk's bitter words on their farewell journey to Galena had needled him enough so that he could see the pattern of conquest. He praised the gallant defense of Santa Anna as well as General Scott's campaign into the Valley of Mexico. His wound had been given him after Cerro Gordo, on the route to Mexico City; he had been sent back into Texas, and from there by slow stages to St. Louis. His horse waited for him not far away, in Hannibal. He had gone up to Galena, remained there for a night, and then come into Wisconsin. He had stopped nowhere, until he reached Mineral Point. And here, learning of the ball, he had been daring enough to come, certain that she would be there.

"You don't have to go back?" she asked anxiously.

"No."

The dance ended. They applauded politely, neither looking away from the other.

"How strange you look in a beard, Nate," she said.

"I don't intend to keep it. I just haven't taken time to cut it."

"I thought at first it was part of your mask."

Over Nate's shoulder, she saw David frowning questioningly at her, but now the music was starting up for a cotillion; so she only smiled reassuringly at him and moved off with Nate, reminding him how like Colonel Bird's ball this was beginning to seem.

"But must we dance?" he asked then, before they took their places in the cotillion. "Can't we just sit down and talk?"

"Of course we can. Look, there are two seats over there. David will probably find us, but that doesn't matter."

They sat down. A few heads turned to glance at them casually, but the cotillion drew all eyes, since it required intricate maneuvering to perform it in the small space available.

"And you, Candace," he asked when they were seated, "how have you been? Your letters told me very little."

"I? Oh, I've been all right."

"You seem more settled somehow."

She laughed. "I don't know that I'll ever be just settled. But I've grown used to Mineral Point, and nobody can help seeing how it's grown. Perhaps some day it may be a great city, just as David's always been telling me. Why, they're even talking of bringing the telegraph in! Do you know, Nate, there are a hundred more houses here now than when you left? And four schools! Several times—since we found out we're not to have any children—I've been tempted to return to teaching. Do you think I ought?"

"Wouldn't you be more distracting than instructive?"

"Oh, Nate!" She went on. "Besides, I got tired of feeling sorry for myself. I had to get out, go places, see people. Aunt Marget kept telling me that; so did everybody else; so I went out. And, of course, you know how it is—I found some pleasure in it. I think David would say I'm 'better'—he'd put it that way, as if I'd been ill. But I think, Nate"—she paused briefly—"in some ways, I haven't changed."

She gave him a direct, almost challenging look. The eyes behind her domino were pooled in dark shadow in which their language was lost.

"I missed you very much, Candace," he said at last.

"And I, you," she answered instantly, and, in a firmer voice, added, "I think we may be attracting attention. But never mind, here comes David. He has Bo-Peep on his arm."

"Tamson," said Nate.

"Can you see past every mask, Nate?" she asked, laughing.

David and Tamson came up. "I wondered where you'd got to, Candy," he said, glancing inquiringly at Parr. "I saw you setting out for the cotillion, but you weren't in it."

She shook her head. "I found such a delightful conversationalist, I couldn't bear to think of wasting my time dancing. May I present him?"

"That's no masquerade costume," said Tamson shrewdly. "That's a real uniform. Oh, David, don't you know who it is? How are you, Nate?" She gave him her hand.

"Nate!" cried David joyously and clapped him on the back. "When did you come? Where are you staying?"

Parr told him as briefly as possible. As to where he was staying—he assumed it would be the Mansion House, as usual, if he did not go to Dodgeville, though that would be uncertain since he had not kept his rooms there during the war.

"Nonsense!" answered David. "You'll have to stay with us. We've furnished our spare bedrooms—we've got two of them—you'll be our first house-guest."

Parr looked toward Candace.

"Of course, Nate," Candace added her voice to David's.

"I don't want to be any trouble," said Parr, hesitating. "Besides, I'm very tired. I may oversleep."

"Must you be somewhere else tomorrow, then?" asked David.

"I want to see the Governor. I understand he's home."

"Then you can sleep as long as you want to. Dodge got home yesterday. The Legislature had just enough of a session to provide for the election of delegates to a new constitutional convention." He turned to Tamson. "Now we can go on dancing—if you'll excuse us."

They moved away to mingle with the crowd once more.

Parr turned to Candace. "Do you really want me to come tonight, Candace?"

"Nate, it will be good to have you under our roof—so good."

She lay listening to sounds from above for a long time after David had gone to sleep at her side. She had put Parr into the bedroom at the head of the stairs, directly above their own room, where she could hear him. He had not gone directly to bed. He had two letters to write, he had said, begging paper. She fancied she heard every scratch made by his pen, just as she heard every footfall, though he had removed his boots and walked about in his stockinged feet.

In the warmth of his proximity, she lay remembering the day he had gone away, the grief she had had to suppress in the face of Aunt Marget's questioning eyes, for the older woman had seen how long Nate had held her hand. She recalled vividly the hollowness that followed his going, the lost feeling, intensified over that earlier feeling of being alien in this Wisconsin wilderness. Yet it had been that very feeling of loss which had helped her to take more active part in the small social gatherings of Mineral Point, and had thus pointed the way for her to enjoy them and to think less often of herself and her isolation.

She marked each sound Nate made, trying to determine what he did. She knew he had placed his boots carefully, one beside the other, near to where he had sat to remove them. He had lifted his chair away from the little desk where he sat to write; he had not scraped it along the floor. He had walked across the floor several times, and when he had finished at the desk, replaced the chair as it had stood before he sat down, and gone over to the bedside, where he removed his clothing. And at last the bed had made its small sounds of protest when he got into it.

She lay, still listening. The night intruded. Owls' cries, crickets churring lazily in the crispness of October, the wind's hush-hush in the unleafing trees. The wind's voice was lulling, soothing.

She turned uneasily; in the darkness her eyes fell upon David's head on the pillow. In the security of the night, she imagined guiltily that it might be Nate lying there beside her.

When she tapped on Parr's door next morning, it was opened at once. Parr stood smiling on the threshold. "You should have called me before, Candace. It's almost ten o'clock."

"David left over two hours ago. I wouldn't have called you now, only your Indian friend is here."

"Trust Soaring Hawk to find out I'm back."

He stepped into the hall, caught hold of Candace's hands. Then he dropped her hands, took her into his arms, and kissed her with all the ardor of long withheld passion.

"Forgive my beard, Candace," he whispered, and kissed her again.

She made no move to repel him, holding to him, her eyes closed, her mouth responding to his. She was in turmoil—the feeling that had grown for Parr and been so rigidly suppressed in the face of her loyalty to David had sprung to full-blown life again.

Releasing her, he said in a low voice, "You haven't forgotten."

"Oh, no!" she cried, her eyes flashing open. "How could I? But it isn't fair to David." She pulled away.

They went downstairs, hands clasped together. In the hall Candace pushed Nate forward. There in the kitchen, Soaring Hawk stood near the door. The Winnebago's eyes flashed his pleasure. Parr threw an arm across his shoulders. It was good to see him, unchanged, as always.

"Hawk! You cunning devil! How did you know I was here? And don't say the wind told you."

"Soaring Hawk know here." He struck his breast. "Soaring Hawk ask himself: where is white brother? He come here."

"Will you have some breakfast, Soaring Hawk?" asked Candace.

The Indian shook his head. He had eaten. He would wait until Parr was ready to go. He knew Parr would want to see the White Chief, Dodge. He would be ready for him. He had fed his horse.

As Parr sat down to the breakfast table, Soaring Hawk made himself comfortable by squatting on the floor nearby, his keen eyes scrutinizing Parr with intent care. The only sign of amusement he made was, on catching Parr's eyes, to gesture, big-eyed, at Parr's beard.

Candace wondered if the Indian ever laughed. She looked at him from time to time. His attention was all for Parr; he did not take his gaze off Parr. She understood that, in his own strange way, Soaring Hawk was devoted to Nate. And Nate, too, seemed fond of Soaring Hawk, for he looked at him now and then and grinned happily. Just like a boy, Candace thought. But, of course, that was it—they were like boys together, each of them was more free than most men.

When Parr had finished his breakfast, he was ready to go. Soaring Hawk hastened outside. Parr kissed Candace and held her for a few moments.

"I'll see you soon again, Candace," he promised.

"I hope so, Nate. Don't let it be too long before you come."

She waved to him from the threshold, under the Indian's inscrutable eyes.

Parr and Soaring Hawk rode out of Mineral Point into the bright, sunny morning. A warm west wind blew, tearing leaves from the trees and scattering them widely over the slopes. Already the claret and maroon colors of late October were fading to sienna and brown.

Though he was filled with questions, Soaring Hawk asked none. He waited for Parr to speak. This Parr presently did. He told the Winnebago about the war, describing the battles with great gusto, knowing Soaring Hawk took pleasure in all such accounts of fighting, though the most peaceful of Indians himself. Parr knew that Soaring Hawk had a streak of darkness in him; he showed it in his frequent mutterings against the lies and injustice of the white men, in his interest in battles and vengeance, in his concern with all the details of any encounter. It was the balance in his nature, Parr often thought; it afforded him a harmless and passive counterpart of all that he had renounced in turning away from savagery, though Parr would never have offended Soaring Hawk by suggesting that any Indian was a savage, for he knew very well that most of the Indians, for all their widespread uncleanliness, sincerely considered their civilization superior to that of the white men, maintaining that their reputed treachery had been taught them by their white brothers.

And what had Soaring Hawk done in his absence?

Nothing but what he had always done, replied the Winnebago. But now there were scarcely any Indians left to watch, and those who remained here were not inclined to jeopardize their precarious freedom of movement in the Territory by doing anything to excite or displease the white men, who were still coming into the Territory in ever greater numbers. The settlers were like these leaves before the wind that blew them up from the south and in from the east; there was no end to them, said Soaring Hawk. There were more of them than there were grains of sand under foot. They came over the lake, they came by wagon train to Galena, and went north and west, they came up the Mississippi on great boats.

Parr listened, as he customarily did, with only half an ear. He was reviewing the ball at the Foster house, the way Candace had looked, the intensity of her greeting, and his pulse beat fast at the recognition that his going away had apparently altered nothing. He had but taken flight from a problem that awaited him on his return. Only one thing had changed: Candace was more sure of herself. Yet it was not possible to measure her affection or her desire any more than it had been to estimate her earlier discontent and the goal of her hopes and ambitions. He had the feeling that, now she had accepted Mineral Point and a new way of life, she was slightly bored. And he was sure that her ambitions were only dormant, ready to come to life at any prompting. And David? Of David he did not want to think; he felt disloyal, even though he had never shown him the open-handed friendship David had always manifested.

As the Governor's farm came into view, Parr thought of the immediate years to come and of his place in the new State of Wisconsin. It was to explore possibilities that he wanted to lose no time in seeing the Governor.

Soaring Hawk grunted. He touched Parr and pointed to the left. On the edge of a wood on Dodge's property, a group of workmen was busy cutting trees. Sitting astride a horse nearby was a rider who could be none other than Dodge. Parr nodded and, turning his horse from the road, skirted a field and rode down the side of a knoll toward the wood.

Dodge hailed him with delight, riding forward to meet him. "If I hadn't seen Soaring Hawk," he cried, "I might have thought you were Byron Kilbourn come to ask still more for his railroad, with all that beard you have. Come along to the house where we can talk." He started off at once, suiting his actions to his words, as always. "Have you taken to wearing a beard now, Nathaniel?" he flung over his shoulder.

"No—I'll shave it off as soon as I can."

"I'll lend you my razor."

At the house, the Governor explained that he was alone for the day; Mrs. Dodge and the children had gone into Madison to stay at the home put at the disposal of the Governor and his family there. He led the way into the kitchen, a small, plain, and very clean room at the rear of the house. Talking animatedly, he took a looking-glass down from the wall, set it up before a chair, and dipped a wash-basin of water out of a pail standing there.

"Being a soldier, you can manage with cold water," he said, his eyes twinkling.

Parr laughed. "I had no idea your dislike of whiskers went this far."

"It adds years to you, Nathaniel. Look at yourself." He held up the glass. "All you have to do is turn down your mouth and frown, and you'll look just like Kilbourn when I tell him he can't have everything he wants. First we'll want scissors."

The Governor disappeared into an inner room, leaving Parr sit where he had put him. Soaring Hawk squatted nearby, gravely interested in the procedure. It was beyond his comprehension that the White Chief should wait upon Parr. But then, many things that white men did could not be fathomed. The Governor came back with the scissors, took hold of Parr's beard, and began to cut it with evident pleasure.

"I'm glad you've come back, Nathaniel. I have several things I want done, if you can spare the time. The most urgent is a little mission to Shullsburg, where John O'Connor is thinking of withdrawing from the field of delegates and leaving it to Billy Hamilton. He must be persuaded not to withdraw. I sympathize with Hamilton, but I confess there are times I could wish Burr had shot him instead of his father. I suspect he had a hand in stirring up those wild Democrats in the last convention. We called them Locofocos, after those highly inflammatory matches."

What had happened? Parr wanted to know. He had thought Wisconsin would have become a state by the time of his return, but not an inch of progress had been made, they were right where they were in the Territory when he had left for the war.

Ah, that was a long story, Dodge explained. Too many members of the convention were green and easily swayed. Such strongly prejudiced men as Edward Ryan of Racine County and Moses Strong, representing Iowa County, had just about taken over the convention, and, excited by the failure of the Mineral Point Bank and Knapp's absconding plus the difficulties of converting bank notes into specie at less than a substantial interest rate, had pushed through an article which would have prevented the state legislature from creating any kind of bank.

"A blow at Alex Mitchell, of course," said Parr.

Dodge nodded. "Almost every newspaper in the Territory damned the proposed constitution and tore it to shreds. After reading them, I wouldn't be surprised if some of the delegates voted against the constitution themselves." He chuckled, stood back, looked at Parr, whose beard was now cut off, and put down the scissors, as Parr began to stir up lather. "This time, though, we'll have more level heads. The party conventions have been nominating good men—Orsamus Cole of Potosi, Judge Dunn, Steve Hollenbeck from Highland, Rufus King from Milwaukee, George Lakin from Platteville, Alex Ramsey from Cassville, Joe Ward from Dodgeville—they're key men. Kilbourn will be there, too, considerably chastened, but I doubt that Moses Strong will make it. For one thing, poor Moses has taken to the bottle."

Parr observed that some of the men the Governor named were not of his party.

"Party be hanged!" exclaimed Dodge angrily. "I'm sick of men who do nothing but vote as their leaders suggest, who think first of their own neighborhoods and damn the state or nation. We've got to have men in government who think of the common welfare. We can do without the narrowly provincial."

Parr completed the stroke of Dodge's straight-edged razor before answering. He turned over what the Governor had said. With the acceptance of the constitution at the polls, the Governor's position would be no more; the pulling of strings in Washington would be a thing of the past, for henceforth the Governor and other state officers would be elected.

"Are you going to stand for your office in the first state election?" he asked.

To his surprise, Dodge shook his head. "No, I believe Nelson Dewey intends to run."

"You're not retiring, Governor?" cried Parr in alarm. "The state, even more than the Territory, needs you."

"No, I'm not retiring. I'll stand for the Senate of the United States. There are many things to be done for Wisconsin in Washington."

Parr smiled. "Your old friend, Doty, intends to be there, too —in Congress."

"I know."

As he shaved, Parr considered his position. If Dodge were away from Madison, his influence for Parr would not be as positive. He cast around in his mind for other anchors, and for a moment was conscious of high alarm—Dodge gone, Doty in Washington, Moses Strong's influence declining—only Judge Dunn was left. The Judge was not an inconsiderable force, but less aggressive than Dodge or Strong might be, and forthright rather than subtle, as Doty was.

As if he were aware of what Parr thought, Dodge asked, "What plans have you made, Nathaniel?"

He turned and faced the Governor frankly. "I had thought of some position in the government. But, to tell the truth, if you aren't to be here, I don't know whether that will be either possible or desirable."

Dodge's eyes, replying to Parr's candid gaze, were affectionate. "I wouldn't forget you, Nathaniel. If I go to Washington—and I have every hope of my election—I'll need someone there, too. For the time being, at least, you could come along as my secretary. Would you like that?"

To hesitate would seem ungracious. "I should like that," answered Parr, "except that there's no guarantee it will last."

"Well, ultimately we'll find something more secure for you, Nathaniel," said Dodge quickly. "Never fear as to that."

But Parr was already adjusting himself to this suggestion of the Governor's. His first thought, that it was dependent solely on the whim of the electorate as well as on Dodge's desire to continue in office and might thus be of short duration, was succeeded by a secondary objection—that it offered him nothing like the position of importance to which he believed himself entitled. These objections, however, were overcome by another possibility—he might be able to take Candace to Washington—*if* Candace's ambitions reached that far and if he had not misjudged her. What he could never do in Wisconsin, he might very well be able to succeed in doing in Washington. He did not doubt that Candace would prefer life in Washington to that in Madison. She would look upon his position as the secretary of the Senator from Wisconsin as only a stepping-stone to something more, as he, too, viewed it.

"I'm sorry I can't suggest anything better at the moment," said the Governor.

"I couldn't imagine anything better, Governor," answered Parr. "I'll enjoy living in Washington—perhaps I'll even be prevailed upon to marry, who knows?"

The Governor smiled. "Do you think you could remain faithful to one woman, Nathaniel?"

He met Dodge's eyes. "I think I could."

"There is such a woman, then! Congratulations, Nathaniel!"

"Thank you, Governor."

Parr finished shaving. His skin was sensitive; he rubbed it where but lately his whiskers had been. He pushed his chair back and got up. He restored the looking-glass to the wall.

"Now you look natural again," said Dodge.

"Thanks to your good offices. I've been in such haste to get home I never stopped at a barber's."

"Let's go into the sitting-room. I have my desk there." Dodge walked out of the kitchen as he spoke. "Another thing you could help us with," he continued, "is the census. It will be taken in November. The sheriffs are supposed to take it, but they're notoriously lax. There are over two hundred thousand people in the Territory. We'll need to know just how many because of the change in our status as soon as the constitution is ratified."

"Aren't you looking ahead rather far, Governor?"

"Not at all. Once drawn up, the constitution need only be submitted to the people—say, next March. As soon as the votes are in, I'll issue a proclamation that the new constitution's in effect. We'll then actually cease to be the Territory and become the State of Wisconsin."

Parr sat down. Soaring Hawk did likewise, near the door, as he habitually did in strange houses, should it prove necessary to leave with dispatch. The Governor preferred to keep to his feet, and walked up and down the small, cozy living-room, with its sturdy, home-made furniture, and its colorful window curtains, his hands clasped behind his back, talking steadily about the affairs of the Territory.

Parr listened. He interjected comments from time to time, but his thoughts were not with the Governor. He was reorientating his plans to fit into the suggestion Dodge had made. If he could bring Candace—if he could persuade her to come with him when the time presented itself—it might be possible to bring the Governor around to acceptance of a *fait accompli.* In his heart he knew that if his absence had accomplished nothing more, it had brought Candace to a definite commitment to him, even if she herself had not yet admitted as much. And from the passive commitment to the act was but a step in time.

Late one November afternoon Soaring Hawk found Parr in Platteville.

He rode on a mission distasteful to him. He had accepted it only because Parr had asked him to serve him. Nevertheless, he conceived that his mission helped Parr to compound treachery, and he resented it. He resented also the attraction Candace held for Parr. He thought it demeaned Parr to desire this woman, for to Soaring Hawk she was an object of pity and perhaps scorn. But he never indulged in pity. He recognized that all women were weak and most of them were unprincipled; he did not expect women to have principles. He thought Candace selfish, despite her attempts to seem not so. He had noticed, on such occasions when he had accompanied Parr, that Candace had betrayed certain small signs of possessiveness, as if she exercised ownership over Parr. They were invisible to all others, thought Soaring Hawk, except the green-eyed one, which was the way in which the Winnebago thought of Tamson Bishop.

Parr had just left the inn at Platteville when Soaring Hawk rode up. Seeing him, he stood before his horse and waited, anticipating what the Indian might have to tell him. He saw by the Winnebago's stolidity that he was not pleased.

Soaring Hawk imparted his message in clipped words that spoke his own distaste. David Pengellen had gone into Milwaukee by stage that morning. He would attend a meeting which would keep him in that city until past midnight and perhaps through the night. He did not add that Candace would be alone; he did not know that she would be, but he assumed it, not being aware of Aunt Marget's or Tamson's habit of coming to spend the night with her when David was not there.

Parr grinned. "Good boy!" he said, and mounted his horse to ride to Mineral Point.

Boy, thought Soaring Hawk bitterly. It was not he who was the boy. It was Parr—Parr with his cursed fawning upon women, his youthful pursuit of love and the hunger of his body. Yet he did not think of Parr in criticism or anger, but rather with indulgent resignation. There was, after all, no way of understanding the curious, complex ways of white men. He rode behind Parr in absolute silence all the way to Belmont, through that settlement, and on to Mineral Point.

It was the edge of evening when Parr rode up to the Mansion House, leaving Soaring Hawk to go on to Dodgeville. He stabled his horse and went into the hotel to arrange for a room, after which he stepped briefly into the tap-room, where a large group of miners was gathered. He was met by a blast of lusty singing, and stopped good-naturedly to listen to an old Cornish song. "*The trees they are so high, The leaves they are so green, The day is past and gone, Sweetheart, That you and I have seen. It is a cold winter's night, You and I must bide alone . . .*"

Colonel Nichols came up behind him and slapped him on the shoulder. "Have a drink, Parr?"

"Not tonight, thanks. I may, if I come back early enough."

"Lend a voice to the singing, then. I have to watch 'em or first thing I know they'll be doing a Furry dance through the place."

But Parr was not inclined to sing. He withdrew presently. It was important that he reach the house and Candace before Aunt Marget or Tamson got there. He had no appetite for supper; so he took none. He was in a state of subdued excitment, because, in a way, this was an opportunity to know to what lengths Candace would go. He walked out of the Mansion House and south on Shake-Rag Street, as once he had gone before, though he knew that tonight he would have to walk more widely out of his way to escape observation and come in toward the house from another side, since the Point had built up so much.

The night was chill. The moon, only a day past the full, made a yellow glow in the east, where it was soon to rise. A steady, crisping wind blew out of the west; it was not a night on which to travel on horse, though the stage would keep any traveler in comfort. Perhaps David would not return in the night; it was more probable that he would come back to the Point tomorrow. However, it made no difference to Parr; he must be back at the Mansion House before midnight.

He startled Candace when he slipped into the kitchen where she sat waiting for Aunt Marget. She jumped to her feet, her fingers to her lips.

"Nate!" she cried. "Aunt Marget's coming any moment."

"Do you need her, Candace?" He walked past her into the dark hall.

"She always stays when David's gone," she answered, following him. "She or Tamson."

In the hall he put his arms around her and kissed her slowly, moving his mouth sensuously on hers until he could feel her quick passion rising.

"Must she stay, Candace?" he pressed. "No one saw me come. I've a room at the Mansion House, and I'll be in it soon."

Her eyes met his, startled, hesitant. At that moment there was a sound on the stoop outside the kitchen door.

"Oh, hide, Nate," she whispered urgently. "Slip upstairs. Hide, please."

He left her side and went silently up the stairs as Candace returned to the kitchen. From the darkness at the head of the stairs he listened. He could not distinguish words. The two women sat talking, talking. The moments dragged like hours. Would they never finish? What could they have found to talk about? What was Candace telling her? She could not ask her to return later; either she must go now, or she must not, in which case he must make his way quietly back to the hotel. But Candace had not told him to go, only to hide.

He sat down on the top step. The step creaked. He smiled mirthlessly at the memory which occurred to him—of his foster-mother telling him that every wrong was ultimately disclosed, every error was found out, every crime uncovered, and a look, a word, a gesture, even a sound betrayed sin. He had tormented her frequently by asking her what kind of sound sin made. Perhaps this was it: the creaking of a stair. He grinned in the darkness. He knew very well that what his foster-mother had told him was only hypothetically true within the boundaries of one body, one soul, not necessarily beyond. He believed that the transgression itself punished the transgressor, inexorably, in one way or another, but he was unafraid, he did not turn away from transgression for all that. A man is what he makes himself, he told himself frequently, nothing more. But deep down inside him he knew that there were forces within every man which moulded him, which drove and compelled him, even as his insatiable compulsion to satisfy his ambition, in a role he believed himself fitted by destiny to play.

A door opened and closed downstairs. That would be Aunt Marget leaving. He listened. No sound. Impatience rose in him, but he dared not move, lest it had not been Aunt Marget. A few minutes passed. He heard someone moving about in the kitchen. Then he heard the bolt snap into place, locking the kitchen door.

The light downstairs went out.

Then Candace came up the stairs in the darkness, feeling her way. He saw her before she saw him, because his eyes were more accustomed to the dark. When she came to the top of the stairs, he took her into his arms.

"Has she gone?"

"Yes. I told her I had to learn to stay by myself sometime."

He kissed her. Her mouth trembled under his. She clung to him, her fingers digging fiercely into him. He held her for a long time, her body locked to his, until he felt her pulse quicken and her lips grow hot. Then he swept her up into his arms and walked catlike into the bedroom.

On election day, knowing that Trelawny was at work at the polls, Aunt Marget stopped in at the store. She chose that hour when Tamson was at home for lunch, and when there would be little to interrupt her. It had taken her a long while to bring herself to speak to David, but she believed it her duty, however reluctant she was to do so. David saw her come and set out a chair for her; that autumn had not been kind to her, for she had begun to show her years, her brown hair had streaks of white, and wrinkles had appeared about her eyes. She squinted a little, unwilling to admit that her sight was not as strong as it had once been, but her eyes were no less soft and friendly. This morning, clearly, they betrayed some distress.

She came into the store and sat down.

"What will it be for you today, Aunt Marget?" David asked.

"Mister Pengellen," she said. "I wisht to talk to 'ee."

"What about?"

" 'Tis not about my own business, I'm feared. But yers."

"Well, talk away," he invited, smiling encouragingly.

Thus urged, Aunt Marget began what she had come to say. She had sent Tamson back with the money he had sent home for her to pay for her work at the house because it included payment for a night spent with Candace. But she had spent no night with Candace.

He interrupted her. "Aren't you forgetting that day I had to go to Milwaukee?"

She shook her head. She was not forgetting. She had gone to spend that night, but Candace had sent her home. She had told her something about it being time she began to spend nights alone—if she had to. And this was true enough.

David was mystified. He felt that there was something behind this, but he could not put his finger on it. He was puzzled, too, because Candace had said nothing to him of spending that night alone. He would have thought that, having accomplished this departure from habit, she could hardly have foregone the pleasure of telling him. That would have been in her nature; she would have been proud of learning to be unafraid.

But all the while Mrs. Pengellen was telling her, Aunt Marget went on in her broad Cornish speech, there was an evasiveness about her. It was something Aunt Marget had felt. It troubled her. It bothered her anew at this moment, for the mere putting it into words seemed somehow to lessen the magnitude of what had built up in the older woman's mind. She skirted the core of what she meant to say, until David's impatience was aroused. Moreover, her recital was interrupted several times by customers who took David from her. But at last she came to what she meant to say: she thought that there had been someone in the house with Candace that night.

"I see," said David. "Well, I'll look into it, Aunt."

She made protestations immediately. She had meant to say nothing, but the matter had troubled her, and when David had sent money to pay her for staying that night, she realized that Candace had not told him.

"She very likely forgot," said David.

Her attitude held little agreement. She said no more, made her excuses, somewhat abashed now, for she was not a woman to carry gossip, and had it not been for this problem preying on her, she would never have spoken, and got up to go.

If David had made no outward sign of it, he was nevertheless puzzled. Aunt Marget had hardly gone when Tamson made her appearance. She had come in the back way during her aunt's recital, and had overheard part of what she said.

"What has Aunt Marget been telling you, David?" she asked.

He told her. "Has she said anything of this to you, Tamson?"

"No. But I could tell something was bothering her."

"What do you think?"

She could not tell him what she thought. "Why don't you

ask Candace, David? It's not my place—or Aunt Marget's either, if it comes to that—to think about it. After all, Aunt Marget doesn't know anything except that Candace sent her home and seemed to act a little strange. That's not very much."

"Your aunt is generally level-headed and fair."

"I wonder sometimes if any woman is always level-headed," answered Tamson, with a wry smile.

David was further baffled. Tamson did not mean for him to guess as to her intention; she did not know herself. He began to feel that things had gone on about him in which he should have had a part, but had none. Tamson was right; he must ask Candace directly; speculation would only lead him into further perplexity.

Since it was his dinner hour, he went home, battling the November wind. He sat down to the table, gazing at Candace from the corners of his eyes. Did he expect to see some physical change? Some alteration in her manner? There was nothing. She talked idly of this and that, and plainly expected no more in the way of conversation from him than the customary recital of events in the routine of the store.

"Candace," he asked suddenly, "why didn't you tell me you sent Aunt Marget home that night I spent in Milwaukee?"

"I suppose I forgot it, David," she answered readily.

"I found out about it just by accident. I sent money up to her with Tamson—to pay her for the last two weeks or so, and she sent part of it back."

"I should have told you. I'm sorry."

He met her eyes. They were bland, direct, almost impersonal. He felt oddly that they represented the outer boundaries of a wall that had grown between them. He smiled confidently.

"I'm afraid Aunt Marget had the idea someone was here with you."

"But she couldn't have seen anyone," she cried.

"Why do you say that, Candy?"

"Because there *was* someone here. Nate had just dropped in. He'd walked up from the Mansion House, where he was staying. I didn't want her to see him, for fear she'd think he had been here longer than he had. So I told him to stand in the hall till she went back home. After she went, he went back to the hotel. I'm quite sure no one saw him; he was careful. I asked him to be. You know people talk."

The explanation was so simple and came so easily that he was surprised. It was only natural that Nate should call; he could hardly know that he was out of town. He thought Candace need not have gone to such a subterfuge, for Aunt Marget could surely be trusted; but she had done so, and there was nothing more to be said.

"And you stood it alone all night, too."

She laughed, pleased. "I'm proud of myself. I had to begin sometime. Just the same, I hope you won't be gone many nights."

"I won't. I didn't build a home to be away from it."

She went on with her dinner and with the usual small talk that prevailed at their meals.

When he got back to the store, he went over to Tamson.

"Tell me, Tamson, did Nate call on you that night I was in Milwaukee?"

"I haven't seen Nate for some time. Certainly not that night."

Where had Nate spent the evening? he wondered. He asked himself this repeatedly throughout the afternoon, but no answer presented itself. Very probably he had been at the Mansion House. He could find out easily enough, but even to make the attempt implied a lack of faith and trust. He would not have entertained the question had it not been for Aunt Marget's attitude; he knew that she would never have made mention of any doubt if she had not believed in her reason for doing so, and he was convinced that she had said less than she had thought about the matter.

Trelawny came in at six. The polls had closed, and he looked fully as tired as he complained of feeling.

"Have the votes been counted?" asked David.

"Yes. If the vote elsewhere in the county is the same, it'll be Charlie Bishop, Joe Ward, and Steve Hollenbeck for the convention."

"That will please the Governor."

"No doubt. But they can have that job! It makes me more tired than a busy day at the store. Had supper?"

"No. I let Tamson go."

"Well, we can close up."

"Better not. Lanyon delivered part of a stock order from Galena this afternoon. I'd better stay and get it ready."

"Well, go home first and get something to eat."

Though he had little inclination to work into the evening, David went home and sat at a supper for which he had no appetite, listening to Candace talk about someone who had come into the Point and bought land on speculation, only to find copper deposits on it. In the midst of her chatter, she became aware of his preoccupation.

"David, do you really think Mineral Point will some day be an important city?" she asked then.

"How can it help but be? Where else are miners getting four and five dollars a day? Lead's three dollars the hundred, and we've been told that it will go to three and a half next year. Every indication is that it'll go even higher before 1850. And you know how people have been flocking in to build."

"I'm afraid we'll be old before Mineral Point ever grows to what you think it might be, David."

"It's twice as big now as when you came," he answered quietly.

"And do you think we'll ever be more than shopkeepers?" she asked.

He was stung, but he did not show it. He said only that they could invest in land and take up farming, thus becoming members of the "landed gentry," if she preferred, though shopkeepers and lead shippers were more secure financially than anyone else in the entire area.

"But I thought you had come to like the Point," he ended.

"I have, David. I only asked."

"Or is it that the old restlessness is stirring in you again?" he demanded hotly.

"Is there a one of us who wouldn't go on to better if he could?" she cried. "I'm no more restless than ever."

"But you want more!"

"Surely everyone wants more out of life, David—no matter what or who he is."

"Well, I guess that's right."

Three hours later, Tamson found him at the store. She had walked out into the cool, snowy night, clad in a snug fur turban and a dress of dark blue velvet, and, seeing the light there, went in. While he peered vainly toward the darkness out of the glow around him, to see who had come in, she reached him and stepped into the lamplight. The stock shipment stood undisturbed, just as it had been left in the store during the afternoon; he had not done a thing to it. Nor was there paper on his desk; so he was not at figures.

"What are you doing, David?"

"I came down to work."

"But you haven't done anything."

"No. I was just sitting here thinking."

"It's almost ten o'clock. It must have been a long thought. Or perhaps you just got here.—But no, it's been snowing for the past two hours and there aren't any footprints turning in. Just sitting and thinking. About what? May I know?"

He sighed. "About everything. About women—and Candace—and the way people change. Yes, and even about you, Tamson."

"Me?" she echoed faintly.

"Yes, did you think I could work with you every day and not see you? And not understand that the way you felt—I felt, too? In these unprincipled times, I'm afraid men of principle are at a disadvantage," he finished bitterly.

"David, have you been making enquiries about Candace?"

"I would not." He shrugged. "It would not become me. If she dissembles, she does it very well. If she doesn't—in what proportion does my own guilt exist?"

"You're talking wildly, David."

He shook his head grimly. "No, I'm not. I know what I'm talking about. She's tried to live the way I want her to live. I've lived as I thought I must. We've had only half a success. If she's ever lain beside me at night wishing I were another—then, I, too, have secretly reflected that wish as it has existed in my own unspoken desire. Perhaps she felt it. Perhaps she understood it. I'm unable to say."

He had not risen. Now she moved closer to him, standing above him, so that the faint scent she wore, combined with the aura of her femininity, enveloped him. He looked up at her from his knees, his eyes troubled and miserable in the yellow light.

"Oh, David," she whispered.

"I'm neither less nor more than human, Tamson."

"I know. I know, David."

He reached out for the lamp, brought it to him, and blew it out.

"Someone might see us here together like this. It isn't as if we were working."

Then he pulled her down to his lap. In the darkness he found her mouth, kissing her hard. The strength with which he held her was no less than her own.

He pulled his lips almost cruelly from hers, but did not release her.

"God forgive me!" he whispered harshly. "I love you, Tamson. I've known it for months—I've been trying to run away from it almost from the beginning."

7. *Lord, We Know What We Are . . .*

Winter, 1848

IN FEBRUARY DAVID WAS CHOSEN TO REPRESENT THE BUSINESSmen of Mineral Point at a meeting with directors of the Milwaukee & Waukesha Railroad Company in Milwaukee. There had been a great deal of futile correspondence. A survey of a sort had been made of the region, and Moses Strong, stubborn and set against any corporation or organization which did not include Mineral Point in its plans, had inveighed so loudly against members of the company in Milwaukee that, even though no single foot of the rail had been laid, it was obvious that Strong, for all his enthusiasm for railroad connections to the outside world, was not the man to be sent to the city. This decision divided the businessmen into two camps—those holding Strong's opinion, and those opposed to his refusal to compromise. As a result, David, who had taken neither side, was elected to meet with Byron Kilbourn, Alexander Mitchell, and Edward Holton in Milwaukee in mid-February, roads permitting.

He was reluctant to go, since Trelawny was alone in the store; Tamson had asked for a week to go on a holiday and had left the village two days before. But there was no help for it, however fruitless the meeting might be; David must go. The snow was not too deep, the roads were open, though the stage, now on a sledge, was not making as many runs as in summer. He left early on the morning of the eleventh for Milwaukee, a distance of over a hundred miles from Mineral Point.

After riding for part of the night and most of the day through the snow-covered landscape, he reached Milwaukee late in the day. He left the inn at which the stage customarily stopped and went to the Fountain House, where he took a room and inquired for something to eat. He was directed to the dining-room, which adjoined the lobby of the hotel; it was a commodious room, though not as large as the somewhat ornate lobby, recently redecorated with gilt paint which failed to conceal its essential roughness.

Both dining-room and lobby were crowded, but David found a place, ordered a meal, and waited upon its arrival. He had ample time before the meeting, which was scheduled for seven o'clock in the lobby of the Fountain House. He sat looking about him at the number of beaver-hatted gentlemen with their gold canes walking in and out of the dining-room and parading about the lobby with the appearance of affluence and importance. He tried in vain to recognize some of them. He imagined that the gentlemen with whom he was shortly to discuss the railroad would be similarly attired.

He ate, taking his time. After he finished, he walked out into the lobby and stood there examining the ornate decorations, thinking that, as Mineral Point grew, that city, too, would have hostelries like this to replace the now popular Mansion and Central Houses. He looked at his watch: six-thirty. He walked over to the desk and spoke to the clerk.

"I'm expecting someone to ask for David Pengellen. I'll be over there," he said, pointing to a recess along the far wall.

"We have a message here for you, Mr. Pengellen. You're asked to call at Room 311. The stairs are over there, sir."

The clerk gave him an oddly arch look. David thanked him. Evidently the men from the railroad company had taken a room for greater privacy. His own room was on the third floor, too; they might as well have met there. He moved through the throng of people to the stairs and mounted to the third floor. He found 311 not far from the head of the stairs and knocked confidently.

The door opened.

It was not the trio of men he had expected to see; it was Tamson who stood there.

"Come in, David." She laughed. "Don't look so startled."

"I'm surprised to see you here, Tamson. I thought you'd gone to Madison."

"No. I went on through Madison. I'm supposed to be visiting Mrs. Trelawny's cousin here, but I haven't found her at home yet. Apparently she went visiting herself, and Mrs. Trelawny didn't think of that when she gave me a letter to her. But, you see, I'm not helpless. I came here directly, and I've been shopping ever since. I'm ready to go home now, though I'll try once more to find Mrs. Corbett."

"But how did you know I was here?"

"I saw you in the dining-room. I know you didn't see me. You went right past me when you came in."

"It's certainly good to see you." He took her hand, pulled her to him, and kissed her.

"But why are you here, David?"

He told her.

"I see. Will that take all evening?"

"I doubt it. Could we meet afterward?"

"I'd like to take a little walk, if nothing else. I've kept to my room every evening since I came. It *is* dull."

"Of course, Tamson. Will you wait here?"

She nodded. Her smile warmed him. He kissed her again.

Downstairs, the three men he had come to see waited for him. He saw them as he came in sight of the lobby, recognizing them only because he had previously met Byron Kilbourn—a tall, dark man, the roundness of whose face was emphasized by a Quaker beard and the high domelike brow which dominated his Roman nose, his habitually grim, down-turned mouth, his wide-set eyes. His companions were, like him, plainly dressed—one standing somewhat shorter than Kilbourn, likewise with a fringe of beard, but considerably less prominent, in a round face dominated by his keen, dark eyes and heavy black eyebrows; the other almost as tall, a man approaching fifty, square-jawed and firm-featured, with pleasant, friendly eyes. He alone of the three men wore a light-colored frock coat and carried a gold-knobbed cane.

Kilbourn recognized him as he came up.

"I trust I haven't kept you gentlemen waiting," said David earnestly.

Kilbourn introduced his companions—the short man was Mitchell, the other, Holton. Holton gave him a narrow-eyed, appraising look, but David had the intuitive knowledge that it was Mitchell who measured him with greater care, though less obtrusively.

"Is there some place we can go?" asked Kilbourn.

"My room, gentlemen?" suggested David.

"Lead the way, sir," said Holton.

David delayed only long enough to order whiskey and mineral water sent up to his room. Then they went up the stairs, Kilbourn explaining carefully that they were in no position to promise anything, but that they would listen to his "proposition." Once settled in the room, it was Mitchell who suggested that they would like to hear what David had to say.

"And we hope you can say it with less intemperance and violence than Moses Strong," added Holton dryly.

"I hope I can," answered David, chuckling. "Gentlemen, the situation is simply this—the lead shippers at Mineral Point believe that any railroad connecting Lake Michigan with the Mississippi by any other route than through the Point and its neighboring cities is a grave error in judgment. Consider, at the present time, for want of adequate connections, lead leaves Mineral Point by wagon for Galena, goes down the Mississippi to New Orleans and so to New York, and from there part of it comes back to Milwaukee—it goes many thousands of miles only to come back to be used in a place less than a hundred fifty miles from its place of origin. Conceive the sum of money lost in useless transportation. Of course, the lead can come to Milwaukee by wagon in summer, oxen or horses can feed on the open prairie, and the entire cost of that transportation is approximately half a dollar a day for every hundred pounds. In other seasons, the cost is doubled for the three or four days it takes. If the millions of pounds of lead produced annually in the region were to be shipped by rail, the income alone would be close to three hundred thousand a year—enough to pay the entire cost of the railroad in a few years' time. And that is to say nothing of the increase in business which would attend such an improvement, and the toll from the passengers. Gentlemen, how else can you proceed with your railroad than by way of Mineral Point?" He paused, challenging them to answer.

"You're a cogent talker, Mr. Pengellen," said Mitchell. "There are other routes."

David had come prepared. He whipped a map of the Territory from his pocket and spread it out on the bed before them, for the room was so sparely furnished that it was necessary for two of them to sit on the bed.

"Look here, gentlemen," he said, tracing his finger over the map from Milwaukee to Waukesha, on to Whitewater and Madison, from Madison through Dodgeville, Mineral Point, and

Platteville to the Mississippi across from Dubuque, "is there a shorter, more direct route? I doubt it."

"Ah, I doubt it, too, Pengellen," agreed Kilbourn heartily. "But—ah, let me say—there is perhaps a less expensive route."

"Expensive!" exclaimed David scornfully. "Gentlemen, balance your expenses against the potential income of the lead region!"

No one answered him. But Alexander Mitchell, who had sat in almost sphinxlike silence, moving not so much as an eyelid, reached out and put an index finger on the map at Milwaukee. He began to mark out the course, saying nothing. To Madison he duplicated the course traced out by David; but from Madison he went not south, but northwest in a straight line to the Wisconsin River, which he touched at Helena, and from there he went on down the river valley to Prairie du Chien.

"You see," explained Holton, "we can take on the lead at Helena, if necessary."

"It's still not Mineral Point, gentlemen," protested David. "And what is there—besides the English Prairie or Muscoday—between Helena and Prairie du Chien?"

"I don't doubt that settlements will follow the railroad," said Kilbourn.

Holton turned to Mitchell. "Show him Edgerton's report, Alex."

Mitchell unfolded a closely written page of script and held it out to David, while Kilbourn explained that B. H. Edgerton, the engineer who had made the survey of Mineral Point, Platteville, and Dodgeville, was an able and conscientious man. David was hardly listening. He read through the report hurriedly; it added up to its central paragraph. "The formation of the mineral region is not adapted to cheap railroad construction. A much greater amount of excavation and embankment will be necessary than in the eastern portion, and it will in most cases be rock, costing six or seven times the price per yard that gravel or sand will cost. Grades and curves must be adopted that would also be objectionable, even on a road designed for local traffic."

"That's the second report, Mr. Pengellen," said Holton. "Mr. Brodhead made a similar report earlier. The Wisconsin River valley is Brodhead's recommendation."

"Gentlemen, the objections are valid enough. But no part of your proposed line does more than touch on the rim of the lead region."

"As to that," said Mitchell, "we have no way of knowing just what need there will be for lead in years to come. Now that the Treaty of Guadalupe-Hidalgo has been signed and the war has ended, the government's purchases of lead will be curtailed. Moreover, we have information that silver is being found in quantity west of Iowa, and there's been another rumor—possibly a wild one—to which few people give any credence, that gold has been found in California." He shrugged eloquently. David was silent. There was nothing he could say. He recognized instantly that any such discovery as Mitchell hinted would empty Mineral Point as fast as the village had filled up with settlers. But no one gave it any credence—Mitchell had said that. Yet rumors had a way of spreading about, with or without credence.

"You see, Mr. Pengellen," Holton went on, in explanation, "the plain fact is that the initial expense of building a road through such terrain as that which maintains in the Mineral Point region isn't likely to be compensated by income from such a road in time to prevent financial collapse. That is the fact Mr. Strong will not see; that is the fact so commonly overlooked by other enthusiasts for the road in your town and its neighbors. There's simply no gainsaying it. I—let me say, *we*—are sorry that it is so, for, believe me, we would very much appreciate the income from the shipment of lead."

David found his voice. "I should add," he said with dignity, "that I'm empowered to say that the businessmen of the lead region are prepared to invest substantially in the road if there is any assurance that the line will pass through our region."

"We cannot give you that assurance," said Mitchell with quiet bluntness.

"I could wish it were possible to do so," added Kilbourn.

David looked from one to another of them. Their faces were adamant, but not uncordial. He still held Edgerton's report in his hand. He glanced at it again. It was plainly written, simple and direct; there was no mistaking its meaning, and he fully understood its cogency, for no one could deny that not only the region about the Point but almost the entire area from the Blue Mounds country down through New Diggings to Galena would afford unprecedented difficulties in the grading of slopes. There was much in the objection that the proposed railroad could well go into receivership before income from such an expensive section of the road could be made to pay the cost of its construction and maintenance. He handed the report back to Mitchell.

"What am I to tell the businessmen of the Point, gentlemen?" he asked simply.

At this, Kilbourn smiled. "Mr. Pengellen, you're a man of considerably more perception than some to whom we've spoken. Pray tell the gentlemen who chose you to represent them that we certainly don't intend to slight Mineral Point. We may not be able to construct our main line through the Point, but be assured that we'll put in a branch just as soon as we can."

"Well, gentlemen, thank you. I'll carry this information back to Mineral Point. I know it will be disappointing—it is so to me —but I understand the difficulties."

"Money is tight," added Holton. "And legislative actions haven't been encouraging to investors."

Mitchell got up; his rising was a signal to the others. Kilbourn downed a last glass of whiskey, from which Mitchell had abstained; Holton reached for another, thought better of it, and refrained.

After they had gone, David put on his beaver and got into his greatcoat. He went down the hall to 311 and knocked gently.

Tamson opened the door at once. "Done already?" she asked. Seeing the glumness in his face, she added, "Oh, whatever it was, it didn't go well for you, did it, David?"

"It doesn't affect me too directly. Let's not talk about it. Shall we go out?"

"Yes, just for a little way. We can't go far—I don't know how safe it is in a strange city."

A light snow fell outside. The night was less cold than damp. A strong musk of water, the smell of the lake, lay in the air; it was not unpleasant and mingled with the fresh moistness of the large flakes drifting through the windless air. Outside the hotel stood several carriages, whose owners were in the tap-room, from which came the sound of music and revelry.

Tamson clung to David's arm as they walked down the dark street. They went for a way in silence. Then Tamson's hold tightened.

"It seems so good to walk here like this with you, David, where no one knows us, and no one would notice," she said.

"Yes, I feel the same way."

"Don't you love to feel snow on your face? David, do you remember the old country? And what a treat snow was there—how seldom it came—how little a time it stayed?"

"Yes, oh, yes!" he said in delight, remembering. His boyhood came back—so far away in time, so close to his heart still in such moments as this. Here was the smell of water, the moisture in the air, almost as of a fog off the sea, something out of a lost time, a time before that coming to America and Mineral Point, before his going to school in Providence, before Candace. It now seemed a halcyon time.

"And were you as lonesome, too, at first?"

"No. I guess the country was so new, so different, and I was young enough to see it without being homesick." This he could say truthfully. He had never known the nostalgia Tamson had evidently known, the longing which had been the common experience of so many Cornish men and women come to Wisconsin Territory for the sea and the skies of Cornwall, and the compact little villages, and the traditions of that old, old land which must indeed have seemed so remote from the perspective of so raw a country as this.

They had turned, not caring to walk to far from the Fountain House. Yet they did not wish to go in. They walked on past in the other direction. Snow came down more thickly than before, enclosing them in a world of white, shutting away everything but the glow of the lamps outside the Fountain House—a soft, strange shining before and behind them, as they walked toward and away from the hotel.

"David," Tamson said, after a longer silence, "did Candace ever say anything to you about me?"

"No, why?"

"Well, that time you were caught in the cave-in—a long time ago now . . ."

"Not so long. Less than two years."

". . . She saw me watching. I think—I'm not sure—she understood then that I felt something more than just friendship for you. I saw it in the way she looked at me. Afterward, in the store, she started to say something; but she didn't."

"No, she said nothing to me, Tamson. I doubt that she would."

"Strange. I could have sworn she had seen enough to make her know. I may have been mistaken."

He did not answer. Perhaps Candace *had* understood. Perhaps she had preferred to say nothing. Perhaps her secret knowledge was in part responsible for the widening rift between them. Yet there had never been any question in her attitude. Perhaps he had simply not noticed, which was symbolic of the chasm which had grown and widened imperceptibly, despite the mutual harmony which prevailed at the house.

"What are you thinking, David?"

"Of Candace."

"David, what was she like before you married her?"

"What was she like? Oh, charming, vivacious, good company. So different from what she is now—at least, so it seems to me now. I'll tell you—she was like a beautiful butterfly coming out of its chrysalis; I thought of her that way every time I called on her. Only, I know now her home wasn't her chrysalis—it was her shell, a part of her she couldn't entirely leave behind. She was so young, so eager to please, so desirous of being loved. I suppose I was young, too—I couldn't help loving her." He stopped in the enclosing snow and faced Tamson. "But I know it wasn't the way I love you, Tamson. It does no harm to say it, because Candace stands between us, and I wouldn't do anything to harm or hurt her."

The cooling snowflakes fell on their faces where they stood, locked in each other's arms. The snow made a hushing sound, sibilant, whispering, all around them, sifting among trees, past buildings. The world was entirely of snow and darkness, with a spectral, deceptive light which existed only in the whiteness of the snow. Mineral Point, the store, the house, Candace, Aunt Marget—all seemed at this moment far away, however strongly they stood on the perimeter of awareness.

They walked on.

"You see," he continued, "I love Candace still. It's not the same as it used to be. But you find out, as you grow older, Tamson, that love is never the same either; it always changes. I'm sorry it's so, but it isn't anything anyone can alter. Candace and I have grown apart without seeming to realize it. She isn't the same woman—she's got so she likes Mineral Point, or at least tolerates it—and what was love has turned into a kind of companionship, as love always does. We've lived together long enough now to have assumed certain responsibilities toward each other—like every married couple."

They turned around once more.

Tamson said, "I've been thinking, David, how this walk of ours is just like living in Mineral Point. We go so far, no farther—from one wall to another."

"Milwaukee's a rough town," said David seriously.

"No rougher than the Point. We've met only one drunkard who probably didn't even see us."

"And besides," he added, laughing, "I don't know my way around. I'm afraid we'd get lost in this snow."

"Lost," she echoed. "Oh, David—we're both lost now." She paused and looked gravely into his eyes. "Don't you know it?"

He answered her gaze soberly. "I know."

They walked for a long time. The snow ceased to fall, the clouds broke, stars shone through, and the first quarter moon glowed low in the west. An eerie light lay upon the city where fading moonlight was reflected in myriad snow crystals. Carriages had begun to move away from the Fountain House when they returned to it, walked past the curious clerk at the desk, and went up the stairs.

He stood at the threshold of her room, holding her in his arms.

"I wish I could ask you in, David."

"I wish I were free to come."

After she had gone into her room, the closed door mocked him. He stood there for a few moments, gazing at it, wavering, but at last he turned and went resolutely to his own room.

From his place of concealment, Soaring Hawk saw Parr leave the Mansion House. The night was almost warm in the valley; the snow that fell was beneficent, good to feel. In his buckskin clothes, the Winnebago was comfortable even though he did not stir. He watched Parr move along Shake-Rag Street with something close to resentment, but his resentment was directed primarily at Candace, to see whom Parr had made it necessary for him to observe her husband's movements and report to him. He knew that Parr, having stabled his horse at the Mansion House and registered there, was now on his way to where Candace waited. Dimly, he recognized that he would soon lose Parr, for this was no ordinary dalliance. Parr did not look on Candace as on those other women he had known so casually as to have been contemptuous of them, once they had satisfied the hunger of his body.

Parr went along the street toward the smelters.

Soaring Hawk was about to begin the journey to Dodgeville when he saw a shadow detach itself from the vicinity of the Mansion House and take the same course as Parr. His instincts aroused, he slipped away in pursuit. If the shadow turned where Parr did, he would be following Parr. The Indian passed in among the smelters in the vicinity of the slag-heaps and picked up a good-sized piece of slag.

The follower turned in Parr's wake, up off Shake-Rag Street.

Soaring Hawk did not wait to see whether he meant to waylay and rob Parr or whether he intended only to ascertain Parr's goal. He moved noiselessly after the follower until he was within easy range; then he flung the slag with unerring accuracy. It struck squarely in the back of the follower's head; he went down without a sound.

Parr was too far ahead to hear.

Soaring Hawk settled himself to wait. He had thrown only to stun, not to kill. He was confident that he had not miscalculated.

He had not. In a few minutes, his quarry moved and sat up. He shook his head, looking around for what had hit him. He found the slag, picked it up, looked at it wonderingly. He dropped it. He scrambled to his feet, peering ahead of him for sight of Parr. Not finding him, he paused to light a match and search for Parr's footprints in the fresh snow. Then he ran eagerly ahead.

Soaring Hawk had forgotten about Parr's tracks.

With a noiseless, loping gait, he started after the follower, sweeping up the discarded slag. Within half a block he had felled his quarry once more. This time he followed to the fallen man, snatched up his hat, which had fallen off, picked him up as easily, and ran back the way he had come, carrying the unconscious form back down to Shake-Rag Street and for two blocks along that street before a groan stopped him. He lowered him into the snow and vanished into the snowy darkness. There he stood waiting.

The follower sat up once more, feeling his head. He rose unsteadily to his feet and stared around him in perplexity. He looked for his hat. Soaring Hawk had dropped it nearby. Groaning, he bent and picked it up. Then he stood peering this way and that into the close-pressing night. He had begun to think about his own pursuer rather than his quarry. He stood for a few minutes looking warily into the darkness, listening for any sound. He heard nothing; Soaring Hawk did not move.

Then he turned and began to run back toward the Mansion House.

Soaring Hawk followed, intent now on discovering to whom the follower might report his adventure. He had marked his features well: a young, ill-shaven man, one white women might think attractive.

But he went into the tap-room of the Mansion House and lost himself in the anonymity of a group of roisterers. He stood for a few moments ruefully rubbing his head. Soaring Hawk settled himself to wait for him to speak to someone, or better, to take his leave and return to whomever had sent him. The fellow was one of the miners, young, sturdy, strong; the Winnebago could not recall having seen him before, but then, white men looked very much alike to him, just as Indians looked to white men.

Parr slipped into the darkened house.

"Is that you, Nate?" asked Candace out of the darkness.

"Yes. Where are you?"

"In here. In the living-room."

"Just a moment till I get used to the dark."

The hall took shape; objects assumed a tenuous reality. He saw Candace standing in the living-room doorway.

"Over here, Nate," she was saying. "I'm right here."

"I see you."

He walked over to her. He kissed her, feeling the intense hunger of her mouth. But his mind was occupied by more than the hour's passion. He led her back into the living-room, found the conversation chair, and urged her into it.

"I want to talk to you, Candace," he said hurriedly, as if he had but a little time before he must go again.

She was disturbed at his insistence. "What is it, Nate?"

"Candace, we can't go on like this," he said with a conviction which grew out of many hours of turning over and over in his thoughts the triangle of which he was a part. "We've got to make a break."

She was apprehensive. "I don't know what you mean, Nate."

"Candace, I've thought it all over. I can't even seem to think straight when I'm away from you too long, when I never have any way of knowing when I'll see you again. I want you to leave Dave—go away with me—divorce him, anything to settle this."

"Nate, how could I?" she protested. "How can I leave David?"

He sat for a long minute saying nothing. What did she mean to say to him? That the security David offered her counted for more than their love?

"Then perhaps I'd better not see you again," he said quietly.

"Oh, Nate. Oh, no!" she cried out at once.

"But don't you see, Candace?" he demanded. "It can't be both of us—it's got to be one. I can't make the choice; I've made it—you know that. The choice must be yours to make—try to understand that."

To live here without Nate, she thought. No, that would be unbearable. She had been only half alive while he was gone. But give up David? That, too, seemed impossible.

"You know how hard it is to get divorce proceedings through the territorial legislature," she protested.

"If you ran away with me, Dave could get a divorce without trouble."

"Ah, and to where, Nate? Where? Out west, where it's wilder than this? Nate, you can't ask that of me. I want you, it's true, I know I want you even more than I ever wanted David—but I'm so confused, perhaps I only think so now. I can't go into another wilderness—it would be the same thing all over again —only much worse."

"I'm not going west," he answered gravely. "I wouldn't think of it. Candace, I'm going to the capital—to Washington."

"Washington!" she exclaimed. "Oh, how wonderful! But what are you going to do there?"

"At the moment, just wait. Dodge is going to run for Senator from Wisconsin—that would be after statehood this year. He's asked me to serve as his secretary in Washington. I have enough money. We could get a place to live in Washington, and we could live very comfortably. I've never been prodigal with my money, Candace. I'm going to transfer some of it to Washington banks next month."

"Washington," she murmured, dazzled. "Oh, Nate! I've always longed to go back east, back to some city where people are civilized. I've never dared to dream of living in Washington." But in a moment her excitement diminished. "David . . ."

"David couldn't come," he said bluntly.

"I know, but. . . ." She hesitated.

"Do you love David, Candace?"

"Nate—in my own way, I do. It's different from this. I'm used to him. I know his ways, I know everything about him, I even know Tamson is in love with him . . ."

"But do you love him, Candace?" he pressed her.

"Oh, don't confuse me. It's bad enough already, Nate, please . . ."

"Do you, Candace?"

She sighed. "I suppose not—not this way—if I love you . . ."

The moon broke through the clouds and a faint illumination entered the room by way of the windows. Moonlight was caught in a brass bowl, reflected from copper candlesticks, lay whitely on the piano keys. Her face emerged more slowly, though his remained in shadow.

"And I do love you, Nate," she added.

She sought his arms. He kissed her, at first gently, moving his mouth from her eyes to her neck and to her lips. In the fragile moonlight reflected upon her face, she had never seemed so entrancing, so beautiful.

"I'm only asking you to think about it, Candace," he said. "We couldn't go now, anyway. Not for weeks. There are many arrangements to be made, and I must make most of them secretly. But I know now I'm going to Washington. I hope and pray you'll be going with me, but I can't force you to go—I can't even say to you that you ought to go. The decision is yours to make. Then, later on, if we come back to Wisconsin to be associated with the state government in Madison, as seems probable, all this will have blown over, people will have forgotten . . ."

She shook her head. "People don't forget that easily, Nate. They only forget your good deeds."

"Is it bad, then, to love each other?" he demanded. "I shouldn't have thought so. I regret being unfair to Dave, I regret the need for this kind of dishonesty." He sighed. "The fact is, I regret a lot of things—but some things are stronger than regret, Candace, and I suppose a really strong man regrets nothing."

"All this talk, Nate," she protested. "I've thought about it—a lot. Sometimes I think I want you both, I need you both, and then I ask myself whether it's true or whether I only think so. David sometimes thinks me selfish; I know Aunt Marget does—she's as much as said so to me."

"I want you to think about it, seriously, Candace. I have to know. And if you decide to go, you must be ready at any time. The opportunity may not come often. I'm for Washington, and, I'll not try to hide it from you, for more beyond that, much more. And I want you, too, Candace."

She said nothing. The vision of Washington rose up in her mind's eye. She had visited there once as a child. The experience was unforgettable, and she saw herself with insidious ease now taking her place in a role of ever increasing importance in that glittering society which moved about the Congress and the White House. An excitement that was almost childish welled up inside her. She began to tremble. Her pulse grew erratic and fast.

"Oh, Nate, Nate," she whispered.

He drew her closer and hushed her whispering with his mouth upon hers.

In an hour, Soaring Hawk's quarry left the Mansion House. The sky was clear, the snow had stopped falling, the westering moon shone yellow. The air was crisp and still, sweet and fresh with the smell of new-fallen snow. A screech-owl called tremulously from the woods northwest of the village.

He stood for a while looking down at the tracks in the snow beyond the Mansion House. The Winnebago divined that he was trying to decide whether enough snow had fallen to obliterate Parr's tracks. He decided that it had, for he went on up High Street.

Soaring Hawk followed silently.

The time was mid-evening. The Indian did not know whether he was bent for home or going elsewhere. He followed up High Street just past the Trelawny & Pengellen store; then he turned to the right, behind Shake-Rag Street. He saw his quarry walk to the door of a lamplit house and knock.

A woman opened the door cautiously; then, seeing who it was there, she stepped outside. Soaring Hawk recognized her. She was the wife of Pengellen's partner. The man spoke to her briefly, explaining with some gestures, and then walked away. The woman went back into the house.

Soaring Hawk was baffled. He could not imagine why it was that Mrs. Trelawny had Parr followed. The ways of white people were forever amazing. He abandoned his quarry and went back to where he had left his horse. He mounted and rode slowly out of town along the moonlit highway to Dodgeville, trying to fix upon some connection between Mrs. Trelawny and Parr. He could not solve his perplexity, but he was not discouraged. What Indian could be expected to penetrate and explain the ways of white people?

Within a week, Candace had a brief note from Parr, brought to her by Soaring Hawk, who did not come to the house with it, but waited until he could meet her on the street and pass on Parr's message without seeming to do more than greet her. She concealed both the note and her astonishment at receiving it, and hastened home as fast as she could.

His message was brief.

My dear,

I am grieved to say that I believe we had better not risk any further meetings for some time. I have it on reliable authority that someone has been watching me whenever I come to Point. Last week I was followed, though fortunately Soaring Hawk was able to prevent anyone from knowing where I had gone. I know the source of the curiosity, but I am unable to learn any reason for it. I need hardly tell you, it is not David, but a married woman of your acquaintance. These ladies, I am given to believe, are far more dangerous than husbands. Meanwhile, I commend again to your most serious thought the proposal I made last week. It may be that at any time I may appear for your decision, and it must be ready when I do. There will be no further time. I dare to send you all my love.

NATE

If it was alarming, it was also perplexing. She read it over several times, carefully, before destroying it. It filled her with anxiety as well as a burning curiosity. She tried to think who Parr could mean, but she could think only that it must be some woman who had an interest in Parr herself—he knew, at least, that David had had nothing to do with having him followed. She grew hot with anger, but this wore away; anger would solve nothing; bitterness took its place, but even this did not hold out before a surging restlessness, and the conviction that her lack of strength led her only from one unpleasant situation into another. There was nothing she could do about anonymous busybodies, or other women Parr might attract.

She resented not being able to see Parr for even those few opportunities which they had taken in the months since his return from war, but there was nothing to be gained by rebellion. She asked herself, quite sensibly, whether it would not be for the best, after all? Parr's wild dream of flight to Washington—his visions of rising in his position—his plans for his future—were they not all dreams which might never materialize but only hold before him as well as her a kind of ephemeral hope? She found it difficult to think of a future without David.

She was walking the very edge of the precipice with Parr, she told herself again and again. The note, now destroyed, assumed gigantic proportions in her mind; it loomed like a signal of danger. She tried to drive its implications out of her mind, so that nothing of its effect on her showed for David to see when he came.

She walked outside and a little way up the slope, until suddenly, ablaze with sunlight, the Mounds loomed upon the skyline ahead of her, far down the sweep of land to the south. She stood for a moment looking at them, until her old feeling about them came back. There they rose, like ever-present guards, the sentinels at the gate, brooding darkly despite their sunlit faces. Her small defiance washed away; she was chilled and shrank within herself. She turned and ran back to the house as if pursued.

On the mid-March day set for the election, Trelawny came hurrying into the store. He was agitated. His customary pleasant face was dark with troubled concern; his usually placid eyes were clouded.

"David, David, did ye hear the news?" he cried, first looking carefully about to be sure no one else was in the store.

"I don't know what news you refer to, Jonathan," answered David. "But it can't be as bad as the look of you."

"Ye doan't knaw the haalf o' et," he replied, lapsing into Cornish speech.

David laughed. "Come , come, Jonathan, you're trembling. Sit down—you've had a shock."

"Indeed, that I have," replied Trelawny emphatically.

He sat down, pulled out his handkerchief, and wiped his forehead. David was surprised to see the perspiration there, for the windy day outside was not warm. A faint prickling of apprehension stung him.

"Now what news?" he asked gravely.

"There's a rumor going about they've discovered gold in California. You know what that means! Half the miners will be off for California like the wind!"

"If it's true, I suppose they will. But is it true? I heard that rumor in Milwaukee last month. Alex Mitchell himself said that few people gave any credence to it. I doubt that our miners will pick up and run on the strength of an idle rumor. Talk's cheap, Jonathan."

"Aye," agreed Trelawny with grim seriousness. "And have you thought—what if it is no rumor?"

"We'll have to trim our sails a bit."

"We certainly will. We've got stock to the ceiling now. I daren't think what it means if they flock away now."

"Where did this rumor come from?" asked David.

"They say some stranger stopped at Nichols' place. He'd had a letter from a relative out there."

"Did anyone see the letter?"

"Not that I know of."

"Fine evidence," said David scornfully. "Who was this stranger? A land-speculator? It would serve such a fellow well indeed to set such a rumor going, Jonathan."

"That's so." Trelawny relaxed a little. He looked thoughtfully dubious.

"Some of the miners take fright easily."

"Aye."

"I'll keep my ears open when I go to vote," David went on. "I'll look up this stranger—*if* there is one, which I doubt."

"Go right now, David," urged Trelawny. "I just heard it. I came right back with the news."

David started out immediately. The streets, as always, were thronged with people in the vicinity of the hostelries, especially now that the opening country made traveling easier and the towns more accessible. At the polls in the Court House people stood in little knots talking about the constitution and the articles in the document. David cast his vote in favor of the constitution and went on down High Street to the Mansion House. He looked around for Abner Nichols, and, seeing him, went over.

"Hello, Dave," Nichols greeted him. "Aren't lost, are you?"

"No, Colonel, I'm not. Lend me your ear a moment, will you?" Nichols obligingly bent for David's whispered enquiry. "I've heard you have a stranger here who talks about gold being discovered in California. Can you point him out to me?"

Nichols indicated with one thumb. "That's the fellow over there. He's waiting for the Milwaukee stage."

David crossed to the stranger. He was a tall, austere-looking man, clean-shaven, with friendly brown eyes. He had anything but the look of a speculator in land.

"Pardon me, sir," said David.

The stranger turned and looked at him with a cool, measuring glance. "Reverend R. P. Lawton, at your service, sir."

David introduced himself. He explained that he had heard of the rumor allegedly begun by the Reverend Lawton in regard to the finding of gold in California. He had been told that there was a confirmatory letter. Had he been correctly informed?

"Quite correctly, Mr. Pengellen," said Lawton. "And I assure you I'm every bit as interested as you, since Mineral Point may well become my home if I return next year to take up the Methodist charge here."

"Might I see that portion of the letter, Reverend?"

"Certainly," replied the minister. He took the letter from his pocket, commenting on the colorful stamps which now decorated the mail since their adoption the previous year, and unfolded it. "Now, let me see," he murmured. "Weather, no, that's not it; topography, no, sir. Ah, here we are." He folded the letter to its concluding paragraph and handed it to David with the adjuration, "Pray overlook my correspondent's errors in grammar and spelling. He's not a lettered man."

David read with mounting apprehension.

"A man named Sutter or Sutler has a mill up nr. Coloma and has discovered gold in the crick at that place. There is wile excitment here, and all are for going up there to stake out clames. They will soon have more clames than gold. I guess I will sit tight here a while and wait till I see some of that gold."

The letter was dated "Erly Feb'y." He handed it back to the Reverend Lawton, thanked him, and excused himself. The refuge from conviction that he took in the thought that no one had as yet recorded the actual sight of gold being panned in California was a slender one. He knew it. Yet he dared not betray to Trelawny the extent of his alarm. This twice-encountered rumor came from something more than mere gossip, he was now certain.

Trelawny beckoned him hopefully to the rear of the store as soon as David came in. Tamson had returned to wait on the trade, and though the store was crowded, David took the time to talk to Trelawny.

"I've seen the letter," he said quietly, "but no one has seen any gold."

"Aha," said Trelawny, readily relieved. "Just as you thought."

"But the stranger was no land-speculator, Jonathan; he's a minister. I spoke with him."

Trelawny's eyes clouded.

"I think, to be on the safe side, we'd better limit our buying of stock for a quarter or so."

Trelawny nodded emphatically. "We'll do it. I'd rather be caught short than long. Nothing at all this next quarter."

David smiled at Trelawny's relief. He went back to work.

But his nagging apprehension was not so readily dismissed. If gold were actually to be had on claims in California, the news would eventually come through. There would be more and more letters like the Reverend Lawton's. Eventually the newspapers would publish the facts, and the rush for California would be on. Tamson noticed his dark mood, but said nothing. Nor was he successful in concealing it from Candace.

"Something's the matter with you tonight, David," she insisted. "Tell me."

"It's nothing of importance."

Perhaps he might have learned of Parr's movements, she thought. "Surely I've a right to know what troubles my husband," she went on. "I'm no child—not any longer."

"No, Candy. There's just not much to say. It's little more than a rumor—hardly that."

She was certain that it concerned herself and Parr. "Then I ought to know it, too. After all, what concerns you concerns me, too."

"Yes, I suppose so. But it's so uncertain—so slight. It's just a wild rumor being circulated that gold's been found in California."

She was so relieved that she laughed. "Oh, is that all! I thought it was something serious."

"It would be serious enough if it were true," he answered. "Don't you understand what it would mean to the Point?"

She gazed at him, wide-eyed, unthinking in the flush of her relief from her alarmed suspicion. "Why, no, David—why would it mean anything?"

"At a conservative estimate, gold in California would take away half of all the miners in and around the Point. That would reduce our business by as much. Candy, if gold has really been found there, mark my words, Mineral Point is finished growing, and we'll all have a stiff time of it. But we'll weather it—we'll have to."

A chill crept into her. For the first time she realized what David was saying. Her face remained impassive, but behind her eyes she was thrown into turmoil. What David implied was that Mineral Point would move backward, not forward, that their own income would be drastically cut. As she sat there, she felt once more—as she had for so long not felt—as if she were in prison, and now its walls were closing in upon her, more solid than ever. That this should happen, too, after the separation from Nate, added to his absence, her loneliness, her desperate hope of resolving her plight without harming David or Nate or herself.

Sitting opposite David, so lost in his own apprehension that he failed to see the depths of her alarm, she reached with angry, confused terror for a way of escape, she cried out with every fibre of her being for Nate, who could take her away from the wilderness to which Mineral Point was turning back. But in a few moments she quieted her confusion. David, Nate—it made no difference which of them, for all that she loved them both—there was no salvation for her but within herself. There was no one else to turn to, only herself. What she had lost could be found only within herself.

How often she had told herself as much. Aunt Marget had been right. She was selfish. Her reaction to David's worry was only worry for herself. She felt contrite, and at the same time resolute—this, too, could be overcome, if she could try hard enough.

"Of course we'll weather it," she said.

8. . . . We Know Not What We May Be

Spring, 1848

ON HIS ARRIVAL AT THE STORE THAT MONDAY MORNING IN April, David found a delegation of merchants and lead shippers waiting on Trelawny. They greeted him with a chorus of cries, until Abner Nichols, who appeared to be their spokesman, assumed leadership, quieted them, and put their case.

They had been reading the recent legislative act supplementary to the incorporation of the Milwaukee and Waukesha Railroad Company, and had taken note that the authority to extend the line from Waukesha to Madison, and thence west to the Mississippi, had been so worded as to permit the railroad company to locate their Mississippi River terminus where they wanted to. They had talked half the night about this at the Mansion House, and, while the specification was for a point somewhere in Grant County, it had seemed to them that the businessmen of Mineral Point ought to make the strongest representations to Nelson Dewey, who was sure to be elected governor in May, to insist that the first State Legislature further define this supplementary act to fix the Mississippi terminus of the road at Cassville, or, failing that, Potosi.

David recognized this as a shrewd move. Dewey's home was in Lancaster, which was on the direct route to Cassville. Either terminal would make the most direct route from Madison come through the lead region.

"I don't think it'll do much good, though," he said frankly. "Dewey can't commit himself at this point."

"We don't want him to," cried Roderick Spensley, a vigorous old man with a white pointed beard. "All we want is for you to talk to him, and find out how he feels about it."

"Me," protested David. "Why should I be the one?"

"You talked to Mitchell and that lot," said Nichols, "and didn't get their dander up—the way Strong always does. You can talk to the government just as well."

"Not a rail has been laid yet," commented David. "Not much prospect of rails being laid, either. I know how they talked. What's the hurry?"

"Well, David," said Nichols, "where politicians are concerned, it's never too early. We don't want a commitment, as Spensley said, but we do want them to start thinking about it. Don't stop at Dewey—go see Jairus Fairchild, too; he's running for state treasurer. No need to trouble about Tweedy—we know where he stands; he'll go along with anything they do in Milwaukee. You won't have to see Jim Brown—he's safe enough. And you needn't bother Dodge—he's getting ready to vacate his office as soon as he's elected to the Senate. Will you represent us?"

"Now?"

"Yes, today. The Governor's proclamation on statehood is being made today—most of the men you'll want to see will be in Madison."

"I've missed the early stage, then."

"You've got a carriage and horses," said Nichols curtly. "You can drive in and come back on your own time. You aren't the only one who missed the stage—Father Mazzuchelli visited a little too long with Father Jouanneault up at St. Paul's. He's on his way to Madison, too. Want to take him along?"

"As long as I'm going, I might as well."

"I'll go down and tell him—or get him back if he's gone up to St. Paul's to wait for the next stage."

David returned to the house to tell Candace where he was going, and harness the horses to the carriage. Candace followed him to the shed and insisted that he change his clothes. How could he think of going into Madison in his everyday clothes? David sighed and complied, though his working clothes were as good as anything he owned. Then he drove off to the Mansion House, where he found the priest waiting.

"One would almost say we were fated to ride together, Mr. Pengellen," said Father Mazzuchelli, his dark, sombre eyes betraying a glint of humor. "If one believed in fate rather than Providence."

"Are they not the same, after all?" asked David.

"By no means. It is Providence that I am now on my way to the capital to take possession of the charter for Sinsinawa Mound College which the Legislature granted us a few weeks ago—not fate, which is only the name applied to the result of man's errors."

The carriage swung out to the Dodgeville road.

Parr made his way down the corridors of the capitol to the Governor's office. The orderly at the door recognized him and waved him in.

Governor Dodge turned at his entrance, smiled, spoke his name, and removed his spectacles. Parr sat down with the ease of long acquaintance.

"I've been working on my proclamation," said Dodge. "I'm not much of a hand to write these things. But the *Argus* wants it for tomorrow's paper. Have you seen their most recent issue?"

"I haven't had time to look at a newspaper," answered Parr.

The Governor picked the *Argus* off his desk and handed it to Parr.

"The Territory of Wisconsin Ceases to Exist," read the headline. "Wisconsin Now a State." Parr dropped the paper.

Dodge thrust the document he had written at him. Parr read this too, dutifully:

To All to Whom These Presents Shall Come, Greeting: Whereas, the people of the Territory of Wisconsin did on the 1st day of February, 1848, by a convention of their delegates, assembled at Madison, the seat of government, form a constitution for a state government, which by the fourteenth article of said constitution was submitted to the qualified electors of said Territory for their acceptance or rejection; and whereas, the said electors did meet at their respective county seats and election precincts on the 13th day of March last, and did then cast their votes for or against the adoption of said constitution; now, therefore, be it known, that from the official returns of said election as made to the executive department, it appears that the whole number of votes cast on the question of the constitution was 22,591, and that the majority was 10,243 in favor of the adoption of said constitution, in testimony whereof, I have hereunto set my hand and caused the Seal of the Territory to be affixed, at Madison this tenth day of April, in the year of our Lord, 1848. Henry Dodge.

"That should do it," said Dodge. "So that battle's over. You saw I'm standing for the Senate, Nathaniel?"

Parr nodded. "You'll be elected easily."

"Now, then," continued Dodge, "I'll be vacating this office very soon. The election is down for May eighth—less than a month off. I'll be going into Washington just as soon as possible once the votes have been counted. Meantime, I wish you'd precede me there and arrange for my living quarters. I can give you some addresses. When could you go?"

"I can leave today, if necessary."

"Excellent!—But *you*'ll need to make arrangements, too."

"I've made them, Governor."

"You'll need money, Nathaniel."

"I have money, thanks."

Something of the growing excitement in Parr communicated itself to the Governor. The older man looked quizzically at him, trying to explore what lay behind his eyes. "And you spoke of marrying, Nathaniel," he said. "Is that it?"

"In good time, Governor. All in good time."

"Good luck with the lady!" Plainly Parr was not communicative. He turned once more to his desk, taking up his proclamation, and calling out for his orderly, who came at once. "Have this set up for my signature and the Seal, Hendon. Copies for the newspapers."

"I hope to have her in Washington," said Parr, after the orderly had gone. "I hope most earnestly that she meets with your approval."

"I'm sure she will, Nathaniel," said Dodge heartily. "I'll expect a paragon of womanhood, too—knowing your proclivities." He had been watching Parr's face as he spoke; Parr's earnestness had seemed anxious. He bent forward, put one hand on Parr's knee, and added, "But, stay! you don't seem easy in mind, Nathaniel? Is anything wrong?"

"Nothing, Governor."

"Aha, I know—you're in love. I should have seen it before this. You have my sympathy, Nathaniel. Love can be a scourge, especially for one like yourself who is far more at his ease on a horse in open country, with an Indian attending. Is the Hawk with you?"

"No, I left him at Dodgeville. He's up to something for the Point shippers."

They sat talking for a while, Dodge suggesting names and

addresses of people for Parr to see in Washington, Parr temporizing with discussion of accommodations and the pertinent facts of finding a place to live in the capital. But over all their conversation hung an aura of change; it was as if, having fought for so long to alter the status of the Territory, both men were reluctant to make the adjustments in their lives to accept that change. It was less so for the Governor; he had been in Washington as a delegate from the Territory, and his position as a senator would be somewhat similar, though one of more power than he had had as a territorial delegate.

But for Parr, this meeting with Dodge was a fateful one. It was possible, he knew, that he would never again see his old friend on quite the same footing; the sense of camaraderie, of kinship, of warm friendship quite above their difference in station, might be lost. If Candace took flight with him, if she came to live with him in Washington, Parr would not predict the Governor's attitude. Dodge had always been an honest man, though not above a questionable device or two when he dealt with the Indians as a young man, when his reputation as an Indian fighter was at its height; but he had always tried to be fair and just. Parr could not guess what he would say about Candace. Perhaps it would be best, if Candace could be persuaded to go with him, to keep their going away together as secret as possible, to keep her hidden in Washington until divorce made their marriage possible. Once that were accomplished, she could be brought into the open; the Governor could then accept or reject, but, while he might have rejected her as an erring wife before her re-marriage, he would be more inclined to accept her as Parr's legal wife.

He dawdled in the office, therefore. He wanted to prolong the pleasant, easy intimacy of their conversation, he wanted to protract the feeling of paternalism in which Dodge habitually indulged with him, yearning toward it himself with all the hunger of one who has never known a real father. He wanted, in fact, to keep the status of the present unchanged; yet he knew that in his heart the decision had been made, the step awaited only the auspicious moment, his career might shatter to ruin by the contemplated step, but he meant to take it, it was too late to turn back.

It was almost noon when he left the Governor.

He rode down to the Madison Hotel. As he dismounted, he caught sight of a familiar figure coming out of the hotel in earnest and, apparently, troubled conversation with Count Augustin Brogmar of Sac Prairie. The big, handsome fellow with his colorful sash was unmistakable; so was his companion. He walked toward them.

"Hello, Dave," he greeted him. "And Count Brogmar. What are you telling Pengellen, Brogmar?"

"Bad news," said the Count, shaking his bearded head. "At least, so he says. I expect to leave for California later this year—with my family. My wife is much upset about it, but it can't be helped."

"Gold in California," said David curtly.

"Not a doubt of it," Brogmar went on complacently. "I heard about it a month ago. Now I've dispatched an agent to Coloma to see for me, and I'm waiting on his report as to the extensiveness of the veins. But it isn't the gold alone." He shrugged expressively. "I can't seem to persuade my grape vines to grow as I'd like on the prairie or the hills along the Wisconsin—some lack in the soil, perhaps—or they need a drier climate like that of California. Pengellen here thinks California's gold means the end of Wisconsin's lead. I doubt it myself—we can't make bullets out of gold—though that depends on the administration, I suppose," he finished, his eyes twinkling.

"Oh, California's far away," said Parr, turning to David. "You're surely not in Madison to gather information on western gold."

David told him why he had come. But he had finished; he had seen Nelson Dewey and Jairus Fairchild. He had had the good luck to run into Alexander Mitchell, also in Madison, who would know more about the railroads than the politicians, though Mitchell was an expert at saying nothing in few words, and his position was unassailable. He was now ready to begin the journey back to Mineral Point.

"Did you take the stage?" asked Parr.

"No. I rode down in my own carriage. The men would have it that way—as if the rails were to be laid tomorrow and only instant intervention would prevent their being laid around the Point, where they'll be laid anyway—all the more so because by this time the Milwaukee men know all about California, and they know what's likely to happen to the miners of the Point and all the neighboring towns."

As David spoke, Parr recognized that perhaps no more favorable time for his departure from Wisconsin would be likely to come. In David's absence, he could ask Candace for the last time to join him; he could reach Mineral Point ahead of David. He felt a twinge of guilty remorse as he thought of doing so in the face of David's worried concern for the future of his village. He excused himself, growing excited at the prospect before him, and entered the hotel, from the windows of which he stood watching David and Count Brogmar.

Both of them went down the street and around the hotel to the carriage sheds. As soon as they were out of sight, Parr came out again, mounted his horse, and rode rapidly out of Madison to the south. He was filled with urgence now—the Governor's words still rang in his ears, the expectation of seeing Candace and persuading her to join him, the shaping of plans for the immediate future excited him. He drove his horse hard along the high road beyond Madison toward Dodgeville, where he must pause to collect such articles as he would need most before going on to Washington. Even the wind, blowing steadily out of the northeast, seemed to hasten him, to press him forward with urgent impatience.

In the afternoon, Candace walked down to the store to get some things she had meant for David to bring; since he was in Madison, she had to go instead, though she disliked to shop. Yet the day was so fine that the freshness of the air and the warmth of the spring sun invigorated her. She walked briskly down High Street and entered the store in good spirits.

Knots of people stood along the street before the Court House and beyond, many drifting down toward the Mansion House. In the store itself, people were similarly congregated. Murmurs of excited conversation rose on all sides. Candace looked from one group to another, recognizing most of the people. Tamson saw her and came around the counter.

"What in the world's going on now?" asked Candace.

"We've had bad news," answered Tamson. "John Ross, Alex Turner, and Bill Tilley are leaving for California. They intend to go down the Mississippi from Galena to New Orleans, then to Panama and up."

"They'll be just the first ones," said Trelawny dolefully, coming up. "Mark my words—they'll go by the hundreds. This town is done."

Soaring Hawk came silently in and passed to the back of the store, where he squatted until Trelawny was ready to talk to him. He was in no hurry, and he looked at the customers who were buying nothing, and listened to their excited talk about gold with an impassive countenance.

On all sides of her Candace heard talk of "going west," as if it were a mere matter of a journey to Dodgeville. She made her purchases and walked out with them. She felt withdrawn, remote from the casual talk in the store. But her high spirits were dampened.

At the house she put away the things she had bought, methodically. She began to pace from room to room, thinking. What would happen to Mineral Point now? "Done," Trelawny had said. But it would surely not be that. Perhaps now was the time to persuade David to go back east and enter into some business there, where life and growth did not depend on circumstances beyond one's own control. But no, he would never go. It was idle to dream of it. She must learn to accept whatever came.

She paced back and forth, trying to think of some resolution of her fears, of some course acceptable to David which would get them both out and away from this rough, frontier town, which had been built up around them like a house of cards and was now evidently to collapse like one. Was she to be imprisoned again when she had only just escaped bondage to her unhappiness? Each time she passed a chair, the piano, the decorations on the walls, she looked upon them as the symbols of her remoteness from the halcyon occasions of her youth.

She thrust self-pity resolutely from her. She had told herself many times that love was just a trap for the unwary. She had fallen into it. She had somehow dreamed she could have David and still retain everything she held dear before he had entered her life. She could not be so deceived again. She could not hold anything once she reached for something more. What was there here in Mineral Point to hold? The cramped white buildings along Shake-Rag Street, the unpleasant smelters, the rough, unclean miners, even the more imposing houses of stone, all receded from her thoughts. There was nothing here, there had never been anything here, and now there would be less than ever, as one by one, in group after group, the miners picked up and left the Point for gold in California.

She grew more confused. It was as if all the reserve of strength and determination which she had built up so carefully had been undermined. She reached for courage in vain. The mood would pass, she was confident, but at the same time she was dismayed to find that her adjustment, despite her sincerity and will, was so unsure. David must not find her like this.

A horseman flashed past the windows from the north and around to the kitchen door. She heard him dismount. Could it be David? But no, he had the carriage. She hurried to the kitchen as she heard the door open and close.

Parr stood there.

With a glad cry, she flew to his arms.

He kissed her quickly, holding her. "Candace," he said urgently, "I've come to say good-bye—or take you with me. I'm on the way to Washington. Will you come, too?"

She broke away from him in a confusion of hope and fear. "Nate! Do you mean it? Now? This moment?"

"This moment. Listen to me. David is driving in now—he must be somewhere near Dodgeville. He set out just after me. I had to stop at Dodgeville. We'll have to ride to Galena and take the stage from there to Vincennes. Then to Cincinnati. We can take a train there for Washington. You can't take many things with you. And I don't know how you can ride."

"Oh, I can ride. But my things!—And David!"

"You'll have to leave a message for him. But don't say you've gone with me—just say you've gone. Otherwise it may reach the Governor's ears, it may jeopardize my position—our position—in Washington."

"We can't both ride one horse, Nate. Oh, how can we go now, like this?"

"We must—if you're going along. I can get another horse. I saw Soaring Hawk's down at the store. I'll go back and get it. Can you be ready when I get back?"

She hesitated. "Oh, Nate. I want to get away. I can't stand it any more—I can't. But—David . . ."

He tightened his arms around her. "I love you, Candace, I love you very much. I want everything to be right with us. If the answer is no, then so it will be. I'll not be back. I'll not ask again."

"Oh, Nate—I love you, too."

He kissed her; the hunger of her mouth came up to meet his.

Her confusion resolved. There would be no more fighting with herself, no more feeling sorry for herself, no more striving to meet people on a footing unfamiliar and treacherous. Of David she tried not to think, nor of her valiant attempts to be the wife she should be, the woman he expected her to be. She pushed back indecision and tumult.

"I'll go," she said.

He slipped away, out of the house, mounted his horse, and rode down to the Trelawny & Pengellen store. He took the Winnebago's horse without leaving his mount, and returned to the house.

He had just dismounted when Candace came out. She had put some things into a small hand-bag, which she put down while she locked and carefully tried the door, a gesture that seemed to Parr unaccountably absurd, as if she were coming back. Then she ran over to where he waited with the horses.

"I left a note for David," she said breathlessly. "Which horse am I to ride?"

"I'm going to put you on my horse, Candace. The Hawk's is a little skittish and needs a firm hand."

He helped her up while he talked.

"We'll try to avoid being seen till we get to Galena. It'll be after nightfall then, and it won't matter so much. Besides, we'll take the first stage out for Vincennes. We'll go around the towns. We'll take the plateau this side of Belmont and come out the other side of Platteville. It'll be slower going, but safer."

He mounted Soaring Hawk's roan. The horse protested, prancing a little, swinging its powerful body around. But it was familiar with Parr and Parr's horse, and Parr remained firm, disciplining him, swinging him over toward his own horse, and he quieted. He leaned over and kissed Candace.

"Are you ready, Candace?"

"I'm ready, Nate."

They rode from the house through what remained of the grove on the slope, and out upon the highway. A few flocculent clouds which had risen out of the west moved toward the zenith, expanding, so that occasional cloud-shadows crossed the landscape, swift before the wind. In the still dry grasses, the wind's voice made a reedy rustling that was constant, unvarying, rising and falling.

They rode silently. The road wound up hill and down, curved along the slopes, and led steadily southwestward. Parr asked once or twice, as they neared Belmont, whether she were tiring. She shook her head.

They reached the edge of the high plateau that swept up to the Belmont and Platte Mounds, and Parr, without hesitation, directed his horse off the road and into the tall dry grass, with the intention of skirting Belmont and shortening their journey by avoiding the more circuitous route between the old capital and Platteville. At the moment of their entry upon the plateau, the entire area, from the road along which they had been riding, to the far horizon, dominated by the two Mounds, lay under the shadow of a cloud, so that it had a dark and forbidding appearance, like a sentient beast lying in wait for anyone venturesome enough to defy it. The grass, most of which lay bent, broken and thickly matted as a result of the winter's heavy snow, was yet in some places as if untouched by the weight of snow; it reached eagerly upward for a distance of over three feet, a lush growth, far down at the roots of which a mist of green showed where new blades pushed from the earth. It rustled and crackled under foot; it slithered and made creaking sounds, as if it protested this invasion; but it parted for them, and did not close after them as green grass might have done. The entire plateau looked at this moment so vast, so dark, so ominous, that Candace felt a surge of fear as she faced it.

At once all her old, unreasoning fascination for and fear of the Mounds themselves sprang back into her consciousness; these ominous sentinels guarding the way of escape seemed alive and angry; the passage of cloud-shadows over their slopes, added to the wind's force among their trees, lent them an appearance of mobility, as if they were stirring portentously out of their long sleep to thwart her flight and wreak their own punishment upon one who had never loved their alien land.

But in a few moments the cloud rode by on the high wind, sunlight bathed the grass, and the face of the plateau seemed to change; it was as bright and inviting now as but an instant ago it had been forbidding and malign; its formidability under cloud changed to a sheen of sunlit gold with a faint haze of green showing here and there, where adventurous blades pushed up between the broken stems of the previous year's growth; and the Mounds, which had seemed so far at their entry upon the plateau, appeared now to beckon them on and were much closer by sunlight. This change, however, did not last. In a little while, cloud-shadow again took possession of the sea of grass, an aura of malignancy and fear once more enveloped the vast expanse undulating toward the Mounds. And the looming Mounds themselves seemed more threatening than ever.

They were now some way into the plateau. They had already

gone well past Belmont in a southwesterly direction, and were riding between the Mounds, with the Belmont Mound on their right. The almost treeless expanse of grass brooded all around them; if Parr had thought of anything but the rapidity of their escape from pursuit, he might have reflected Candace's feeling of insignificance, for the vast plateau dwarfed them, the towering Mounds, like two survivors from a dark, unknown, prehistoric era, reduced them to motes in this ocean of grass, from which arose under the sun the faint, sweet aroma of dried blades, so that they were not aware of the fragrance of April, but rather of the strong, pungent smells of drying stems and blades which belonged to November.

In addition to the feeling of insignificance she had, Candace felt a spreading satisfaction, for they were now actually riding between the Mounds, out the gate past the sentinels which had guarded the way of escape for so long. But her feeling of satisfaction was short-lived; with escape now all but accomplished, with freedom before her, the satisfaction she felt was eclipsed by an insidious note of error that came with the thought of everything she had left behind her—of David. The insignificance she felt before the great Mounds and the far-reaching plateau aroused a belated humility, and the thought of David—seen now from this perspective of what seemed to her freedom—filled her with shame and remorse.

What would he think of the woman he had loved and trusted? How selfish and wilful she had been—and still was! She was overwhelmed with sudden, violent hatred for herself. What right had she to think only of herself? David deserved better of her than this. And did she not deserve better of herself, too? In that moment she saw herself more clearly than ever before—her past was irretrievably gone, save only in her memory; her present was David and Mineral Point; her future was uncertain.

With mounting conviction, the decision she had made only

so little a while ago now seemed to her monstrous. She was speeding headstrong from a situation that might have been a mistake—but surely one that she had met successfully—into one that could be catastrophic not only for herself, but also for Nate. She closed her eyes, pressing her lids together, in an effort to blind herself to the image of David before her mind's eye, to shut herself away from the shame she felt so pitilessly. All was in vain. Her relief at escape had brought her only to the certainty that she fled a vague dissatisfaction for an unknown life begun under a pall. A wave of helplessness came over her; she began to fight back tears.

They were approaching the first of the streams that ran through the plateau. Like all the others, it was swollen, and Parr tried to guess at which point it would be easiest to cross. While he glanced up and down the river and debated with himself, he heard Candace call.

"Nate! Nate!"

He reined in his mount and turned.

Candace rode up. He saw with amazement that her face was streaked with tears.

"Oh, Nate! Nate! I can't go on," she cried.

"What are you saying, Candace?" he asked, almost roughly.

"I'm sorry—I'm terribly sorry, Nate. I can't do this to David—to you—to myself. It's not the way . . ."

For a moment he said nothing. Was this a sudden whim? Or was it the inevitable goal of all her indecision, arrived at at the moment of freedom, when escape seemed illusion?

"You mean you want to stay with David—is that it?"

She looked at his face, now white with anger. How grimly his lips were pressed together! Her eyes did not falter. "Yes, Nate."

"That's your final decision, then?"

She nodded. "We've got to get back before David finds that

dreadful note I left for him," she said urgently. "Forgive me, Nate.—You surprised me, you came so suddenly just when I had bad news—I didn't have time to think. But I know now this isn't the right way . . ."

"Then there's no time to lose," he said quietly, accepting her decision.

He dug his heels into the sides of the Hawk's mount and rode back the way he had come.

She rode after, weak with relief.

They had not gone twenty steps when Parr heard her sudden cry of terror, and, turning, saw her catapulted over the head of her horse. He was down instantly, filled with high alarm. He knew at once what had happened; Candace's mount had gone through into a gopher hole, for the plateau was overrun with rodents whose tunnels crossed and recrossed under the grass. The horse had pulled its leg free, but now stood three-legged, holding its right fore-foot above the ground.

He came to his knees at Candace's side. She was already struggling to get up.

"Candace, are you hurt?" he cried, helping her to her feet.

"No, I don't think so."

But that she was, was clear in a moment, for she could not walk. Some injury had been done one of her legs. She sat down again, biting her lip.

"Oh, Nate—what shall we do now?"

"Never mind. It will be all right. Perhaps we can get back to Belmont—or on to Platteville."

"No, no—back, please."

"Back, then. One place is as close as the other."

He turned to her mount, his own horse. He could not feel that the leg was broken, but it was injured; perhaps a tendon had been pulled. The horse could not be ridden. They would both have to ride Soaring Hawk's horse, difficult as it would be. Fortunately, they were not yet too far from Belmont, even though, he guessed, they were closer to Platteville.

Parr was not hopeful. He was immediately aware of the magnitude of the accident, and he cursed himself now for taking the risk of crossing the plateau; he had known the danger, but he had set too high a value on secrecy, in maintaining his position in Washington and all that went with it; all seemed now of the utmost unimportance.

"We'll have to try somehow to get on the one horse," he said. "If nothing else, you can ride him. I'll walk and lead my horse."

"Oh, Nate! The letter! If David gets there . . ."

"I'm sorry. It can't be helped."

He moved toward Soaring Hawk's horse. The horse reared and ran. Fifty yards away it stood, legs spread and ready, its tail and mane blowing in the wind. Parr walked toward it slowly, coaxing and wheedling.

At this moment Soaring Hawk arrived at the point of their entry upon the plateau. He had emerged from the store not very long after Parr had taken his horse. The discovery that his horse had been stolen filled him with a slow, growing rage. Believing that Parr was in Madison, he had not the slightest intimation that it was Parr who had taken the horse. He went at once to the Mansion House to borrow Abner Nichols' fastest mount and set out in pursuit. He lingered only long enough to ascertain that travelers coming in from the north had not seen his roan. Then he started for Belmont. On the road he found the prints which showed that two mounted horses had gone that way but a relatively short time before.

He rode with all possible speed into the southwest. He was puzzled. He had not thought his roan would go with anyone but himself; he had believed the horse would balk at any other rider. Perhaps he would have tolerated Parr; he did not know; but Parr was in Madison, Parr would be in the capital all that day and perhaps the next; so he had told Soaring Hawk. He wished Parr were here; the two of them would have no trouble rounding up the horse-thief.

The Winnebago had borne insults and scorn without complaint; he was not moved by the racial superiority assumed by most of the white men, being secure in his own superiority; he took no umbrage at the servile positions he was often required to take because of the color of his skin; but this outrage upon his horse violated a deep-seated principle and shook the affection he had for the roan. He rode in fury, burning with a desire for vengeance.

When he came to the place where tracks indicated that two horses had entered upon the plateau, he was filled with additional anger. He knew what danger gopher holes and rodent runways offered to horses traveling there. But in a moment he arrived at the reason for this hazardous course; obviously the thief did not want to be seen; he and his companion—if indeed the burden on the second horse were another rider—meant to avoid Belmont and Platteville, perhaps other villages, too, on their way to Galena or Dubuque.

He got down to examine the earth with minute care. How long before had the tracks been made? He thought not long. He would not endanger Nichols' horse by following them; he might be able to overtake them in the vicinity of Platteville. He mounted again and rode like the wind through Belmont, following the highway which crossed through the plateau beyond the village.

Not far beyond Belmont, his keen eyes caught sight of his quarry. He could not ascertain why there was no movement in the group. He was too distant to determine anything but the presence of two horses, quite far apart, of one human being, in pursuit of one of the horses, of another sitting on the ground near the first horse. Evidently they were resting there. The opportunity lay before him to go in over the plateau, but Soaring Hawk would not risk his mount there. It would be better to drive his quarry back to the road. He calculated the strength and direction of the wind, rode back a little way, and dismounted.

He began to pull up dry stalks of grass, rapidly fashioning himself a torch. This he lit. Then he touched fire to the grass at that point, mounted with agility, and rode swiftly along the rim of the plateau, touching fire to two other places, before he was forced to throw the torch away. He made another and repeated the process. By the time he had finished, the wind was whipping the flames through the dry grass with an ever-increasing snapping and crackling and a growing roar.

He sat for a moment trying to fix upon the place where his quarry was most likely to emerge. He determined that it would be close to where the road crossed the stream, the course of which he identified by the trees growing along its banks and extending almost as far as the eye could see on both sides of the road, plainly marking the meandering course of the small river. He dug his heels into his mount and rode toward the bridge which he descried up ahead, unmindful of the billowing columns of grey and white smoke which rolled high up the wind to tower tall in heaven above the leaping flames, now a wall of fire bearing down between and toward the Mounds.

Parr smelled the smoke and turned. For an instant he was too horrified to move. He was some distance from Candace, still trying to coax Soaring Hawk's roan within reach. The roan was still balking him, running ahead a little way, turning, waiting, then running again, tirelessly. He calculated the velocity of the wind, and knew there was no time to be lost.

He ran back to Candace as fast as he could.

The roan, perversely, followed him.

By the time he reached Candace's side, she, too, was terror-stricken. The fire made an advancing wall whipped to additional height by the wind, and the smoke was now dense. She was coughing.

"Candace, I've got to put you into the water. It'll be cold. But it's our only chance."

She nodded, afraid to speak.

He picked her up and walked over to the bank of the stream. He thought for a hopeful moment that it might be possible to cross the river, but the fire had already leaped it in several places. He thought of following the course of the river along the bank, but this way to the road was already cut off by the flames.

"There's an overhanging limb, Candace. Hang on to that."

"Don't worry, Nate. I can swim."

He kissed her, unwilling to leave her. Then he walked part way into the water with her, pulled down the limb of the young tree, and held it for her. Only when she had taken it in both hands did he lower her into the water. Her face whitened, with pain or cold, he could not tell: it did not matter; in a few moments the heat would be unbearable.

Yet he must save the horses. He ran back for his own horse, but the mount had come almost to the bank of the stream. He led him down and pushed him into the water, trusting that he would have enough sense to escape the flames. Then he wet his handkerchief and ran back up the bank to the plateau after Soaring Hawk's horse. The roan still stood as he had left him. He ran toward him, holding his wet handkerchief over his nose and mouth. The roan veered away. But the horse was nervous and tense in the face of the fire. He retreated from Parr. It seemed to Parr that he went less far. He renewed his efforts to reach the roan.

Perversely, the horse ran toward the advancing flames. Parr

hesitated. The roan turned, whinnying and neighing in terror. Choking and gasping, Parr made a final effort to reach the roan. The horse waited until he was almost upon him; then he turned, screaming, and bolted directly for the fire, running with ever-increasing speed. He leaped through it, still screaming.

Parr turned to run back to the little river.

But fire was racing down along the bank. He was cut off directly from Candace. There was still a chance that he might reach the shore below her. He ran, stumblingly, half blinded by smoke. The heat had dried his handkerchief; but he still held it to his face, so that he might keep from his lungs the sparks and ashes which filled the air all around him. He stepped into a tunnel and fell. The heat was scorching; heat and smoke together seemed to suck the air from his mouth and throat. He staggered to his feet and ran blindly. It was not until he dared to open his eyes that he saw he had been running toward the central wall of fire coming in on the northwest wind.

He turned. The fire along the bank of the stream had begun to cut in toward him. He was in a vortex of smoke, flame, and ashes. He tore at his clothes, which had caught fire in several places from flying stems of burning grass. He took a few uncertain steps, fighting for breath. Then he fell to his knees. He slid forward to his face. He made one attempt to rise, another to crawl forward, out of the terrible heat which seared his flesh.

Then the wall of fire swept over him.

Candace, raising her head above water, saw Parr go down. She screamed once, shrilly. Far up along the stream the waiting and now somewhat apprehensive Soaring Hawk recognized a woman's voice, and was shaken with premonitory fear.

Candace strove to go to Parr's assistance. She no longer felt the pain in her leg. She thought only of Parr. The fire had passed her; the bank and the plateau were a smouldering blackness. She tried to pull herself closer to the shore by means of the limb to which she had been holding, calling frantically, "Nate! Nate! I'm coming! Nate!" but the roots of the tree, weakened by the eroding waters of the swollen stream, suddenly gave way.

She fell back, struggling against going under. Her struggles brought her head into the direct line of the falling bole, which struck her a stunning blow along her right temple. Nate's name died in a swirl of water rushing into her mouth.

She went down.

Far up the river, the Winnebago began to pick his way over the burned plateau along the bank.

David saw the towering pillar of smoke above the plateau at the Mounds as he drove into Mineral Point. He viewed it with vexation, knowing that the fire was an extensive one, or else the smoke would not have been visible more than a dozen miles away; he was vexed because it was late to burn over grass-land —already woodcocks, prairie chickens, partridges, and other grass-nesting birds had begun to lay eggs.

He rode through the Point by the old road from Dodgeville, up High Street, to his home. He would have gone directly to unharness the horses, had it not been that he saw the hoofprints around the back door. His first thought was that Parr was visiting; he knew that Parr had left Madison before him. But then, if Parr were here, his horse would be here, too. He came down from the carriage and went to the door.

To his surprise, it was locked.

He unlocked it and went in. He found Candace's note at once; she had left it on the kitchen table, where he could not fail to find it.

Dear David, I am sorry, but I am going away. I am going back east. Please get a divorce as soon as you can. I want nothing, except maybe some of my clothes I will send for. You don't owe me anything. Perhaps it is I who owe you. Please forgive me. I did try—I thought for a while I had come to like Point and the way we lived—but now, with everything happening the way it is, and Point certain to stop growing. . . . But it is not that alone, I guess—it's my own weakness. Please think of me sometimes as a woman who loved you, but was not strong enough to love both you and the place where you belonged. Candace.

He was astounded and incredulous. He had been so inured to Candace's dissatisfaction that he could not believe she would actually act upon that dissatisfaction. He had seen little sign of rebellion, and nothing of despair, even of displeasure for such a long time that he was satisfied that her adjustment was a settled thing. He searched the house before he could bring himself to believe what she had written. It was surely a cruel joke, nothing more.

But when he did not find her, he stood considering what he must do. How had she gone? Could she have gone alone? Candace had always liked someone to lean on; it was improbable that she had gone alone. He went outside and examined the tracks before the house. Two or three horses. He walked a little way on each side and discovered the twin trails leading toward the grove. So there were two of them. And on horseback? His incredulousness grew. He got back into the carriage and drove down to the store.

Tamson saw how strange he looked. He seemed both stricken and angry, both hesitant and forthright; he walked as in a dream. She came to meet him, holding back her questions.

"Tamson, have you seen Candace?" he asked.

"Why she was in here hardly three hours ago. She bought some things for the house."

"Did she say anything about her plans?"

"Why, no."

"She's gone."

"Oh, no! Did you look at Aunt Marget's? She seemed upset

because she heard that three Pointers were setting out for California."

He unclenched his hand and showed her Candace's note.

She read it. She looked into his eyes. Plainly, he did not know what to believe. But she knew what had happened. The disappearance of Soaring Hawk's horse was now clear to her. She folded the note and slipped it into his pocket. Then she went back for her hat and coat, paused to tell Trelawny that she had to go with David, and, before the older man could protest, had gone back to where David stood, taken his arm, and half-led him from the store.

Outside, she asked, "David, what are you going to do?"

"I want to know who she went with."

"I'm afraid it was Nate, David."

"How could it be? He was in Madison. . . ." He faltered, remembering something withdrawn and remote in Parr. "He could have got back here before I did. But I heard he was on his way to Washington."

"Candace would like Washington," said Tamson quietly. "But other people don't have to know until it can't be kept hidden any longer, David. They can't have gone far. They'll make for Galena. If we can get there, we can stop them by telegraph if they go east. Soaring Hawk has already gone after them." She explained about the Indian's roan.

"Come on, then!" cried David, and leaped to the carriage, pulling her up after him.

They rolled out of Mineral Point as fast as the horses could go with the encumbrance of the carriage. From the ridge they saw that the smoke above the plateau was even more dense than before; it rode the wind high up and spread over a wide and widening area; the fire was advancing in a broad swath toward the Mounds. The pall of smoke had a menacing appearance.

They rode in anxious silence, looking as far as the road permitted at every height, every curve. But they looked in vain. They swept past the trail into the plateau before Belmont without noticing it. They went through Belmont, past the place where the fire had started. Far in the southwest the flames still leaped skyward beyond the Mounds, following the course of the river there. They came at last to the bridge. The horse Soaring Hawk had ridden stood there.

"That's one of Nichols' horses," cried David, reining in.

"It must be the one Soaring Hawk borrowed." Tamson turned to follow the course of the stream with her eyes. "Oh, look—there's someone out there. And a horse."

"Wait here." He jumped from the carriage.

She took the reins, backed the carriage a little, and drew it off the highway. The horse left by the Winnebago whinnied a welcome to David's horses.

David made his way rapidly along the bank of the stream. He was alarmed now; he was afraid that the Indian's mount standing deserted beside the road boded no good. What could have happened? He went in as fast as he could, running, skirting still smouldering areas, where old stumps or fallen limbs burned. The air was acrid, but slowly the fragrance of April was beginning to permeate the smoky pungence.

He heard Soaring Hawk before he came to him. Seeing him, he stopped in horrified amazement. The Indian knelt upon the ground, rocking his body back and forth, keening in an eerie, forlorn voice, his arms, fists clenched, crossed upon his chest, his head bent almost to the ground. It was not until David walked up close that he saw what lay there—Parr, badly burned, turned over on his back, motionless and dead. The horse that stood beyond, as unmoving as Parr, and burned, too, but not badly, was the Winnebago's roan; it stood waiting mutely for its master.

"Hawk!" he cried.

The Indian raised his grief-stricken face.

"Where's Candace?"

Soaring Hawk gestured wordlessly toward the river.

David turned and saw her. She had been carried down and lodged against the tree which had been the instrument of her death. Her body lay awash, partly supported by the tree, her long dark hair moving gently in the water, which murmured and laughed among the branches of the fallen tree, with the westering sunlight dancing upon it. He walked into the water. He did not feel its chill. He extricated her gently from the limbs which imprisoned her.

He carried her out of the river.

Soaring Hawk watched him. He had ceased his keening, but still knelt there, not knowing what to do. He waited on David.

"Bring him, Hawk," said David.

Tamson saw them coming—David first, carrying Candace, then Soaring Hawk, carrying Parr, and at last the horse, alone. David's face was terrible to see, like a stone image with the epitome of pain forever engraved upon it. He said nothing; there was no need to speak. He got into the carriage, still holding Candace's body.

Without a word, Tamson turned the horses and set out along the road for Mineral Point. She knew how deeply he was hurt, how the grief he felt was locked in lost faith in himself as well as in Candace. It would take a long time to bring him back to what he was, back to the man about whom Aunt Marget had so often written.

She resolved that he must never be hurt like this again.

In the evening of an early June day, Tamson found David in the cemetery. He was just leaving Candace's grave. She stood with him to look back. There were flowers on Candace's grave, and there were flowers, too, on another grave not far away.

"I was at the house, David," she explained. "I thought you might be here. Aunt Marget sent over a pasty. I left it there."

"Thanks. Perhaps you'll join me in eating it. I thought I ought to come up and see how the flowers I planted were growing."

"People think it strange how you tend Nate's grave, too."

"Do they?" He shrugged. "I suppose they suspect what happened. But they'll never know. I burned her note. I said they'd gone out for a ride together. And Soaring Hawk has gone—he's out west, somewhere across the Missouri. Besides, I don't harbor any ill feeling toward Nate. Just the opposite. He saved my life once, Tamson—I'm sorry I wasn't able to save his."

He took her hand in his, and together they walked back down toward the village, their shadows long in the light of the setting sun.

"You know," he went on, "I often think of that morning when I left for Madison. Some people say they have premonitions of coming events. That's foolish, of course. Just the same, that morning I took Father Mazzuchelli into Madison with me. He was talking about the difference between Providence and fate. Fate, he said, was a name applied to the result of man's errors. So I've told myself since that day, it was fate that everything happened as it did. But the errors weren't Nate's and Candace's alone, Tamson. They were mine, too. If theirs was the positive sin, mine was the negative. Who is to say which is worse? No, don't object, don't stop me. I know it here." He struck his breast. "And Providence is that which is intended by God to happen. So it was fate that determined what must happen to Candace and Nate—and it is Providence that I must remain to remember."

"Aren't you being morbid, David?"

He shook his head and smiled. "No, Tamson. Because, even if I believe every word of it—and I do, truthfully—that same

Providence has ordained that you, too, are left to walk here at my side."

They had reached a knoll, from which they could look down upon the village where the June dusk already lay. The sun had gone under the rim of earth. A light west wind blew, heavy with the fragrance of wild crabapple blossoms, carrying petals from the trees that stood in great groves of pink clouds everywhere on the slopes.

David sat down and pulled Tamson down beside him.

"Let's watch for the moon, Tamson. It should show in just a little while."

They sat in contemplative silence, his fingers tightening about her hand and holding there, while the afterglow drew down the western heaven and the night came in with darkness and the first light of the moon silvering the slopes of the dark Mounds, sleeping on the rim of sky.